to Betty Lee — enjoy

TH

HANDLESS
MAIDEN

A Lakota Mystery

Dorothy Black Crow

Dorothy Black Crow

A Lucky Bat Book

The Handless Maiden: A Lakota Mystery
Copyright 2014 by Dorothy Black Crow

Cover Design by Nuno Moreira
http://www.nmdesign.org

See more titles by Dorothy Black Crow at
http://dorothyblackcrow.com/

Published by Lucky Bat Books
10 9 8 7 6 5 4 3 2 1
http://LuckyBatBooks.com

ISBN-10: 1939051886
ISBN-13: 978-1-939051-88-2

Also available in digital formats.

Dedication
to

Taté Eaglestaff, grand-niece
&
for all the handless ones
Napeshni & descendants
Che Guevara
Taj Mahal architect
Apache Jar of Hands
and
Joanna Joe
a character from the Spirit World

Acknowledgements

The following writers helped this novel find its shape:

Paul Amundsen, Kris Ayer, Sara Backer, Orpha Barry, Nancy Boutin, Steve Brown, Sharon Cannon, Susan Clayton-Goldner, Alison Clement, Carole Cole, Emily Lambert Dalton, Susan Dominguez, Jean Esteve, Lily Gardner-Butts, John Ginn, April Henry, Lynn Jeffress, Art Johnson, Susan Kelly, Liz Kracht, Patsy Lally, David Lambert, Robert Lambert, Sue Lick, Elizabeth Lyon, Nancy McLaughlin, Lloyd Meeker, Martha Miller, Judy O'Neill, Carla Perry, Jeffrey Phillips, Martha Ragland, Rae Richen, Scott Rosin, Ann Warren Smith, Susanna Solomon, Dan Stein, Elaine Taylor, Joe Telafici, Pam Wegner, Theresa Wisner, Eric Witchey, and most of all, mentor James N. Frey.

Disclaimer

My husband Selo Black Crow said that if I ever wrote
about the res, it'd be all lies.

He was right.

This story is Fiction, since Truth is seldom believable.
Thus names and places have been changed.

*Proceeds from this book will go to Native American civil
rights projects.*

Lakota Words in the Story

To help readers understand how Lakota is spoken, I choose to write out pronunciation rather than use linguistic symbols, such as like č for *ch* or š for *sh* or ġ for *gh*. Also I use marks to indicate which syllable is accented. Otherwise, readers might think that *ate* means to have eaten, but *até* means father, or that *ina*, mother, would be pronounced eye-nah instead of *iná*. Worse yet, readers might think that *waste* means waste, as in waste time or waste money, but *washté* means good.

Words are listed by frequency in the story and grouped by type. If used only once or twice, their English meaning follows directly. Sacred words and names are capitalized.

nape—hand
Napeshni—no-hands
Woluta—small red ball tobacco tie prayer
Wanaghi—spirit being, ghost
Wakan Tanka—Great Mystery, big sacred
Tunkashila—grandfather, Grandfather God
Tunkashila unshimaleye—prayer: Grandfather God, help me
Yuwipi—finding ceremony, they-tie-him
Ieska—translator, go-between-worlds
Hanblechia—vision quest, cry for vision
Hochoka—sacred circle
Inipi—sweat lodge, reborn ceremony
Chanunpa—sacred Pipe
Kinnick-kinnick—sacred tobacco, red willow bark shavings
higna—husband
mihigina—my husband
taichu—wife
mitaichu—my wife

mielo—it's me
kola—male friend
hokshila—boy
tahanshi—cousin
ohan—yes, okay
hiya—no
washté—good
shicha—bad
hau—greetings
pilamaya—thanks
unshika—humbly pitiful, a sorry lot
tokiya he/hwo?—Who's there?
hechetuelo—so be it, the end
wana—now
wana wota—now eat
kabuk bread—flat pan bread, unleavened
wojapi—berry pudding
washichu—White person, greedy, takes-the-fat
Mako Shicha—Bad Lands
Paha Sapa—sacred Black Hills
chetan—hawk
Chetan Yuhomini—Turning Hawk

Map of South Lakota, Eagle Nest and Camp Crazy Horse

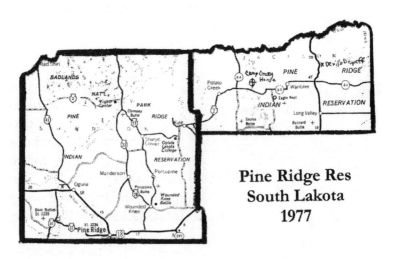

**Pine Ridge Res
South Lakota
1977**

CHAPTER 1

ALEX

Pine Ridge Reservation, South Dakota
Camp Crazy Horse
Winter 1977

WIND WHISTLED in the eaves of the log cabin, like an old man crying. Alex Turning Hawk was only twenty, a medicine-man-in-training, but he prayed to the Great Mystery for help as he sat at his workbench and whittled a cedar stem to fit into the red stone bowl of a fasting Pipe. He worried about where AIM—the American Indian Movement—was heading. He wasn't sure he was up to the task. Four years ago his traditional elders had asked urban AIMs to help bring justice to the Res. Civil rights and treaty rights, the sacred Black Hills, were at stake. They'd chosen him as their young spiritual leader.

On the wall behind him hung the large Turning Hawk treaty Pipe, so long-stemmed only grown men could smoke it. Across from him, lit by the kerosene lamp, sat his wife, Tate, just turned eighteen, writing Lakota words on cards: *higná*, husband, *taichu*, wife. Although he spoke Lakota slowly to her, she learned the language more easily by writing words down. He loved the close silence between them.

The outhouse door banged, startling him. No one lived nearby, and snowdrifts blocked the road. Maybe a *wanaghi*, a ghost. Or a lost wino. He yanked open the heavy door to face a snow-covered figure wearing a parka and navy ski mask. Only ice-coated eyelashes and lips showed.

Stepping inside, she demanded in Lakota, "Where'd you put my rifle?"

He recognized Joanna Joe, the AIM warrior who last year had exposed an FBI informer, then hid her gun underneath his outhouse, and disappeared. He'd worried about her since. She'd been brave to come back, and must be exhausted from walking in. Relieved to see her, he said in Lakota, "Thought we'd lost you." He switched to English. "Tate, it's your old AIM friend."

Joanna Joe had brought more than snow in with her. She took off her ski mask and unzipped her army parka. "I need my gun," she repeated.

Tate jumped up and hugged her old friend from Minneapolis AIM and brushed melting ice from her eyelashes and cheeks like a mother bear. "JJ, sit by the fire to get warm."

Joanna Joe wasn't dressed for the Res. City clothes, thin jeans and an AIM T-shirt. She hadn't changed, just thinner arms, hollow cheeks, dark glowing eyes. He saw her eyes flash at him like a laser beam. Indian way, you didn't look directly at someone unless you were angry.

She leaned over the woodstove. "You took it into town?"

"This is sacred ground. No guns at Camp Crazy Horse." Medicine men weren't allowed to touch guns. He'd had George, their American Indian Movement leader, take it away. Every morning, with his Pipe prayer—sacred breath—he *became* the Land. He wasn't surprised that she'd broken tradition by hiding a gun in the outhouse. Four years ago, at the Wounded Knee Occupation, he'd carried his sacred Pipe; she'd carried her gun.

"You took it into town?" she asked. She took off her gloves, leaned close and flicked her hands at him.

He stared at her knuckles. RED POWER spelled across both hands. Inside Wounded Knee, she'd used red ink to tattoo the letters. Some even said she used her own blood. He grabbed her cold hands and pulled her towards the woodstove to warm them.

Tate, bringing a wool sweater for Joanna Joe, saw the flashes of red. "JJ, are your hands bleeding? What—tattoos? When? Why?"

Joanna Joe spread her hands out over the woodstove. "If you believe it, you have to live it, show it, make it part of you."

Some of Joanna Joe's words seemed right to him, the *live it, make it part of you*. But to *show it*, like a walking billboard? You could take off a t-shirt or a bumper sticker, but not an in-your-face tattoo. He remembered that Grandpa Emmett wore a tattoo all his life after he came home from Carlisle Indian School, a crude blue ink E on his forehead. "E for Empty," the older boys teased.

Tate touched Joanna Joe's arm. A turquoise-and-silver bracelet shone on her wrist, a turquoise ring glowed on a chain from her neck. "These are new as well. Do you have an admirer?"

Joanna Joe laughed. "My jewelry is my bank account."

Tate looked puzzled. She hadn't learned much Lakota yet, nor ways on the Res, but she was trying in a way that Joanna Joe, who'd adopted urban Indian ways, had not.

"No banks on the Res," Joanna Joe said. "I hock them when I need to."

Tate said, "You don't need to sell them. JJ, you must stay with us." She sat her old friend on a stump seat by the woodstove and peeled off her army parka, cowboy boots and socks. Wet wool smell filled the cabin.

His wife had learned Indian hospitality, but Joanna Joe carried trouble with her. She was too thin, too hyper. She needed to eat, talk, and rest. He ladled out three bowls of beef-and-potato stew and carried them to the table. "*Wana wota.*" Come, eat.

Tate brought spoons and a plate of frybread, and they all sat down.

Rich earthy aromas rose from the table. They ate in silence, Indian way. Tasting each bite.

Then Tate leaned forward. "We've been so worried! We missed you at our wedding."

Chewing on frybread, Joanna Joe asked, "Your foster parents let you get married?"

Both his mother and Tate's parents had tried to stop them. Tate was too young and wild, and he had no job, not with his long hair and darker skin. And his mother had already chosen a suitable mate for a young medicine-man-in-training.

"I'm of age now." Tate said. "So we got married Indian way with the sacred Pipe."

Joanna Joe turned toward him and asked in Lakota, "What about the wife your mother picked out for you?"

Still asking blunt questions. Asking questions on the Res got you lies, silence, or danger. Indian way, you told stories about *another* town, *another* girl, subtly making a point. Instead of answering, he brought Joanna Joe hot coffee.

Tate replied in English, "Alex didn't like that girl because she was too bossy."

Alex laughed. His wife was learning Lakota fast. She'd met his mother's choice and saw that the girl had tried to own him.

Joanna Joe paced back and forth, skittish as an unbroke horse eyeing a gate. With a throaty laugh, she pointed and said, "Dammit, Alex! You've gone soft and taken up the piano."

He was tired of the Lakota joshing about his wife's shiny black machine sitting on the dirt floor. The piano was her security blanket, the only thing she'd brought with her from Minneapolis after the wedding. When Tate played, her body swayed as if the notes came from inside her and filled the cabin with strange, passionate music. She'd said her soul was in the strings.

"Get her to play for you," he said. "She plays every night to lull me to sleep."

"No time for that. I could borrow your axe. Or a switchblade?"

How desperate had she become? Switchblades on the Res? Carry an axe over her shoulder into town? He shook his head, no.

Tate brought Joanna Joe dry jeans, socks, and fur-lined boots. She slipped wool socks over Joanna Joe's icy feet, and kept talking non-stop, as if words could warm her. "JJ, I missed you at the Red School-house where we worked. The kids did, too. I learned to drive the van myself to take them on field trips."

Joanna Joe tried the boots on and paced back and forth. He sensed that she was going to bolt, like a mustang, skittish from being corraled. Maybe their closeness was too much for her. He'd have to calm her down. He'd give her the only protection he knew—prayers that would reach the Great Mystery.

Alex stoked the fire with another dry log, sat at his workbench, and opened his tin box. He laid out twenty small red cloth squares and dropped a pinch of loose tobacco on each. From across the room, Tate and Joanna Joe looked alike enough to be sisters: straight black hair parted in the middle and tucked behind the ears, high cheekbones and dark eyes. Yet how different inside. Joanna Joe tough, older, cynical, relentless, an AIM firebrand who fought in the trenches. Tate raised White, still trusting and tender-hearted.

Concentrating on his sacred task, he twisted each red cloth square into a tiny ball and looped each onto string, one after the other like a miniature kite tail more than a foot long. With each tobacco tie, he prayed for Joanna Joe's safety.

As Joanna Joe circled the cabin, Tate talked to her. "JJ, we can start a Red Schoolhouse here on the Res. These kids don't know their own Lakota history."

"When I return. Right now I need to talk to Alex. Alone."

People came to him in confidence, and like a priest or psychiatrist, he couldn't reveal their personal secrets. Tate knew this, but Joanna Joe's rebuff surely hurt her feelings.

Joanna Joe sat down opposite him at his workbench in Tate's chair, pushing Tate's word cards aside. She said in Lakota, "I'm on the trail of the *second* FBI informer. Here on the Res."

His own thoughts exactly: so am I. A chill permeated the room, rising from the floor. This was not a personal problem. Tate needed to know how dangerous this was. She'd known only city cops who upheld the law.

He said in English, "Tate, join us. We're all together in this struggle for our rights." He pulled her close to him on the crowded workbench. "There's a second FBI informer on the Res spying on AIM. We have to be on guard or our whole way of life could be destroyed."

Tate looked surprised. "Another one?"

Joanna Joe reached her tattooed hands across the table. "FBIs always plant two, just in case. I caught the first one, but AIM just kicked him off-Res. This time, don't worry. I'm onto him."

Tate asked, "Who? How do we find him?"

He knew Joanna Joe wouldn't answer. He said to her, "You must be careful. The first one threatened to kill you."

"Last time AIM didn't believe me when I caught him. I need clear proof. And I'll get it."

"*I* believed you," he said. She was a loner, but now she needed help. "We'll set up a trap." From the fierce look on her face he knew she wasn't out to *trap* the informer, but *waste* him. He must find the traitor first, so that AIM could ban him from the Res and publicly shame the FBIs, as they'd done before.

"Bad idea." Joanna Joe stood up. "You're AIM's spiritual leader, not an AIM warrior."

"I'm a different kind of warrior, he said." A spiritual warrior walking the Big Red Road.

Tate said, "JJ, you must stay here. It's too dangerous in town." She hugged Joanna Joe, as if that could stop her from leaving.

Joanna Joe shrugged out of the embrace. "I'm a danger to you if I stay. FBIs are after me, and they'll search here like they did before."

"It's too cold and dark out, Tate said. "I'll play the piano for you. At least stay overnight."

Joanna Joe grinned. "Night is my time. I make myself invisible, like you, Alex."

He winced. She'd had no training to hide her energy. She'd be visible to someone hidden inside AIM. And she'd be vulnerable because she had a one-track mind for vengeance. He warned her, "FBIs still raid the AIM houses, late at night."

"George has my gun." Joanna Joe had figured out where it was. "I'm going to get it."

Tate tried once more. "JJ, it's too far to walk."

Alex stood in front of the door barring her path. "Be reasonable. I'll walk with you into town in the morning."

"Tonight!" She flung her hands in his face.

No one could stop her. Joanna Joe was on a deadly mission. "At least take these *wolutas* with you," he said, and laid the tobacco ties in her hands. Even though she was blind to any other kind of force, she needed his prayers that went with them. "*Wolutas* for your protection."

Sniffing the string of small red bundles, she knotted the ends of the prayer ties and slipped them over her head. "*Pilamaya.*" Thanks.

He hid his dismay. Instead of hiding them in a traditional place like a pocket or next to her heart, she'd turned them into a necklace. Would the *wolutas* still protect her? Would his prayers keep her safe? He couldn't throw her in a corral like a wild horse. He could only protect Tate.

He stepped aside and held his trembling wife in his arms.

When Joanna Joe lifted the door's bar, a cold gust of wind pushed the heavy door open, whining and wailing, and blew out the kerosene lamp.

Down by the creek, a coyote howled. Standing on the threshold, Alex called, *kree–kree–*, for his hawk spirit to watch over and guide her. But Joanna Joe, dressed again in dry boots, parka and ski mask, laughed at the cry on the wind and plunged into the night.

CHAPTER 2
TATE

Two weeks later
Badlands, Redstone Basin

CAMP CRAZY HORSE had run out of food. Tate Turning Hawk did her best to keep the AIM guys' stomachs full, but their monthly rations of government commodities had lasted only two weeks. Alex always said, "Feed them and they will come." So after a Sweat Lodge ceremony, she fed the AIM warriors and they stayed out of trouble at the Camp.

After she dropped Alex off at his Law & Order meeting in town, she drove off-Res to Kadoka and filled their rusty red Ford pickup with propane, kerosene, food, and firewood. Low clouds hid the western sun, but she didn't worry about running late. She'd been used to cold winters in Minneapolis, and after three months she knew the Res roads. She shifted into four-wheel drive and headed south to the Reservation line and on toward Camp Crazy Horse. Even though her husband's eagle feather above the dash was supposed to protect her, she wasn't afraid of the Pine Ridge Agency Goons or Kadoka rednecks who might try to run her off the road.

So many factions. Whose side were you on? The Res was so confusing. So far, she'd figured out that some wanted to live the Old Ways, the Traditionals like her husband. Others wanted to live the New Ways, the Assimilateds like the Indian Affairs employees. And she had chosen to change from her Pederson White world to his Turning Hawk Red world.

Down in Redstone Basin she faced a wall of swirling snow. Damn! She hated ground blizzards. Nothing had prepared her for ground blizzards sweeping for miles across the open prairie.

Winds shook the pickup and whipped the snowdrifts horizontally so that flakes seeped through the rust holes in the floorboards. Icy white needles hit the windshield and stuck. She flicked the clogged wipers off and drove slowly into the grayness, hugging the centerline. This road had little traffic, and she'd see a semi's powerful lights in time to pull over.

Alex had warned her about Dead Man's Drop-off, how many cars had missed the turn, how ghosts with energy like giant magnets pulled careless Indians off into the deep gully where they crashed and died. It wasn't ghosts, though, that made the Drop-off dangerous, but a sharp narrow bend in the road where even the semis wrecked.

She saw a dark figure loom in the middle of the road, arms akimbo. It must be another Indian stumbling home from the Kadoka bar, if he didn't freeze first, get run off the road by rednecks, or stuffed in the trunk of a car. Alex always rescued Indians on this stretch, brought them back to the Res to safety, brushed them off with his eagle feather and prayed for their lost souls before he let them out in Eagle Nest.

She couldn't pass the man by, though she hated alcohol fumes in the cab. She slowed to a stop, opened the far door, and yelled, "Hurry up and get in!"

She called again over the noise of the throbbing engine. He moved so slowly that he must need help. She pulled up the brake and opened her door. A gust ripped it out of her hands. She tumbled into the blizzard, regained her balance, and walked in front of the pickup. The wind whistled around her. Sheltering her face with a gloved hand, she peered into the swirling snow. The dark figure floated at the edge of the gully, side-lit by the headlights, one hand raised, one knee bent, as if ready to flee.

This did not feel right. Indians caught in a blizzard always wanted a ride. "Don't be afraid!" she called. "I'll give you a ride." She reached out to him, but he backed over the edge of the snow bank, slipped, and vanished.

She ran to the bank and stared down into the gully thirty feet below. Between the gusts she could make out the man, sprawled face down, flat and unnatural, on a tableland of grass stubble blown free of snow by the biting wind.

"Halloo—" She wasn't surprised when he didn't answer. The fall must have knocked him unconscious. She couldn't find where he'd plunged over the edge. There were no footprints in the snow bank. He must have been really afraid if he'd leaped over.

She kicked steps into the bank, a downward path into the gully. Though partly blinded by the snowflakes, she couldn't have missed his trail. Below her a dark form lay face-down on the icy ground. She slid halfway down to a ledge above him. The man seemed smaller. He wore a large navy peacoat and a wool cap. Long black hair swirled around the shoulders, some strands loose in the wind, some iced into the snow. He must be a Long-hair, an Indian cowboy. How strange.

Minutes before, he'd stood in the center of the road up above, but now his arms reached out, half-frozen in the snow, as if he'd dug deep into the icy crust to escape. He must know she wouldn't harm him. Was he hurt? No one could survive this cold, not even pickled.

She struggled through the drifts to the bottom of the gully until she reached him, his hair blue-black in the dusk. A Red Power fist glowed on the back of the coat—American Indian Movement. He was an AIM warrior—a Brother. She read the letters below it: Wounded Knee '73, and stiffened. There weren't many of these jackets around, since only three hundred AIMs had occupied the village of Wounded Knee four years ago to reclaim their Treaty Rights.

He lay so still. Had he been knocked unconscious? He'd be hard to haul to the pickup. She bent down and grabbed his shoulder, stiff under the large coat, so stiff she couldn't flip him over. She stood, confused. This wasn't the man who'd flagged her down. He was frozen. Dead.

She wasn't supposed to touch the dead. Alex said they could take you away, take your mind away to the Spirit World. But she didn't believe that. Besides, she wore gloves. She wanted to get the hell out of there, but she needed to know which AIM guy he was, so she kicked snow loose and heaved the frozen man onto his back. Gray fur-lined boots emerged from the snow. Like her boots, but they couldn't be. She stared down at—not a long-hair Indian cowboy, but a small woman.

Frost coated the lips and cheeks and lashes, almost hiding her dark empty eyes, her familiar face. Fine snow swirled around JJ's frozen body, swirled around Tate as she dropped to her knees beside JJ and rocked back and forth, unable to look at her friend. She'd hugged her only last month. JJ had sat by their woodstove only a few weeks ago, teasing them about their marriage vows.

Finally, she forced herself to look closer. Her tears had fallen on JJ's face. She took off her glove—it didn't matter now—and gently brushed the tears off the cheeks carved of ice. She wanted to cradle JJ, warm her back to life with her own body heat, take her hand and pull her into the world of the living. Even in a ground-blizzard, such things must be possible. But as she knelt there to gather strength, her own body stiffened. The cold prairie seeped through her denim jeans at the knees. Something else was wrong besides the purple bruises on JJ's neck.

She stared at the long sleeves of the navy peacoat. There was no way to check for a pulse.

No blood.

No hands.

RED POWER cut off.

~~~

Tate stared at her own hands, one gloved, one not, and her childhood nightmare buried deep inside swirled before her against the snow: hands chopped off, the fairy princess sent to wander helpless in the dark woods. The scary story her mother read to her to teach her to protect her chubby piano fingers, and as her mother's fierce voice filled the bedroom, Tate always became the fairy princess, changing the story by running away before anyone could catch her, running out of her nightmare, out of the Badlands to Alex, who'd know what to do.

Tate shook her head to banish the old images and put her glove back on. Her hands felt numb from the cold. She clenched them over and over. This was now, and it was JJ, handless—in the Badlands. She looked around. She was alone in the dusk. She searched amid the snow-flailed drifts for the hands, almost wishing she wouldn't find them. On the road above a semi-truck rumbled past as it geared down the hill. Then silence. She was alone with JJ.

Alex had told her about staying with a body to guard it. It was called *Keeping the body*. As the wind whipped across the prairie stubble, she caught a flash of brightness in Joanna's black hair. She brushed it back. As she touched a tiny bit of red cloth tied into the strands above the nape, she felt a jolt of power surge through her, like static electricity. Startled, she let go and flexed her fingers. A single prayer tie, one small square of red cloth filled with shreds of tobacco, tied together with plain string, glowed as if alive. It must have been static electricity. She reached in again, felt nothing this time, and gently slid the tie into her own jacket pocket. It looked like one from the string that Alex had made for JJ to protect her. Though it hadn't worked, Alex would know what to do with it. Alex, who waited for her to pick him up. Though she'd worn her watch, she'd lost track of time.

～～～

Tires crunched in the snowy road above. Engines revved, doors slammed, voices swore. The semi-truck must have called in about an abandoned pickup, or perhaps had seen her with JJ in the gully. Yet how could one tow truck make such a racket? How had several vehicles arrived so quickly? This was a deserted stretch of road through the Badlands.

Above her, blue and white and red dome lights whirled amid the snowflakes. Doors slammed, one after the other. Her lips felt frozen, her mind numb. How could there be so many vehicles here so soon? She stared up at six or eight dark figures haloed by headlights and searchlights. Their beams blinded her more than the ground-blizzard. She raised her arm to protect herself from the glare. Voices shouted down at her, but she heard only the wail of the wind.

Two of the shadowy figures came to the edge of the road and climbed down toward her. The looked like EMTs, help at last. She pulled herself upright and raised her hands to block the searchlight beams.

"What're you doing down there?" asked the first figure as he walked across the road.

She didn't answer. They weren't EMTs. Under their long black overcoats they probably wore white shirts and black ties, and under their fur hats, short hair. They looked like Mutt and Jeff, but well-dressed and very efficient FBIs. She pointed to JJ's body.

Agent One, the shorter man with short dark hair and deep frown lines, walked over to JJ. He held himself erect as he looked down. She could tell he was the Alpha male, in charge of the scene. He'd go by the book.

Agent Two, the tall tanned man, bent down and shined a small flashlight onto JJ's face. Strands of a blond forelock fell over his face. He brushed them back under his fur hat. Both his longer-than-regulation hair and his loose and lanky gait suggested that he might have been a California surfer, loose and lanky. Perhaps he was along for the ride.

Agent One focused on her. "You must have accidentally hit a drunk Indian hitchhiker."

His words reverberated in her brain until her AIM protest training kicked in: *Volunteer nothing. Keep your mouth shut.* She'd never been stopped by cops, never faced the Law alone, and she trembled. When AIM picketed the Minneapolis courthouse during the trials, the whole group drummed and chanted, and the FBIs didn't frisk them, only snapped photos. Though the FBIs tried to put AIM leaders in jail on trumped-up charges, they acted polite. This one did not.

He strode closer, as if by dominating the space he could force her to speak. "Surely you didn't try CPR?" The wind blew his coat open to reveal white shirt, dark tie, and shoulder holster.

Never say nothing to FBIs, Alex always said. She backed off and shook her head.

"So you dumped the body."

He was using accusations, blaming the witness. Though she should protect JJ's body, she backed toward the embankment, ready to bolt up to the road. "I just found her."

Her words floated in the frozen air. How empty they'd sound to a White man who didn't understand that you stayed with a dead person, four days if you could, so the loved one didn't pass alone into the Spirit World. But JJ had no relatives, only AIM. She'd be alone in a hearse, on a mortuary slab, in a wooden box.

They'd come to take her friend away, and she didn't see how she could stop them. How had they gotten here so fast? Had they followed Alex's pickup from Kadoka because it had Tribal plates?

She should have left sooner.

Agent Two looked up at Agent One. "Take it easy. She's in tears. Just get her out of here." He waved his arm in a dismissive gesture.

Before Agent One could grab her, she scrambled on all fours up the embankment. She slipped past the other hooded figures and headed for the pickup, surrounded by white Blazers and black-and-whites, cruisers and more cruisers. FBIs, Highway Patrol, BIA cops from the Res, federal marshals, even the Kadoka Sheriff. She was stunned. Why did so many cops want to see one dead Indian? She trembled, but not from the cold. She should've gotten Alex right away.

She opened the driver-side door so it didn't creak and slid in. Someone had turned off the engine and lights, but had left the keys in the ignition. She patted the dashboard and crooned, "Good truck." It started, as if it knew it was time to get the hell out.

Boxed in by vehicles, that didn't stop her. She rolled down her window to check the cruiser behind her, and cut the steering wheel. She backed up until a shadow blocked the open window, a shadow with a voice.

"Whoa, not so fast." Agent One rested his gloved hands on the door frame and leaned in. "You found the body. What made you stop?"

She lifted her foot off the gas pedal. They'd never believe she saw a hitchhiker. She had to say something, or they'd never let her go. "I thought I saw something on the road."

"In this ground-blizzard?" He continued to stare.

She stared back. It was un-Indian to stare at someone, but he was FBI. "We've missed some ponies—" She stopped. He looked as if he didn't believe her.

"And?"

"It wasn't a pony."

"Anyone you know?"

Pickup in idle, close to escape, she couldn't open her mouth, though her silence denied JJ.

He waited and leaned closer. "I know, all Indians look alike."

If it weren't so painful, she'd laugh. Everyone in Minneapolis had said she and JJ looked enough alike to be sisters. Ahead of her the Eagle Nest ambulance pulled off the road and one of Alex's cousins jumped out. He'd help. She waved at him, but he turned away.

Agent One signaled the ambulance driver to back up above the gully. Then he turned to her, all business. "Name? Registration. Driver's license."

She echoed his intonation: "Name? FBI badge number."

He glared at her. "Not clever." He waited.

She waited. "Identification, please." At last he reached into an inside pocket, flipped open his badge, and flashed its shiny metal for a moment, long enough for her to read his name.

"Agent Trask," she said, without trembling at the name. He was the one who hated Indians the most because his partner had been killed at the Jumping Bull shootout. He was on a personal vendetta out to destroy AIM. He and Alex had a history, a bad history. Now she was part of it.

"Hand me your ID," he said.

She reached for the glove compartment to get her purse, but he cut her off with a curt "Uh-uh." She froze in mid-motion. He thought all Indians carried a gun. He hadn't noticed the eagle feather that protected their pickup. Reaching in her jeans for her wallet, she reluctantly handed over her license.

"Tatiana Pedersen, Minneapolis, Minnesota. Obviously stolen." Trask looked at her, then her photograph, then back to her. "Pedersen, you dye your hair black?"

Her name didn't match her dark features. He didn't know whether she was Indian or not.

Finally he smiled, tight-lipped. "You're Turning Hawk's new wife. You brought a piano into Camp Crazy Horse." He smiled again. "A baby grand full of guns smuggled in for AIM."

She'd have laughed if she weren't so afraid.

"We want to question you more, Tatiana Pedersen."

"Tate Turning Hawk."

"By either alias, stick around."

As if he knew her mind, he reached in, switched off the ignition, and removed the key.

She hadn't grabbed his sleeve, too slow to react, as numb as JJ, frozen in the snow.

"Don't leave the scene," he said.

Like hell she'd stay, even if Trask had her license—and the pickup key. Alex had taught her how to hot-wire the pickup, so she fished the screwdriver from under the seat, touched the loose wires, and started the engine again. Slowly she nudged the pickup past the bumper in front and turned in an arc across the highway.

A huge figure in a Stetson loomed in her headlights, waving his arms as if to stop her. She headed for him anyway, but when he jumped aside, she noticed his cruiser blocking the highway. She slid sideways across the blacktop into a snowdrift on the other side of the road. As he came toward her, she saw his name, Jelenik, and his brown mustache, gold badge, tan uniform, and gun holstered on his belt. Why was he here? He had no jurisdiction on the Res.

"Where're you going, squaw?" he shouted and lunged around the hood for her door.

She wasn't going to answer to *squaw*. She revved the engine instead.

"FBI said you'd sneak away." He braced his arms on the door frame. The pickup creaked.

She rolled up her window, but the door locks were long since broken.

He yanked the pickup door open and leaned in. "Hey, whazzat? You got a turkey feather?"

He said *turkey* with a jeer, so he must have recognized a white eagle feather, white tipped in black. He reached past her before she could block his arm and yanked at the feather.

"Don't touch that! It's sacred." She held her breath, willed him to let go. It wasn't a decoration or a talisman, but the feather Alex used for healing.

With a snap the red thread wrapped around the quill broke and the feather came loose in his hand. "That so, squaw?"

She grabbed his leather jacket arm and hung on to it.

He backed out, waved the feather aloft, and shook her loose as a coyote shakes off a dog.

She scrambled to her feet and jumped up to reach the eagle feather. "You can't take that!"

He backed away. "Yup. Gen-u-ine eagle feather. Yours, eh?" He dangled it above her head. "Against the law to possess the feather of an endangered species. I could arrest you for that, squaw, but I won't, 'cause I bet it's your old man's."

"He has a permit. Give it back!" She couldn't stop herself. She leaped in the air, grabbed the feather out of his hand, and shoved his chest away from her.

Caught off guard, he slipped on the icy road and almost fell, but regained his balance. His eyes went wide. Probably no squaw had ever pushed him around. As if time had frozen her stiff, he grabbed her arms, flipped her around against the hood, and cuffed her arms behind her to the pickup mirror.

"Help!" she screamed. "You fucking bastard!" She tried to kick him in the knee. Several cops turned to look, squinting through the snow.

"Fucking Indian squaw!" the sheriff called out to his audience. "You see her hit me? Assaulting an officer! Can't I admire this feather?" He dangled it in front of her.

She lunged toward him to kick him. "Fucking bastard stole my eagle feather!"

The cops didn't move. They took it all in, nudged each other and laughed.

"Thief!" she yelled.

Amidst the snow flurries, Agent Trask appeared next to the sheriff and took the feather from him. She could hardly believe Trask was coming to her rescue. She turned to thank him, but instead she said, "That sheriff's the thief, and he has no jurisdiction here. He can't arrest me!"

"He just has," Trask snapped at her, and turned abruptly away toward the sheriff, emphasizing each word. "You. Don't. Need. This. Sheriff." Then he dropped the feather at the sheriff's feet and ground it into the slush with his boot.

She felt the veins of the feather shiver and break, as if its life had been crushed out. The wind whistled and blew flakes over the feather's black tip. She could barely see it, beyond her reach.

Alex's feather was more than an object or good luck talisman. He used it to heal people. Trask had no idea what he'd done, what he'd brought upon himself. Then she saw the hard glint in his eyes. He knew what he'd done. It was as if he'd taken a crucifix from a church and smashed it to pieces. No wonder Alex hated him.

"Okay, Sheriff, take her into your little jail. She's first at the scene, keep her for questioning. We'll be back later." Trask turned abruptly, strode back toward the ambulance driver.

Furious, Tate threw herself backwards into the mirror's brace, which held, though the mirror broke and cut her hands. She swung her body forward, stretched her boot toward Alex's trampled feather to scoot it nearer.

The Sheriff said, "Uh, uh, you tricky squaw. That's for my collection." He dragged her up erect, released the handcuffs from the mirror brace, shoved her into the back of his cruiser, and slammed the door, which locked automatically. Then he picked up the feather, blew off the snow and grit, tucked it in an inside breast pocket, got into his cruiser, and drove her away.

The rear doors had no handles. A metal grille kept her from attacking the driver. Caged in, she huddled down in the rear seat. She should have left right away to tell Alex so they could drive to Pine Ridge Agency to identify JJ and claim her body. Instead she'd freaked out because of the missing hands. She dreaded what Alex's mom might say. Already Iná thought her a poor wife for a medicine-man-in-training, without manners or knowledge of Traditional ways. And Alex—he'd wait and worry, and then—no pickup. She saw the deserted pickup in the Badlands, its bed full of wood and kerosene and food, a temptation for every passerby. Soon it would be stripped, even the tires and battery gone—all they had. He would understand, but his mother Iná would blame her. She sank deeper.

At least the cruiser warmed her, and Alex's feather was nearby. She'd get it back. She felt a chill as they neared the invisible line at the river and left the Res. The Reservation might be dangerous, but it was safer than out in the White man's world where she'd been raised. As the cruiser crossed the White River, the Sheriff turned and said, "The FBI, they're transporting another dead Indian whore. But me, I got me a live one, a real prize—the local medicine man's shack-up."

She pulled into herself, wrapping her AIM armor around her so his words couldn't seep in. When they pulled into the jail parking lot, she told him the AIM refrain, "I know my rights. I demand a phone call." She must claim JJ's body. But who could she call? No one on the Res had phones. All the relatives used the Moccasin Telegraph—invisible gossip lines across the Res—and it didn't reach this far.

CHAPTER 3
ALEX

ALEX TURNING HAWK would apply to be an *Akichita*, a warrior in the old Kit Fox Society to protect the young and old, if he weren't a medicine-man-in-training sworn never to touch a gun. The elders had gathered to create a traditional Reservation Law & Order, to protect and serve the *People*. The old BIA cops—Bureau of Indian Affairs, or *Boss-Indians-Around*—were gone.

The new Board met in the Eagle Nest CAP round house, more like a large yurt than a tipi. In the big room its seats formed a semi-circle, round the Lakota way, with no dark corners for negativity to gather and spoil the harmony of consensus. On the Res, you solved problems slowly, chose your words carefully, spoke slowly without interruptions, in a sweeping cadence. You considered all aspects and took no rash steps until the path of action became clear. Unlike the *ewashichus,* the fast-talkers that came on the Res with a salesmen's pitch that you couldn't trust.

He was honored and humbled to be among a dozen elders, descendents of the 1861 Treaty signers. He dressed for the occasion, wearing a red pearl-button shirt, beaded vest, eagle plume tied in his braided hair, and his new alligator boots. Filling the room with the fragrance of sage and cedar, he opened the meeting with a Traditional Pipe prayer.

None of the AIM warriors had applied for the Kit Fox Society. They didn't want to become cops; they hated cops. Yet how else could the image of police as brutal enemies be changed to camp protectors? He nominated Tim New Holy, recent graduate of Crazy Horse School, for the Tribal Police Academy.

As the elders examined the papers before them, the CAP door banged open. Jerry Slow Bear, the ambulance driver, his burly, slow-talking cousin and rodeo-tough buddy, pointed his lips at Alex, silently calling him to come near. Outside, the ambulance's red flashers spun around. An emergency, probably someone who needed doctoring.

Jerry said, loud enough for all to hear, "Yer pickup's stalled by Dead Man's Drop-off. Better get it before it's stripped." He let go of the wooden door and turned toward the ambulance.

Alex apologized to the old gents, grabbed his parka and Pipe bag, and left. Outside, he looked for Tate in the passenger seat, but saw only a covered stretcher in the back. He caught his breath, grabbed Jerry's jacket. "That's not my wife, is it?"

Jerry shrugged. "Leggo, cuz. Just a dead body I gotta deliver to Pine Ridge before midnight."

Alex relaxed his hold. "So where is Tate?"

Jerry climbed into the ambulance and closed the door.

For some reason, Jerry wouldn't answer. Alex leaped on the running board and yanked it open. "Cuz, tell me straight—"

"Hey, I didn't hafta stop, but you're my relation." Jerry pulled his door shut, locked it, and yelled as he left, "Sheriff hauled her off to Kadoka jail."

Alex jumped off in a flurry of snow. No wonder Jerry was embarrassed for him. How could Tate have been arrested?

He caught a ride, kept silent the whole ground-blizzard way, praying that Tate hadn't been hurt in an accident, or accosted on the road home. Off-Res, Indian women were easy targets. Or had she said something rash while in the hands of the County Sheriff, who could make any Indian's words sound suspicious enough to be an excuse for a fine?

He'd have to rescue the pickup first. Drive to Kadoka. Hock something at the local bar for cash to bail her out. At last his ride's high beams shone on his deserted pickup, surrounded by a cross hatch of tire tracks in the snowdrifts, both sides of the road. As the driver slowed, Alex thanked his ride and got out at Devil's Drop-off, a sharp turn in the road that pulled drivers into Redstone Basin's deep gullies.

Many vehicles had come and gone. Lots of tire tracks in the snow. What had happened here? Deserted now, except for his faithful pickup, tires on. Propane, kerosene, food and firewood in the bed. He lifted the hood: battery still there. He slid in and hot-wired the pickup. He pumped the gas, revved the engine, and thanked the Great Mystery for protecting their supplies for a month.

Only then did he notice his eagle feather was gone. Strange, the Great Mystery had kept everything else safe. No wonder inside the pickup felt empty. Without it, he didn't feel complete. He'd have to find it. He used it in doctoring to brush off darkness. Was he losing his power? Its presence hadn't kept Tate safe. Or had she taken it with her to protect her in jail? The County Sheriff knew better than to arrest an Indian on the Res. Tribal jurisdiction. Indians were safe inside their prison on Res land. It must be federal.

Tate didn't drink, and wasn't a fool. But she was used to Minneapolis justice, Law and Order in the White world. The South Dakota Governor said publicly that, "The only good Indian is six feet under." Many had gone six-feet-under since Wounded Knee Occupation, eighty on the Res.

At the edge of town, he turned right, and pulled in behind a row of pickups parked outside the Kadoka Bar. It was long and thin like an old red boxcar. He tucked his Pipe bag behind the driver's seat. Part of him hated to go inside, clogged with alcohol fumes, but when he needed cash for bail, Wally the bartender knew him as a regular customer.

He opened the heavy door and scanned the room. Overhead hung rodeo hats, cowboy gear, coiled ropes, and old barbwire along with a grainy TV. The built-in booths and red vinyl stools in front of a long plank bar were empty. Too near dinnertime. Only a few regulars in the smoky back room played pool. He could talk to Wally privately.

He'd known Wally from his own rodeo days. Wally was a tough bronc rider who ran a mixed bar, both Indians and White ranchers welcome. As a White man, Wally could get away with it. Together he and Wally worked to keep Indians out of the Kadoka jail. Wally paid a fair price for valuable beadwork and quillwork, so Alex could rescue full-bloods and take them back to the Res before they fought two or three ranchers, broke all the bottles in the bar, or passed out.

Wally smiled to see him. "Hey, Saint Alex, whatchu gonna hock tonight?"

Old friends always joshed each other—friendly insults. Alex responded in mock-Injun-talk. "Long time no see-um. I need fifty bucks." The usual bail. "You want to hold this parka for me?"

Wally wrinkled his nose. "Jeez, Alex, what drunken relative you gonna rescue this time from our Indian-lover sheriff? You know I only take in good stuff. What about your beaded Pipe bag?"

Medicine men never hocked their sacred belongings. Only desperate drunks sank so low. But Wally liked to josh. Alex bent down, pulled off one alligator boot, and thunked it on the beer-soaked bar counter. "How about a new pair? They're worth three hundred." A wedding present from Tate's parents that he'd never worn until today. Movie star boots, too tight and thin. Her parents would approve of the boots rescuing Tate.

Wally whistled, looked at the boot, looked at Alex, and laughed. "Chief, where'd you get these Hollywood boots? Always knew you Indians was poor, but you'd be desperate to walk around with no boots in this goddam ground-blizzard."

Alex joshed right back. "My wool socks don't have no holes, and they're better'n Chief Big Foot's rags." He took off his other boot, pocketed the fifty bucks, and walked out sock-footed. He ignored the snow and ice. When he was six, his grandpa had taught him to turn on his internal heater. Part of his medicine training.

He drove two blocks to the County Courthouse on Main Street and parked in front of the familiar two-story white frame building with a cement foundation. He limped down to the basement door and entered the Sheriff's office. Inside, behind a metal door with a glass window came a droning twangy voice muffled by concrete walls.

He walked across the tiled floor and headed for the curio cabinet where the Sheriff kept his collection of beadwork and Indian artifacts. He turned the knob, but the glass door, which fit flush with the frame, was locked. Through the glass he saw beaded baby moccasins, braided horsehair ties, and several eagle feathers. Alex called to his, and felt a red glow draw him to where it lay beneath the others, just the tip of its shaft showing, beaded in a red-white-black vision hill design. Ruffled and damp, it waited for his hands to stroke it smooth again.

"Injun, what're you doing, breaking and entering?" The sheriff stood quietly behind him.

Alex turned around. "Come to get my wife."

"Who?"

The sheriff knew who. Wanted him beg. "Tate Turning Hawk."

"Can't release her to you." The Sheriff backed him out and shut the inner door, but not before Alex heard a muffled cry.

"*Mi-hi-gi-na!*"

Alex smiled, relieved. Tate was inside, and she knew the most important word in Lakota: *mihigna*, my husband. He stepped toward the door to the cells.

The sheriff barred his way. "She's drunk and disorderly."

"We both know she doesn't drink. What are the charges?"

"Disorderly conduct. Assaulting an officer." He pointed to his chest. "Me."

"This occurred at Dead Man's Drop-off, where I found my pick-up? And Dead Man's Drop-off is ten miles inside the Res?"

The sheriff huffed and hemmed.

"—which means it's under Tri-bal jur-is-dic-tion—" Alex emphasized the word.

"FBI said to hold her for questioning."

Alex became formal in his speech. "Illegal. Do you want to release her now and pursue this in Tribal Court, or shall I call in our AIM lawyers?"

Pause. "Her bail's set at fifty bucks."

The usual he paid for bailing out Indian drunks to bring back to the Res for purifying sweats. Alex waved the wrinkled bill in the air. "Receipt. Please."

"No receipt. Take it or leave it."

Alex let the bill float to the floor. "Take it or leave it. Please."

The Sheriff hesitated, then bent down to pick it up. He stared at Alex's feet. "Jeez, no shoes. You sneaky Redskins. No wonder I didn't hear you sneak in to rob me."

"Unlock her cell." He'd get Tate first, then come back later for his eagle feather.

~~~

Alex put his arm around Tate's shoulder, walked her out the basement door, and wrapped her in an old horse blanket kept behind the pickup seat. "Did anyone hit you, beat you, or try to rape you? I was so worried."

Tears streaked down her face. He couldn't tell whether she was trembling from fear, cold, or anger. As he headed home, he listened to her backwards story: anger at her arrest for pushing the sheriff who stole his eagle feather; fear of questioning by the FBI, who must have shadowed their pickup. They shadowed any pickup with Tribal plates or AIM bumper stickers saying *Custer wore Arrow shirts* or *Blessed with a Bilingual Mind*.

With each layer of story, he felt waves of disaster coming for AIM. He needed to sort out her tale. He went inside himself, became the turning hawk that flew above it all and saw everything. "Start at the beginning."

She burst out, "JJ's been killed." Tate frowned. "Don't you feel anything? I feel like I've lost an older sister. She was my best friend in Minneapolis AIM, long before I met you!"

He sucked in his breath. No wonder she'd been crying. And she'd said the name aloud, which called the dead to you. He drove one-handed, took her hands in his to comfort her. She had no idea he'd known Joanna Joe longer, that he had his own memories. He'd grieve later in a mourn sweat. Softly he said, "We don't speak the name of the dead aloud. Just call her *Our Lost One*."

Perhaps they were the last ones to see Joanna Joe alive. She must have found the second FBI informer. She'd been like a snapping turtle that never lets go of prey. The tobacco ties he'd made hadn't protected her. He'd let her walk out into the night to her death. If only his will had been stronger than hers. Now it was up to him, using the slow deliberate ways of the elders who examined every aspect of trouble before choosing a course of action.

Tate turned away and pulled the blanket tighter around her, as if anger could block tears. At last she said, cold and clear, "A hitchhiker stopped me." He leaped over the edge and fell. When I got down, he wasn't there. I found JJ instead. I don't know where he went."

No wonder she was upset. She'd seen a *wanaghi,* and tried to make sense of a ghost. Joanna Joe's spirit had floated onto the Badlands road to stop an AIM car. But Tate wouldn't believe that.

She stared at him. "Her hands were cut off. No blood."

So Joanna Joe hadn't bled to death. Maybe raped, killed, hands cut off, and dumped at Dead Man's Drop-off. Someone had wanted Joanna Joe's hands. A chill swept through him, as if her hands had reached out to him now, icy cold. How he'd pulled her inside to get warm by the woodstove in his cabin. Had a redneck collector wanted an AIM trophy? The act sent a message: *RED POWER cut off.* How easily this could happen to AIM, to George, to himself.

Tate shook her head, as if it was her fault. "She was in the snow. I looked for her hands but I couldn't find them anywhere."

He took one hand off the steering wheel and stroked her cheek. "Don't cry, They were already taken away. But I will find them and bring them back." Hands were sacred, powerful. Hands could zap someone, send them negative energy or blame. Images flashed in his head: fingers dropped off from frostbite, like Jake White Magpie who had only stumps from the Blizzard of '49. But to have no hands at all—to be denied what makes people human—how terrible. Without fingers and thumbs, no one could hold onto anything. A reminder of ultimate helplessness? She must have been like Chief No-Hands, *Napeshni*, who sacrificed himself for the People.

But hands were evidence. Dump them in a trash can, burn them in a fire, or throw them in a pond at the gravel pit. Had they been cut off because they might reveal tight cuff marks and torture?

Tate interrupted his thoughts. "Your favorite FBI Agent came, Trask, and dozens of cops."

He clutched the steering wheel to keep from swerving off the road. State Troopers and County Sheriffs never came on the Res—no jurisdiction—only FBIs and tribal cops. And they never came when you needed them. An APB must have alerted them, but it wasn't curiosity that roused them in the middle of the night to go nowhere in a ground-blizzard. Trask must have called law and order for a hundred miles to be witnesses. For a dead Indian woman dumped on the Res. Maybe they'd already been on alert. Alert for AIM's reaction. A set-up.

Tate said, "That bastard Trask called her a drunk Indian whore."

He sensed a trap. Joanna Joe's body dumped on the Res meant tribal jurisdiction and tribal cops, yet the FBI had taken charge of the scene, which meant they considered it a major crime—murder. How convenient for Trask and Slade, who'd been after Joanna Joe for months, to arrive so timely at the scene. They'd have recognized her face, even without her tell-tale hands.

Now the trap made sense. The FBI wanted control of the body, to erase any evidence of rape or beatings, any kind of mistreatment. Had a cop been ordered to find the body? Had a *wanaghi* wrecked that plan and guided Tate there first?

As Tate relived her tale, she became more frantic. "They hauled her to Pine Ridge Agency. Alex, we have to go and claim her. She has no relatives."

He disagreed. He needed to see the scene to study the dark energy at Dead Man's Drop-off. Then go directly to tell George, their AIM leader. Avoid a Pine Ridge trap. He slowed at the turn in the road.

Tate cried, "Stop here! The hitchhiker. We have to find him!"

There'd be no hitchhiker. Alex tried to reassure her. "He'll have caught a ride."

Tate glared at him. "I saw a real man on the road. He's still out there in the Badlands." She opened her door a crack. "I'm getting out."

He must check out where Joanna Joe had died, so he pulled beside drifts on the side of the slope. Tate was like Grandpa Little Thunder, who always threatened to jump out if he didn't get his way. High beams revealed tire tracks on the edges of the road, but left the gully in darkness.

She opened the glove compartment and turned on the flashlight. "I'll show you." She jumped out and shined the light down over the snowdrifts. "See, no ghosts here."

No yellow crime scene tapes, either. He put the brakes on, left the pickup in neutral and got out sock-footed. His feet were warm. "I believe you!" The FBI had probably wiped out any clues. Before he could reach her, she'd climbed down into the gully and wandered in the dark with a flashlight that could die any minute.

She called up to him, "See? The hitchhiker jumped down here."

He slid down after her, felt the snow harden and the air thicken as if pushing through a wall. They shouldn't be here. Joanna Joe's body was gone, but her *wanaghi* remained.

Tate shined the light over footprints in the snow, back and forth. Dozens of boot prints, thick work boots, pointy-toed cowboy boots, round-toed trooper boots with heels, waffle-soled boots, ripple-soled sneakers. The flat prairie was trampled with boot prints over boot prints. And everywhere, ghost footprints.

"What are you looking for?" he asked.

She bent over small square indentations in the snow. "My boot-prints. *Our Lost One* wore my boots." Then she turned the flashlight on him. "You don't have any boots on. Your socks are full of ice. How could you have lost your new alligator boots?"

She'd forgotten that he could turn on his body-heater, send sparks of energy down into his toes. Uncle Jasper had taught him long before he found out it was a special skill. Touched by his wife's concern, he caught her in his arms and warmed her with his body until their breaths became one. Silence surrounded them and the Great Bear shone overhead. "We'll be okay," he said.

After Tate was warm, he searched with the flashlight for the imprint of Joanna Joe's body. He'd been trained to study people's bodies, living ones, for clues about which herbs to use. "Did you see any bullet holes? Knife wounds?" he asked.

"I—I didn't look You told me we're not supposed to touch a dead body."

But she could have looked. "Any bruises on her neck?"

In reply, Tate pulled out a small red bundle from her pocket. "This was hidden in her hair."

She handed it to him. "Is it one you gave her?"

As soon as he touched the *woluta* he knew it was from his prayer offering for Joanna Joe. His protection had failed, the string broken apart, this one retied and strange. Vibrant no fragrant tobacco smell, more like something flowery, sweet. Where were the rest of the tobacco ties? Had she torn the necklace apart, desperate for a smoke? No wonder they hadn't protected her. How could one get caught in her hair? The small *woluta* chilled his hand. Cold and stiff, yet he felt it crinkle to the touch. Not a *woluta*, though it looked like one. No tobacco inside, more like a scrap of paper. Perhaps a message. Too dark to see in the dim flashlight, he pocketed it to check out later.

He regretted so much. He'd let Joanna Joe rush out into the night in search of the second FBI informer. If only he'd found the traitor first.

"This is serious, Tate," he said. "You touched death, in a place sur-rounded by evil." He felt its darkness swirl around and fill the air. "You need a sweat to purify you and keep you strong." He put his arm around her and led her to her seat in the pickup. Once inside, he revved the engine, headed up Quiver Hill and on to Eagle Nest.

She tossed her head. "If it makes any difference, I wore gloves."

He barely heard her. If they went to claim the body, the FBIs would blame AIM. His wife worried about the hitchhiker-ghost, Joanna Joe's body, his lost eagle feather, her own arrest—minor problems. He worried about more than another AIM warrior lost. A deadly trap had been set to destroy AIM: reclaim the body in Pine Ridge and provoke another firefight with the Pine Ridge Agency Goons, the tribal president's private Indian bodyguards. Then the FBIs would swoop in. Only they had jurisdiction for capital crime on the Res. AIM would be framed.

First they took you in for questioning and then you'd disappear, like Joanna Joe. The FBIs sucked you into a black hole. They took you to motel rooms to interview. And kept you there, no calls to lawyers. They gave the guys wine, women, and dope. They sweet-talked you until you confessed, or told them what they wanted to hear. Threat-ened your family. Beat you up. Vengeance for their two agents killed in 75. Whatever it took to *get their man*. Disaster for AIM. For Camp Crazy Horse. For George and the Turning Hawks.

Tate asleep in the blanket, leaned against him. The FBIs would try to pin Joanna Joe's death on AIM. Instead, he vowed to expose their informer as the killer and bring him to justice.

~~~

Midnight. Alex raced to tell George, their AIM leader, that Joanna Joe had been killed. Eagle Nest wasn't much of a town: water tower, school, clinic, post office, tribal office, American Legion Hall, and one store. Alex drove past empty cabins and shacks, past darkened houses and trailers of eight missionaries and eleven bootleggers, up to the newest of all, the seventy-two Bureau of Indian Affairs housing circle planted on the open prairie, prefabs clustered together just like prairie dogs sleeping. Two weeks ago Pine Ridge Agency Goons had started a firefight and shot out all of the housing circle's street and yard lights. Broken windows ply-boarded, since the scaredy-cat government employees didn't come into an AIM town. Quiet now. No dogs barked, no doors opened, no clicks of rifles cocked in windows. Only the wind whistled through the broken swings of the housing's central playground.

Their headlights lit up the AIM house, black graffiti spray-painted over the AIM logo—a Red Power fist planted in the center of an upside-down American flag. He cut the lights and engine, coasted into the driveway and stopped behind a bullet-riddled blue Chevy pickup.

Tate stirred but didn't wake. He re-tucked the red blanket around her and climbed out.

Alex felt closest to George, who'd been raised in the city and didn't speak Lakota.

George Lonehill had been chosen as AIM's leader by age, experience and command, even though his school had been the streets and prison. He'd emerged scarred but not hardened, his rage focused like a laser on Indian Treaty rights. He'd let go of alcohol and drugs along with anger, then married and had a kid with Shuta. Now George followed the sacred Pipe and walked the Red Road of Peace.

Alex tramped through the snowdrifts to the back corner of the AIM house. He rapped lightly on the frost-coated glass of George's bedroom window, the AIM S-O-S knock. George hated to be woken up in the middle of the night. Too many times it had been the cops breaking in.

He heard a groan. Someone stirred. He knocked again. A shadow drew the sheet curtain aside. A hand wiped a circle in the frost. Alex whispered, "*Hau, kolá, miyelo.*" Hi, friend, it's me.

George's head loomed, puffy-eyed and ratty-haired. "Shit, Alex, it's the middle of the night!"

No way not to say her name to get George's mind to snap open. "Joanna Joe."

"Jeez, Alex, why'd you bring her here? I can't let her in. Shuta'd kill me."

"Outside, we have to talk."

"Lemme get dressed. Don't want to wake Shuta." George disappeared.

Alex didn't want to wake Shuta, either. He prayed all the way back to the pickup to keep all hell from breaking loose. Unless they put themselves in the Great Mystery's hands, more AIM warriors would die.

The kitchen door opened. George, in red long johns and short braids, loomed in the doorway with a flashlight. His square face, weathered and frowning, made him seem older. He stepped barefoot onto the cold cement steps. "Damn, bro, don't bring her here."

Alex walked up the steps and shook George's hand, the AIM brothers' handshake, then dropped it and embraced him. In his ear he whispered, "She's gone, George."

George looked confused. "She's not in the pickup?" He shone the flashlight into the cab. "Damn, looks like her." He stared. "But that's your wife."

A blast of wind rattled the house windows and the cars in the driveway. The half-open kitchen door slammed shut. Alex shook his head to find his voice. He couldn't look George in the face, so he bowed his head. "Gone to the Spirit World."

For a moment, silence. Then George, his face contorted, whispered, "Last year I sent her away." George pushed Alex out of the way into a snow bank, groaned like a wounded buffalo, and ran out onto the dark open prairie beyond the housing circle.

At the sound, Tate woke up, startled. She climbed out of the pickup. "George has gone crazy! Go after him!"

Alex brushed himself off. Joanna Joe hadn't made it into town, at least not to George. But Alex hadn't expected George to go wild with grief before he could talk sense into him and they could strategize to keep AIM safe. "He needs to run into the wind, run out his sorrow."

Tate shook her head. "He's barefoot—like you. I'll go get him."

He put his hand out to block her. "Don't go near. He'll hit at anything in his way. That's how Indian men grieve."

She stamped her boots. "Let's go inside." She climbed up the stairs and tried the door.

After the firefight, everyone locked their doors. "We wait. He's our leader."

Finally Tate sat down on the steps below him. He held her shoulders between his knees, rocked her back and forth, and quietly sang a mourning song. Starlight transformed the sleeping houses into ghostly shapes of long-lost wolves and buffalo, antelope and elk, kit fox and coyote. Yip-yips in the distance reminded him that coyotes were still around, waiting for prairie dog dawn.

At last George returned, limping and winded but tearless. Blood dripped onto the steps. George had cut his feet and ankles on the stubble, or on rusty tin cans and broken wine bottles dumped behind the housing circle.

"She wanted her gun," Alex said, "to track down a second FBI informer."

"Shit," George said, brushing off his bloody soles. "So he got to her first."

Tate stood up and tried to wrap her blanket around George's feet. "You're bleeding!"

George shook the blanket off and turned to Alex. "Anybody else know?"

Alex shook his head. Medicine men kept the secrets of the people, but he had no idea who would betray AIM, even though some in Eagle Nest had blamed AIM for the shootout.

George asked him, "You found her?"

"Tate did, and got held for questioning. I bailed her out." He counted off the cops present at the scene: BIA cops, State Troopers, County Sheriff, FBIs.

George looked up warily, assessing the situation. "So it's a Tribal case."

"Federal. Agent Trask took her body to Pine Ridge—"

Tate interrupted, "No! The killer cut off her hands."

George flinched. "You saw?" He reached out and took Tate's hand. "You're cold. We'll go inside where it's warm, get some hot coffee and stew. Then we'll head out to get her back. Then *we'll* cut off some hands!"

Alex grabbed George by his long johns, nearly ripping them. "*Witkótko!*" Fool. "Just what they want! The old AIM way—the fist. Violence for violence. We'll end up arrested or killed—"

"I don't know any other way. Survival. I always use my fists." George held up his bloodied hands and shook his head like a buffalo testing the wind.

"You know another way—the Pipe." Alex took George's hands in his own. "When you came here, I gave you a sacred Pipe. You carry the AIM Pipe now. You must pray."

George jerked his hands loose. "I've prayed. Now my heart is black."

"George is right!" Tate interrupted. "We have to go to Pine Ridge and claim her body, demand an investigation, make the FBI find the killer—"

George stared at her. "The FBI *are* the killers!"

Tate stared back at him. "How do you know?"

"We've been roughed up and jerked around by the FBIs for years. They are out to destroy AIM, just like they did to the Black Panthers and Martin Luther King."

"Aren't you jumping to conclusions? Looking in the wrong place?" asked Tate.

His wife was right. "We must be wise as the buffalo, sharp as the hawk, to trap the FBIs into revealing their second informer."

George, tight-lipped, turned to him. "We won't fall into any FBIs' trap. I'm already under indictment, and have to stay clear."

Alex pointed to the basement where the AIM warriors stayed. "*They* won't. When they hear we lost another warrior, they're gonna go for their rifles. They've been trigger-happy ever since the Pine Ridge Agency Goons shot up this town."

He blurted out his plan, hoping George agreed. "We have to stall them. Use your AIM Pipe, they'll recognize that. We'll pray for her, then drag them to Camp Crazy Horse for a mourn sweat so hot, it'll wipe their anger out."

George nodded. "Keep them busy chopping firewood and fixing fence out in the country where it's safe."

They'd last about a day. The AIM warriors couldn't be stopped so easily from seeking revenge. He hoped George, who'd gone to a medicine man for help before the AIM trials, would be open to *yuwípi*, a Lakota *finding* ceremony. "We need the Spirit People to tell us who killed her."

"Yes," George said slowly. "Otherwise we'll turn against each other."

"You keep the warriors busy, chop firewood for the sweat, prepare tobacco ties for the ceremony. I'll bring back Old Sam from Oglala—"

"What? We're not going to Pine Ridge Agency?" Tate cried.

George stared at her. She'd forgotten not to interrupt, not yet used to Res rhythm, slow talking, pauses, wait and listen.

"It's cold," Alex said. "Let's go in and gather the AIM guys, cool them down with strategy.

Tate frowned. "We have to wake somebody, since we're locked out."

George gave her another look, fished a key from his long johns, and opened the door.

CHAPTER 4

TATE

AIMs VERSUS GOONS. On one side—her side—she was AIM, the American Indian Movement, urban Indians plus Tradtional Res Indians, like her husband, working together for Indian Treaty and Civil Rights. On the other side were Pine Ridge Agency Goons, a law unto themselves, plus the Bureau of Indian Affairs employees, who wanted to keep their jobs. Watching them all were the FBIs.

The AIM House was easy to find. It sat at the far end of the Eagle Nest housing circle, its brick wall painted red and black with the AIM logo, a warrior's profile, his head topped with two eagle feathers. She entered the side door, which opened to a large open area Four bedrooms for George and his wife Shuta, and older men, and a large basement bunkroom for the young warriors.

Tate welcomed the hot steamy kitchen. People in Eagle Nest Housing got free heat, so they kept it hot for the kids, who ran around in diapers all winter and caught colds from the least bit of snow and wind. Her friend Shuta, George's wife, stood in a striped wrapper, tall and broad-shouldered, with tangled hair. Shuta poured boiling water into the coffeepot and flashed her eyes at them, silent. She pointed at George. "You moaning around outside! Who's killed now?"

"*Our Lost One*," Tate blurted out. "We've got to go—" She looked at George. His broad face loomed like a ghost, his eyes dark holes.

George said, "We got a full house, wait—"

What was wrong with Shuta? Indian women spoke out. They even ran AIM meetings in the city. Was it because she'd interrupted George?

In a low voice George said, "Joanna Joe."

Tate looked at Alex. George had said her name aloud. He should know better.

"Aiyee!" Shuta wailed and spun around, spraying hot coffee across the room. The pot hit the floor with a thud and rolled across the linoleum.

George reached out to catch Shuta, but she broke away and kept screeching. Her high loud wails, *ai-yi-yi*, pierced the air, over and over.

Tate had never heard such high-pitched screams, not even when babysitting. She glanced at Alex. Was this Traditional keening, when women slashed their arms and legs? Tate ducked out of the way as Shuta tossed her hair over her face, threw herself into the walls and against the gas stove, where her long wild hair caught fire. She'd never seen Shuta so distraught, screaming and running her hands through her singed hair, her wide face smudged with soot and tears.

Perhaps JJ's death on top of Shuta's miscarriage, was too much. But as Shuta's hysterics continued, they sounded forced. Tate peered into the darkness of the living room. Teenage boys wrapped in blankets, some on the three couches, some on the rug in front of the TV, rolled over and covered their heads. Others stood up, hands over their ears, or rubbed their eyes.

Alex spoke to them over the keening, "Don't get scared, she's in mourn."

George caught Shuta from behind, beat the flames out with a wet dishrag, and held her arms down in a tight hug. She kicked his legs and banged her head back against his chin.

Tate ran to help Shuta, but Alex stopped her, pulling her into the open living room. "Let George handle it."

As the AIM warriors stomped up from the basement into the living room, wide-eyed and alert for trouble, Lester strode past Alex and said, "Turn off the lights! No more bullet holes in our house." He took Shuta from George, and talking in Lakota, calmed her down.

When Tate looked surprised, Alex said, "He speaks Lakota. He's her brother."

When Shuta's cries stopped, Lester walked her toward their bedroom.

Shuta shook her head, her singed hair flying loose. "I'm staying."

Just like that, Shuta had closed off her grief, back in control, sullen and resentful.

Alex whispered to Tate, "If you take her back into the bedroom, you can tell her firsthand, and George can start the meeting. Only men at AIM strategy meetings."

Alex said that on the Res men worked with men, women with women, because men and women spoke Lakota differently, each with their own special words. But this was the 20th Century. Men and women needed to work together. She'd found the body, but the men ignored her eye-witness account. Only Alex's second-hand version counted.

The real reason was that Shuta was still bleeding from her miscarriage, and couldn't be near the sacred Pipe, and Alex wanted to smoke the sacred Pipe together to start their strategy meeting. Tate could have stayed, but she needed to help Alex. Tight-lipped, she told Alex, "All right. We women will have our own AIM strategy meeting." Shuta was the strongest AIM woman, tough as iron. She'd been through a lot. She'd know who'd been out to get JJ.

Tate took Shuta's arm, pulled her to the bedroom door. Behind it, she heard their three-year-old son crying. Kids didn't need chaos and violence.

Shuta rattled the door. "Tokeya, open up. It's me."

Inside, more crying, a heavy object scraping the floor, a click, and the door swung open.

Tate stepped around an elk-hide AIM drum as large as Tokeya, who'd dragged it over to block the door. Long drumsticks spilled out of a bag. He picked up a drumstick as tall as he was, ready to beat on any intruder. He was all elbows and knees and long braids down his small back.

"It's just me, Tate. Don't beat me," she said, flailing her arms, pretending to be afraid. Three-year-old Tokeya was so energetic, jumping into the midst of the grownups and climbing on their laps, even hers. She'd loved it, his trust, his arms clinging tightly. She'd had no brothers or sisters to play with, and her foster parents hadn't allowed her to babysit. She missed the playfulness.

Sure enough, he dropped the drumstick and leaped into her arms.

"You're my drummer boy," she said, brushing away his tears. She picked his small drum up from the floor and handed it to him. At three, she'd banged out tunes on her miniature piano. Now Tokeya was banging on his drum. "Where's your drumstick?" she asked.

"Big one." He pointed to the one on the floor.

Shuta shut the door, picked the drumstick up, and put it back in the large drum bag. "That's George's," she said. "Don't touch your father's things." She took Tokeya and sat him on the bed. "Men's toys," she said to Tate.

In a drum group, each man had his own drumstick. Better the drumstick than the gun. There were too many guns in the basement with children around.

Tokeya cried, "I want my Daddy."

"Shhh." Shuta wrapped him in a star quilt and lay beside him. "Lakota boys cry *Hoka hey*, like Crazy Horse. Be quiet now, your father's in a meeting and I want to hear." To Tate she said, "Bring me some hot tea, and leave the door open a crack."

Tate slipped out for tea, brought back two steaming cups of peppermint, closed the door, and set them near a small tipi lamp on the bedside table. On the wall overhead hung a poster of AIM warriors at Wounded Knee Occupation '73. In the dim light she could make out George, who stood in the center of a bunch of men, wearing a headband and carrying the AIM banner, and near the edge, Shuta standing tall. Tate pointed to a second woman in the poster.

Beside Shuta, a foot shorter, stood JJ. How brave she'd been then, how shrunken and cold now.

When she'd found JJ, Tate had cried hard, but not like Shuta. Now too much had happened for her to cry. Yet she couldn't erase the memory of JJ's stretched-out body in the gully beside the road. "I knew her, but you knew her better. You must miss her a lot."

Shuta sat up on the bed next to Tokeya. "Just because you saw me cry, you think I'm weak. I lost a baby, and I'm still strong." She picked up her cup of tea.

Tate sat at the end of the bed and drank hers. Of course Shuta grieved. JJ was the first AIM woman killed. Shuta might know who did it. Tate asked, "Wasn't she your best friend?"

"We been through a lot together, arrested and jailed." Shuta sat on the bed and gulped down the tea. Leaving Tokeya, half-asleep on the bed, she went to the doorway. "Shhh. I need to know their plans. Men are so stupid. So macho they think they can shoot off their guns and make things okay. But we have to protect our kids." She listened a moment, then asked, "Are you pregnant yet?"

"Not yet. I have no symptoms." Symptoms, as if pregnancy were a disease. She wasn't sure what the symptoms were. She'd only heard complaints from other AIM women. But she and Alex were still on their honeymoon.

"Too bad." Some women just can't have kids.

Tate picked up the empty teacups. She didn't mind the suggestion. She loved kids, but she wanted to get used to the Res, meet all her Turning Hawk relatives, and learn Lakota first. She'd take her time so she'd not to miscarry like Shuta. She joined Shuta at the door.

Shuta said, "They're still passing around the Pipe. Indian prayers take forever."

"Let's sit back down, then." She wanted to ask about JJ, but it was awkward without mentioning her name aloud. "I don't care what the men do. We have to claim *her* body from the Pine Ridge Agency before the FBIs bury *her* in an unmarked grave."

Shuta sat on the bed with her. "No we don't. We have to track down the killer, and he ain't at Pine Ridge!" She handed Tate a hairbrush and turned her back toward her. "Brush my hair, get the burned part out."

Shuta had reverted to her bossy self, as if to erase a moment of weakness. She might talk more freely if Tate sat behind her, out of sight, and could watch her face in the mirror. "George thinks the FBIs did it. Do you?"

"FBIs don't waste time on women. They're after AIM leaders like George." Shuta jerked her head. "Only one bastard goes after us."

Tate thought the FBI were bastards enough. "Who?"

Shuta spat out the words. "*Her* driver."

Tate brushed Shuta's hair and waited. Then Tate asked, "Who drove *her*?" Silence. She stroked, stroked, to calm Shuta down, as if the brush could bring out answers. Tate phrased it differently. "Who drove *her* when she went underground?" More silence. Stroke, stroke. Tate tried again. "Who'd cut off *her* hands?"

At last Shuta responded, as if from deep inside. "He'd do anything."

"What's his name?"

Shuta hesitated, as if she didn't want to bring his presence into the room. "Night Cloud."

Though Tate could watch Shuta's face twist into a snarl in the mirror, she couldn't tell what Shuta felt. Shuta's tough armor made it hard to be friends, but Tate felt sorry for her, the AIM leader's wife. She didn't think George brushed and braided Shuta's hair, as she and Alex did. Tate put her hand on Shuta's head and gently pulled out the singed hair.

"Careful. Put it over there, in the hair bag. Hair is power. We keep burned hair, too."

Tate reached for the bag. "What's Night Cloud's first name?"

"You never heard of him because you weren't around. He was an FBI informer inside Wounded Knee Occupation. *She* caught onto him right away, dyeing his hair!" Shuta burst into harsh laughter. "None of us in the trenches had time to wash ours!"

Why hadn't Alex noticed Night Cloud in the sweats at Wounded Knee Occupation? "Maybe he was a wannabe."

"Not a chance." Shuta pointed her lips and chin, Indian style, toward the poster. "But *she* collected evidence. He was slick, though. He accused *her* of being the FBI informer, said *she* was always around when AIM got in trouble."

"Not in Minneapolis."

"*She* caught him stealing a million dollars of donations from AIM."

Tate would have heard about that much of a loss. "Did George want the crime kept quiet?"

Shuta spit out, "George finally caught Night Cloud meeting with the FBIs."

"What'd the FBIs say?"

"Nothing. AIMs kicked Night Cloud off the Res, told him he's dead if he returns." Shuta knotted her fists. "If you don't kill a rattler, he'll come back to bite you. Your *peace-loving* husband worked on George's mind. Now AIM won't kill him, even if he comes back for more *squaws*."

Tokeya whimpered in his sleep.

Tate whispered, "He's still around?"

Shuta paused, looked at her son, and continued in a low voice. "He's a killer. Young girls are his specialty. He shacked up with my teenage cousin, got her drunk, and ran over her on the highway to Nebraska. 'Dead by exposure,' the authorities said."

Taken aback, Tate asked, "What's your cousin's name?"

Shuta turned away. "Francine Running Deer killed, hit-and-run on Nebraska highway. And he raped more of us women than her."

Shocked, Tate asked, "Did he ever get to you?"

"What do you think my name means in Lakota? *Tough*. "You think I'm not tough? I survived it all. Shuta glanced up at the poster. "He didn't get to me, like he got to *her*."

It was clear that Shuta thought Night Cloud had killed JJ. "Didn't anybody prosecute this Night Cloud?"

Shuta jerked toward her, eyes fierce. "Are you kidding? Nothing! *No evidence.*"

Tate's brush had filled Shuta's dark hair with electricity, haloing her puffy face. She looked like a banshee, a woman on the warpath. So vehement, perhaps Shuta'd exaggerated Night Cloud's crimes. Alex had never mentioned him. She'd find out more about this first informer, the one out to get JJ. She could ask questions, find out things, not blinded by anti-White prejudice. Shuta hadn't convinced her that Night Cloud was the killer.

"Night Cloud swore he'd get *her.* He's around. Near enough to dump *her* on the Res and cut off *her* hands as a trophy." Shuta flicked her fingers toward an invisible enemy outside the window. "This time he won't get away. I've got kids and can't hunt him down. You find the fucker, you get him for me!"

She'd do it for JJ, for AIM, not just Shuta. She'd investigate this Night Cloud person on her own. She didn't believe all Shuta said, who was so biased and so bitter. Tate had been in Minneapolis with AIM and had never heard of him. Besides, he'd been run off the Res a while ago. She'd ask Lester.

Meanwhile, at the strategy meeting in the living room, the AIM warriors were eager to take on the FBIs themselves, who could harass, interrogate, and threaten. But would the FBIs choke someone out, in a close personal attack? Surely they wouldn't cut off hands to steal JJ's jewelry?

She hadn't forgotten that a second FBI informer lurked on the Res. Together she and Alex must find him and bring him to justice.

CHAPTER 5
ALEX

WHEN TATE AND SHUTA went in the bedroom, Alex and George rounded up the AIM warriors for a strategy meeting. Warrior energy filled the room. "Nobody's shooting at us," Alex said. "Calm down." On the Res, Traditionals took things slowly, no rash action. They spoke slowly and listened rather than interrupted. Called it *ewashichu,* like a fast-talking salesman. But the urban AIMs had to learn patience. On the Res, you took things slowly, spoke slowly without interruptions, with a Res cadence. You considered all aspects of a problem and took no rash actions until all was clear.

Alex's goal was to keep the peace, to avoid senseless vengeance and death. He had to reconnect the AIM warriors with the sacred Pipe. As he looked around the room, he wondered if one of them could be the second FBI informer. Hard to imagine. He'd been with them inside Wounded Knee Occupation, and knew each one well. No AIM warrior would betray his brothers. Nor kill a woman. Someone else on the Res had taken the FBIs bribe money.

Lester Bear Heart stood beside George. A Vietnam vet, he carried his rifle in his hands. Alex said, "Put it down. No guns with the Pipe." Burned out by Vietnam, Lester had sundanced to learn the old Lakota ways of living to heal his heart. He'd become George's right-hand man.

Old Louie was next. Louie Bad Wound, the oldest, descendent of the Great Sioux Nation Treaty signers, a Traditional with a long gray ponytail sticking out of his beaded baseball cap. Alex needed him, a

Lakota orator who could recite from memory the Treaty articles, history, and stories of the People. Old Louie kept youthful by hanging with the young bloods. He wouldn't take a money settlement for the Black Hills, let alone from the FBIs.

Chaské, the youngest, Alex's hot-headed nephew, a teenager, awkward around the edges from an inch-a-month growth, bounding like a frisky colt. A few years ago Alex had felt like that, embarrassed that his body felt beyond his control, all disjointed arms and legs. Chaské had cut his hair short, but left long bangs, which he tossed back to impress the girls, Arapaho style. He might be attracted to money, but he was too young to legally drive off-Res.

Smokey, Alex's rodeo buddy, solid and stubborn, glued to saddle broncs and bulls, while he, Alex, lightning-quick, rode bareback and roped anything that moved. Smokey had seen it all on the Indian rodeo circuit, gained his reputation as a ladies' man, elusive as smoke, his gray eyes that pulled them in—but he'd tired of it and came back to the Res to fight for Indian rights. He'd see through any attempt at bribery, unless he'd gambled away lots of money. No casinos here on-Res.

Then the other AIM warriors who'd stayed in town after Wounded Knee Occupation—Dave, Willie, Ben, Vietnam vets from different tribes. Alex didn't know them well, so he'd watch them closely to see if they left Camp Crazy Horse or Eagle Nest for a rendezvous with the FBIs. Last, the Locals: Chappa, the Beaver, with his big front teeth; Yamini, the third in his family. Dressed alike in cowboy boots, worn jeans and t-shirts, with long hair bound back by red bandanas, and leather belts with sheathed knives. No bows and arrows or slingshots, just deer rifles in the basement. Both raised families in town, poor but proud, too proud to turn against AIM.

As he surveyed the room, Alex was proud of the AIM warriors and Camp Crazy Horse. He didn't see anyone he'd suspect as an FBI informer.

Only Sonny remained below, sleeping it off, Shuta's harmless brother, the one Alex couldn't stand, always drunk. The FBIs didn't use winos as informers, much as winos would grab at the chance.

George turned to them. "Brothers, I've called an AIM strategy meeting—" He paused.

"Remember, we start by smoking the Pipe." He took Lester's rifle and put it in the coat closet.

The warriors shifted and shuffled to seats. Finally Chaské asked, "Who got killed?"

Silence. Then Alex replied for George. "The one who exposed the first FBI informer."

Some of the warriors bent over, some let out moans, while others stiffened. Old Louie choked back a sob and bowed his head.

Alex felt nervous energy scatter about the room. Chaské, always impatient, wanted to know what they were going to do. So did Lester Bear Heart, who paced back and forth among them. Tough, disciplined, and loyal, he could be counted on to keep the warriors in line. He'd survived 'Nam, and knew how to strategize.

"Time to get this meeting started," Lester said.

George's job. But George came out from the kitchen. He carried an enamel coffeepot and an ice cream bucket full of cups, serving Lester first. "Gotta wake up, brothers. Long night ahead."

Alex grabbed the coffeepot and followed George around the room until the circle of warriors all had coffee. He felt humbled by a true leader—the first to feed, the last to eat.

Nothing tasted better than a mouthful of dark boiled Res coffee. More than a custom, it was a shared cup before battle. His AIM brothers, ten long-hairs, milled around the room, some sleepy, some ready for action. Alex counted hot heads and cool dudes. How to reach them all?

After everyone had settled, George spoke quietly. "Brothers, come make a Hoop." They gathered in a tight circle, shoulders touching. George waited until all stood still. "We lost a fighter, one of AIM's best. Some of you knew *her* from inside Wounded Knee Occupation."

George raised his hand to halt talk. "Brothers, there's been a trap set for us. So first we're gonna smoke our AIM Pipe and pray for *her* spirit." He motioned to Alex. "Lead the prayers."

Chaské nudged Alex. "We need action!"

Alex, next to Chaské, shrilled his hawk cry, *kree–kree–*, into his nephew's ear. The *Hochoka*, the tight circle of brothers, had been broken. Like George earlier, the warriors needed to release their anger, fear, and grief. Alex laid the AIM Pipe back on its bed of sage. "Brothers, we can't lose any more of us. First we have to strategize."

Alex gave details about Joanna Joe and named inconsistencies: ten cops immediately at the scene, the body dumped on the Res for tribal jurisdiction, the FBIs' takeover for capital crimes.

Some warriors sprawled on the couches, chairs, or floor. Others milled around, ready to bolt. George, next to him, raised his hand. "Speak one at a time, Brothers."

"I say we go get her." Lester's loud voice filled the room. "Get her out of the morgue tonight before they bury her as a Jane Doe."

Old Louie lit a cigarette. "She's one of us. We gotta fight for her."

Alex asked, "Louie, what's the best way to fight for her? Walk into a trap?"

"Head out now," Chaské said. "Raise hell, four carloads, hit 'em before daylight!"

"Who're you gonna shoot?" Smokey asked. "Chop off Pine Ridge Agency Goon hands?"

Chaské stared back. "Why can't we go down and steal her back?"

Silence. Alex groaned. "Chaské, half of AIM is on trial right now for Wounded Knee Occupation. Shuta's on probation. Others are in jail, out on bond, or hiding in Canada, threatened with extradition. George has to lay low. We're all that's left. We gotta keep ourselves alive and safe."

Old Louie said, "You young'uns don't remember how our gov'nr said the only way to deal with AIM was to put a gun to our heads and pull the trigger. He wants all of us in jail, or under it."

Lester stood up. "I'll go alone. I've been on this kind of mission before. Break into the morgue before they autopsy her. We can bury her at Camp Crazy Horse."

Alex knew how badly George wanted to see her one last time. Yet George only said, "Lester, you could get her, but she's dead. I need you here. I count on you."

Alex said, "We need to find her killer right away." The second FBI informer, he thought.

"If the FBIs want to write off her death, how the hell will they explain her hands cut off—" George choked up.

Lester asked, as if he couldn't believe it, "You sure her hands were cut off?"

Smokey jumped in. "They'll say someone came along to steal her frozen-on jewelry, and cut off her hands. That's FBIs' logic."

"Maybe the FBIs hired a killer and wanted proof." Old Louie said in a deep whiskey voice, "Bring back a body part, then they'll pay you."

"Bloody bastards want a trophy!" said Chaské.

Alex disagreed. "They cut off her hands so there'd be no more RED POWER."

"Trask got her at last," said Old Louie, "like he said."

Smoky replied, "If the FBIs wanted her disappeared, she must have had something on them. Hidden somewhere. We need to find it."

Old Louie looked up at George. "If the FBIs want to crush AIM in their trap, us hunters are too smart to fall for it."

George stared into the swirling blackness of his coffee cup, as if it might swallow him up, as if the grounds could give him guidance and prophesy events to come.

Alex watched George turn the cup round and round as he spoke. "First, we lay low. Stay outta Pine Ridge Agency. That's an order. Forget the firefight. The Pine Ridge Agency Goon squad is still on the loose. Nothing's changed until we get our own cops and bring back the Traditional Kit Fox Society to protect our women and children."

Alex looked around for signs of resistance. Silence.

George continued, "Next, we take a mourn sweat to honor *her* memory; to protect us and prepare us. We put on a *yuwipi* ceremony to find out who did it. Only then do we send out the hunters."

Old Louie said, "*Ohan*. Yes. Bring back that old ceremony to ask the Spirit People for help."

~~~

The town's energy was frustration bottled up, but out in the country, Camp Crazy Horse was peaceful. Building the sweat, sitting around the fire, hearing the old *Napeshni* story would help them become of one mind and stay together in safety. In the sacred Sweat Lodge, there were no lies. Each warrior prayed for purification of body, mind, and soul.

Alex stood with the other AIM warriors around the fire pit beside the Camp Crazy Horse Sweat Lodge. Some smoked hand-rolled cigarettes, some dozed upright, and others paced, restless that they had left their rifles behind. Pine boughs crackled and smoke rose straight up to the stars overhead. Inside the upright logs he could see big rocks set on bigger logs. George had built it right.

Alex treasured this men's-world talk before the sweat as they thawed their hands and feet. At first his body always felt like two separate parts, his backside frozen stiff while his front roasted from the flames. Then he'd turn and roast his butt while his face and hands grew cold. He hoped that together they could talk and turn until they were as warm and ready as the rocks.

Smokey, one of the coolest warriors, took him aside by the Sweat Lodge altar. "Rumor going around town, person last seen with *Our Lost One* was you in your red pickup."

Alex shriveled inside. Rumor was a powerful destroyer. Once started, it only grew and grew. Someone was out to get him. He breathed deeply of the cool night air to let his fear escape.

"I don't believe it, though," Smokey added.

Alex leaned down to the altar and picked up the AIM Pipe, holding it to calm himself. That meant the second informer *was* in town. Someone must have driven past his old red pickup left in the Badlands, or else stopped at the crime scene. Or was called to the crime scene. Jerry probably told his wife Eliza that he saw Tate in Alex's red pickup in the Badlands, and Eliza turned it into a Joanna Joe rumor. Eliza had never liked him since Alex and Jerry became rodeo buddies.

The FBIs always targeted AIM leaders. First George, now him. In the sweat ceremony he'd see if anyone else had heard the rumor, or knew the source.

Chaské, the youngest, hauled a metal pail filled with icy water to the altar. He stared at the rocks glowing in the fire pit. "Uncle, how come so many?"

Alex remembered when he, too, asked too many questions, before he learned to sit quietly and figure things out. "You ever taken a mourn sweat before?"

"Sure!" said Chaské, but Alex recognized the bluff.

Old Louie looked disgusted. "Kid, he dumps the whole pail of water on them forty rocks, and you mourn! You mourn that you're inside, with the door flap closed and you can't get out. So you cry from the heat, you cry for the dead."

Alex called out to Smokey, "Douse the headlights so we can see the stars." As the pickup lights flicked off, he looked up at the star people twinkling in the immense blackness overhead, so far yet so close. "See all the stars overhead? Once we were star people."

Chaské replied, "Yeah, right."

"Some Lakotas over in Spring Creek keep the name Star Boy," Alex said. He stood by Chaské and pointed. "See *Na-pé*, the Hand, up above?"

They all looked up at flickering lights far above. George said, "That's Orion the Hunter."

Alex replied, "White-man astronomy calls it Orion. We know it as *The Hand*. See the three stars in a row? *Wrist,* not Orion's Belt." He pointed lower in the sky. "The three stars hanging down in a line? *Thumb,* not Orion's Sword. And that bright star below? White man calls it Rigel. We know it as *First Finger*. Way over on the other side is *Little Finger*. Now you can see the whole *Hand*."

"Hand Stars!" said George. "We gotta teach the young ones our own astronomy."

Old Louie spit in the snow. "Ain't it just like us, looking for a handout in the stars!"

"Handout wasn't always there," Alex said. "We only think that way since we got boxed onto the Res, waiting for the dole. Long time ago *The Open Hand* meant giving. Giving yourself to the People, giving yourself to the Creator."

Old Louie replied in Lakota, "Already know the Star Boy story."

It was a very sacred story, only told in winter. Besides Old Louie, only he and Lester spoke Lakota. The others were Chippewa or Navajo, or like Chaské, raised by TV, not their elders.

Old Louie stared at the fire pit until everyone quieted. He told the ancient story in Lakota and Alex translated:

"Long time ago, *Na-pé*, the Hand Stars, disappeared and life on Earth almost ended. A greedy time and people forgot to share."

Alex copied the same gestures as Old Louie, who spread his hands to indicate how long ago and pursed his lips to point at the stars above, the way old-timers made the story come alive.

Old Louie waited before continuing in Lakota, "This stingy chief kept all the buffalo meat for himself. He never fed the old and the sick, or the orphans. He wouldn't sacrifice his blood for the People each year to renew the Earth. So the Thunder Beings got mad and swept down in a terrible *wamini-omini*—" Old Louie and Alex spun their hands in the air. "Thunder, lightning, hail."

"Whirlwind," Lester added.

"The Thunder Beings ripped off the chief's arm and hid it in the clouds. That night *Na-pé*, the Hand Stars, disappeared and the people were ashamed of their stingy chief and called him *Na-pé-shni*, the Handless One. And they were all afraid, because if *Na-pé* didn't shine in the winter sky, the Earth wouldn't warm up, and the plants wouldn't grow. We'd all starve and life would end." Old Louie and Alex spread their hands over barren earth.

"Then one warrior named Star Boy got brave and said he would climb to the sky and fight the Thunder Beings. But the people didn't believe him, because how could he reach the sky, and if he did, how could he fight them when they were so big and powerful?" Old Louie and Alex's hands climbed skyward.

"Star Boy had special powers. He turned himself into a small bird and flew down the smoke hole of the Thunder Beings' tipi. Before they saw him, he grabbed the chief's arm and flew back out the smoke hole all the way back to *Na-pé-shni*." Their four storytelling hands became small birds that dipped and flew over the fire pit.

"Then the people were happy. Not because the selfish chief got his arm back. Not because Star Boy got to marry the chief's daughter. They were happy because the Hand Stars reappeared in the night sky. So by bravery and sacrifice, balance was restored. Spring came and the plants and animals and people filled the Earth again. *Hechetuelo*." So it is.

The fire pit coals pulsed red. "That's all?" Chaské asked.

Annoyed, Alex added, "No, it's about why we Sundance. The Old Ones say that every year, in the summer the Thunder Beings tear off the chief's arm again and hide the Hand in the sky and wait for us to sacrifice ourselves. That's why we pull from the Tree of Life, why we give flesh offering at the Sundance, to bring the Hand back into the night sky each winter, so Mother Earth will renew herself each spring." Alex watched Chaské looking at the dark sky, probably wondering whether Thunder Beings were around today.

George rapped Chaské on the head. "Listen, it's about us right now." His voice floated out over the Sundance grounds. "The last four years we've had a greedy leader in Pine Ridge, and our Mother Earth is dying, soaked with Indian blood. In the dead of winter we are here to mourn a sister, small and bright like a star. Unselfish, always worked for the People. Now she has sacrificed her hands."

In front of the AIM warriors the fire hissed and crackled, behind them the leaves of the sundance tree rustled, and overhead Alex heard his night hawk calling, "*kree-kree-*," on the wind.

When the call faded, Alex asked, "Ready to sacrifice yourselves in the mourn sweat for Star Girl?" When they nodded, he added, "We'll smoke the AIM Pipe inside before the rocks are brought in and we close the door. Once we're in, that's it—we sweat, we cry, we weep. We suffer, we mourn *Our Lost One*. We pour out of ourselves, we purify ourselves, die and emerge reborn."

~·~·~

Starting before dawn, Alex drove a hundred miles into the snowy yard in front of Old Sam's shack near Oglala at the western edge of the Res. Old Sam, his mentor, was a finder with the power of medicine passed down from his grandfather. The power to travel between worlds, like a spider in the rafters of a room, to listen and know where things hid, to hear what Spirit People said. Through Old Sam's *Yuwipi* ceremony, They'd tell him who had killed Joanna Joe. Then George, their leader, would know who to bring to justice.

The old man's faded green sedan rested next to the outhouse, up on blocks, covered with snow. It needed engine work. He pulled up in front of the shack and waited. If Old Sam wanted visitors, he'd come to the door. Wanjí, the old man's scruffy dog, bounded up to the side of the pickup to check Alex out and whined in recognition. This time he'd brought no food, only the Turning Hawk sacred Pipe. Disappointed, the dog leaped down the path to the outhouse.

The old man hovered in the outhouse doorway, pushed Wanjí away, and pulled up his suspenders. He wore no coat, but a battered black fedora—Old Sam came from a time when the old gents wore fedoras, not navy wool Scotch caps, rodeo Stetsons or beaded baseball caps. His ears splayed out from underneath, and below them, wispy gray braids.

The Spirits had timed things right. He'd caught Old Sam before he hitched into town for his noon meal at the Senior Center.

"*Hau, tunkashila.*" Alex used the respectful address, *grandfather*, to honor his elder who spoke the old-time Lakota language.

Old Sam nodded and continued in Lakota, "*Hau, hokshila.* You caught me at a good time." He waved to Alex to follow him up the steps and inside the clapboard shack.

Even though Alex was a man at twenty, Old Sam called him *hokshila*, boy, not *wichasha*, man, meaning still a medicine-man-in-training. He shook his head, embarrassed. He'd visited the old man many times, but he'd been inside only once, a long time ago as a boy. This time a blast of dry heat blew him backwards. The woodstove blazed away, Old Sam's cure for rheumatism.

At one end a kerosene lamp sat on a wooden table with two chairs, and at the other, a cot covered with a denim quilt. Nothing to show that this ordinary shack held powerful medicine. Underneath the cot, a small cardboard suitcase contained ancient gourds and eagle fans, sacred gopher hill dirt, round stones and medicine bundles passed down for generations. True medicine men always lived simply without show. Alex felt humbled.

He tripped over a cream can full of water by the door, and almost fell onto the woodstove. He hung onto the Turning Hawk Pipe bag with one hand and with the other grabbed at flannel shirts and a parka that hung from nails in the wall overhead. A Wall Drugstore calendar fell down. Hoping Old Sam hadn't noticed, he bent down and picked the calendar off the wood slab floor—1966—the year Old Sam's wife Sadie died.

Old Sam tapped an old enamel coffeepot on the woodstove. "You must want Sadie's calendar. She used to tell me the date. As if I didn't know."

Alex turned away, ashamed of his clumsiness. He couldn't say, sorry. People didn't apologize, they learned to do things right. He hung the calendar back on its nail. Probably the only physical memory Old Sam had left of Sadie. Everything else of hers had been given away.

"Don't like the famous Wall Drug calendar? Let's see what else I have." Old Sam turned and lifted the lid of an old steamer trunk next to the woodstove. He motioned Alex to come.

Alex stayed by the door. "I don't need anything." As soon as he blurted it out, he recognized the mistake. Old Sam had insisted on giving him something: Indian hospitality.

55

"You young ones always want something. Alex, come look." Old Sam held the lid open.

He had no choice. Old Sam had called him by name. Another test. He took three steps across the room and peered in. Almost empty, one denim quilt at the bottom. Old Sam lifted it out and put it into his hands, forcing the quilt upon him, all because he'd been clumsy and knocked down Sadie's calendar. Probably the wily old man wanted something better, maybe a chief's blanket. Luckily, he carried his father's old Hudson Bay blanket with him behind the pickup seat. Old and faded, but with three black Chief stripes woven into the red wool, left behind when his father had disappeared. Alex said to Old Sam, "Grandfather, I've brought you a blanket."

"Oh? Where is it?"

Feeling foolish, he went outside to his pickup. He brushed straw off the blanket and folded it neatly over his arm so the three stripes showed. Careful not to trip over the threshold, he held the blanket out to Old Sam. "Grandfather, I bring you an antique Hudson Bay blanket."

"Antique, huh. I've seen this before." Old Sam reached out to stroke the wool. "I believe it belonged to your father. You should keep it."

He should have known the old man had seen it before. Alex's father had been in training with Old Sam, too, but he'd been a failure as a medicine man. Clearly his father's blanket wasn't good enough. "I'll bring you a new one."

"*Hiya!*" Old Sam smiled. "No, I like this antique—that is, if you're ready to let it go."

How'd the old man know it was all he had left of his father, the smell of sage and cedar? He unfolded the blanket and tried to wrap it around the old man, but Old Sam shrugged it off. "It's hot in here. Put it in the trunk. It's an antique, too."

The old trunk did smell of sage and cedar. Alex refolded the blanket in the bottom.

56

Old Sam dropped the lid with a thud and sat down at the kitchen table. "*Washté.*" Good.

Alex relaxed. At last he could offer him the Pipe. He laid the beaded Pipe bag on the red and white oilcloth. He kept his hands on it as if it, too, might disappear.

"Take your coat off." Old Sam took off his fedora and set it aside. Alex shrugged off his parka. He'd forgotten how rude it was to leave it on.

"Hurry-hurry," Old Sam muttered. "White time you're on. No time for piss, no time for coffee. Terrible way to live. Painful, too." He pulled at his crotch and smiled.

Old Sam always joshed him like a cousin-in-law, which embarrassed him. Only cousins-in-law could josh each other. He wanted to laugh, and he knew Old Sam wanted him to laugh, too, but he couldn't. He felt like a boy. He stared down at his hands that gripped the wrapped leather.

"Coffee first. He lifted two mugs down from the shelf. "Can't drink the Pipe—though some people try. When they pour alcohol in the bowl, they find out the Pipe and alcohol don't mix."

Alex remembered the last time he'd had Old Sam's black medicine, coffee brought by White men. Old Sam moved toward the woodstove. The old man poured his boiled black mud into the mugs and added spoonfuls of sugar to each.

Alex swallowed his coffee medicine and answered the customary questions about his Eagle Nest relatives. He managed to drink all his coffee as he relayed current Moccasin Telegraph gossip.

Then the old man got up for refills. Alex didn't dare put a hand over his mug to refuse, so Old Sam poured him more mud. "So you run from the new wife?"

Alex shook his head. Joanna Joe's face floated before him, but no words came.

"I could give you advice while you take me to lunch. I'm pretty hungry—"

Of course he'd take Old Sam to lunch. He opened his mouth. "We—"

"Maybe you come to tell me your AIM boys are gonna fix my jalopy?"

Alex flinched. The old man had deliberately interrupted him. So un-Indian, so rude. Old Sam was echoing his own bad behavior, so he'd learn not to interrupt. "We need a ceremony—"

"When my jalopy runs—"

"—tonight, before my AIM warriors go out with guns—"

"When my jalopy runs," the old man repeated, "I can drive away from all them that come to my door for a ceremony. Always too cold out and too far."

Old Sam was right. Alex wished he had a newer pickup. Or a heater that worked. "We'll bring you a car that runs. New," he added, though he didn't know if he could find a new one.

"I like my antique jalopy." Then he frowned. "What makes you think I can stop a carload of AIM warriors gunning for Pine Ridge Agency Goons? You think I can put out a roadblock so they turn into my place and tarpaper my leaky roof? You think I can feed them so they stay and put in a new engine and wheels on my jalopy? You think I'm that powerful? All I do is *Yuwipi* ceremony."

Alex smiled. He liked Old Sam's roadblock plan.

"Go somewhere else. Haven't you heard? I've lost my touch." Old Sam paused. "I'm merely a translator for the Spirit People, and hard of hearing."

Not with those big ears. The old man came up with more excuses, played at being pitiful. Old Sam knew that other medicine men didn't accept AIM Pipes—because of AIM's violent, in-your-face reputation. Urban Indians with no respect for traditions.

Alex had enough. He joshed back. "I felt your power when you were in the outhouse."

"My sacred shithouse. When people get in deep shit, they always come to me, desperate to find something, desperate to know." Old

Sam leaned across the table, intent. "You don't want to know. Think, now, what that knowledge will bring—"

"George sent me." He hesitated. "We lost one of ours. We don't want to fight. But the warriors are hot-heads for gun revenge. We have to turn their energy around." We need lots of help. There's a second FBI informer in Eagle Nest who may be the killer. We need to expose him and kick him off the res, Indian justice, like we did before. If he is the killer, we'll turn him in.

Old Sam shook his head. "They expect me in Oglala tonight."

Alex saw Joanna Joe's ghost wandering the Badlands, looking for her hands. Desperate, he leaned forward. "Put them off. I'll bring you back tomorrow. She's *Napeshni*! No hands! We have to find them and bury them with her body, so her *wanaghi* will quit haunting the Badlands. I bring you the Turning Hawk Pipe." He lifted the heavy beaded Pipe bag onto the table.

Old Sam put up his hands. "That Pipe bag sat there all this time?"

At last Old Sam was ready. Yet he was so unpredictable, he might not accept the sacred Pipe and listen to their grief. Before dawn Alex had prayed as he filled the Turning Hawk Pipe with sacred tobacco, wrapped it in sage and red felt, and slid it into his grandpa's beaded Pipe bag. The filled Pipe was his prayer request, which must be offered properly, held flat in both palms and given to the medicine man four times. The first three times were ritual. The fourth was the important time, to show you offered your life. If Old Sam didn't accept it then, he'd have failed. That couldn't happen.

Alex pulled out the Pipe wrapped in sage and red felt, closed his eyes and thrust it across the table four times. He steadied his hands and prayed for Joanna Joe. Waited. Clung to the Pipe. The fourth time, when he felt rough thick fingers grasp the Pipe from above, he let go at last. His numb hands tingled and filled with blood again. He'd done it. Old Sam would come.

Old Sam turned the red felt around and held the Pipe in his arms, cradling it like a baby.

He unwrapped the red felt and took out the Pipe, touched the bowl with its spread hawk wings, then removed the sage plug and lit the sacred tobacco. "Haven't seen this Pipe since you came as a small boy begging for teachings." He paused. "Your dead woman—"

How could Old Sam know? Tate had just found Joanna Joe. Had Spirit People told him?

Old Sam looked at him. "I hear these things." He lit the Pipe, touched the bowl to the four directions, took a puff and blew the sweet-scented smoke across the table so it surrounded Alex. "Spirits give me big ears. Quiet enough out here to know what happens at Pine Ridge Agency." Old Sam blew out more sweet smoke. "At the morgue."

The morgue? Why did they always have to cut up Indians, dead or alive? He knew the answer, lots of money with each autopsy for the butcher turned mortician.

Old Sam tamped down the sacred tobacco for one last puff. "You will find her hands. "Spirit People will help you so her soul can rest." Old Sam finished smoking the Pipe and handed the two parts back to him. "*Hechetuelo.* So be it."

While Alex laid the Turning Hawk Pipe back in its bag, Old Sam put on his parka. "The ceremony must be kept secret," he said. "My shack is too close to Pine Ridge Agency."

Cold wind entered the room. Alex had involved Old Sam, and sooner or later the Moccasin Telegraph would label him as AIM. They'd have to protect Old Sam. Couldn't leave him alone in the middle of nowhere. He lived too close to Pine Ridge Agency with its Goon squad.

It was easy to hijack Old Sam from the Senior Center and order him a steak at Kyle Café on the way back to Camp Crazy Horse. It would be easy to find tarpaper to fix the old man's roof, bring him a load of firewood. Harder to find car parts so the AIM warriors could tackle Old Sam's jalopy. The small tests: find him a *new* car. Find the hands. The big test: find the killer before he killed again.

CHAPTER 6
TATE

WHEN ALEX BROUGHT Old Sam into the log cabin at Camp Crazy Horse, Tate thought he wasn't much to look at. He was small and thin, a stooped old man in baggy clothes, straggly white ponytail, deep wrinkles, big ears and gnarled hands. He wore a silly black fedora, something out of the 30s films. He didn't say anything, just shook her hand with eyes averted, and nodded. She'd get used to such an old-fashioned greeting. If she'd been male, he might have said, "*Hau.*"

As he ate, she watched his eyes—their deep black that shifted from opaque to shiny, as if he had black shades or another eyelid like a cat to close off this world from his penetrating glance. His sagging eyebrows couldn't hide their gleam, eyes that saw both ways, inwards and out. Alex said Old Sam could see in the dark, see through things, see into other worlds. No wonder people feared him.

She didn't believe in Old Sam's power, but she'd treat him with respect. She didn't believe in oracles, unlike some of her school friends who swore by astrology or palmistry or Tarot or I Ching. How could Spirits find the diseased mind of a murderer? To find him you got out there and dug up the facts, unearthed the clues, chased him down, caught him red-handed. Facts, logic, motives, cause and effect, all led to capture. It seemed like she was the only one who thought so.

Alex believed in ceremonies, believed only in ceremonies for crucial knowledge. She had the wrong attitude for the wife of a medicine-man-in-training: *ta-wa-chin shi-cha, self-doubt,* which could ruin any ceremony. She'd work at clearing her mind, so she could help Alex in his work. .

~~~

Grandfather Turning Hawk's Ceremony House at Camp Crazy Horse sat several yards behind the cabin, long and narrow with a step up to the door. Earlier Tate had washed the plank floor clean and smudged the room with sage. Its log walls were plain, with no decorations. In the center sat a small wood stove. Wood benches hugged the four sides. The room was warm and fragrant. Old Sam's beady eyes took in everyone in the room. But Alex looked tired, as if the trip to bring Old Sam to Camp Crazy Horse had taken all his energy. She smiled as she handed him the lit kerosene lamp. He set it down beside the woodstove in the center and shoveled the last of the coals into a bucket. Not one coal could remain. Then he covered the two end windows with blankets and nailed them tight so no light could seep in.

The women sundancers laughed and gossiped as they came near the house, but fell silent at the door. They carried in paper bags of frybread, pots of beef stew and hot coffee to set by the woodstove, then shuffled around the room to the women's side, where they sat on pillows and blankets against the west wall.

She wanted to sit next to Alex so he could translate and tell her what went on, but in ceremony, men sat with men, women with women. So she sat on cushions between the two oldest women, Nellie White Owl and Frances Looks Twice, who'd elbow her awake if she slept. She tucked her legs under her shawl. She'd been warned to keep her arms and legs in close so not to trip up a Spirit Person—or whoever walked around in the darkness with magic tricks.

At last the men entered and sat against the east wall. Old Louie, the drummer, sat nearest the door, opposite her. Old Sam came in last with his battered suitcase, took off his boots and sat barefoot in the center of the room. Alex and George barred the door and nailed the last blanket in place. No chance to leave. Once in a ceremony, whatever happened, you stayed in. The lantern shadowed the faces around her and cast strange elongated shapes on the far walls. She felt the women around her stiff with fear. Spirit People were supposed to enter the room, but she knew no Spirit could name the killer. She was just curious because she'd never been to a *yuwupi* ceremony.

George walked around the room swinging the smudge bucket to purify everyone with cedar smoke. Alex handed people sprigs of sage to put behind their ears. She wanted to touch his hand as he put sage behind her left ear, but he moved on as if he'd walked into another world.

Alex handed Old Sam a coffee tin of dirt. Old Sam leaned forward, facing north to dump the dirt in a pile before the woodstove. Alex said they used gopher hill dirt because gophers travelled underground and knew which roots to eat. They had *underground medicine*. Old Sam took an eagle feather out, stroked it, and spread the pile of dirt in a flat circle until it became a round earth altar. She'd made sand piles like it at the beach.

Alex handed Old Sam a long string of red ties. She recognized them as those she'd made for the ceremony earlier from small red cotton squares containing a pinch of tobacco. Each tie had become a remembered moment with JJ. She'd looped string around each bundle and tied them together like a long kite tail. She'd prayed in her own way for JJ's soul.

Old Sam draped the red ties around the circular altar. He made designs in the dirt with his index finger. She looked away because she'd been told not to stare—like visual eavesdropping. Your mind might go funny, seeing Old Sam's Vision Hill designs that gave him power.

He knelt in front of the round altar and laid out a board with holes for offering flags, small sticks painted red and black, tied on top with red felt. He filled his sacred Pipe with tobacco, offering a pinch to each of the four directions, and laid it down on a bed of sage. Then he rubbed his hands with more sage and called, "*Ho. Wana.*" He was ready.

But then he stood up. This didn't seem right. Old Sam was supposed to sit before the altar. But no one said anything. No one looked on directly, yet everyone watched. Alex took a huge ball of red tobacco ties wound up like yarn. Someone had worked all day to make them. Alex laid the red strands on the floor in a large square around Old Sam. As Alex walked, his boots came so close to her, she could almost reach out and touch his ankle. When he moved beyond her to the south side of the square, he laid the ball of ties on the floor. Together Alex and George stepped inside the square of tobacco ties and wrapped a worn quilt around Old Sam, top to bottom. Then they laced him up tight with a rawhide rope so he couldn't move. Tied up, he'd be helpless. Then she remembered, *Yuwipi* also meant *they tie him—they tie him up and he goes into the Spirit World blind and the Spirit People untie him and he seeks and finds the answer.*

Alex knotted each loop and George tucked a sprig of sage in each one. Then they laid Old Sam facedown on a bed of sage near his altar. She wondered how he could breathe, let alone see or hear Spirit People. If only they hadn't been so solemn, she'd have laughed at the absurdity of two large men trying not to step over lines of red tobacco ties on the floor.

They backed out of the center, and Alex unrolled the last of the tobacco ties on the south side that closed *the sacred fence* around the medicine man. Alex said that once *the gate* was closed, Old Sam went into the Spirit World.

When Alex blew out the lamp, she couldn't see anything. The room was pitch-black, not shadowy-dark like in the Sweat Lodge lit with hot rocks. She heard sighs around her as well as a deep regular drumbeat. A ragged voice started the ancient Lakota songs to call in the Spirits. Men's voices joined in. She recognized Alex's strong tenor voice coming from the opposite wall, but understood only *Tun-ka-shi-la*, Grandfather, and *un-shi-ma-le-ye*, take pity on me. In the darkness the endless Lakota songs and prayers wrapped around her. In spite of the elders next to her, she dozed off until a winter chill, certainly not a Spirit wind, jolted her awake.

A loud falsetto voice from the center of the darkness repeated *na-pe-shni, na-pe-shni*. It sounded like Old Sam's voice. She didn't believe in Spirit People and they certainly couldn't talk. JJ's spirit might wander the Badlands, but not inside the Ceremony House.

A cold wind blew through the room, as if someone had turned on a fan powerful enough to shake the rafters, or a huge condor had flown in overhead. She was surrounded by rattling noises and something rapped her forehead sharply. She braced her head against the log wall. The rattling moved to the sides of her head, above her ears and thrummed, so loud and rapid that she couldn't hear the drum opposite her. Then the rattling knocked on the back of her head. It hurt, but worse, she couldn't sense anyone in front of her. She stretched her feet out, though she'd been told not to—nothing. Then she heard nothing.

As if electricity had pulsed through her brain, ear to ear, she lifted and flew, flew without wings, pulled up and out into the night sky. She could see far below the Ceremony House with no smoke rising from its smoke hole. How curious, like a hash trip, everything remote and exquisitely detailed, as if she had eagle eyes. She floated over the pastures and the pines into the Badlands. She felt disconnected from her body, but she didn't worry because flying was so glorious. Was this the Spirit World that Old Sam had entered? Someone had used rattles to grab her above the ears and pull her away. She felt pressure on her temples as she flew. It was no hallucination.

Below lay the asphalt road that wound through Redstone Basin. Dots of light crept along it. Below her she saw the Rock Sisters, three sentinels guarding the trail to Wounded Knee. Their heads sheltered red scaffolds poking up from the snow, burial sites for warriors no vandals could reach. She flew over weather-beaten buffalo hides and moccasins with beaded soles exposed by the wind.

Below the Rock Sisters, below the curve at Dead Man's Drop-off, stood a dark shadow at the gully where she'd found JJ. As she zoomed closer to see, her eyes grew blurry, like a telescope out of focus. Not the ghostly hitchhiker, arms akimbo. Instead a giant in a hooded army parka knelt in the snow on top of JJ's tiny body, gloved hands still at her throat.

She willed herself closer, to circle around straining to see the killer's face, fearful that he'd be the stranger, Night Cloud, whom she'd not recognize, or worse, that she would know him. As she squeezed her eyelids wide open to sharpen the images, she crash-landed in the dark Ceremony House. After-images flitted on her eyelids, but not the face of the hooded killer in the Badlands.

Light blinded her eyes. A kerosene lamp was lit beside the altar. She was too dizzy to stand, her legs cramped, her hands numb. Had a bolt of electricity zapped her? Something hard bumped her ankles, leaving tingles like frostbite thawing. She pulled her numb legs in by reflex. The songs and drum had stopped.

The aunties on either side of her stretched and rubbed their eyes. In the center sat Old Sam, cross-legged and grinning. Perhaps he'd been gone, too, and the ceremony a success. People meant it when they talked about out-of-body experiences. Had Old Sam seen the killer's face? She only knew what she'd experienced in her exhausted over-wrought mind. She couldn't deny what she'd seen, but it didn't fit it into her world of reason and logic. Later, she'd sort it all out.

The room had been transformed. In front of her sat the can of yellow ceremony flags. Its yellow blazed like liquid sunlight. The other flags, red, white and black, sat in front of other people around the room. She'd never received any of the sacred flags after a ceremony, but it felt like a gift, almost like flowers. She'd ask Alex what to do with them.

Somehow the tobacco ties of the *fence* had been rolled back up into a ball in front of George, and the *yuwipi* quilt had landed by the altar, neatly folded with its rawhide rope coiled on top. She couldn't ask anyone around her what had happened, but the aunties seemed relieved.

Everyone waited silently while Old Sam lit his sacred Pipe and puffed to the four directions. He tapped the ashes into the stove, took the Pipe apart and put it in its beaded bag. But no one could move yet. Ceremony food, blessed at the altar, must be eaten. Alex said it was to ground you, fill your stomach so you'd go home sleepy and happy. The men stretched and stood while the aunties fetched Tupperware dishes that had been tucked under benches.

The ceremony—perhaps all that flying—had made her ravenous. She sniffed the air—meat and potato stew, yeasty frybread. She took out two bowls and a big plate. When Chaské ladled out soup, she made sure he filled her bowl, and when he passed around frybread from a bag, she grabbed two pieces. Then Alex ladled out *wojapi*, the old-fashioned pudding she'd made earlier, chokecherries ground up into a sweet purple-gray nutty pudding. Good ceremonies must make you hungry. But what had happened? She could barely swallow her impatience.

People all around her found their voices again. She could hear them, as if from afar, and she watched George remove the blanket from over the door as if through a telescope. Perhaps she hadn't returned yet. Perhaps her ceremony wasn't over.

George unlatched the door. Outside the stars were dim in the night sky. In the pre-dawn air people headed to the outhouse or their cars to warm them up for the drive home. Stiff, she climbed into their pickup. Sitting on the faded cold seat covers, she felt safe, grounded at last.

Alex climbed in beside her and took her cold hands. "Tate, you okay?"

She barely felt his fingers. As if from afar, she said, "I had a vision, no, a dream—"

Someone knocked on the passenger side window, the one that didn't roll down. George wanted in. She opened the door for him, scooted over and straddled the gearshift.

George squeezed in next to her and shut the door against the wind, bringing the smell of sage and cedar with him. "Brother, I'm glad I caught you. What did Old Sam say in Lakota?"

Alex replied, "Spirit People say—"

"No, no," she asked. "What did *Old Sam* say?"

"*Old Sam* didn't say anything. He just listens." He's the *i-es-ka*, the go-between, the translator—the intercessor—" Alex paused.

"So what did he *hear*?"

"Spirit People say, *two white men*—"

"Two?" asked George.

Alex added, "—*and one reluctant Indian.*"

It took three people to kill one small woman? She said, "I don't believe this! That message only confuses things." This was no way to solve a mystery.

"We found out what we needed to know." Alex said. "Spirit People don't help by naming names, they just point in the right direction, and let you do the rest."

"That's not evidence, that's just the word of Old Sam."

Alex stared at her. "Spirit People are more reliable than witnesses," he said. "Spirits don't lie. Facts and people can lie, but Spirits give us truth."

"George, you've been raised in the city," she said. "You just want the ceremony to be true?"

"When I was in the prison Sweat Lodge, I learned to believe."

Believers surrounded her on both sides. "All right," she said, "if we're going to trust the ceremony, listen to *me* as well as Old Sam. I had a dream, but was a flying vision. There was a big man without a face hovering over *Our Lost One*—who could be the reluctant Indian. Believe *me* like you believe Old Sam. Maybe he what I saw. Ask him."

In Alex's eyes she saw sacrilege. Instead of reprimanding her, Alex said, "Tell me more. How do you know it was her? Where exactly in the Badlands was this? What was the man wearing? Did he have a weapon in his hands?"

"I don't know. I'm just *pointing the direction,* like Old Sam."

George stayed out of it.

"We could try a Ouija board or a Tarot deck or the I Ching."

"I know you don't believe in Spirit People," Alex replied. "But we trust Their guidance."

He looked sad, but she couldn't change her beliefs to make him happy. Even though she'd had a dream about the killer, it was just a dream. "I want facts," she replied. "I want to see the autopsy, the death certificate, the crime scene report." I want to check alibis to see who was where, when and why, to eliminate those who couldn't have done it."

"All right," said George. "Suppose we do that. What about the two White men?"

"Those two White men—wait a minute, we're already assuming there were three killers?" Sneaky George.

"We have to start somewhere," George said. "No surprises that it's FBI vs. FBI." Then he turned to her. "Federal Bureau of Investigation versus Full-Blood Indians."

As if she didn't know. George was mocking her already. She said, "Those two White men could have been White ranchers passing through. Or the local Kadoka sheriff and his deputy. Or perhaps your candidates, the FBIs."

Indian prejudice immediately blamed the FBIs, who were too busy to be killers. Threatening, yes. Arresting Indians, yes. Killers, no. She'd already dealt with missionaries in Minneapolis who tried to save her soul. It was no use arguing, since they knew *for a fact* what God's Will was. Prejudice wasn't so much a question of blindness as arrogance of will.

Then George's deep voice turned serious. "That those two FBI agents came upon the crime scene so quickly is very suspicious. They already knew something, and were waiting for the body to be discovered. Your take on the FBI is naïve. Hasn't Alex warned you that there's a second informer on the Res? Do you know how many AIMs have been held unjustly by the FBI as a result? I know from experience. I'm on trial for something I could not stop, yet I was there. I took the blame so that others can continue AIM."

Squeezed between the two men, Tate felt overwhelmed by their experiences. The pickup windows had clouded up from their arguments, and she couldn't see a way out. Let them investigate the FBIs.

"The killer is one man," she said. "My bet's on Night Cloud, the *reluctant Indian* you drove off the Res, who hated *Our Lost One* because she exposed him as an FBI informer."

"Night Cloud isn't Indian," Alex said. "The *reluctant Indian* is the second informer."

Tate said, The FBIs wouldn't waste money on a second informer, they'd reuse the first in a different way. Shuta says he's come back."

George shook his head. "Once outed, they're useless. We'd recognize him. No, they've planted a new informer here on the Res."

"I'm honing in close," Alex said. "I know the Res. I can catch him because I speak the language, I know who's related, and I know their secrets."

"Alex," George said, "I need you to get evidence on the FBI."

"Evidence?" Alex said. "It's hopeless. No court will ever hear of their crimes. No jury will find them guilty, no matter how much evidence. We'll never pin anything on the FBIs."

George put his arm on the backrest to reach around her to pound on Alex's shoulder, as if she weren't there. "You don't understand. I'm sending you off-Res on a mission. You have to investigate the FBIs to stop them from investigating *you*. Shadow Trask and Slade, check out their office in Rapid City and where they stay. Do it for AIM." George paused. "Old Sam told me you're the only one who can."

Alex looked worried. She rested her hand in his lap, letting him know that she *was* there.

"It's not a good idea to split up forces," Alex said.

George frowned. "Alex, you're the only one I can trust. No one else can become invisible. And you have Hawk Power to find her hands. Only you can bring back RED POWER."

Alex said, "I don't know the White-man World, never been in a bank or business office."

She turned around, surprised. Alex wasn't afraid of anything. He'd been fine in Minneapolis, where they'd met and gotten married. He must be afraid to leave her alone at the camp. George didn't know that Agent Trask had her driver's license, and soon he'd question her about finding JJ.

"Then it's up to you, George, to find the *reluctant Indian,*" Alex replied.

But George was gone much of the time to Custer Courthouse. She'd never seen Alex so depressed. "Don't worry, I'll run the Camp Crazy Horse while you're gone."

George was almost in her face, yet he didn't look at her. "I'll send the AIM warriors out. My brother-in-law Lester can run the Camp. Alex, I don't expect White-man justice. Spook 'em, drive 'em crazy, get 'em transferred out of here, so the FBIs'll leave us alone, and I'll be happy."

"Stay at Camp, Tate," Alex said, worried. "Night Cloud can't come back on the Res."

But Night Cloud could have sneaked over the Res line to put the blame on AIM. She'd go wherever she needed to find JJ's killer, whether it was Night Cloud or not. And she still had to retrieve JJ's body in Pine Ridge Agency.

CHAPTER 7
ALEX

ALTHOUGH ALEX had been up all night in ceremony, he had to stop the red-pickup rumor about him and Joanna Joe. If it spread, the FBIs would come after him, and with AIM's spiritual leader in custody, the young bloods would run crazy, drink and shoot up the Pine Ridge Agency Goons. Bar fights would wipe out AIM. Traditional Indians would shun AIM and the White world would call them criminals.

Alex suspected the source was Jerry Slow Bear's wife. She'd do anything to protect Jerry from losing his job as ambulance driver. Jerry must have used the ambulance as a hearse, and gotten in trouble. There were several reddish pickups in town, but Eliza hated living in an AIM town.

Alex drove past Eagle Nest's frozen water tower to Jerry's fancy yard fence of peeled pine, and turned in under the tall ranch gate topped with an eight-point elk rack. Jerry pretended to be a mechanic, but mostly he traded car parts. Once it had been a horse corral, but now it was filled with used parts. Driving the ambulance, Jerry got to accidents first, which gave him first chance at the wrecks. Jerry had a transmission for sale. Alex parked beside the ambulance, which was supposed to be kept at the police substation, but there it sat, as if Jerry owned it.

Alex walked to the door of the BIA split-level prefab. A *sell-out-to-the-Government* home, four bedrooms, shiny new pickup, overstuffed couches, Navajo rung on the floor, Santa Fe paintings on

the wall, and two government jobs to pay for it all. Jerry's wife had
dollar signs for eyes and never spoke Lakota. She always covered for
Jerry. She gave up after three months of coaching him for his driver's
license, people said, and took the written test for him. But working
together, they could be the second FBI informer.

Every time Alex came to visit his cousin he could see the fear in
Eliza's eyes, fear of his Lakota words and ways, fear that he'd get her
husband away from her, into that strong, man's Lakota world, with its
own grammar and words.

Alex knocked loudly, *rat-a-tat-tat-tat-tat*, the AIM knock on the
split-level's door. With her permed hair and polyester pantsuit, the
wife answered, as if on guard duty. Although her short solid body
blocked the doorway, he could still see into the living room where
Jerry watched sports TV. She didn't welcome him inside.

"Jerry *tokiyahe*?" Alex asked for Jerry in Lakota, hoping he'd come
to the door himself.

She stared at him. "Why are you here?"

"I heard he has a tranny for sale." That should get her, a possible
sale.

She turned away and said, "Jerry, quit that game. You have a customer."

Jerry came to the door, his face beefy as ever, brush-cut skinned
almost to the skull, pearl buttons on his Western shirt too small for
his belly, rodeo trophy belt buckle hung low. He shook hands so hard
that his Black Hills gold ring cut into Alex's hand. Last time he'd talked to Jerry, he'd felt that ring against his chin. Jerry had a short tem-
per if you didn't buy or trade something.

"*Hau*, buddy," Jerry said in a deep raspy voice.

Alex responded in Lakota, men-speaking-to-men grammar.
"Outside, we can talk."

"*Ohan*." Yes. Jerry pulled on a dark blue down parka and wool
cap, fancy medic issue. They went outside near the engine hoist, surrounded by snow banks. Car parts sat nearby in an open shed, one
a transmission.

"Cuz," Alex began in a friendly way. "Appreciate you stopping by the CAP office to tell me about my wife. Women!"

"So you come to thank me by getting a tranny." Jerry reached over and brushed the snow off the transmission. "Your wife screamed and swore at all of us, knocked the Sheriff down. You got a hot-head there." Jerry sniggered. "You ain't got her trained yet. You like her that way?"

Alex ignored Jerry's innuendo. "Ten cop cars at the scene. Too much attention for a dead drunk Indian. You knew her?"

"Nah. I try not to look at 'em. Dead bodies all look the same. Besides, my wife don't let me hang around AIM chicks. Dead or alive."

So Jerry knew Joanna Joe was AIM. Trask must have told him. "So Agent Trask ordered you to use our tribal ambulance as a hearse. I bet it wasn't the first time."

"I just do my job, cuz. They call me, I come."

"You drove ten miles, they drove a hundred. How'd they get there so fast?"

"They're the law. They can speed a hundred miles an hour."

He tried another tack. "You don't care if they mess up your ambulance with corpses?"

"I don't stick my nose in."

Alex walked over to the ambulance and opened the rear doors. "No blood in here now."

"Always keep my ambulance clean." Jerry closed the rear doors and locked them. "Hey, I go where I'm told."

Time to put the pressure on. "You didn't do your job two weeks ago when the firefight broke out. Shuta miscarried because you weren't here."

Jerry looked down at his boots. "I must'a been busy on another run."

"Cuz, that's why I'm asking you exactly where you were."

Jerry kicked a snowdrift loose and turned around to go back inside.

Alex grabbed Jerry's parka. "Your wife ain't here, cuz. So you tell me."

Jerry pulled away, looked down at his boots. "Hell, on a run up to Kadoka for gas."

Another excuse. "Substation, where the ambulance's supposed to be parked, always got gas."

Jerry stamped his work boots, crushing the snow. "Cuz, I didn't have to tell you that your wife was in jail." Jerry paced back to the car parts under the tarp. "You want this tranny or not? Don't waste my time. I got a game to watch."

"So you just happened to take your daughter to Kadoka to work. Against tribal regulations, cuz." Alex strode over to the ambulance and brushed snow off the driver's round mirror. "A man over to Rosebud lost his ambulance 'cause he forgot his relations, too greedy making money, big salary and free gas for luxury trips."

Jerry lunged at him, knocking off Alex's navy wool Scotch cap. "I could drop a tranny on your foot," he shouted in Alex's face, spewing pork chop breath.

Alex backed away and picked up his cap. "You forgot this is Eagle Nest's ambulance, a community ambulance that's never around when we need it." He jammed the cap back on. "You didn't take Shuta in too-early labor, and you didn't take Rodney bleeding to death on the highway. All you got here is a death-mobile, a hearse painted white." He thumped the metal door. "I'd hate to see young AIMs paint it red, turn it into an Indian ambulance to serve all the people."

"Cuz, I keep it runnin' which ain't easy. Ambulance ain't like a regular car, it's complicated, got lots of extra gadgets."

"We need somebody to drive it who can read, who knows CPR."

Jerry stepped toward him and pushed Alex's chest. "Cuz, I'm real good at pounding chests for heart attack. I took a class, got a certificate hanging on the wall inside!" Jerry waved toward the lighted windows, then shoved him against the ambulance.

Alex, ready for the punch, ducked to his left and pushed Jerry sideways so that his beefy fist slammed into the ambulance mirror, splintering it.

Jerry looked at the cracked mirror, then looked at his fist. "God-dam! See what you made me do!" He lunged again at Alex.

But Alex had already slipped behind the ambulance. He ran to the open shed, where he grabbed a rodeo rope hanging there, coiled several loops in his hands, and turned to face Jerry. "You win at bull riding. I win at roping."

Jerry halted, backed out of range, and spread his arms wide. His face red, his eyes wide. "Why'd you come here?"

Alex twirled the rope in front of Jerry, then flicked it out to knock snow off the engine hoist onto Jerry. "Cuz, I don't fight relatives. I ask them for help."

"Gonna fix my mirror?" Jerry brushed snow off his pearl-button shirt. "Whatchu want?"

Alex re-coiled the rope, walked up to Jerry and thrust it at him. "I heard you're real good at telling the FBIs stories about my bro-ken-down red pickup. It don't help me, Jerry, when you spread ru-mors about me and the dead woman."

Jerry took the coiled rope. "Not my idea."

"Tell the FBIs your wife got it wrong. Our blood is stronger."

Jerry frowned.

Alex waited. Slow minds work slowly. Finally he tapped Jerry on the chest, not hard as Jerry had done to him, and said, "I'd hate to see AIM take over my own cousin's ambulance here in Eagle Nest. Like you don't want to see me locked up, which you know they never could do because I'd give 'em the slip, come back and haunt you." Alex grinned. Why not bully a bully? "Course, you don't believe in ghosts and spirits and superstitious stuff."

"Not me."

"Everybody but the FBIs know the other beat-up red pickup is over to Oglala at Leo's Camp. Get Leo mad at you, he'll send dead bodies to drive you off the road into the deepest Badlands gully." Alex waved his hands at Jerry. "No one'd find you, even with them flashing red lights going round and round, not for days. Leo'd wrap you in Black Spirit fog."

Jerry fiddled with the rope in his hands.

Alex knew he'd hit home. Jerry'd just realized that he'd sicced the FBI onto Alex, and now Alex was mad. The difficulty was that bullies like Jerry were dangerous when provoked. To make peace, Alex shoved the rope aside and shook Jerry's hand. "Cuz, you want to keep this ambulance. I do, too. You and I, we're long-lived, all our relatives are long-lived." And to make sure of his own long life, he had to go right home and take a sweat to pray for protection and invisibility. He could feel the FBIs coming.

~~~

The other AIM warriors thought one sweat purified you for a week, or even a month. Alex had little time to take a sweat, but he must purify himself for his mission off-Res. He didn't mind being alone with the Great Mystery to pray every day for renewal and protection. Take the time, no rush to run away. He had a plan. But he couldn't tell it to Tate, or it wouldn't work.

As they built the sweat together, he told her about Jerry' rumor: Joanna Joe last seen with Alex in a red pickup. The FBIs had a warrant out on him, and were coming to arrest him.

Alarmed, Tate said, "Now? I'll help you pack."

"I need to take sweat and pray first, so the Great Mystery will guide me." He wasn't sure of his own power any more. His tobacco ties hadn't protected Joanna Joe. It was as if, by not stopping her that night, he'd sent her to her death. And he'd had no time to examine Joanna Joe's odd tobacco tie in private, in a sacred space.

Now in front of his altar, he untied the *woluta,* damp from the snow, and peeled back the red material. No pinches of tobacco, just the fragrance remained. Instead, he stared at a wrinkled piece of plastic-coated white paper about two inches wide. The paper smelled faintly of perfume. He unfolded it and held it up to the light from the door. In pale blue script he read part of a word, *Springv*—. What kind of message had Joanna Joe hidden in her hair? He imagined her cutting a *woluta* loose from the string he'd made for her, desperate to leave a clue for help. He handed Tate the scrap of paper hidden in Joanna Joe's hair.

"It's part of a soap wrapper," she said, "from a motel. Perhaps it's where she was kept in Rapid City. You must find it. Leave now."

No, first I must apologize for not stopping her. My *wolutas* didn't protect her. I must take sweat to pray. Take sweat with me. It's safe in here. If they pull out their guns, the bullets will drop. If they reach inside, the steam will burn their hands."

She picked up the pitchfork to haul in the rocks. "Not in daytime. I'll guard the door."

He smiled. She was more afraid of the Sweat Lodge than the FBIs. She was afraid of the close darkness. Another time, he'd share a slow, warm sweat with her, just for two.

She said, "I'll get their guns away from the altar and keep them occupied. They won't bother you. They're after me because Trask kept my driver's license so he could question me."

Alex bolted out of the Sweat Lodge and embraced her, including the pitchfork. "I' won't leave you, I'll stay and call the AIM lawyer to defend you."

She hugged him back. "I guess they're after both of us. But you have a sacred mission. First you must go off-Res to find the killer and bring back her hands."

He was grateful she understood Turning Hawk Honor. He could not fail George and AIM.

"If I leave and the FBIs try to scare you, the AIM lawyer's number is in the Pipe bag. Don't go around the Res alone." It would be bad for both their reputations, but he didn't want to say that, so he added, "You don't know the language, so go with Shuta or Iná."

"I might go with Shuta, but Iná, who hates me, is out of the question. I'll guard the Camp. Since you can't be two places at once, I'll smoke out the second FBI informer hiding on the Res."

He smiled. "Remember, Iná will scare off even the FBIs with her broom and house full of black widow midwives." Eventually his mother would come around, waiting to be a grandmother. "Are you sure you're not pregnant?"

She rubbed against him and whispered in his ear, "Check me out. No bulge. Besides, I don't have morning sickness. Just the opposite, I'm very hungry and *everything* tastes good." She hesitated, coming on to him at the Sweat Lodge. Then she laughed. It's probably this fresh country air."

He caught her evasion. If she'd said yes, she knew he would stay, and Turning Hawk Honor would suffer. He was both relieved and horny. Pregnant women didn't want sex, did they? Before he left, he'd find out, one way or the other. "You know, Lakota way, we don't seal a marriage until a child comes, and I've been hoping—"

"No, no," she stopped him. "I want kids, just not now." She walked over to the fire pit with the pitchfork, ready to haul rocks into the sweat.

She could be as proud and stubborn as Joanna Joe. She thought that tracking Agents Trask and Slade for evidence was crazy, but she'd never let herself stop his mission for AIM. George said he'd send the AIM warriors out to the Camp so she wouldn't be alone. And the Turning Hawk treaty Pipe would protect her and the land. He captured her in his arms. "Keep the Turning Hawk Pipe near you at all times."

She kissed him and ran her fingers through his long hair, as if gathering strength from the strands to hold onto the moment.

Finally he let go and crawled back inside the Sweat Lodge. He needed to concentrate on the task ahead. Undressing, he handed out his clothes, which she folded neatly by the altar. Then she pitchforked the hot rocks in and closed the door flap. He hung two strings of red prayer ties over the willow frame overhead, one for his journey and the other for her safety with the FBIs coming.

Crouched in the Sweat Lodge, he felt like *Iktomi*, the spider trickster, inside a web he'd spun while waiting. He could feel the FBIs coming, pulled by his prayers and the medicine bundle on the altar. Many times the FBIs had come out to Crazy Horse Camp to harass him. They saw the sign at the gate, *No guns*, but they always wore their sidearms when they came on sacred land. Back in June '75 had been the worst. A class had come to learn about the Sundance, and he'd taken them into the Sweat Lodge. In the midst of an ancient song, they'd heard the whap-whap of a helicopter overhead, louder and louder until it landed nearby. He stopped singing and opened the door flap. A grey-green helicopter gunship rested in the tall prairie grass next to the Sundance arbor. Out poured a camouflaged SWAT team like a swarm of hornets. They dropped and rolled, assault rifles in hand, then dodged through the Sundance arbor to the Sweat Lodge and surrounded it. The leader—name tag *Trask* on his shirt—pointed his rifle into Alex's face and yelled, "Come out!"

He'd no idea what had happened to unleash such firepower. The big AIM camp was on the other side of the Res, eighty miles away. Some kind of mistake. He'd tucked his wet towel around himself, ducked out and raised his hands high.

Then one by one semi-naked college students and one bearded professor emerged, dripping sweat from their wet blond or brown hair. If a rifle hadn't been pointed at his bare chest, Alex might have laughed at the FBIs' expressions. Swearing, the SWAT team tore apart his Sweat Lodge, ripped off canvas and blankets, smashed the willow frame, and kicked the smoldering rocks out of the center. Agent Trask turned to the altar, tossed the buffalo skull into the fire pit, and trampled on Alex's sacred Pipe.

He'd watched in helpless anger. While the professor tried to reason with Agent Trask, the SWAT team brought shovels from the helicopter and dug up the fire pit, hot coals and all, searching for a gun cache. Res rumors run wild.

Later Alex heard about the shoot-out at the big AIM camp—an Indian and two FBIs dead, one of them Trask's partner. Trask, a hundred miles away on a routine prisoner transport, had listened to his buddy's frantic cry for help over the CB—then gunshots—then silence. Trask must have relived those minutes over and over, and hated Indians ever since. Driven by regret or guilt, he vented his fury on AIM, swore a personal vendetta to nail an AIM leader to avenge his partner.

Alex found it hard not to hate back, but it was fatal to feed on hatred. Growing up on the Res, he'd watched it destroy too many souls. AIM must not become like the FBIs by seeking blind vengeance for Joanna Joe's death.

He always invited the FBI to take sweat with him. A great honor, he told them. He'd invited them politely, teased them, taunted them, begged them—*Come on in*—but they never did. They'd never take off their clothes, vulnerable in a skimpy towel, nor lay their guns down beside the altar, even if empty of bullets. They were afraid of close dark places, afraid of the earth, afraid of long-haired wild Indians, afraid of what they didn't believe in—the power of the Great Mystery.

Let them come for him. He felt the earth tremble slightly, as if faraway tires gouged into the gumbo and sprayed mud into the ditches. "They coming?" he asked Tate, though he already knew Agent Trask was coming with his new FBI partner, Agent Slade.

He peered out. She was leaning on the pitchfork by the fire pit, warming her hands. The ashes, a rippled bed of warmth, glowed even at midday. "Nobody."

"Thought I heard a car plow through the mud."

"I don't hear anything." She paused. "Wait, no, it's that white Bronco covered with shitty yellow mud."

He peered out the open door. "I'll ask them to sweat with me." She didn't understand that he'd drawn them here with his mind. She'd be furious, calling it *playing with fire*. But he had a plan.

"Alex, you know they'll never take sweat with you!"

He laughed. "Can't you see them strip off their suits and lay their guns on the altar?" Then he saw that she was afraid.

"Goddam Agent Trask," she cried. "I told you he'd come to get us!" She wiped her lips as if she thought she could take back the words. "Sorry, I know I shouldn't swear."

Words had power. Once released to the world, they came alive and couldn't be taken back. He saw fear in her way of holding the pitchfork in front of her. "Tate, they're not coming for you."

"How can you be sure they're not coming for me? It's me they suspect, it's me they want to question."

He shook his head. "*Hiya.*" No.

He felt her warm hand on his bare shoulder as she leaned in.

She removed her hand and stood up stiffly. "Certainly. Here they come."

He heard car doors slam. She stood there with the pitchfork in her hands. His brave wife, ready to take on the FBIs so he could escape. He prayed that she'd find him later and bring the things he needed for his journey. He closed the door flap and sang the first Sweat Lodge song.

CHAPTER 8

TATE

TATE STOOD in the cabin doorway with the pitchfork. She hated being polite to monsters, but Alex needed her to lure the two FBIs away from his altar. She'd be brave. It wasn't his fault that she was the one who'd stopped beside the road and found JJ. "My husband's praying now, but he'll be in soon. Please have some coffee."

The FBI agents entered the shadowy cabin, stomped mud off their shoes but kept their overcoats on to hide their guns. She set two mugs on the table, her hands steady, her mind concentrated on the manila envelope in Agent Trask's hands that she almost missed the pile of Alex's clothes and moccasins in Agent Slade's hands.

Agent Trask laid the envelope on the table and sat down. She wanted to throw it in the woodstove. Instead, she poured hot black coffee into their mugs. They'd just issue another copy of the warrant.

"Sit down," Trask said. "The woman you found, when was she here?"

Tate sat down opposite him. "I knew her when I lived in Minneapolis. I recognized her when I found her body. What did you do with it? Where is she buried?"

Trask continued. "Why did she stop here?"

How did Trask know? Or was he guessing? Was he looking for her rifle? "I don't know, she said. "She didn't come to our wedding."

"What was she doing on the Res?"

Tate leaned forward. "She has no relatives, only AIM. May we see the autopsy report and her death certificate?"

Trask, undeterred, asked, "Do you know where she went?"

"I was her best friend." She didn't care if Trask didn't answer her questions. She didn't answer his, either. She'd get the documents at Pine Ridge Agency when she claimed her body. "We ran the kids program at the Red Schoolhouse in Minneapolis. That's when I last saw her—alive."

"But what was she here for?"

This she could answer. "Treaty rights, civil rights, Indian justice."

Trask said, "We have photos of you and her at the AIM trials."

Probably pictures of Alex, too. "Yes, she was my friend." Metal and leather crashed to the floor behind her. She jerked her head around to see if anything was broken.

Agent Slade, sun-tanned and blond, had wandered around the cabin to the worktable, perhaps to avoid the strong, boiled coffee. More likely, he was casing the cabin for anything to use as evidence. Ignoring the bridle he'd brushed to the floor, he laid Alex's clothes on the workbench and picked up a hawk feather with his black leather gloves.

"Look, but don't touch!" she said, adding *goddammit* under her breath. Control the anger and you control the fear. Keep them occupied.

Slade dropped the feather, but continued inspecting. His gloves stroked her beadwork loom, then Alex's half-finished bone breastplate, and beside it, a porcupine tail headdress for Chaské, AIM's young grass dancer. As if by touching them, Slade could possess them.

She rushed to the worktable. Agent Slade had picked up the nearest sharp tool.

"That's my awl," she said. "Put it down." She reached across to grab it, but hesitated. She remembered the AIM drill: never touch an FBI agent because they'll charge you with assault and battery. Slowly he held the awl aloft. "Stiletto. Weapon. Evidence."

"Do you have a search warrant?" she demanded, though it didn't matter on the Res. Let them take her awl. She'd get another. Resigned, she walked toward Trask at the table. "I'm ready."

"Pardon, ma'am?" asked Trask.

"You can serve me your warrant."

Trask pulled papers from the envelope. "Alex Turning Hawk. It's your husband we want."

"It's a mistake!" She grabbed the papers from Trask. They trembled in her hands. Alex was innocent, a man of peace. How could she live without him?

Trask took the papers back. "No mistake. We have orders."

She was shocked, even relieved for a moment. Then she was ashamed at being relieved. At last she found her voice. "He hasn't done anything! He's a holy man!"

Trask replied, "He's a person of interest."

She said nothing, just folded her arms across her chest. Had Old Sam told Alex more than the English translation? Had someone in the ceremony told the FBIs about the prophecy? They couldn't arrest Alex on hearsay. Besides, Camp Crazy Horse was a sanctuary on the Res, as sacred as a church. Then she remembered that murder on the Res was under federal jurisdiction. She said, "You have to read him his rights, after he comes out of the sweat."

She heard Alex in the Sweat Lodge. His songs started high and pure and ended deep in the throat, a cry for the Great Mystery to take pity. She'd come to love the old songs, the way they dropped down the scale deep into the earth, a wail turned into a caress.

Trask looked at his watch. "How long does this caterwauling go on in that pup tent?"

FBIs mocked the Indian songs, the high-pitched *ai-yi-yi* and *yippie-i-o,* as if they were cowboy roundup songs or nursery school chants.

"He can't last much longer," Slade drawled, "or he'll fry his brains in that sauna."

She heard Alex singing the Fourth Round asking for protection and blessings. The last song. He'd come out soon, wrapped in a wet towel.

Trask stood up. "Better get him cuffed."

Tate, armed with Alex's clothes and moccasins, ducked beneath Trask's arm as he opened the door. She yelled, "Alex, they're coming for you!"

Pushing her aside, Trask ran to the Sweat Lodge, yanked open the canvas doorflap, and dropped to his knees. "Damn! He's gone!"

She followed Trask to the Sweat Lodge, amazed, then relieved, then scared. Alex was gone, but where could he go, how could he get away? Did he really have the power to vanish? Or did he use a trick, like Houdini? She never imagined he had such power.

Trask dashed toward the Ceremony House behind the log cabin, threw open the door, and ran inside, all the time yelling at Slade, "Check the shacks, the woodshed!"

Slade skidded to a stop in the snow beside the Sweat Lodge. Before she could stop him, he'd ripped off the canvas layers until only the bare willow frame revealed a pile of warm rocks, an empty water pail, a soaked towel. "Jesus, the bastard ran off naked!" Slade knelt down and examined the snow banks around the Sweat Lodge. "Not a goddam footprint!"

Tate stared at the smooth snowdrifts. No clothes, no footprints, no noise! Alex had disappeared like Houdini. She kept her face stiff, her smile hidden. Alex had ridden bareback since he could hang onto a mane. Up and away, he'd bend close to Bloketu's warm body and head for the Vision Cave hidden in the Badlands Wall. He'd flown away! Hawk medicine! They'd never believe it.

The Ceremony House door burst open. Trask raced to the woodshed beside the engine hoist. He threw firewood out onto the snow until satisfied that no one lurked inside. Then he dashed back to Slade by the Sweat Lodge. "Did you check the outhouse?"

"Hell, he ain't in the outhouse. It's only go three sides."

Trask grabbed Tate's shoulders and shook her. "Where'd he go?"

Her jaw locked. "I—don't know—let go of me." She jerked free from his grasp.

Trask kicked the small Pipe off the altar in front of the Sweat Lodge, stamped on the buffalo skull in a fury, and scattered strings of red tobacco ties in the snow.

"Stop! It's sacred!" she cried, bending down to rescue the Pipe from the muddy snow. She brushed off the mud and cradled it, full of fresh tobacco, in her arms. Alex hadn't smoked it. He'd known they'd come for him, not her. Yet he'd worried about her, made prayer ties for her as well. She picked them, mud and all, and wrapped them next to her heart.

Slade knelt behind the Sweat Lodge. "Calm down, partner," he said. "See where the fucker brushed away his tracks? By now he's wading buck naked in the creek to throw us off his trail."

Tate drew in her breath. Alex had run to the streambed by the horse corral.

Trask started toward the Bronco. "Son of a bitch! Get down there and cut him off."

"I'll finish here first." Slade tore the red strips loose that held the bent willows until the whole frame collapsed. "Let him run to the Badlands flats before we nab him."

"Leave it!" Trask revved the Bronco engine, and Slade jumped in.

Tate, furious at the sacrilege, ran beside them. "You just witnessed Hawk Power!"

Slade rolled down his window. "Watch the U.S. eagle hunt down the hawk."

Trask's face was grim. "We'll be back."

Slade said in a low, confidential tone, "If he comes back to you, you let us know."

"Fucking fat chance!" She kicked the running board.

Slade smiled. "Better to turn himself in than be hunted down by helicopters and a SWAT team. Out in the Badlands he'll starve, freeze, or get riddled with bullets. You want him to die?"

Even naked, Alex could turn on his inside heater.

Trask gunned the engine, spinning mud backwards onto the log cabin wall. The Bronco slid out the gate of the fenced yard. She watched them turn down the muddy path to the Sundance grounds beside the creek. They ploughed through shallow windswept drifts. The *hrmm-hrmm* of the engine floated back up to her. With each futile, erratic loop, the Bronco dug deeper ruts into the land. The FBIs looked small and harmless, trapped inside a white metal windup toy that circled round and round the Sundance arbor. But they were not.

Still, she'd survived Trask's interrogation. He'd only questioned her, not taken her in. He'd found out nothing about JJ, and Agent Slade had found nothing of JJ's in the cabin to use as evidence. She felt a great energy fill her and surround her. Alex was gone, but she had a good idea where he was.

CHAPTER 9
ALEX

NAKED, ALEX CREPT onto the ledge overlooking the Badlands. Past the pile of ancient Sweat Lodge rocks, old bent willow branches, a wooden bucket, faded red vision flags and a buffalo skull altar, lay his refuge, the Turning Hawk Vision Cave dug from layers of ochre and lavender shale.

He worried about Tate. He regretted leaving her alone with the FBIs. He trusted her to figure out where he'd gone, and that she'd wait until it was safe to ride out to bring him clothes and food. He worried more when she didn't arrive by nightfall. Perhaps she hadn't caught Midnight, her skittish horse. Wading through the deep drifts, maybe she'd exhausted herself with a heavy load.

He withstood the cold, trained to stand day and night in the wind with only a blanket around him, trained to turn his body-heater up. Not Tate. He couldn't signal to her with a lit fire to dry her off when she came. In the crisp cold he heard the grinding gears of a four-wheeler stuck somewhere far below in Redstone Basin. The FBIs out with a search crew—madness—then another sound, nearby and above. He knelt, ready to spring. Pebbles ricocheted down the Badlands Wall, then paces of a person who stumbled and slid. Then silence. He peered out into the dusk. Nothing.

Wind blew the leather door flap open, air too cold and clear for snow. Overhead the stars of The Hand pulsed brightly, and from a distance coyotes yipped in the Badlands. No one was near.

"*Kree–kree–!*" He sent the Turning Hawk call out into the night, so Tate would turn his way, stay on the path and find the Vision Cave.

He heard Lakota on the wind. "*Tokiya?*" Who? Alex braced himself against the loose rock wall, ready to throw any intruder down. He heard footsteps on the ledge above. He held his breath.

"Alex? Where are you?"

Tate. He reached up to keep her from falling over with the heavy pack, but she crouched down beyond him. He asked, "Are you alone?"

"Who else, *mihigina?*"

"*Mitaichu*, this way." He caught her gloved hand and pulled her to safety, the snow-covered pack bumping into his legs. "You could have fallen. The trail drops off."

"Good thing I couldn't see. Your Great Mystery must have guided me."

He wrapped her in his arms and pulled her into the Vision Cave, away from the FBIs' search. The moon had risen, best to burrow in and stay hidden. He pulled off the heavy pack, then her frozen parka and held her next to his heart. He put her icy hands under his armpits and licked away her sudden tears. Pulled off her snow pants and let her thighs warm his swelling *ché*. He held her tight and rocked back and forth in the small dark cave while she cried in his arms. Tate rarely cried, sometimes just from joy. He stroked her hair, moved his hands down her thighs and pulled her close. He let his *ché* throb against her belly until her sobs slowed.

When she stopped shivering, he pulled her down onto the Vision Cave blanket, pulled her down on top of him and tucked the blanket around her and back underneath him, the way they always wrapped blankets around themselves to keep warm. "*Washté*," he said. "We're together."

"I worried," she said. "They took your clothes—"

Her mouth rattled on a mile a minute, *iwashichu*, fast-talker, Tate being raised White man way. He put a hand over her mouth to stop her. The Great Mystery took care of them, safe on sacred ground, close to the Spirit World. No FBIs could find them now, invisible to the outside world. In the Vision Cave they had nothing to fear.

He sang, "*Tunkashila, unshimalaye...*" over and over until she stopped shaking and joined in. She remembered the words he'd taught her. When the song ended they kept breathing with its beat, the earth's heartbeat, becoming of one heartbeat as they always did before becoming of one body.

He felt her touch his chest scars like she always did, caressing them as if they were unhealed wounds which she could smooth away. She still didn't understand that he gave his flesh to the Great Mystery, his yearly sacrifice for the People. He pulled her hands away and down to his crotch where his *ché* throbbed. His longings and fears deep inside his chest washed away in a wave of heat.

He reached between her thighs and found her little man-in-the-boat hidden between her folds, and circled it gently until it swelled and she swayed her hips down onto him. His *ché* rose inside her, and with a soft cry, "*krrrrr,*" in her ear, he rolled them over and dove into her again and again, down deep into her darkness, deep into her wet earth, until he became earth, too, and they shuddered together, check against cheek until their trembling stopped.

He wrapped his arms around her thighs tight so his *ché* wouldn't slip away, and she hung onto him. Even though spent, he felt full, their bodies woven together as if laced into a single cradleboard, watched over by the Great Mystery, safe and secure from all harm.

He woke in the pre-dawn while Tate slept beside him. He'd fallen asleep feeling great, but now he was overcome with worry. Tate thought him strong. Not afraid of snakes or horses, not even bucking broncos. Not afraid of cold, or heat, or chest-piercing. He'd been trained since childhood to undergo physical ordeals. Not afraid of FBIs on the Res. All this time he'd hidden from her what really scared him. Since birth he'd never been left alone, always on Grandma Unchi's lap, in his Mama Iná's arms, at Uncle Lekshi's side. Relatives surrounded him, so he could never get away even if he'd wanted. He'd been watched, protected, driven to and from ceremonies. He'd barely escaped to ride bareback in the Indian rodeos. At sixteen, he went on *Hanblechia*, alone on the Vision Hill. He welcomed the silence and space, standing out in the open, exposed, all alone, waiting for the Spirit People to lead him to the Other Side.

But after the third day and night, he'd become so lonely he could barely pray. He felt protected by the fence of *wolutas* around him. He knew that back home Iná and Old Sam kept the Sweat Lodge fire going night and day to pray for him. But when the Spirit People came, wings beating, circling around him, thrusting power into his chest that burned all the way to his hands, and he became a night hawk, sending out his lonely cry—only then did he begin to understand how much lonelier he would become as a medicine man. Respected by all, but feared for his powers, even by his own mother.

Tate, who didn't believe, had no fear of him. Not when he met her at the AIM trial in Minneapolis, and not here on the Res. He hadn't felt lonely since. He wrapped the Vision Cave blanket tighter around her back, and pulled her hands inside. *Unshika* Tate, raised in a thick-carpet home. Here her hands were always cold. She had a saying, though, *Cold hands, warm heart.*

She didn't wake, nestled next to his heart, her breath slow and heavy. Her hair tickled his neck, so he gently brushed it aside and lay down, not wanting to leave her, yet planning his mission, readying himself to be lonely again.

CHAPTER 10
TATE

TATE WOKE UP cold in the Vision Cave. Wrapped in their blanket, she heard Alex outside. Last night the outside world had dropped away, faded into nothing but the two of them lit by their own warm glow. If only it could have lasted, the closeness deeper than words. She put her arms around herself to keep the warmth of him with her.

Leaning in, he handed her a thermos of cold coffee and *kabuk* bread. He sat beside her and ate. The cold didn't affect his appetite, nor hers.

She should have insisted George send Smokey, who knew the off-Res world, instead.

"It's all very well to be noble," she said, "but when it comes right down to it, what about me?"

"When it comes right down to it, why didn't you tell me sooner that you were pregnant?"

She shifted away from him. I'm sorry," she said. "No one ever told me anything good about being pregnant. To be honest, I'm scared. I'm not ready to be pregnant, not ready to be a mother. I never had a real mother to learn from. My foster mother was never pregnant and never wanted to be pregnant. First you can't eat and then you throw up, and then you get fat and can't do anything, especially tie your shoes, and no sex, because that would hurt the baby. And then the pains come, worse than anything. I'm afraid I'll be like her, never a mother, always a bride."

His face became sad. He wanted children, many children for a big family. Indian way, having a child bonded the marriage. He was worried. No children meant no bonded marriage.

But instead of being sympathetic, he laughed, which made her feel worse. "I'm afraid to tell anyone, because then they'll take me in to stay with Iná the Terrible, away from you. JJ's gone and there's no one else to help me, not Shuta, who's so tough. Just you. And now— " She choked up.

"I hate to leave you alone and pregnant." He reached out to embrace her.

She leaned back against the Vision Cave wall. "Oh yes! But you will leave. Turning Hawk Honor is at stake."

"If I'm not back in ten days, you must move into town with Iná, who's a midwife."

She refused to think of that possibility. "Not yet. You know she doesn't like me."

"She'll like you when you give her a grandson."

"And if it's a girl?" Or if I miscarry, like Shuta?" She hugged her knees, as to protect her belly from him.

He had no answer. Instead, he began stuffing clothes into his pack.

She grabbed the pack and searched his face for a reaction. "Whether you stay or go is not the question," she said. "The question is how do you solve a murder? How do you find the killer? It's one thing to have a ceremony to bless the mission. It's another to follow voices on the wind. You are being sent off on a wild goose chase. You won't find anything out about the FBI. You won't even get close. You should stay here and sniff out the second FBI informer while I look for the first. Then we could work as a team. I wouldn't be just a left-behind wife."

He sat against the opposite wall. "I brought Old Sam here. I believe in his powers, in what Spirit People say. I needed his blessing for the journey. For that *yuwipi* ceremony I promised him a pickup. I can't change the path I'm on."

"I could go with you. I know the city better."

"One person can vanish. Not two."

"You think the FBIs won't notice you, but they have x-ray vision."
He closed his pack and laced it shut.

"Finding the informer hidden inside AIM is more important. If I stay to guard the Camp, I'll track down the killer."

"That's what I'm afraid of. You don't know many people in town."

She didn't know the language well, either, but that wouldn't stop her.

"Listen to George, then. Trust only him." He hauled his pack outside the Vision Cave, and leaned back in. "Angry as you are, I need you to cut my hair."

Medicine men never cut their hair. "You can't," she said. "It's your power, your medicine—"

He pointed to his chest. "My medicine's in here."

"But why cut your hair?" He'd need his power to shadow the FBIs and find JJ's hands.

"Off-Res I'll be a target as a long-haired Indian. Instead, I'll turn into Harold Goggle Eyes, an ordinary urban Indian, so no one will notice me. Wear glasses, V-neck sweater and a school jacket, maybe a tie. The right clothes will get me in anywhere."

What a terrible idea. He was heading into danger, joking around. He'd never pass as a student. "If you have to, get a haircut."

"If people ask, I'll say that I'm in mourn. I *am* in mourn."

He meant, for Joanna Joe. Still, it was a bad idea. "I don't have any scissors."

He lifted a small knife from the dirt altar and thrust it toward her. "Use this fasting knife."

She picked up the rusty knife. What a weapon. She was tired of doing wrong things, pretending to believe in his mission. The icy handle froze in her hands. "I can't do it."

He shifted to sit in front of her. "You're my wife. Must I cut my own hair?"

Only a wife could braid a man's hair, so only the wife could shear a man's hair. She loved to touch his long thick hair, shiny blue-black.

Reluctantly she picked up a handful and let it slip between her fingers, so magical, so alive. Shearing it off felt so wrong.

"Don't worry, it'll grow back."

Steeling herself, she grabbed a hank near his ear and sliced close to his scalp. It came loose in a great clump, leaving black bristles above his ear. She picked up the lifeless hair. It was as if she had cut off its power. "I hate this."

She grabbed another hank and leaning close, cut away another swath of blue-black. Again and again she sliced, watching the long strands fall into the air, down onto the rock ledge. She turned his head, now showing a raggedy brush cut, and continued on the other side. This was very wrong. His lap filled with lopped hair, resilient. He looked like a waif or a monk. She didn't know whether to laugh or cry. His big ears stuck out, almost like hawk wings. She touched them and giggled. "Are you ready to fly off, Hawk-man?" She was glad there was no mirror. "You look awful."

"*Pilamaya, mitaichu,*" he said. Thank you, my wife. "I must leave my hair here. No one must know. Burn it at my Sweat Lodge fire pit." He'd become formal, distancing himself from her.

But why not save the hanks in his hair bag? Doing things right was important. She'd repair the FBI's damage to his Sweat Lodge and altar as well.

"You keep the Turning Hawk Pipe," he added.

"Alex! You need it for protection!"

"*Hiya.* No. You must hang it on the cabin wall to protect you. I'm taking my grandpa's little fasting Pipe, the one I left here last summer. You keep the treaty Pipe at home to guard the Camp."

Tate picked up the big Turning Hawk Pipe she'd brought him. Only men had carried it. It was heavy with responsibility, and duty. She could guard it, but did she believe it would bring protection as well? She must stay and guard Camp Crazy Horse, keep it going for AIM. It was always harder in winter, so cold and remote. Just as he'd turned cold and remote.

"George will send the AIM warriors out to help you." He shouldered his backpack and started down the trail down to the Badlands.

When she ran to kiss him goodbye, he turned around and said, "Don't worry, the FBIs quit searching and went home to sleep. But they'll be back, so I need an early start." Then he relented and said, "I'll send you hawk feathers so you'll know I'm okay."

She wondered how, but he could do many things, including closing his heart to her words.

He left so silently it was as if he'd flown down into the Badlands and they'd swallowed him up.

How close they'd been last night, so why had they argued? They were so different. He believed in prayers and divine guidance from the Great Mystery—which was in itself a mystery to her. She believed in facts, do-it-yourself investigation, logic and reason. They were going on different paths. Would they ever rejoin to solve the crime? To raise a family?

She held up the ball of Alex's hair. What did it mean, to burn it at the altar? Great changes were coming, and she had no ability to see the future.

~~~

She nestled the Turning Hawk Pipe in her daypack and started home. She'd miss Alex., but she felt so good. Was it the afterglow? She was so full of energy she felt she could run for miles. If this was pregnancy, she'd be fine. Agent Trask had only questioned her, not taken her in. He'd found nothing about JJ, and Agent Slade had found nothing of JJ's in the cabin to use as evidence. She felt a great energy fill her and surround her. Physically, she could run Camp Crazy Horse.

Now she could go to Pine Ridge Agency and claim JJ's body. Since JJ had no relatives, AIM had been her family. The Bureau of Indian Affairs cops had no power to investigate major crimes, and the FBIs were too busy pursuing their own cases. She'd track down the evidence and find the FBI informer who had threatened to kill JJ, even if George had banned AIM from Pine Ridge because it was, he said, *too dangerous.*

CHAPTER 11
ALEX

ALEX TURNING HAWK knew there are no *goodbyes* in Lakota, only *so-longs*. Saying goodbye meant you thought you'd never see that person again. He waded through the deep snowdrifts on the old trail down to Redstone Basin. George had sent him out into the White World, *Mainstream of Insanity*, with so many tasks: find evidence that two FBI agents killed her; find Joanna Joe's hands so she could be buried whole; spook the FBIs to drive them away from plotting against AIM. He had his own agenda: expose the second FBI informer. He prayed to the Great mystery for help.

Though the trail was drifted over, he was never lost. Every snow-covered arroyo might look the same to outsiders, but he knew the Badlands from childhood, chasing lost Indian ponies back home. In the clear air he heard gears shifting from a semi-truck below. In half an hour, he reached the paved road.

He waited for an Indian car to stop and pick him up, take him north to the thruway, and if he got lucky, take him all the way to Rapid City and Lakota Homes. Even if eight people rode inside, they'd stop. Indians never left another Indian standing beside the road because they might be related. Or, these days, a target for racists. He'd wait for someone driving to K-Mart to restock supplies. He preferred a pickup, better than crowding into a back seat full of kids. He'd be glad to ride in a cold pickup bed.

The day was sunny, if early for traffic. Four semis whooshed by, and two fancy new cars from off-Res. Finally a battered blue pickup appeared, speeding past, but then it slowed and slid to a halt, spewing gravel. It looked like Yellow Elks from Kyle. Eager to catch up with relatives, Alex leaped through waist-high drifts along the edge of the road. He slowed to see who drove the pickup.

The passenger door creaked open and a young ranch hand in coveralls and cowboy hat climbed out. "Get in, Redskin."

Alex hesitated, drew back. His family had worked with White ranchers, leased land to them, traded horses with them, worked together to put out prairie fires threatening their pastures. None of them had ever called him "Redskin." He shook his head and backed away.

The cowboy lunged forward, grabbed Alex's parka, and pulled him toward the pickup. "Come on, Tonto. We're heading for the Kadoka Bar, and we're lonesome."

Alex pulled loose, but before he could back away farther, the guy yanked his pack off and tossed it in the hay-strewn pickup bed, near a yellow wire stretcher and a rusted branding iron. Alex leaned into the pickup to grab it back.

"Nah, we'll give you a ride. All the way to the Kadoka Bar; that's where you're headed, right?" The cowboy towered over him, turned him around and heaved him into the cab. Alex rubbed his bruised knee and stared up at an even larger, meaner-looking cowboy with a stubble beard and dirt-stained hands. They smelled as if they'd spent the night branding cattle.

"We been waitin' for a Bud," the partner said, shoving Alex over. "Sit in the middle."

Alex straddled the gearshift, feeling overpowered and uneasy. Crushed beer cans littered the floor beneath him. The reek of whiskey hit his nose, almost making him gag.

"We're rednecks and redskins, yeah. In a good ole' red pickup. Red Power, right on!"

"It's too lonesome, only the two of us. Besides, we're brothers."

Alex sat silent, counting the miles to the thruway, praying that his fasting Pipe inside the backpack on the pickup bed protected him from these drunken rude ranch hands.

"Your name's not Tonto, I can tell. You don't like that name. So what is it?"

"Harold," he said. Harold Goggle Eyes was an AIM joke on the FBI, used on 302 forms as a signature for made-up testimony. He left off the Goggle Eyes part.

"Well, Harold, we're gonna have a good old time...."

"Thanks. But I'm due in Rapid City this morning."

"We'll take you all the way. Detour to get a little fuel in our bellies for the ride."

Alex kept silent. He knew better than to tell them he didn't drink, had never had a drink, hated alcohol ever since his alcoholic father ran off and disappeared in shame. That would egg them on to try to get him passed-out drunk. His cousins had already tried that on him.

"Wanna beer?"

"No, thanks, too cold."

"That's good. We're out."

"We'll get you something that'll heat up your insides, real soon. Meanwhile, have a joint. You're pretty uptight. Relax, Tonto, we'll get you there, all right."

Alex shifted in his seat. "I roll my own, thanks. Later."

"Our weed's not good enough for you? Bet you raise better stuff on the Res, easier there, with those BIA cops on the take. Bet you got some in that backpack, taking it to Rapid to deal."

Alex kept silent. They crossed the White River, off-Res now. Ten miles to go.

But instead of climbing up to the flats where Kadoka sat, high above Redstone Basin, the driver pulled off the highway into a grove of willows beside the river. "Now we're off-Res, let's us have a little talk. You gonna give us your stash, or we gonna take it off you?"

Alex braced himself, sandwiched between two cowboys ready to beat him up. He could outrun the half-sloshed, uncoordinated guys. But he'd never been in a fight. He wasn't supposed to fight, not allowed to fight. Not the medicine way. He'd always been protected by his uncles, driven to ceremonies on other Reservations, always with a bunch of braves whenever they went off-Res. He'd wrestled with cousins and pinned them in the dust. He'd played stickball, been in contests to lift the heaviest cedar fence post. He'd run miles chasing ponies, strengthened his muscles riding bareback, thrown off, getting back on. He'd never had to fight a person.

The driver put the pickup in park, opened the door, and slid out. "Come-ee here, Har-old." His brother kicked Alex in the back and shoved him out of the pickup.

Alex hit the ground, slid on the ice, and grabbed the side of the pickup bed to reach for his backpack. A large arm threw him down flat beside the rear wheels. He scrambled underneath, dug his boots in the ice and headed for the legs of the other cowboy.

The driver jumped back in the pickup and revved the engine. "Get 'im," he yelled.

Alex crawled to the other side, yanked the cowboy flat and pulled him halfway under.

"Walt, stop! I'm under the pickup!"

Alex slithered out the rear and ran for the river before they could turn around and run him down. He'd had no chance to pray himself up like he had in the sweat or put on his cloak of silence to make him invisible. It'd been so easy to disappear before the FBIs, but two cowboy punks angry as rutting bulls were out to get him. And he was deserting his sacred Pipe.

They came after him, the driver backing up the pickup on the bridge, the other man on foot. Alex swerved away from the bridge into the river, nimble on his feet, avoiding the slippery rocks and ice chunks. Behind him he heard the guy on foot crash and fall into the river. Alex plunged up to his thighs in the open water, desperate to reach safety on the Res side. He'd never been alone to experience mean-spirited mindless bating.

Before he could crawl out of the water, he heard the pickup whine in reverse, squeal of brakes, and a door slam. The driver loomed overhead, ten feet away, tire iron raised, boots tromping down. Alex rolled away from him and under the bridge. From the corner of his eye he saw the first guy in the river struggling against the current. Then a blow from behind knocked him to his knees. His parka hood fell back, leaving no long hair to cushion it.

"C'mon," the driver yelled. "Shit, got no campfire to heat this tire iron and brand 'im."

Alex crawled farther under the bridge. Some blows, even though deflected by his thick parka, stunned him. As he lost consciousness he felt hands stripping off his parka, boots, and even his rodeo belt before the blows to his head drove him into blackness.

~~~

Out of the blackness his mother's blurry face drifted above Alex. He opened his mouth to call to Iná, but as he raised his head, flashes of light crackled his brain. Gradually the pain became the throb of a powwow drumbeat. Then he remembered: lying between worlds, Under-the-Bridge over the river that divided the Res from the rest of South Dakota.

Icicles dripped from a concrete slab above him, splat, splat. He couldn't move his arm. He couldn't lift his head. He had no energy left to hate. The Great Mystery hadn't protected him. He closed his eyes in shame, lay back and sank deep into his darkness.

The redneck cowboys had been mad because their lighter ran out of fluid. They couldn't start a bonfire, couldn't torch him after they poured beer on his parka, so they stripped him, left the worn-out sweatshirt, patched jeans and worthless boots. Took everything else.

Iná, Tate, George, Joanna Joe—he'd failed them all, wiped out before he'd started. He'd never been beaten before. He'd learned to dispel evil spirits, but he'd been protected from evil people. Never again would he be caught off guard.

"*Tunkashila, unshimaleye, Wakan Tanka* help me!" He concentrated on the pains in his body, talked to them, willed them to go away. At last he stood up under the bridge. He looked around. No parka. No pack. No belt with conchos and rodeo buckle. No wallet.

No Pipe bag. He stopped himself—no broken bones, either—though he reeked of alcohol and his mouth tasted foul.

Overhead the sky was as gray as Badlands slate, late afternoon. He'd been knocked out for hours. His body felt stiffer than when he'd fasted for days on top of Eagle Nest butte. If only he could crawl into a steamy Sweat Lodge. But he must keep going. He willed himself to climb onto the bridge, head north off the Res and limp toward Kadoka and the thruway ten miles away.

No cars stopped in the dusk for a wet stumbling figure. He didn't trust a ride, anyway, not even if it looked like a beat-up Indian car.

At the edge of town he came to a row of narrow log cabins, igloos built after WWII for Indians who'd lost their land and moved off-Res to find ranch work. Auntie Rose's had been abandoned for storage, its roof covered with a blue tarp. He crawled through the barbwire fence to it, forced open the heavy slab door. Inside everything had rusted and rotted, mold covered papers and rags. Rats had eaten all the commodity flour. No commodity cans. No food. No boots. No parka. His body wanted to lie down and rest, but he couldn't stop there.

He pulled himself tall. The bleeding around his ears had stopped. He needed a parka, he needed a sweat to get rid of the liquor smell that made him sick. His hair—his braids cut off, and with it, his power. He felt helpless for a moment, then told himself, no, not helpless, just weak. He'd be strong again. He prayed to the Great Mystery, to fill him with new power.

He forced himself to concentrate. He couldn't show himself to his relatives in town. They'd never believe he hadn't gone on a drunk. He staggered along the darkening alleys until he came to the Kadoka Bar. Several muddy pickups parked at an angle in front. Among them sat the redneck cowboys' battered red pickup. They'd be inside drinking up his money. He ducked between pickups until he reached theirs. In the back lay a spare tire, a yellow wire stretcher, and a bloody tire iron. Also, his pack, flattened. Empty. But maybe not. No, empty. He peered in the cab, lit dimly from the neon bar sign. On the dashboard lay his Pipe bag. They hadn't hocked it yet for booze. He thanked the Great Mystery for protecting it.

The pickup was locked. That didn't stop him. With the tire iron he pried open the driver's side door, which had been banged up already and didn't fit tightly. The door screeched when he pulled it open, but he reached in, and like magnetism, the Pipe bag flew into his open hand. His Pipe knew where it belonged, even if he reeked of booze and blood.

He felt the urge to smash the windshield out, but laid the tire iron on the front seat instead, and deflated all four tires. He had his fasting Pipe. It was all he needed.

Alex disappeared into the dark alley and shuffled toward Uncle Homer's house on the corner of Main Street. His uncle wasn't AIM. Town Indians worked jobs for Whites and got along.

He couldn't let them see him all beaten up, with a warrant out on him.

In the open garage behind it, full of half-dismantled cars below engine hoists, Homer's elbow-patched greasy parka with a broken zipper hung on a hook by the side door. His uncle wouldn't care if he'd return it later, or, better yet, bring him a new one. He wrapped himself in it, so warm and sturdy, reeking of honest hard work, oil, diesel fuel and gas—not of alcohol. He felt better already. In the back yard he washed up in a snow bank, then chewed some juniper berries fresh off the bushes below the dining room window.

Inside, his Charging Elk relatives gathered around the big table for supper. He smelled beef stew and frybread, but he didn't dare go in. They'd recognize him, even without braids, and he'd have to explain why. These relatives didn't belong to AIM. No Red Power fists on their pickups or front doors. They fixed Indian cars, worked at the town laundry, cleaned motels and washed dishes at the diner. Reliable, quiet, always on time, never no trouble.

Alex was proud, not hungry. Back at the Vision Cave he'd had a breakfast of dry meat, Indian jerky. He'd survive. He turned away and limped toward the thruway on-ramp. He must go on. Otherwise he might lie down in a ditch and sleep forever. He'd never been so dirty, not when he rode broncs in the Rosebud Indian rodeo and made his mother scream with fear. He'd never been without long hair. He felt naked, scalped, though he'd forced Tate to cut it. He remembered how he'd stood on the Vision Hill against the wind and rain, how the Great Mystery's power had flowed into him through his hair, and that power still lived inside him, braids or no braids.

The Great Mystery must have heard his prayers, though he'd shivered as he prayed, because he had no problem hitching a ride. Truckers, late night drivers, often wanted company, and picked up men alongside the road who traveled light. He hid his Pipe bag inside his parka. The trucker who picked him up didn't mind him with an old oily parka, didn't bother to ask him for his life story, turned up the radio country westerns until the trucker woke him and said, "Lakota Housing exit."

Where his Auntie lived. She'd feed him and find clothes for him without telling anyone else he was in town. When he'd ridden bareback in the Rapid City Rodeo she'd helped outfit him, paid his entry fees and cheered him on from the bleachers. Tomorrow he'd shadow Trask and Slade.

All night long cars drove around the Lakota Homes Housing. Old drunks and young bloods cruised, making it hard for Alex to sneak up to Auntie Agatha's house before dawn, when blackness turned to charcoal. He shuffled down the alley and called softly to Red Dog, who whined in response. The four-legged person recognized him, and didn't bark. He opened the yard gate beside tipi poles and walked to the back door. He waited until the light came on in her kitchen. Auntie Agatha was a Traditional, an early-riser up to greet the dawn. She'd put a pot of coffee on and heat the skillet to make *kabuk* bread. He knocked on the screen door. "*Tanké, miyelo.*" Auntie, it's me.

"Eh?" she replied. She came to the door, unlocked it, and opened it a crack. "Go away, drunk. Leila don't live here no more." She grabbed the door knob. "Nothing here for you. I call the cops." She paused, then switched on the back porch light. "*Tokiyahe*?" Who is it?

Alex pulled at the hooked screen door. "Auntie, it's me, Alex Turning Hawk, your nephew." He shook off his parka hood so she could see him better.

"Eh," she cried, "*Iteshni*!" Can't be. She peered out at him, then pulled back. "You got no braids." She had her braids, a white crown around her head.

"It is me, Auntie, Iná's son."

She leaned back, opened the door a bit more and stared through the screen. She looked him up and down, then poked her nose to the screen and sniffed. She drew back, startled. "*Iktomini*!" She switched to English. "Drunk and been in a fight. Don't come around here!"

She didn't recognize him. As a last resort he tried the baby name she'd always called him, Little Bear. "Auntie, you forgot your own *Mato Chikala*?"

She stared at him. "Alex, you always a good boy. So don't come around me now like this and spoil things. Go down Under-the-Bridge with all them other winos. That's where your father went. Like father, like son."

"Auntie, please, I need to stay—"

"Not here. This house full of women. Girls. Your cousins go to school. Get over to the AIM house, they drink over there."

He couldn't be seen at the urban AIM house, full of hard drinkers and fighters. He wouldn't be undercover for long. "Auntie, it's not what you think. I don't drink—" He scrunched his shoulders down and looked hangdog apologetic, hoping to hit her soft side, with no one else around to see. Traditional aunties were supposed to take care of their nephews, no matter what, not shut the door on them. At least let them in and feed them.

"*Hiya*." No.

He tried one last time, the blood sister appeal. "Auntie, do it for my mom."

"Hah." That's all she said, but she hesitated, then unlatched the screen door.

He slid in and sat at the oilcloth table. She harrumphed and fussed at the stove, but brought him a hot cup of coffee, then plopped a tin plate of eggs over easy and hot *kabuk* bread in front of him. "I never see you like this again," she said.

He hung his head, ate silently and half-listened to her harangue. His teeth ached from the hot coffee, but the black medicine revived him. "You won't," he promised, between bites. "Please don't tell my mom," he added. "She'd die from shame."

"Humph. Gettin' light. You gotta go before the girls get up."

He took his grandpa's little fasting Pipe out from under his parka and laid it on the table. She stiffened and moved away, wide-eyed. "I'm not drunk, just beaten up and rolled. No one knows I'm here. Swear by the Pipe you won't tell anyone, not even your sister."

She gave him that dead-eye piercing look. "*Hiya.* Pipe and alcohol don't mix. I don't touch a wino's pipe, no way. I won't say I seen you. But I'm on your case. Gonna pray and watch out for you, send you to detox if I have to."

"Thanks, Auntie, I can use lots of prayers."

"I can't believe it, my best nephew, a sundancer, now like your father, fallen into evil ways."

"It's not what you think."

"Go, take this." She pushed a bundle of hot *kabuk* bread into his hands. Her right hand slid underneath her apron to her dress pocket and she pulled out a folded bill. "Just this once. I may be an old fool, but you're my sister's boy. I know you gonna go buy more wine, but nephew, watch out. It's cold and dangerous out there in the White world." She locked the back door behind him and flipped off the porch light. "Don't come back."

He knew he couldn't. His plan to hide in the basement, get a college haircut, old-fashioned black framed glasses and a backpack, to become Harold Goggle Eyes evaporated with her final flick of the porch light. His own auntie hadn't recognized him until he used his baby name, so maybe being a drunken bum was the best cover of all.

~~~~

Midnight. Alex headed downtown, to find *Under-the-Bridge*. In Rapid City the homeless hid away from the cops, out of the wind and snow, under the I-90 thruway. He didn't mind the fresh air and clean Rapid River water. As a child Iná had told him that's where his father had gone, but he'd had no idea then what *Under-the-Bridge* meant. He only knew that his father, Até, shell-shocked by the Korean War, had disappeared. He dreaded the possibility of finding him, looking just as dirty and beat-up as he was himself, but passed-out drunk.

He walked the back streets and across the city park, listened for the sound of the Rapid River, and walked along its banks until he came to the six-lane concrete thruway bridge looming in the grayness. As he drew nearer, the rapids drowned out the sound of any traffic above, and grew louder as the river rushed underneath, its roar bouncing off the concrete bulwarks.

He scrambled down the embankment and stopped. Although he'd been only four when the river had drowned so many Indians, he remembered Iná crying over losing Uncle Bernard in the great flood. More than three hundred drowned as it thundered down from the Black Hills. All the bums Under-the-Bridge had been lost, leaving their *wanaghi* to haunt the place, so only the dregs stayed there now. There'd be space for him.

He ducked past the low willows and into the shadows under the thruway. In front of him he saw shapes wrapped in khaki blankets, cardboard boxes, packing crates and car hood lean-tos clustered next to the concrete walls, away from the cold stream and icy rocks. A stench of human waste, alcohol and gasoline filled his nose. He gagged. Opposite side, more huddled winos.

He slipped on the icy cinders, falling on his knees. He landed on a caved-in cardboard box with Sears printed on its side. Above the roar of the river he heard a groan. The box rolled sideways and a figure crawled out. The wino had a dark red beard and long wild hair. Below the beard Alex saw a red plaid jacket and dirty red long johns with feet in them.

"Fucking watch where yer goin'!" The wino raised an arm to grab him, but Alex rolled to the side, jumped up and backed out of reach.

The wino peered up at him. "Hey, Injun." He staggered to his feet, at least six-four, and blocked the way. "Hey, guys, we got us an Injun."

Alex turned around. In the darkness, bearded men stumbled out of crates and boxes, blanketed men rose and menaced—knives, sticks, tire irons. Round-toed work boots, pointy-toed cowboy boots. A rodeo belt buckle glinted on one.

Red-beard said, "Git 'im before he gits us."

Alex tensed his muscles, ready to spring. Not this time.

The cowboy sized him up. "Nah, he's got nothin'. He don't know he's on the wrong side. Throw 'im in the river so he can swim over to Injun Hell."

Alex didn't give them the chance. He swung around, grabbed Red-beard by his jacket and flung him into the wino behind, then ran up the embankment onto the thruway, crossed over, and dropped down to the Indian side. He didn't know why he thought it'd be any different Under-the-Bridge: always two worlds, Indian and White, always a river apart.

He wanted to be anywhere than with hundreds of bums. They had no honor, no pride. He stumbled over a sleeping body and huddled against hard cement and damp earth, too cold to sleep. He ached all over, and couldn't stand the reek of cheap wine and piss. As a small child all he could remember was the smell of alcohol, of being tossed in the air, as if he had wings and flew, squealing, Até, Até, until caught in sweaty arms. Over and over, until he was dropped, and his mother lay on the floor. Later, Iná had told him his father drank himself to death. He hadn't believed it, waited years for Até to return from the Outside World, and when he didn't, Alex had never forgiven him.

Had the Great Mystery led him here to find his father? No, the Great Mystery was leading him to find *two white men* who'd killed

Joanna Joe's and stolen her hands. He'd be on his journey after sunup. He didn't need a cardboard box. He'd not be back.

He tried to sleep. Last summer he'd soaked his sore feet in a glacial stream as he came down from his vision quest on Bear Butte. Now the spray from the rapids froze him and his body-heater refused to send sparks into his fingers and toes. He felt naked without hair to wrap around his face. The north wind blew through, sucked like a cyclone, a bone-chilling, heart-stopping cold, a wind from the dead. A faint "*kree–kree–*" floated in the air above. Too far for his hawk. It was as if a *wanaghi* haunted Under-the-Bridge, echoing off the ceiling, a lonely "*kree–kree–.*"

Finally Alex dozed off. He dreamed of home and Tate. In his sleep he heard a Sundance song, its notes dropping from high to low, down into the earth. It poured out into the darkness and filled his heart. His pulse slowed to the beat as the ancient words wrapped around his aching body. The Great Mystery had sent him a song. Under his breath, half-asleep, he sang along. The song repeated over and over, like a stuck record. He roused himself enough to keep the song a-going.

Then The Great Mystery's voice, low and hoarse, joined in again, as if retrieving the old-time words from a deep well. Alex stirred and woke, enough to realize he wasn't home at the Sundance grounds, but in Rapid City Under-the-Bridge. It wasn't The Great Mystery singing, and these songs couldn't be sung anywhere but on sacred grounds. One of the *wanaghi*, a ghost sundancer, must have been singing to lure him into the Spirit World. Or had his father's ghost come to haunt him?

In the moonlight, the Under-the-Bridge shacks and cardboard boxes lay still, a frozen landscape, except for the tumbling river. The sacred song continued somewhere to his left. He listened. It faded, then rose again, stronger than ever. He got up stiffly, followed the sound and stumbled closer. It came from one of the cardboard refrigerator boxes. He nudged the top flap.

"*Hnnn.*" Someone inside stirred. "*Tokiyahe?*" Who is it?

He answered in Lakota. "You're singing a Sundance song."

The box shook, wobbled, and sang another line.

Alex smelled peppermint schnapps. He waited.

Pages of crumpled newspaper shook loose at the entrance. A white-haired head and sunken black eyes appeared. A cracked toothless mouth sang the phrase again.

Sacrilege. Singing a sacred song outside the *Hochoka*, the sacred Sundance circle, and in winter, while stinking drunk.

The drunk pulled himself partway out of his cardboard box and sat up. "Got any?"

Alex didn't understand.

"Gotta bottle to share?"

"*Hiya*, I don't drink." Alex didn't want to explain what a fool he'd been, to get beaten and pass out, then doused with drink and left to freeze.

"Gotta smoke?"

"*Hiya*." He'd saved a small amount of red willow tobacco to make prayer ties.

"Why you here, freezing? Your girl ditch you? You got robbed and beat up, cops dumped you off in the river 'cause you a full-blood Injun? Safe here, they leave us alone, we leave 'em alone."

Alex shook his head. No bottle. No smokes. No girl. His wife at home, worried about him.

The old bum spat, then reached into a pocket. He struck a match, sheltered it in his gloved hands from the wind, and leaned out to stare. "*Ohan*. Yes, what I said. Beat up. You got a big shiner there, broken nose, cut lip. Even with bad eyes I can see it. Beat up bad. Not a sundancer, not with that whacked-off hair. How'd you learn them songs?"

Alex had almost forgotten his hair, and he didn't want to explain anything.

"Where you from?" The old wino grilled him, not directly by asking his name, but Traditional way, indirect, honing in on his *tiyoshpaya*, his clan.

Silent, Alex wanted nothing to do with someone who slaughtered the sacred songs.

"*Hokshila*, you don't look so great yourself. Got your name beat outta you."

Alex turned away. The old wino called him *boy*, like Old Sam, and insisted that he reveal his name, when he must know that full-bloods didn't give their name to strangers.

The old man shook. "What's a matter, you too proud to tell an old wino your name?"

Alex wasn't ashamed of his Turning Hawk lineage, but he wasn't about to tell a wino his name. "Harold, *mielo*." It's me.

"*Hau*, Harold Whacked-off Hair, you must be in mourn. Barely know your name. They call me Badger, and I ain't ashamed of it.

The old man dug like a badger, sharp-clawed. Let him. "Goggle Eyes," Alex replied. "Harold Goggle Eyes, *mielo*."

Badger hacked, coughed and cackled until out of breath, then heaved and belched. "Haw, haw, thought I heard 'em all. Thought you could fool an old man with a made-up tribal name." He sank back into his cardboard box. From inside came a wheezy voice. "*Hokshila*, how come you ain't home with your mother?"

It was Tate he missed. He hadn't left her enough firewood or enough oats for the horses. Just his hair to burn. Alex was pissed enough to pee on Badger's box. Instead, he kicked it four times and shouted, "I'm trying to sleep, but your singing keeps me awake."

"*Hokshila*, shut up and sleep in that empty box across from me. It's safe."

The refrigerator box was bent and scuffed, but warmer than the ground. Alex crawled in.

"*Washté*," Badger mumbled. "Good. You knock four times, the sacred number. I sing them sacred songs, nobody comes near me. I don't get robbed."

CHAPTER 12
TATE

AT THE CABIN at Camp Crazy Horse, Tate reached for Alex, but his pillow was cold. He always got up early to re-stoke the fire. Then she remembered: she'd had two hours of sleep. Her joints ached from slogging through snowdrifts, her cheeks tingled from windburn. She stared at the heavy Turning Hawk Pipe bag on the far wall, her protection and her responsibility. No Alex, no morning prayers to the Great Mystery. At least she'd burn his hair. Then on to Pine Ridge for JJ's body.

The silence was broken by the thunk of ax on wood. *Thunk. Thunk.*

Had Alex come back to help her? He shouldn't have. She was glad, anyway. She slipped into her ski suit and opened the heavy door. A figure bent over by the woodpile. "Alex!" she called.

A tall man wearing an army parka, black boots and hat, turned mid-stroke and smiled. He was George's right hand man, a Vietnam veteran, older, with a war-weary military bearing.

Disappointed, then relieved that Alex hadn't given up his quest, she asked, "Lester Bear Heart, what are you doing here?"

"Chopping firewood."

She turned away so he didn't see her tears. "When did you get here?"

"George sent me to keep the Camp going." He paused, split another log. "To guard it."

"I'm guarding the place. I chop my own firewood." She stood in the cabin doorway, hands on her hips. "I feed our horses, care for the Sundance grounds."

"George wants me to help out. I mean, help you out. Help you move into town." He looked directly at her. "You know you should move into town with your mother-in-law."

She glared back. "You tell George I'm staying. This is my home." She loved the Turning Hawk land, the Sweat Lodges, Sundance grounds, Vision Caves, all built by Alex's great-grandfather, and the Ceremony House and log cabin built by his grandfather. Now the cabin belonged to Alex.

Lester hoisted the ax and split another log. "Needs a man here. You can't stay alone."

She couldn't let him—or George—force her out. "If you think you can move into Alex's cabin—" She grabbed the broom by the door and thwacked it on the threshold.

He laughed. "You got the broom, I got the ax."

She glared at him. "Hah."

He wedged the ax into the chopping block. "Look, Tate, no one wants to live out here. No faucets for hot and cold. No hot air heat. No TV. Freeze their butt off in a tipi? Cook over an open fire?" He spread his hands open and laughed. "Just me. I respect the old ways."

He picked up a load of kindling and brushed against her. She grabbed his arm to stop him from squeezing past into the cabin, but he dropped the wood on the floor and came in.

He'd gotten inside, and she resented the intrusion. As he bent down to pick up the kindling, she stood over him. "You better stack that up!"

He stacked the wood neatly beside the woodstove. "Put the broom away, Tate. I won't bite." He stood up and smiled at her. His sweaty presence seemed to fill the cabin.

"Don't think you can take Alex's place!"

"I know my place. Down by the Sundance grounds." He walked out.

Relieved, she turned back to her chores. She missed instant hot water, but now her life was back to essentials. She piled empty ten-gallon cream cans onto the wooden sledge, shouldered the rope harness, and pulled the sledge down the snowy path to the creek. The horses had broken through the ice to drink, making it easy to dump cream cans into the stream until submerged. It was harder to haul them out by their icy handles, harder still to keep them from tipping over.

She remembered how the FBIs had dragged JJ up the slope and dumped her like firewood into the ambulance. George had ordered AIM to stay away from Pine Ridge, but AIM was JJ's only family. She'd claim the body to make sure JJ was buried Indian way.

The sledge stuck to a wet patch of snow. She yanked on the harness to loosen it, felt it jerk free and the load lighten. A cream can tipped, spilling water as it rolled into the creek. She grabbed the other cream can, steadied it, and slogged into the creek to rescue the first.

Before she could get to it, an arm reached out from the willows and hauled it ashore. Lester. He was supposed to be at the Sundance grounds. She watched him turn, smile at her, fill the cream can, and carry it up to her.

"Let me haul that sledge. You hold the cream cans on."

"I can do it myself. You watch the cream cans." She pulled on the rope traces, but the sledge didn't move. How had it gotten so heavy? She'd hauled two cream cans every day. She glared at him. Had he put his foot on the sledge?

"Time to switch places." He lifted the rope harness over her head and put it on. With a jerk he pulled the sledge uphill, and she followed beside it, holding the cream cans in place. He made her feel clumsy and ridiculous, and didn't let her lift the cream cans by the washstand.

He warmed his wet hands over the woodstove. "Teamwork's better."

Wet and cold, she stood opposite him and studied his smile, trying to gauge his motives. Let Lester work for Camp Crazy Horse by hauling water and chopping firewood. He was like the big brother she'd always wanted, bossy, and sometimes helpful.

Lester handed her a paper sack. "You're outta soap. My cousin works in motels, saves me soap, toilet paper, even towels for the Sweat Lodge."

Lester had thought of everything. She stacked the soap bars beside the wash basin and put her coat on. Two days had passed, and Pine Ridge Agency was a hundred miles away. "Take care of the horses while I'm gone."

"Drive careful," he said and walked away.

She brushed the snow off the pickup windshield and climbed in. Damn Agent Trask who'd taken the keys. Alex hadn't gotten a second set, like her careful parents in Minneapolis. She bent down to hot-wire the pickup. She pumped the gas. It didn't turn over. She couldn't tell if the tank was empty, since the gas gauge never worked. She got out, dipped the siphon hose into the tank and withdrew it. She had half a tankful. Maybe one of the FBI agents had disabled it when they'd been here. Maybe the battery had died. She wished she knew more about cars, like Alex.

She walked to the Sundance grounds to Lester's pickup. She'd never paid attention to it before. It was brand new, like a fire truck to the rescue, all shiny red and chrome, with snow tires, large engine and jacked up wheels. Lester was loading a chainsaw and red gas can in the bed. He called it *Red Power*.

"I need to borrow your pickup," she said.

"You think firewood grows on trees," he said. Ignoring her, he climbed in.

She ran in front of the grill. "As leader of the Camp, I'm commandeering it." Through the windshield she saw his mouth twist in refusal, then slide into a knowing grin.

"What's so important, *Sergeant* Turning Hawk?"

Would Lester go against George's AIM orders? Her style was to go her own way and take the consequences later—and if she brought

JJ back, George would be glad. "I'm going to Pine Ridge, to get her body from the Agency."

"Off limits. 'General' George outranks you." He revved the engine.

If he shifted into first, she'd climb on the grill and pound on the windshield. Before he could try, she darted to the passenger door, yanked it open and climbed in. She'd rather have gone alone, but she had no choice but to shame him into driving her. "*Private* Bear Heart, no one else will claim her body. She's an orphan."

Lester said nothing as he sped like a maniac hell-bent for Pine Ridge Agency down the wide-open country road stretching for miles. Tate wished she hadn't called Lester *Private*. He must have been at least a Sergeant in Vietnam. His engine had so much power. But the heater worked, the wipers worked, the doors closed and locked, and the radio played Indian country western, Willie Nelson and Buddy Red Bow. She enjoyed the luxury for a moment before turning down the music so she could ask him about JJ. "How did you know *Our Lost One*?"

Lester stared ahead. "It's not right, the FBIs keeping her body."

She tried again, "Didn't she fight in the trenches with you guys?"

"She was a loyal AIM warrior."

Trenches were close quarters. He'd known her, but he didn't want to talk. "Why did you agree to drive me to Pine Ridge Agency if you think it's a trap?"

"Nobody ever stopped me from rescuing a warrior. I did it in 'Nam, and I can do it here."

"So you taught her to fire a rifle?"

He laughed. "Sarge, she already knew. She was a fighter, not a spoiled princess."

Just because Alex chose her to marry, some AIM women thought her spoiled. Lester had picked up the gossip. Tate glared at him. "You have no idea how I was *spoiled*!" She slapped the dashboard. "I was my foster mother's adopted toy, her black-eyed baby doll. I didn't look like her, so she pretended I was a lost Hungarian princess. She read me fairy tales, sent me to piano lessons and French class. I believed it until one day my father got mad at her and told me I was Indian, came wrapped in a blanket from the Reservation. I felt so cheated, I ran away and joined AIM to be Indian. *Our Lost One* found me, said I looked just like her, that we were lost orphan sisters. AIM and the Red Schoolhouse were our family."

"Okay, Sarge, we'll rescue your lost sister."

Maybe he felt sorry for her, maybe for both of them. After they passed Sharp's Corners, she tried again to ask about JJ. "Where'd she go after Wounded Knee Occupation?"

"Lost track of her, she jumped bail—" He turned and stared.

She stared back. "Who saw her last?"

"Sarge, from now on your name is *Question Box.*"

If she'd gone underground, someone in AIM must know. She'd ask George.

Lester slowed down at the shell of a church on a hill and burned-out store below.

"This isn't Pine Ridge Agency. Why are you stopping?"

"Question Box, welcome to Wounded Knee," he announced in a tour-guide voice. "My AIM brothers are buried here. We took over the church cemetery, up there. Bunkers everywhere, some filled in now, grassed over."

She stared at the iron-grilled arch of the cemetery, expecting to get out.

Instead, he pulled across the road, stopped abruptly on the wrong side. "But the real cemetery is this gully."

She stared at the snowdrifts. "Why here?"

"You want to get her body because she had no family. My family is here. At the *first* Wounded Knee in 1890, Chief Big Foot's band got gunned down—343 women and children—dumped in a common pit grave." He climbed down the snowplowed drifts, took a string of red tobacco ties from his parka, and laid them on the white snow in the gully, as if underneath there was a roadside shrine like those that marked car accidents.

When he came back, he slammed the door and revved the engine. "Nothing there now but snow—grass under the snow, and Spirits." He looked grim and determined. "It's a powerful place. I can see you don't feel it."

What could she say? She'd read about the original massacre in a book. She'd heard about the Occupation of Wounded Knee when she joined AIM two years ago. Her only connection now was through Alex.

Tate said, "Head toward Pine Ridge Hospital."

"Why go there?"

"Isn't the morgue there?."

"Okay, Question Box." He turned past the Bureau of Indian Affairs offices, the Tribal building, headed up to the Indian Public Health Hospital, and parked in the lot. They got out and went in the main entrance to the information desk.

She spoke politely to the clerk dressed in hospital greens. "I'm here to identify a person brought in two days ago by the Eagle Nest ambulance."

The woman looked up over her half-glasses. "Name?"

She hesitated to say it aloud. "Joanna Joe."

The clerk bowed her head to look in her admission book. Then she looked up. "No record. None for Eagle Nest. Did you try the outpatient clinic?"

"Jerry Slow Bear brought a body here—"

The clerk frowned. "This is a hospital."

"The morgue isn't here? Then where do you identify bodies?"

"You have to go to the Black Funeral Parlor." The clerk turned away. "Don't you have documents? Go to the BIA offices first."

Tate walked away. Outside on the steps, she turned and grabbed Lester by the arms, ready to shake him. "Why didn't you tell me? We're wasting time."

"Question Box," he said, backing off, "You boss me around, drive here, drive there, like I'm your personal chauffeur to do anything you say, stupid or not."

Clearly Lester couldn't take orders from females. She wondered if he'd followed men's orders in 'Nam. He'd disobeyed George, too. Since they were both rebels, maybe they could work together. "It's your pickup, your Res. You know things. Take over."

Lester laughed. "You just got the *Pine Ridge Run-around*. You talk and sound White. Here you have to keep asking questions. Those BIA *Apples*—red on outside, white on inside—pay attention to you, not to an AIM longhair *blanket Indian* like me."

His laugh had sounded bitter, but she laughed, too. "Okay, Lester Long Hair, find this Black funeral parlor."

"Ain't no funeral *parlors* on the Res. The Tribe don't do bodies. They send 'em off-Res to Nebraska to be embalmed and put in expensive caskets for the Tribe to bury. That mortician gets rich off our dead. He's famous for his *died of exposure* autopsies on Indians."

"They're going to ask for documents."

"Nah, she wasn't from Pine Ridge. All you need is money. Enough to pay for the ambulance, embalming and casket."

Lots of money, but she must try. "So drive me to Nebraska!"

"Only two miles to White Clay, border town for booze and burials. Known as *Death Road*."

At the Res border three buzz-cut Indians wearing camouflage outfits and black gun belts manned a roadblock. "Pine Ridge Agency Goons—Guardians of the Oglala Nation, what a laugh," said Lester. "Look straight ahead, say nothing." He rolled down the window and opened his wallet.

Pocketing the bills, one said, "Even AIMs gotta have booze. Pass through."

She expected White Clay, Nebraska, to be more than a strip of highway lined with bars, pawnshops, and a fast-food joint. "Where is the town?"

"Hang on, Question Box. Funeral home's three blocks away."

He turned onto a residential street lined with trees, turned at a brick ranch house, turned into a large paved driveway, and parked in front of a loading dock and a pair of double doors. Beside it, steps led up to a door labeled *Office*.

Tate climbed the steps and went in, Lester behind her. The office was small, cramped, and steamy hot. A built-in registration counter blocked the hallway to rooms behind it. "Is anybody here?" Her words echoed down the hallway. She called again.

At last a woman in a business suit and bouffant hairdo entered the hall and walked down to the counter. "It's after closing time."

Tate reached across the counter to her. "We've driven over a hundred miles to identify an Indian woman delivered here two days ago."

The clerk sighed, retrieved a ledger book from a shelf and flipped it open. "Name?"

"Joanna Joe. Indian."

The clerk looked up. "Don't toy with me. She came in as a Jane Doe?"

"Has anyone else been here to identify her?"

The clerk closed the ledger. "Miss, we've had several Jane Does. All Indians."

"You'd remember. She had no hands."

"I don't know about that."

"I'm her sister. I'm here to identify her body."

"Let me check." The clerk walked back down the hall and disappeared behind a metal door. Almost immediately she returned with a fixed smile. "I'm sorry. All our Jane Does have been sent back to Pine Ridge Cemetery already."

Tate's face flushed. JJ wasn't a Jane Doe. How could the FBIs label her so?

"I'm sorry. We're closed now. I'm locking up." The clerk lifted the hinged countertop, walked past them and opened the office door for them.

Lester stood, eager to leave, eager to tell her that this time it was *The White Clay Run-around*. She couldn't move, overcome with the feeling that JJ's body must be inside. She bolted past the open counter, down the long hall and burst into the room beyond the steel door. In the cold autopsy room lit by an overhead light lay a bloated form draped under a sheet on a gurney. She shrank from the mixture of formaldehyde, blood, and sweat.

Lester, right behind her, caught the door, closed it and flipped the lock. "You crazy?"

Tate ran over to the gurney. "That clerk's lying. JJ's here." She lifted the sheet. A bald potbellied man with a Y stitched in his chest with black thread. Frantic, she ran to the wall of refrigerated shelves and yanked them open, one by one. Empty. She stood, paralyzed.

The clerk banged on the steel door of the room, but Tate couldn't hear what she said.

Lester grabbed her arm. "We're outta here!" He unlatched the double doors and pushed her outside onto the loading platform. They ran to Red Power. He spun onto the highway back to Pine Ridge before the woman could call the cops. He whistled. "Now who's the hothead?"

Tate sighed. "I was so sure. I felt her there. And now she's disappeared!"

"Only the FBIs have any authority around here. Case closed."

"Where do they send the dead bodies?"

Lester shrugged. "Back to the Res, to the Unknown Graveyard, beyond the Pine Ridge Housing. Probably a priest from Holy Rosary prayed over her."

"She wasn't Catholic."

"Doesn't matter. You gotta be Catholic or Episcopal, one cemetery or the other. You can't get buried out on the land or up on a red scaffold. It's illegal."

She shook her head. Everything was illegal. She'd heard Pine Ridge was lawless, run by Goons, but she thought that disappearing a person happened only in foreign dictatorships. A trickle of fear seeped into her bones.

At the state border ahead loomed the same Goon roadblock, barricaded now with sawhorses marked with reflecting tape. Had the mortuary clerk seen their red pickup and called the Pine Ridge Goons? "Don't stop," she said.

Instead, Lester halted and rolled down his window. "We came through for a quickie trip."

Tate slumped down and pulled her hood over her face.

"Road's closed now. Curfew." One of the Goons yanked at the driver's locked door. "Get out so I can search the vehicle."

Lester muttered, "—for booze, yeah. Ain't got none." One Goon reached in to haul the driver out, but Lester held onto the steering wheel and waved a wad of bills. "Get it yourself."

While the three Goons divided the stash, Lester eased the furthest sawhorse aside with his front bumper, slithered through the unofficial roadblock and sped back onto the Res.

Bribery was bad, but in this case it had worked. "We could have been arrested," she said.

Lester laughed. "If I'd plowed through, we'd have BIA cops on our tail, red lights flashing. Those camouflage Pine Ridge Agency Goons are just on the Booze Patrol."

So far they'd gotten nowhere: no death certificate, no autopsy report, no burial site, nothing.

They reached Pine Ridge Cemetery at dusk. Lester looked across at her. "You okay? Graveyard's closed, too." He circled the Pine Ridge cemetery to its open back gate, drove in and parked in front of a fresh grave, dirt humped high, white cross on top.

She climbed out and stumbled over the curb to the grave. No name, no date, no plastic flowers. It wasn't necessarily JJ's. Everything she investigated was *not necessarily*. It was so frustrating. Lester wasn't getting out. Maybe this wasn't it. Maybe it was and he didn't want to see. Wind whistled through the pines. It was getting too dark to see. There were other white-crossed mounds, but none as newly-dug. The whole trip felt like a dead-end wall of snow, soft and smothering.

From a distance raucous laughter and a metallic whine drifted upward on the wind. She saw headlights at the cemetery's chained front gate, heard the groan and clang of metal chains bursting.

Spotlights lit up gravestones below. It was like a scene from *Invasion of the Body Snatchers,* except it wasn't funny.

Behind them, in front of them, all around them, loomed high-center jacked-up pickups with hunting strobe lights on top. Like deer, they were caught in the beams and hemmed in. Doors slammed, men got out.

Lester backed the pickup onto the grass, swung around, and opened her door. "Get in!"

As she ran to Lester's pickup, a dark shadow grabbed her hair and yanked her back. She elbowed him in the gut and broke loose, leaving a fistful of hair in his hands. She flung herself onto the passenger seat, slammed the door, and locked it. Her scalp stung.

Her attacker, hooded in a dark sweatshirt, banged on her window. She flinched and slid over toward Lester.

"Hey, who's your chick? You her pimp? How 'bout a freebie, seeing as we'll let you go without smashing your shiny red wagon."

Lester said in a low tense voice, "Hang on. They're young punks, gung-ho half-breeds born to raise hell, but never been to war like me. Red Power can outrun them."

At his window a young Indian wearing a black cowboy hat and flak jacket yelled, "Who you looking for, Chief? Only bums and whores buried here." The punk banged on the pickup's fender, window, and side mirror. He held his beer bottle high and slugged the last of it down.

Lester jerked the pickup in reverse, smashed into a pickup that had come up behind them, and revved the engine in first. He turned sharply past a black pickup that blocked them in front.

The punk, startled, stepped forward and crashed his empty bottle against Lester's pickup, raking the broken end along the side as they headed downhill across grass and graves.

On Tate's side, the hooded Indian hung onto the door handle, hooked a cowboy boot over the edge and hoisted himself into the pickup bed. She screamed, "He's climbed in the back!"

"Made a mistake, riding with me. I'll bounce him out, or get him later on."

The guy pounded on the rear window. "Always causing trouble, you AIM bastards."

Lester swerved around gravestones, bumped over graves and headed to the front entrance. More headlights blocked the road. "Too many damn fucking spotlights!" He jerked onto the gravel road that circled the cemetery, cut his headlights and zoomed toward the back gate where they'd come in. Behind them, pickups careened through the cemetery, knocked over gravestones and sank in muddy sloughs. Strobe lights and curses filled the air.

"He's trying to kick in the rear window," Tate yelled.

Lester braked sharply, rocking the pickup back and forth. "Good. Stay put." He leaped out, climbed into the pickup bed, and jerked the drunk upright. He spit in his face and said, "You're right, I am a French trapper's bastard!" and threw him over the far side.

When Lester climbed back in, Tate cried, "Ohmygod, did you kill him?"

"Drunks always land loose, like bronc riders when they get bucked off." He revved the engine, pulled out of Pine Ridge the back way and headed toward Wounded Knee, going sixty, then seventy, driving by half-moon light and instinct for the lay of the land.

Behind them headlights shone from afar. When they came to Holy Rosary Mission, Tate said, "Turn in here, the priests will protect us. We can find the priest who buried her."

He stepped on the gas, hitting eighty on the straightaway through the dark countryside. "Those holy men don't open doors at night. Red Power can outrun them punks. We keep going."

Her heart raced. Churches always provided sanctuary, but here on the Res it seemed as if even the priests feared hired guns. Far ahead she could see lights, road crew spotlights and flashing red cop lights. "Is it an accident? Drive on by!"

"Hell, it's the real curfew. BIA cop roadblock." He surged through the dark at ninety and barreled through the barriers, leaving splintered wood in the roadway. "Get down, brace yourself!"

Bam! The rear window shattered. Fragments showered on them. Tate huddled on the floorboard. She heard sirens, more gunshots. Flashes of red and blue strobes lit up the cab.

She curled up tighter, hands over he eyes. "Ohmygod, they'll kill us."

Lester slowed to seventy, screamed past Sharp's Corners to Kyle. "Brush the glass off me."

She reached up to sweep broken shards off his arms as Red Power jerked ahead. Bang! Behind them a BIA cop car smashed into the rear fender to force them off the road. But Red Power surged ahead. They seemed to float above the road, he drove so fast. As they raced past Kyle and onto open prairie, she climbed back up and brushed more glass off Lester's shoulders. No headlights behind them. She breathed deeply. "It's a miracle!"

"No miracle. That BIA cop radioed ahead. We ain't home free." Lester slowed, turned onto a gravel track down to a creek and pulled behind a grove of cottonwoods. He pulled out a camouflage tarp from behind the seat and covered the pickup before the BIA cop car zoomed past, spewing gravel.

"He won't make it into the Badlands on this gravel track with no guard rails. He'll skid at the first curve and go over the edge two hundred feet down." Lester lit a smoke.

Her scalp hurt. She shivered, thinking of what she'd started. George had been right. The Pine Ridge Agency was too dangerous. She needed to apologize, to explain—no, she'd say nothing. Silence meant you'd done wrong. It was no use trying to justify it with words.

Lester drove home without lights. She felt numb as she stumbled into her cold, dark cabin. She barred the door and fell directly into bed. What a disaster. She had no idea the Res was so disorganized and lawless. Even Minneapolis wasn't this dangerous. Alex had warned her there was no law and order here, but she'd brushed it aside. Everybody made their own laws. So no Pipe or prayer ties could make her safe.

Lester's Red Power was wrecked, all her fault. How could she get it fixed? No wonder Lester was mad. And if Alex found out, he'd be mad, too. She wondered if he were safe somewhere, not discouraged and miserable. He was probably at one of his aunties', warm and well-fed.

CHAPTER 13
ALEX

SOMEONE SHOOK ALEX'S cardboard box. He covered his ears. He was Under-the-Bridge.

"Wake up, Harold. It's me, Badger. Don't like being called *Tonto*, ennit? That Harold Goggle Eyes shit ain't gonna work."

Alex looked out. He could barely see Badger, who leaned on an old split baseball bat. Just what he needed to bash Badger's mouth shut. He jumped out, grabbed the bat, but managed not to yank it away. Although Badger didn't know it yet, the old wino was going to be his new teacher.

"Can't have my bat," Badger snarled. "Don't know what you're after, but you ain't no wino. Dirty and ragged, but you ain't passed out. I can tell, you been a good boy to your mother."

Alex let go. "That's right, Badger. When I've been off-Res, it was only to Lakota ceremonies or AIM courtroom trials, never to ordinary places like banks or libraries. I need you. Teach me to survive in White-Man World." Otherwise, he'd never be able to shadow the FBIs.

"*Hiya*. No. Got my own territory." Badger backed away, swinging his bat. "You stay off'n it." He picked up a duffle bag and started up the embankment.

"You get out early, but the strong ones take it all from you, ennit?" He'd hit the old man's weak spot. "With me along, nobody could grab your stuff. You could take it easy."

Badger turned and sneered. "You? All beat up?"

"I got muscles, Badger. Bareback rodeo-riding muscles." Alex flexed his pecs. "And you got street-smarts." He grabbed Badger and lifted him off the ground. He let him flail the air.

"Hey!" Badger squealed, as if Alex had tickled him. "Goddam, I'll bat yer brains out."

Holding Badger aloft, Alex kicked the bat loose from the wino's right hand. It rolled down the bank into the river and floated downstream. "That one's split. We'll get a new one, you show me how." He put Badger down and bowed. "From now on, I'm your *hokshila*."

Badger sat down on his duffle bag, suspicious. "Ain't done nothin' wrong. Lemme be." He opened his coat and laid out a cigarette paper. "Why you wanna be a bum?"

"Got my reasons. I want to walk around out there invisible."

Badger laughed. "That ain't hard. Share me some tobacco."

The old wino must have tobacco radar, otherwise, how'd he know about the red-willow tobacco saved for offerings? Alex gave up two pinches of it, sat down beside Badger in front of his box, lit the hand-rolled smoke, and accepted his share, the butt end. Two Lakota men establish a bond by sharing a single smoke.

When done, Badger stood up. "*Wana, hokshila*. Ready to become a bum?" He pulled a tin washbasin from his cardboard box. "Fill it in the stream. Gotta wash up, look neat."

Orders already. Just like his mother. Alex bent down to the cold water, slipped on the icy edge and almost lost the basin to the strong current.

"Hey, don't let that 'un get away!" Badger squatted on the ground, handed him a small bar of Ivory soap. "Wet down your sticking-up hair. Gotta let that hair grow so you can cover your face."

Alex took off his parka and stared at the soap wrapper. "Where'd you get this?"

"Wha'ja mean? In the motel dumpster."

"You go around to all the motels?" Alex asked, excited. Badger knew the places he needed to check out Joanna Joe's motel soap-wrapper hidden inside a tobacco tie. "You know all the motels in Rapid?"

"You want more soap? I got my routes. Tomorrow, I'll take you on that 'un."

Alex pulled out the torn soap wrapper from his sweatshirt pocket, the name in faded blue, *Springv*. "Ever heard of one called *Springvale*? *Springview*?"

Badger peered at the faded paper. "*Hiya*. No. Thought I knew 'em all. Must be new—hmm, looks old, maybe closed down. I'll ask around."

As Alex took the wrapper back, Badger grabbed him and yelled, "Take off that greasy sweatshirt! Gotta wear a cotton one till you get a new parka." He rummaged in his cardboard box for a button-down blue shirt.

Alex hesitated. He was shy around strangers because his chest was scarred from pulling free from the Sundance tree.

But Badger had already guessed. "Don't believe yer line. Wanna see them piercing scars."

Alex didn't brag up his Sundance scars, front and back, his personal offering to the Great Mystery. But he saw no way around Badger's nosy look, so he took off his sweatshirt, washed up in the cold river and put on the thin blue shirt.

Badger nodded. "You got a shiner all right. Time for them good old Salvation Army prayers." He led Alex to a large padlocked crate high under the cement bridge, unlocked it, and took out a beat-up shopping cart. In it sat empty cartons, pop cans and bottles. Badger covered it all with an old once-blue tarp. "*Hokshila*, help me push it up to the street."

Alex pushed the squeaky cart up the embankment. Two wheels turned and froze.

"*Shh!* Squeaky wheel gets all the attention. Gotta lift me some oil later on." Badger led Alex down frost-covered streets to a blinking neon sign, *Jesus Saves*.

Alex knew about the Salvation Army. Once when he was little, Iná took him shopping at K-Mart. A fat red-suited man stood outside with a big kettle, ringing a bell for coins, and blocked their way. He'd called the man *White-Man-Santa-Claus*, but the man became angry and said no, this was his uniform and he was a *Soldier-for-Christ*.

Shadowy figures stood in line before the chapel door. Dark and anonymous, shrouded in khaki army parkas, they shuffled in worn work boots and muttered greetings to Badger, who took his role as teacher seriously: "They lock the doors, so we can't sneak in late. You gotta get here on time, sit through hell-and-damnation to get the bacon. So, *hokshila*, look down, shuffle, sit down quiet. Don't fall asleep and snore like some that get kicked out. Pay attention and say *Amen* loud and clear. When the ladies hand you a booklet, pretend you can read it and say, 'Thank you, Ma'am.'"

Badger didn't know that Alex's grandpa Turning Hawk, medicine man, also had been an Episcopal lay reader. As a young boy Alex had sat on hard benches in the log church, learning to doze upright while others sang off-key hymns translated into Lakota, long and slow like a wake. When he came of age at sixteen, he'd chosen the Sweat Lodge as his church—a purifying sauna, confession booth, and head-shrinker's couch—all in one hot, dark, and short ceremony.

Inside the chapel, Alex half-listened to Badger, then the sermon. Sin and hellfire, so different from his grandpa's Bible stories of Jesus' love. And different from the Catholic funerals where they chanted in a sing-song foreign language, whether about hell or heaven, you couldn't tell. Except that you must kneel—up-down, up-down, no dozing off—until you were worn out before the meal. As the last chords of a pump organ echoed throughout the evangelist hall— nothing like Tate's piano—he worried that she'd be so lonely, she'd play music all day and forget to feed the horses, or file the chain saw blade, or put new wicks in the kerosene lamps.

As they filed into the basement soup kitchen, Badger nudged him into the line for a tray of oatmeal, scrambled eggs, toast, and best of all, hot coffee. Badger negotiated his way to a table at the end of the room. "Some sit closer to get leftovers. But here by the door you can see what's comin' and get out fast before a fight breaks out, which is not allowed but sometimes happens and we all get blamed and banned for a week."

Maybe Badger had enemies. Alex, who'd already eaten up the food Auntie'd sent with him, ate in silence, grateful.

Not Badger. Food fueled his tongue. "See this basement? When it gets twenty or thirty below, they fold up the tables, lay down mattresses and let us sleep here till it gets warmer outside. But you got to go up and be saved by Jesus in their prayer meetings. I been saved every cold snap."

Alex marveled that Badger could talk non-stop and still demolish his breakfast. He seemed to have forgotten that Traditional Indians don't talk while eating, so you can taste the food. Maybe hunger Under-the-Bridge had changed him.

Badger hadn't finished yet. "Gotta have a cart for work. When the cops raid us Under-the-Bridge, you skeddadle with all your gear. You hang on and ride 'er downhill. Worse comes to worse, you crawl in, wrap yourself in blankets and tarp, and sleep."

Alex couldn't imagine curling himself tight enough to fit in a two-foot by three-foot cart, but at least he knew how to turn up his body-heater to keep warm.

They walked back from the mission to K-Mart at the south edge of town, surrounded by a huge asphalt parking lot. Badger ducked around to the rear alley lined with large gray dumpsters, but no shopping carts. "Hell, no rejects today. Have to try strategy." He dug into one of his bags and drew out a bundle of shiny orange straps. "Gimme your parka, put this on."

Alex straightened out the bundle and grinned. The old guy had found a K-Mart employee vest. He shed his old parka, pulled the vest on and tugged it in place.

"Stand up straight. Now you look official, like you come outta the store," Badger said. He led the way to the front parking lot. A few shoppers pushed carts toward pickups. Badger leaned on his cart and pointed. "Stand by that lane, wait till that old couple loads their bags in their trunk. Then go up to them and say, "Ma'am, may I return your cart for you?" And she'll give it to you. But don't take it inside, you slip around the corner."

Alex wondered about the difference between borrowing and stealing. After he thanked the woman, he pushed the cart behind the store to Badger, took off the vest, and put on his parka.

Barger said, "I can see lifting a cart bothers you, so when you head back home, you can leave it here, good as new."

Alex followed Badger down the back alleys until they reached the rear of a Goodwill store.

Badger knocked on the back door. "*Hokshila*, you gotta have a parka that zips. Cold front coming in, my bones feel it. Free to Indians on Wednesday, but that's in Spearfish, have to hitch a ride with some of us 'skins. Weekend, St. Vincent DePaul for army blankets and good parkas. But today we only got Goodwill. Park our carts in the alley, go in the back, find the 10¢ bin."

An employee answered, a big stocky girl with long black hair parted in the middle and a no-nonsense stance. "Hello, Badger. You sober?"

"You bet, Sophie. Neat and clean as a whistle." He waved a voucher beneath her nose. "My friend Harold here needs a parka. Cold front coming, might freeze himself to death. Wool hat, socks, gloves, snow boots, too."

"You get ten items each, as you know." She handed them each a large plastic bag.

"Can we throw in a few from the 10¢ bin." It wasn't a question.

Sophie shook her head. "Ten items." Badger must look like one of her grandpas.

Alex roamed the aisles, choosing plaid flannel shirts, jeans, padded jumpsuit, work boots.

Badger came alongside. He pulled out the flannel shirts. "No bright reds and yellows, you're a bum now, you want no attention." Badger filled the bag with dark flannel plaids, then pulled something shiny and black from his own bag and shook it loose.

After the dust settled, Alex saw a woman's long black-haired wig.

"Gotta make you into a long-hair wino, cover your face lying in the alley."

Alex picked up the wig and sniffed. Perfume, makeup grease. No way he'd put it on. He shook his head, "*Hiya*," and tossed it into the nearest bin.

Badger retrieved it and stuffed it into Alex's bag. "Mine's full. Got no nits, it'll do." Badger's bag bulged with wool scarves, socks and gloves, topped by a clean fur-fringed army parka. In only a few minutes Badger could clean out a store.

While Alex replaced the bright plaid shirts on their hangers, Badger ducked down another aisle and disappeared for a moment. He popped back up wearing a black wool topcoat over his parka. Badger only needed a top hat and cane.

"Ready to go, Harold?"

Alex nodded. *In-and-out, in-and-out.* Another of Badger's rules.

Badger grabbed his arm and led to the rear. "This coat's for you. You do need it, Harold."

Alex wrestled his arm loose. "I gave up that student disguise."

"Never know when to look like a store owner, Indian lawyer, FBI, to get in anywhere."

Sophie blocked their way. "Ten items, Badger."

He smiled broadly. "I can add, Sweetie. Ten and ten makes twenty." He handed her a packet. Then Badger shivered violently. "Cold snap coming in." He gestured toward Alex. "He needs one of them army blankets you got back here."

Sophie looked Alex up and down, then pulled a khaki blanket off a high shelf.

He smiled and thanked her. She looked like his cousin Cora. Outside, he asked Badger, "What's inside the packet?"

Badger shrugged. "Stuff. She's my Sweetie, remember?"

Badger must have lots of Sweeties. Alex reached for his new parka, but Badger held on.

"Now you wear the old one. Me, too." He peeled off the black topcoat and laid it in Alex's cart. "After lunch, we switch."

He didn't understand Badger's idea of when to wear clean or dirty clothes, but he'd find out soon enough. They walked the back alleys toward downtown, past McDonalds—no good scrounging food there—to the rear of Royal Fork steak house. Badger pushed his cart to the edge of the dumpster. "Climb up, *hokshila*, you're skinny."

Alex climbed onto the cart, then stepped on the rim and lifted the heavy lid. Burned grease, rotten meat, sour beans from the thick swill filled his nose. He gagged. Then he forced himself to look down. A pile of unpeeled boiled potatoes. Lettuce heads bobbed in slimy cheese sauces swirling in the bottom.

"We look for steak. Rib-eye. See any?" Badger handed up a Good-will plastic bag.

Alex held his breath, controlled his stomach muscles. Rotten food.

"Near empty? Somebody get here last night? Climb in and find something."

No wonder Badger hadn't given him the new parka. Alex stepped gingerly on a crate of rotten oranges, squishing it down. The lid dropped down onto his head. His eyes adjusted to the semi-darkness. Pancakes, dripping syrup. Eggshells. French fries. Congealed sausage patties. Sourdough bread. For a moment the smells overwhelmed him, as if he had grown a giant nose and was caught in a garbage hell, unable to claw his way out. He'd asked for this, but hadn't realized dumpster-diving was part of being a bum. He exhaled and picked the topmost items to fill the bag. A second breakfast for lunch. If he could eat any of it.

A door banged. The lid rose, letting in light. He felt smothered by a heavy plastic tarp.

Badger's voice nearby warned, "Duck down, pull it over you. I'm outta here."

Footsteps dragging a garbage bin came near. "Get away, you bum," a man yelled.

Badger's cart squeaked away rapidly down the alley. Deserted in a dumpster by a bum.

The dumpster lid opened again. Crouching immobile under the tarp, Alex held his nose. Otherwise, he'd cough or choke on the smell, hoping the tarp had no rips or holes. Garbage sloshed in on top of the plastic tarp. Alex held his breath until the lid clanked down, foot-steps retreated and the door banged shut. Not the FBIs this time. He'd heard that sometimes they searched dumpsters for phone bills and credit card bills. But they'd never eat garbage for lunch. He felt ridiculous. Surely this wasn't one of the Great Mystery's tests. If only George could see him now, sunk so low, he'd be horrified. He imag-ined Tate, still in the honeymoon stage of love, laughing and forcing him to take a long shower, maybe even scandalize Iná and take it with him, just to make sure he was really clean.

Step by cautious step Alex slid out from under the tarp, stood on the rotten orange crate, lifted the lid, and took a deep breath. Before he could climb out, he saw chicken-shit Badger coming.

"Wait," Badger cried. "The tarp! You caught it all fresh. Lift it out to me."

Alex looked at his hands smeared with ketchup and coffee grounds. Nothing mattered, everything filthy. So he grabbed the tarp's edges and hoisted it out to Badger's waiting hands.

"Sorry," Badger said. "Bad timing. But you did good, hid so the guy didn't call the cops."

Alex climbed out, wiped his hands on the old parka, and watched Badger kneel on the tarp, picking pieces of steak from it. Repulsed, he said, "You're not gonna eat that."

"*Ohan.* You will, too. Until we work to get some cash."

"*Hiya.*" Never. Yet he put the bag of pancakes and scrambled eggs into his cart.

Together they wheeled their carts out of the alley and headed toward the downtown park. The stone drinking fountain had been turned off in winter, so Alex wiped his hands on the dead grass while Badger laid out his spread on a picnic table and divided it in two.

"That pile of shit is all yours." Alex took out his bag of pancakes and scraped off the gravy.

Badger waved his hands over the table, as if blessing the food. "You get used to it. Timing is everything. Get there seconds after they shut the back door, it's unspoiled and delicious."

Alex was not convinced. He longed for a cup of hot coffee.

After Badger had chewed his steak pieces, he wiped his mouth, took out a pouch of Bull Durham, and rolled two cigarettes. He handed one to Alex. So the old fox had tobacco all the time.

"Knew you'd take a cig. Better'n coffee. Relax and listen. You wanna go unnoticed, learn to be a wino, a passed-out drunk Injun, harmless as hell. They look at us, they look away. Cops leave us alone in the dark alleys and dumpsters. Last thing they want is to frisk a stinkin' wino."

The more Badger spoke, the more Alex retreated to sullen silence. He was learning more than he'd bargained for, his new teacher compressing knowledge of a lifetime into one day.

"Listen up, *hokshila*. There's two kinds of winos: *Passed-Out Wino* and *Sober-Sinner Wino*. Number One, you got to stink, shuffle, mutter, keep your head down, hair mussed, fall in gutter, lay in the back alley, but keep your hand on the broken bottle hidden and ready. Number Two, you gotta look repentant, confess your sins. Look neat, but let your hands shake, say *amen* and *thank you* loud and clear. They feed you—after they save your soul."

Badger was a great teacher. Alex could see him in Holy Rosary Boarding School cueing six-year-old orphans on how to survive.

Badger stood up. "End of lesson. Need to piss, wash up, get warm."

He had to piss, too, so he followed Badger directly into the Men's Room of the public library.

Next to him, Badger spurted away. "Never piss in an alley. They'll get you for indecent exposure. Come in here instead, piss and shit and clean up."

Alex turned on the hot water in the sink and let it flow over his hands. A glass globe dispensed soap. He scrubbed himself and his clothes clean, raked his chopped-off hair flat in the mirror and grinned. No one could recognize him as Alex Turning Hawk.

Badger had slicked back his hair, put on wire-rimmed glasses, and carried a folded newspaper in his hands. "Now we claim an easy chair, read the news, take a little afternoon nap. Don't snore, or we get kicked out in the cold." Badger chose a chair furthest from the front desk and beckoned Alex to join him.

He couldn't stay mad at Badger, but he needed to know more about the FBIs. He scanned the room full of bookshelves until he saw the "Reference" sign, and asked for a telephone book. He found the address and number for the local FBI office and memorized it. Then he found hotel and motel names similar to the soap wrapper he carried and memorized them as well. He tapped the nodding Badger on his shoulder. "Gotta dime?"

Badger jerked awake, stood up, pocketed his glasses, dropped the newspaper in a trashcan and headed toward the door. "Time for work, Harold, collect cans out in the cold."

He should have known. He'd come back tomorrow to read about the FBIs operations. Snow fell all afternoon, coating the streets, hiding the pop cans. Alex watched Badger, learned to see the outlines of cans and bottles alongside the road, in trash barrels and bins in the city park. They walked, heads down. They filled plastic bags with cans and bottles, tied them to the cart handles, slid them underneath, piled them on top of their stash of clothes until the carts could scarcely move. As dusk came on, the snow fell heavier.

"Time to check out and get cash, *hokshila*." Badger had a route, one that started downtown at the bridge, then wove throughout the city and ended at the city dump on the outskirts. Packs of dogs rooted in the hills of garbage. They pushed their full carts to the recycling booth at the entrance, dumped their trophies into a bin. The man behind the counter greeted Badger. "Got a young'un along today. Maybe I should give him half—more'n half, looks like—"

Badger pushed Alex out of the way. "He don't know nothing. I teach him, so I get the cash." He spread his arms on the counter. The man tallied the cans and bottles, turned and unlocked a drawer. He counted out bills and change, then shoved them at Badger.

"Whooee, *hokshila*, almost ten bucks! We're rich for supper." Badger danced a little jig.

Alex thought of beef, smelled the juices, fried potatoes, gravy-sopped *kabuk* bread. He followed Badger headed back downtown for food. Finally they stopped.

"Watch my cart," Badger said, and went into a corner liquor store.

Alex looked in the window. Badger, with all the money, stocked up on wine. Red Turkey. When Alex went in, the bell over the door jangled.

Badger turned, hiding his wine bottles. He handed Alex some coins. "There's enough left for McDonalds. See you back at the bridge."

Alex looked at the coins. "There's enough for two."

"Ain't hungry, just thirsty."

Alex paused. After dark, and Badger had lots of wine. Better if they went back together.

"You go on ahead." Badger said. "I'll sneak back later and hide my cart."

Alex noticed Badger's trembling hands. It had been a long, hard day.

"Go on, git." Badger waved him away.

Alex realized his teacher was embarrassed, had worked hard all day in order to go on a binge—alone. "Want me to take your cart back, too?"

Badger shook his head. Reaching into his cart, he handed Alex a piece of clothesline. "Tie yourself to your new cart. Tomorrow we go to the all-you-can-eat dumpsters. The Episcopal soup kitchen. St. Vincent DePaul, the best. *Hokshila*, stick with me and you'll never starve."

Alex swallowed. But he might die of food poisoning. Empty promises. Badger'd not make it past the winos lining the alley, sleep through the next day. He'd disappear for at least a day or two—if he didn't end up rolled in a ditch, or in detox at the jail. Or just vanish like Até, his father. He took the flimsy rope, so different from his lasso at home. He'd use it, if only as a clothesline.

As he pushed his new cart full of Goodwill trophies through the snow-covered alleys down to Under-the-Bridge, he missed Badger's rough whiskey voice and squeaky cart. He'd walked all over on cement in a cold wind. Being a bum was hard and dirty work. No wonder Badger called him *boy*. "I'll take care of you till you get on your feet, get your cuts and bruises healed," he'd said. Yet Alex felt grateful. He had dry clothes, warm boots, and two blankets. Tomorrow he'd shadow the FBIs and find Joanna Joe's motel. Check the alleys for Badger as well—if he wanted to be found.

When Alex returned to his cardboard box at dusk, a cluster of Indian bums surrounded him to check out his new cart and clothes. Last night he'd arrived so late, and Badger had roused him so early, he hadn't seen the Indian side of Under-the-Bridge: men straight from second-hand bins: ripped, patched, dirty, mismatched, and paint-splattered. Some with shirttails hung out; others with pants belted high. He looked down at their feet: scuffed cowboy boots, combat boots, steel-toed work boots, unlaced sneakers, bedroom slippers, worn moccasins, even bare feet.

They wore their belongings in layers to survive the cold: Army parkas, wool peacoats, coveralls, camouflage suits on top of biker jackets, leather vests, bib overalls, jeans all shades of washed-out blue, sweatshirts, t-shirts, plaid flannel shirts, on top of red flannel underwear. Underneath the padding, he could sense broken battle-scarred men: a useless arm, a badly-set ankle, bum knee, bent noses, gimpy eyes, shaky hands.

Why were the bums here? On the Res, they'd be fed, never locked out to die. Unless—had Iná locked the door on Até? It was shameful being a drunken hang-around, or worse, having a frozen locked-down heart that kept drunks away, both ways bringing dishonor to the family. At least, Under-the-Bridge the bums were anonymous.

"Survived a whole day with Radio, did ye?" asked a wrinkled geezer, still black haired. "He's a non-stop station."

Alex laughed. Badger, the non-stop talking machine, had hidden his nickname.

A grizzled half-breed with a straggly beard grabbed the handle of his new cart. "I could trade my box for this."

Alex pulled his cart back, coiled the clothesline around his arm and tied one end to the cart. Working all day for it, he'd become attached. His cart and cardboard box were all he had—but his box, which he'd put next to Badger's, was gone. He uncoiled the clothesline and flicked the loose end in a circle around his cart to drive back the bums. "Where's my box?"

A sloshed teen in camos with a long pony tail challenged him. "Looking for another box?"

Alex re-coiled his clothesline, ready to flick a joint from the surly boy's mouth.

Just then a powwow wino leaped out with a war-whoop. "Ever wonder why it was empty?" He pigeon-stepped in a circle toward Alex and cackled, "Thought it was waiting for you?"

Alex lassoed him before he could reach the cart. He recognized the man, once a champion grass dancer, now mocking one that honored warriors in battle. He regretted tightening the rope.

Before he could release the man, a wind-burned ranch hand in oily coveralls had stepped forward and released the loop. He tossed the rope back and strong-armed the wheezing wino into the crowd. Clearly the Under-the-Bridge leader, the Indian cowboy explained to Alex. "They hauled him away yesterday, before dark. Died in there, so we gotta burn it."

Alex shuddered. He'd slept in a dead man's box turned into a coffin.

"Burn all his things, too," cried a biker bum in black leather jacket and boots.

Yet the box had been empty, thought Alex. They must have taken the dead man's clothes and belongings before he'd arrived. "Yeah, which one of you is wearing his shirt? His parka? His cap? You're all guilty!"

The circle broke up and turned away from his accusations. Four of them dragged the dead man's cardboard box toward their hobo campfire by the embankment. That's how they kept warm. Fortunately, he already knew how to keep his body warm. He pushed his cart toward Badger's empty cardboard box. He unloaded his new clothes inside, pulled the cart to block the entrance, and retied himself to the cart. As he tried to sleep, the earflaps of his new cap couldn't block out the raunchy punch lines and off-key powwow snagging songs that filled the night. Away from home for only two days, he'd learned to be wary of everyone and everything.

He'd been raised to see the good in everyone, the Everywhere Spirit all around him. Now he'd lost his protection—his power, his hair. He remembered how it felt against the back of his neck, the weight of it down his back, pulling his chin up level, so he stood tall and straight. Uncut since childhood, braided down to his waist, thick and healthy. Gone, in mourn, now burned at the Sweat Lodge—if Tate had finished the task. Hair took years to grow long enough to braid down to his waist. Meanwhile he felt naked and vulnerable, as if people could see into his skull and read his thoughts. He wore a wool cap pulled over his ears for warmth, but useless as protection from the FBIs he sought.

In Badger's cracked mirror he looked like a skinned possum, big beady eyes, face all bones and hollows, chunks and tufts of hair sticking out all over. Badger'd said if bums got too fat, they'd accuse you of stealing someone else's stash. Always on guard, suspicious, alone.

CHAPTER 14
TATE

AT CAMP CRAZY HORSE it was still dark, but a chain saw buzzed nearby. The *hnnn-hnnn* buzzed in her brain, reminding her that her head hurt, her body hurt, her knees and arms were bruised. The image of exploded glass fragments sprinkling her face and hair rose before her eyes. Lester Bear Heart was running his chain saw down by the creek at the Sundance grounds. She guessed he was taking out his anger and frustration on the downed trees.

She sank back into the covers, reminded of how she'd failed to bring back JJ, who was already buried without an autopsy, as if that closed the case. Well, it wasn't closed for her. If only she and JJ had been related, she could have ordered an autopsy and buried her in the AIM cemetery at Wounded Knee.

Now she'd focus on catching the killer that Shuta insisted was Night Cloud. She hugged Alex's pillow, sniffing it for the comfort of his sage fragrance. Underneath lay Alex's hair. She'd forgotten it, had come home too tired even to take off her jeans and sweater. She took the bundle of hair from under his pillow, grabbed kindling, and went outside in the gray pre-dawn.

She lit a small blaze in Alex's fire pit. When the wood caught she crouched down and placed the bundle on top. While the hair burned she looked away, unable to watch the flames swallow the strands, gagged by the singed smell. It was as if she could feel Alex's power vanishing in smoke. Had he run into trouble off-Res? She sang the only Sweat Lodge song she knew, sang it for him. Then she raked the ashes into a tin can, carried them down to the creek, and scattered them on the rippled water. At least she'd done something right, even if she'd failed to bring back JJ's body.

When she walked back to the cabin, Lester stood in front of the door, his banged-up Red Power behind him. She hoped he hadn't seen her down by the creek. He probably wanted breakfast.

He said, "Cut you some fire wood. Alex left your woodpile down when he ran away."

"He didn't run away." She almost said more when she realized George sent Alex in secret. Lester didn't know, even though he was George's right-hand man. "I know how to use a chain saw."

He said, "You owe me a rear window." He cursed louder. "Damn expensive trip. Shit knows why I let you talk me into it."

She was annoyed that he was right. If she'd been in Alex's pick-up, without door locks or a powerful engine, she'd never have gotten back alive. "I apologize. It's my fault."

Lester nodded, accepting her apology. "Before the cops come looking, I gotta repaint my pickup, change the plates, take off the chrome." He stared at his battered pickup. "Black's the only color that'll cover Red Power."

"Not now. I need to track down Night Cloud, the FBI informer out for revenge, even though I don't know what he looks like."

Lester shrugged. "How could you not see him? He was in Minneapolis to spy on AIM, tried to make us believe *she* was the informer."

"I was there at the AIM trials. But I don't remember anyone grabbing a mike at AIM press conferences. That was Night Cloud? Where's he now?"

Lester spat. "You were too busy snagging Alex. Night Cloud ain't on the Res. We kicked him off a year ago—permanently. She exposed him, caught him stealing AIM donations. Turns out, the FBIs paid him a thousand a month to spy on us. We had our own AIM trial. Maybe we should'a killed him, like they kill us."

"He has to be around. She hasn't been dead that long."

"You don't want to find him. He's a vicious killer. Worse than the FBIs."

"You're trying to scare me off."

"Don't believe me? I knew the bastard." He looked at her. "Gotta get to Big Ed's garage in Kyle before daylight. You pay for the paint and the window, and I'll introduce you to a 'Nam buddy of mine runs the college archives. He'll give you facts—"

She wasn't sure she should trust him, but she'd pay for the damage. Grabbing her parka and daypack, Tate climbed into the pickup. This time Lester had the headlights on. Despite the bumpy road, she dozed. When he pulled into a compound near Kyle, she woke. Barking dogs surrounded them. Dawn lit up a large barn, and beyond it, glints from broken headlights in a car graveyard. Indian ponies whinnied in a rough corral, and beside it stood a gigantic Sweat Lodge that could hold twenty people, built so low the bent willow frame barely reached her waist.

A big man in an army parka walked from the barn to the rolled-down window and gave Lester the AIM handshake. "Hau!" Then he nodded at her and said something in slurred Lakota.

She replied, "Tate Turning Hawk."

"*Ohan. Alex-taichu.*" He looked her over, pointed at himself and said, "*Tanka.* Big Ed. I know your old man." Then he opened the barn doors.

Lester parked under a work light hung from the rafters. Ed's old barn had been made into a garage, converted from hayloft and horse stalls into engine hoists and grease pits.

She couldn't figure Big Ed out. Although he had black buzz-cut hair, he wasn't a Goon, just ex-military. With his huge Sweat Lodge, Indian ponies, and Lakota-accented English, he must be a Traditional Indian, one who followed the old ways.

While Lester masked the pickup windows and headlights, getting ready to repaint, Big Ed drove her to the college center down the road.

As she got out Big Ed asked, "Alex know you're looking for the FBI informer?"

She didn't answer. On the Res, no answer meant *no*.

Big Ed waved her on. "Leon's in the basement."

The College Center was a round concrete building with side wings curled upwards to the sky like a giant bird resting momentarily on the barren prairie. The building was stunningly modern with seams deliberately left un-sanded. She pushed against the carved eagle door. Inside a wide ramp circled around the open meeting hall, leading up to second story balcony and offices. She found the basement stairs and descended to dry cement, warmer than outside. Dim light came from a string of overhead bulbs. It felt like an underground tomb. She walked down the curved corridor to an open door. In front of a large, cluttered desk she saw the back of a wheelchair. Long black braids hung down over a denim jacket decorated with an upside-down flag.

"Hi," she called out. "Lester Bear Heart sent me."

Slowly the braids and wheelchair spun toward her. "Can I help you?"

Only one hand had turned the wheelchair. The second sleeve of the red ribbon shirt dangled loosely. Her mouth went dry. She tried not to stare. Below the cuff hung a curved metal hook.

He raised his hook and broke the silence. "I can help you, you know."

"I'm sorry," she said, blushing. She knew better.

"It's okay, everybody stares. I got blown to bits in 'Nam, but the Great Mystery pieced me back together, brought me home safe. Now I work for AIM and Indian Treaty Rights. I collect documents. Leon Bordeaux."

She reached across and shook his left hand, trying to ignore the deep scars on his face. "Tate Turning Hawk, from Eagle Nest. Documents are what I need."

He wheeled around and waved toward the corridor that curved around into the depths of the basement. "Got lots of Lakota history here, facsimiles of the 1851 and 1868 Fort Laramie Treaties, tribal winter counts, Old Treaty Council minutes, beef ration issue lists,

Vine Deloria Senior's sermons, all in Lakota. Pay rosters from Buffalo Bill's Wild West Show."

"What about—" Tate paused, then said the name aloud: "Joanna Joe?"

He wheeled back and stared at her as if she were transparent and he could see into her mind.

How else could she explain what she needed? "William Night Cloud?" she added.

At last Leon said, "Please sit down. In the armchair. You're Alex's wife?"

She nodded.

"You haven't lived here long." He wheeled behind his desk. "It's not safe down here."

"Alex isn't safe, either. The FBIs are trying to pin her murder on him."

"Those sons-a-bitches." Leon banged his hook against the wheelchair arm.

She leaned forward. "I'm the one who found her. Alex is in hiding. Please help me."

He raised his hand. "You? Be careful. You're too new to know who to trust."

"Lester says you have information about Night Cloud."

Leon laughed. "That information's scarce. Someone stole our booklet."

She stood up, disappointed.

He opened a locked cabinet underneath his desk, "I have my own AIM files." He took a key from his belt, unlocked it, and handed her a worn blue booklet. "The FBI confiscated all copies. So you can't have seen this."

She held it carefully. A few mimeographed pages stapled together. It didn't feel like dynamite. The cover read *William Night Cloud, Agent Provocateur*. So he wasn't just an informer, but a provoker of violence.

"You stay here. I'll get some coffee. You like yours black?" Before she could reply, he wheeled down the corridor to an elevator.

He'd surprised her, a man bringing a woman coffee. Perhaps he was giving her privacy, perhaps just shy. In an oral culture, who visited a subterranean storehouse of written documents? Only anthropologists and historians would come here. Any Lakota would ask relatives instead of reading what White newspapers, books and treatises said. They'd go to the town crier or the town historian. But Leon must have had Lakota visitors, at least 'Nam buddies.

She read about Night Cloud: *Marines, Bay of Pigs*. That meant training as a CIA operative, maybe with Operation CHAOS, domestic spy-and-disrupt. She turned the page. *Head of organized crime. Trained city police in undercover work*. Could he be both Mafia and CIA? Was he untouchable?

In her notebook she wrote down the details, then skimmed ahead. *Private pilot for AIM*. He'd learned to fly to get near George. *Exposed as FBI informer by AIM. Pay: $1000 a month*. Hearing a slight whoosh in the hallway, she hid the booklet and stood up. What had Leon said about missing files?

Someone was coming. She braced herself. She was the intruder. She didn't work at the college, and she wasn't a student. When Leon wheeled back into the office, she sat back down, relieved.

"Here's your coffee." He handed her a mug held sideways with his hook.

She took the mug, accidentally grazing the cold metal. "This is scary stuff."

Leon laughed bitterly. "You got to where Night Cloud became head of AIM security?"

She nodded. She'd read enough. The coffee warmed away the chill of the archives.

He reached for the pamphlet with his hook and immediately locked it in his safe. "Can you believe it, AIM let him go!" He wheeled directly in front of her. His voice dropped lower. "She caught onto him early. Ribbon shirt, beads and headband didn't fool her. Caught him dyeing his hair black, using contact lenses to make his eyes dark, taking pictures of bunkers inside Wounded Knee and at the AIM Sundance. But he said she lied, and nobody believed her until too late."

Tate closed her eyes and saw JJ lying in the snow. She shivered, then shook off the image. "Who took Night Cloud's place as AIM security?"

He stared at her. "Didn't Lester send you here? My old 'Nam buddy, George's right-hand man. Stick with him and you'll be safe. He's after that FBI informer bastard, too."

Tate traded the chill of the archives for below-zero winds outside. As she strode along the road back to Ed's garage, she digested what she'd learned, first from Shuta, and now—more than enough to suspect Night Cloud, with no idea how to find him. She needed a private detective.

When she yanked open the barn door, she didn't recognize Red Power. Its shiny red paint, flashy Sioux borders and spoke wheels had disappeared. Now the pickup looked like any other battered Res pickup, flat-black with tailgate and rear fender banged into place.

She watched as Lester put on the last of some old unmatched hubcaps.

Ed screwed in old South Dakota plates. "You wanna save these Tribal plates?"

"*Ohan*." Yes. Lester looked at her. "Believe me now, that Night Cloud's dangerous?"

"He's not dangerous until I find him. But I don't know where to begin." She tossed her daypack into the pickup cab.

Lester snorted. "Begin with Auntie in Rosebud." He paused, "Or let him find you."

"Why would he want to find me?"

Big Ed said, "Not a good idea."

"Sure it is. We'd spread word around that you found Joanna Joe's diary full of incriminating papers. Lure him back to the Res and we'd have him."

"Jeez," Big Ed said, "if you're gonna use Alex's wife as a decoy, you might as well put her in high boots and miniskirt, stick her out on the state highway with her thumb out." He looked Tate up and down. "You look like her, so be careful."

Tate didn't think she looked like JJ, but everyone else did. So why not use it? Why not set a trap? She'd talk with Lester's aunt. No one else but Lester cared.

Lester touched the hood. "Paint's pretty dry. Help me peel off the masking tape."

She started with the cab windows, then noticed the rear window. "Hey, it's not fixed."

Big Ed laughed. "Indian air conditioning. Try the next Res over, too modern for here."

~~~

On the way back to Camp, Lester said, "Too early to visit Auntie. Rosebud's on Fast Time. Different zone, an hour ahead."

Why was he putting her off? "It's still morning," she argued. If only Alex's pickup had started, she'd have driven over to Rosebud herself. She could see it, though—she didn't know where Lester's aunt lived, and the Res didn't have street signs or house numbers. If she asked someone, they'd shrug or misdirect her, and even if she found the house, the old lady didn't let in strangers.

He must have sensed her frustration. "Auntie hits the bottle after dark. You want to meet her in the afternoon."

"No problem. We'll get there before then."

"With a hangover, you sleep till noon," he said. Lester maneuvered the four-wheeler through ruts and hillocks of the old road to Corn Creek and on to Norris. "Up to you, barging in."

She ignored his words. "Francine Running Deer was killed on a Nebraska highway." She paused. "That's far away from where JJ was killed. How does that connect to Night Cloud?"

"He kept Francine as his woman," Lester said. "Ask Auntie. She'll tell you first-hand. After AIM drove him off the Res, Auntie tried to get him jailed, but he slipped away into a Witness Protection Program—" He pounded the steering wheel. "Shit! As if *he* needs protection!"

"Did AIM find out his real name? Night Cloud's so obvious an alias," she said.

"Auntie's kept track. She's never forgiven him for killing her granddaughter."

Lester drove through Parmelee, past the closed-down gas station, its sign riddled with bullet holes, spray-painted *lots of free air.*

"This Res isn't so safe, either," said Tate.

"It's an old sign, just target practice. Nobody died there, like at Wounded Knee."

He pulled into a dirt driveway in front of a porch attached to a WWII Army surplus igloo house. A pack of dogs rounded the corner and barked at them. "Wait. She'll shoo her dogs away."

A hand pulled a curtain back from the window. At last the front door opened slightly. A tall stooped woman peered out. "*He tuwa he?*" Who is it?

Lester laughed and waved. "Mielo, *tunwin.*" It's me, Auntie. He turned to Tate. "She don't recognize this black pickup, she's looking for Red Power." He opened the pickup door and stepped out, patting the pack's alpha dog on the head.

The tall stooped woman wore her white braids as a crown around her head. She stepped onto the wooden porch, shooed the dogs away, and folded her arms across her apron like a barrier that said *come no farther.*

Lester climbed the three steps and spoke in rapid Lakota, waving toward the pickup. When his aunt went back inside, he motioned Tate to come on.

Tate hesitated. "She doesn't want me here."

He laughed. "You don't get it. She thinks you're my new girl-friend." When she didn't move, he walked back and jerked open the pickup door. "So she'll size you up, but she'll talk to you. Don't worry, she speaks English."

"She's Francine's mother?"

"Grandmother. Call her *Auntie*, ask her about *the granddaughter*."

She let him guide her to the porch and into the kitchen. Then he left to find a rear window for the pickup. She sat down at the wooden table and waited. Traditionals didn't shake hands, embrace, or ask your name. Auntie handed her a cup of coffee and put a sugar bowl on the table. Spoons sat in an old tin can. She tried her Lakota. "*Mniskuya-sni, pilamaya*." I don't use sugar, thanks.

Auntie brought over a Tupperware bowl of frybread, sat down, spooned sugar into her own coffee, muttered something, and finally said aloud, "Lester promised me a deer. Remind him."

Tate startled. She'd dragged Lester to Pine Ridge, and he'd been angry ever since, maybe because he'd had no time to hunt. Or maybe he'd forgotten.

Auntie stared directly at her, which wasn't polite. "You look like her."

Tate shifted in her chair. "Like your granddaughter?"

"*Hiya*. No. The AIM woman you found." She reached across the table and took Tate's hand. "*She* tried to help my granddaughter get away."

Tate thought only Pine Ridge AIM knew about Joanna Joe, but the Moccasin Telegraph had reached Rosebud as well. Or maybe Lester had just told her. She hesitated, tears filling her eyes. "I found her—was it just yesterday? Or was it the day before?"

Auntie threw her apron over her head and shook the table with her sobs. She keened in a high tone, different from the women's *li-li-li* of victory. When she lowered her apron, her tears had dried. She took pins out of her hair and shook her long braids loose. "Why are you here?"

"I want to find my friend's killer, William Night Cloud." Tate reached across the table to take Auntie's hand. "Lester said you'd know where to find him."

"You're Turning Hawk *taichu*." She shook her hand free, got up and walked over to a photo on the dresser at the far end of the living room. She picked it up and brought it to the table. A young girl had stared at the camera, dressed in buckskin, shawl, and necklace of long hollow shells. Her eyes were set wide apart with thick brows, and a low hairline. Not like JJ.

Auntie held the frame against her heart. "He met her at an AIM rally, drove her around, bought her things. Beat her up, too. I told her to leave him, but he took her off where we couldn't find her. She said he was going to marry her—" Auntie put the photo back down "—as soon as he recovered from a deadly illness. *Unshika.*"

Tate nodded. It was sad, what young girls believed.

"Somebody saw her on the road to Valentine. When I come home, I went and found her body in the snow, all bruised and beaten. Tears froze to her cheeks like crystals. Her arms and legs broken. *An accident,* they said. *Hit-and-run,* they said. We complained, but nothing come of it because she died off-Res, in Nebraska. *Another drunk Indian whore in the ditch.*"

In her mind Tate saw the FBIs dumping JJ into the ambulance.

After a pause Auntie said, "Your friend came to help us with photos of the bruises. Somebody saw my granddaughter get picked up by a dark-haired man in a white car. Not many on the Res. Night Cloud drove a white car. But they said, *Lotsa white cars around, lotsa dark-haired men.*"

"No proof?" Tate asked.

"No investigation." Auntie slid a ripped piece of yellow paper folded in quarters from under the sugar bowl. "I shop in Valentine. See this on a telephone pole. Rip it off."

Tate opened it. A poster for the John Birch Society National Lecture Tour. Black letters caught her eye: *AIM Exposed: The Inside Scandal.* She hesitated. Who could have betrayed AIM? In the center was a black-and-white photo of a man in a three-piece suit, short haircut, light hair. He looked conservative, more like a banker or stockbroker than a redneck farmer or rancher. Not Night Cloud. There was a different name, Patrick Stewart. Was it another alias? She read farther: *Gordon Grange Hall Sunday 7pm.* The speaker had been to Chicago, Omaha and Lincoln.

Auntie pointed her finger at the photo. "He's back. You show to Lester. So he'll get 'im."

Tate examined the poster more closely. The eyes, dark and fierce, glowered. They reminded her of the man she saw fighting with JJ for the mike at an AIM rally in Minneapolis. Mentally she dyed the man's hair black and stretched it into a long ponytail, took off the business suit and tie, put a ribbon shirt on him and had him slouch with a wise-ass grin. Was this the same man? George had let Night Cloud go, on condition that he stay off-Res. But Night Cloud did anything for pay, and probably was still undercover for the FBI with a new alias. What a way to get revenge, to go on a national speaking tour to discredit AIM.

Tate shook her head. Shuta had been right. JJ had been out to get Night Cloud for the death of Francine. Instead, JJ'd been dumped the same way as Francine.

"Not unusual. Lotsa Indian women who see too much get dumped in the snow."

"Do you have a picture of Night Cloud?" Tate asked.

"*Hiya.* No. He always took the photos. That way he wasn't in them."

"But you know what he looks like."

"Ain't seen 'im. Don't want to, 'cause I know what I'd do." With a grimace she swept her fingers across her own throat. Then she rose and placed her granddaughter's photo back on the dresser. "Moccasin Telegraph says he's around. Be careful. He's got a thing for Indian women."

~~~

Lester didn't come in, just honked his horn, probably because of the deer he hadn't brought as promised. Tate shook Auntie's hand and said, "We'll go hear him speak."

As they drove back to Camp Crazy Horse, Tate waved Auntie's poster in his face. "Look what's all over Nebraska."

He squinted. "Can't see good."

She flipped on the cab light. "It's a John Birch Society Speaking Tour against AIM. Is that Night Cloud? Is *Patrick Stewart* his new cover?"

"Patrick Stewart." Lester laughed bitterly.

"He could cut his hair, dye it, switch jeans and cowboy shirt for a three-piece suit," she said, "but you'd know his voice."

Lester frowned. "His voice." He handed the poster back to her.

"What about rumors that *Our Lost One* was an FBI informer?" asked Tate.

"Night Cloud's idea. He turned the tables on her, accused her of being the FBI informant to get back at her because she caught him stealing AIM funds. He tried to make all the good she did look bad, got people to say, *Look at that woman. She's always traveling. Wherever something happens, she's there. She must be the informer.*"

"But *he* was the informer."

"Yeah. We caught him meeting with the FBI in Rapid City, and exposed him in the press."

"And then?"

"Nothing." Lester thumped the steering wheel. "We kicked him off the Res."

"How could you do nothing, when he betrayed AIM?"

"The FBIs wanted us to kill him—so they could nab us warriors and destroy AIM. We turned him loose so the FBIs got bad publicity and they had to disappear a used-up informer."

Tate found his story hard to believe. As if you turn a rattlesnake loose. So it can kill you next time. "That bastard," she said. "You turned him loose, and he got his revenge. He tried to turn AIM against JJ, and when that didn't work, he killed her!"

Lester gripped the steering wheel and sped up.

She could see wheels churn in his head, but she'd already made up her mind. "We have to crash that John Bircher lecture, take over the mike, and tell those Nebraska ranchers the truth." The AIM warriors would need little convincing. They'd have a great time, counting coup.

When he turned at the camp gate, Tate cried, "Stop. We have to show George this poster."

Lester pulled onto the cattle guard. "You want to start a prairie fire?"

"It's time to call an AIM strategy meeting."

"Only George can do that, and he's not home."

"Alex isn't, either, so I'll do it." Tate opened her door, ready to get out. "I told Auntie we'd stop that liar before he gets any farther."

"George won't like going off-Res. That rally could be another FBI trap."

She'd promised Shuta and Auntie. Normally she'd keep a friend's secret, but if she told Lester, it would prod him into action. "Night Cloud raped Shuta, too."

Lester looked surprised. "Who told you?"

"Shuta, when she told me he was the killer."

"She never told me." He thumped the steering wheel. "I'd have gone after him myself."

"Women don't talk to men about those things. She was afraid George might kill him. Then he'd go to jail and AIM could die."

Lester's face grew taut. "My sister got raped," he said, as if it couldn't be true. He swerved on the road, his mind elsewhere.

Tate could feel the tension in his fisted hands. She'd never had a brother to protect her. But then, she'd never been raped. The street-wise Minneapolis AIM boys had taunted her, but left her alone because her White parents could threaten them for contributing to the delinquency of a minor. Then she'd met Alex, so polite she'd had to chase him.

Lester said, "You just told me that to get me mad so I'd go after Night Cloud."

"I don't lie." But she'd lied to Trask, only to protect Alex.

Finally Lester said, "If you think the AIM warriors will follow you, you're crazy."

"I—and Shuta. We women, we'll go."

Lester looked sideways at her. "She won't go." He frowned. "You really want to risk it?"

"Night Cloud doesn't know me. I'll walk up to him, smile and take the mike away."

Lester said nothing. He pulled up to the Sundance grounds and parked. The AIM guys stood around the blazing Sweat Lodge fire pit. "Just in time," he said, breaking the silence between them. "Gotta steam that paint spray outta my lungs." He jumped out of the pickup, grabbed his towel from behind the seat. He looked across at her. "I suppose you want one, too."

"I don't take sweats with men." She longed for showers. Though her body ached, she never went in the Sweat Lodge, not even with the women. She'd gone in only once with Alex, before their wedding. That had been scary enough, sacred as it was. Even the memory of it made her claustrophobic.

"Women's sweats are new age stuff," Lester said. "In the old days women didn't take sweat, stayed out of men's affairs. Now they want to tie themselves to the tree, like men. They don't understand they already sacrifice their lives giving birth."

Was he trying to scare her? In the olden days women did die in childbirth. Not now. She touched her still-flat belly. Iná was one of the old-fashioned midwives, but she'd go to the modern hospital at the Pine Ridge Agency. "No thanks," she said. "Instead, I'll have stew ready for you guys."

She walked from the Sundance grounds to the cabin. At the wood-pile beside the door she picked up two logs to rekindle the banked coals of the woodstove. Then she lit the kerosene lamps, one by the sink, one near the piano, and one at the workbench. All she had was leftover *kabuk* bread, black beans and warmed-over coffee. She emp-tied cans of beef, peas, and carrots into the iron skillet and set it on the woodstove. Commodity rations would have to do.

She listened for the men's songs at the Sundance grounds, but a cold wind swept in from the north and whistled in the eaves, drown-ing out anything else. Then she heard a pickup—too soon for the sweat to be finished—which stopped outside, engine running. Maybe the AIM guys were offering her a ride into town. She heard a playful rat-a-tat-tat, not like the AIM knock. She hesitated. Only Lester stood there, face flushed, hair steaming from the sweat. She wasn't sure she had enough energy to withstand his overbearing presence. "Where are the rest of the guys?" she asked.

"Gone into town."

"What?" She'd hoped to catch a ride and call an AIM meeting about Night Cloud.

He held a covered pot in his hands, and the rich aroma drifted in, thick and salty. "Elk stew. Drymeat left from last fall." He stepped over the threshold, stamped his boots free of snow, and handed her the pot.

It was a peace offering, hot in her hands, but she didn't let it drop. She placed it on the woodstove between the skillet and coffeepot. Why hadn't the AIM guys come? Were they shy? Did they hate commodities? Maybe Lester had sent them away.

He hung up his parka on a peg by the door, poured himself a cup of coffee from the woodstove, sat down at the table, and stretched his legs. Waves of steam rose from his body, filling the room with the smell of sage. He brushed his damp hair back and drank coffee in one swallow.

She dished out two servings of elk stew into enamel bowls, set them at the table, and sat down opposite him. She waited for Lester to pray over the food, as Alex did, but instead he started right in. "Better than canned commodity beef, *ennit*?"

She had to admit it was delicious elk meat rich with dried *timpsila* and wild potatoes. It was much better than what she'd be eating for days. After they'd eaten, Lester said nothing, just stared at her as if she should talk to him. She missed Alex, who always talked to her.

Lester laid his packet of Bull Durham on his thigh and rolled a smoke. His hands were black from chain saw oil. "Heard from Alex yet?" he asked.

She shook her head. "I don't expect to, either." She'd hide how lonely she felt, and wouldn't complain about the hawk feathers Alex promised to send that never came.

"Gotta talk to your old man." Lester insisted.

"I already told you I don't know where he is."

"Learned something at Big Ed's. I got urgent business with Alex, so let me know."

"And what is more urgent than finding Night Cloud?"

"Men's business." Standing up, he brought her his empty coffee cup. His hands touched hers, slippery from soapy water, and she fumbled to grab its handle. "*Pilamaya*," he said as he caught it, smiled at her, brushed against her apron, and dropped the cup in the dishpan with a clunk. As if he could get her to talk.

Before she could turn around, he'd bounded across the cabin, filled with new energy as if they were two positive magnets repelling each other. He bent over Alex's worktable piled with leather, beads and bone for a half-finished breastplate. Taking his bowie knife from its sheath on his belt, he tested it against his thumb. "Could use some sharpening."

His shadow from the kerosene lamp loomed huge on the log wall. She breathed in, taken aback. "Don't touch Alex's things! He likes everything just so."

"His sacred workbench. I'll be careful. I'll need my knife soon as I catch a deer." He picked up Alex's whetstone, sat down on the work stool by the table, and smoothed the blade over the stone in steady strokes. *Rasp, rasp.*

She tried to ignore the rasping, as if with each stroke he was asking, *Where's Alex? Where's Alex?* She left the sink and walked over to face him directly.

Rasp, rasp. He kept his head down, intent on the knife. "Alex got relations all over the Res who'd welcome him if he showed up."

The Moccasin Telegraph would let everyone know. Alex wasn't stupid.

"Oglala, Manderson, Rosebud—" Lester paused. "If I ran from the FBIs, I'd hide out in *Maká Shíca*, the Badlands. They'd never find me, miles of Badlands arroyos all the same."

She walked over to the workbench and picked up a half-finished bone breastplate to rescue it from the fragrant cedar shavings. "What are you making?"

Lester thrust a chunk of rounded red cedar at her, the foot-long length sawed neatly in half, releasing the fragrance of freshly-cut wood. "Soon, I'll play for you. First, you play for me."

Did her music carry all the way to the Sundance grounds?

"I don't want to disturb you." He smiled again. "Or scare you. I only want to listen."

No one in Eagle Nest, let alone the whole Res, liked classical music with its complex chords and harmonies. Alex listened politely, but he didn't understand it, feel it the way she did. He sang Lakota style and turned on KILI or St. Francis radio every morning, not only to hear Lakota spoken, but to hear it sung the old way, not half-way-Indian-country-western.

Lester might have heard her at her wildest abandon, playing Chopin's tempestuous mazurkas. She sat down at the piano and settled into her world of notes. She'd give him a recital. He deserved it after sawing wood all day. She played pieces from her high school concert, before she'd joined AIM to claim her Indian heritage. When she finished, she looked up. He stood at the piano, leaned on the curve of the top, and swayed slightly, holding the cedar pieces in his hands.

"Play more. Never heard anything like it, like the wind blowing through the pines before a storm from the west." He moved closer, around to the keyboard and her fingers. "No book. How do you remember all the notes?"

"It takes practice, but it's just black and white keys."

"But you make them into stories, stories on the wind, some lively, some lonesome."

She became self-conscious as he leaned nearer. "Pay attention to your cedar." She motioned him back. "I'm grateful for the elk stew." She handed him a flashlight.

"Don't need it. Remember, I can see in the dark." He grinned. "And drive by moonlight."

So could Alex, who'd left his pickup for her to use. Even if Alex were going the wrong direction to find JJ's killer, she hoped he'd found someplace warm and safe to sleep.

CHAPTER 15
ALEX

RODEO DREAMS. A calf wiggled loose from its ties and pulled Alex into the dirt. A rope tied around his waist dragged him from his sleeping box. He jerked awake. He was Under-the-Bridge. He'd tied himself to his shopping cart. In the pre-dawn he couldn't see which of the bums had tried to steal it. He braced his feet, hauled in the rope and yelled, "Drop it!"

The hooded figure turned and tugged at the cart.

Alex lunged for him, knocked his gloved hands off the handle and pummeled him to the ground. "*Mitawa.*" It's mine. He stared into the ancient man's wrinkled and toothless face. His eyes were cloudy, his nose lined with veins.

The man cowered. "Thought you was Radio." He backed away. "Yer in his box."

Only one day and he'd started to act like them, as if overnight his disguise had sunk beneath his skin and into his veins. How easily he'd slipped into their world. He'd be careful to keep his two identities separate, AIM man-on-a-mission from Indian bum, just as Badger separated *Passed-Out Wino* from *Sober-Sinner Wino.*

Alex pulled the man up and gave him a cigarette from Badger's hoard. Today he'd look like this bum on the outside, the stinkin' Injun that everybody saw and nobody noticed. No name, no wallet, no cards, no past and no future. Harmless. The perfect disguise.

He untied the rope and loaded his clothes in the cart. Badger's routine: wash up, comb hair, dress worn but neat. Collect enough cans to buy fresh clean food. He put on his clean worn parka, wool cap and gloves, and left the protection of Under-the-Bridge. Overhead, snow fell, piling up along the edges of the highway. He pushed his cart through snow until he came to red neon *Jesus Saves* that beckoned him into breakfast.

No shopping carts. Yesterday he hadn't noticed the sign when they went into the church. Badger must have left his in the vestibule, but it'd been nearly empty. No wonder Badger had built himself a locked cache underneath the bridge. Alex hid his rope underneath his clothes and laid the greasy ripped parka on top so that no one coming in could be tempted to rip him off.

After breakfast, he found his cart still there. He searched the Rapid City motels. Sidewalks hadn't been shoveled, and most stores hadn't opened yet. He tried a corner café.

"Get your cart outta here. We don't hire bums off the street."

He wasn't job-hunting, he was FBI-hunting. He'd forgotten how he looked: bruised face turned purplish yellow, hacked-off hair. He needed scissors and a knife. But he wouldn't steal.

The lobby of the Rapid City Inn was open. He parked his cart behind a pillar, walked in and stood by the empty front desk. He saw a round metal bell, and dinged. After a moment a clerk in a blue and white uniform emerged from behind an inside door. She looked him up and down. "You want to book a room? Come back at checkout time, 11am."

He took out the wrinkled soap wrapper and handed it across the counter. "Please. I'm looking for this motel. Can you tell me where it is?"

Without touching it she examined it. "It's a soap wrapper. Could be from anywhere."

He took off his glove and pointed to the writing. "Do you know what motel this is?"

She squinted at the faded lettering. "*S-p-r-i-n-g*—it's the soap brand the cheap motels use."

He didn't think so. "Not like *Ivory*. Doesn't it look like *Springview*? Maybe *Spring Valley*?"

"No motels like that around here. I say it's Spring Fresh. Soap." She tossed the wrapper at him, but it wafted down to the floor beside him.

He picked up the wrapper, tucked it in his parka pocket, and walked to the lobby's phones.

"Those are house phones," she said loudly. "Pay phone booth's outside around the corner." She called toward the open door behind the front desk. "Gilbert! Get out here!"

"Thank you, Ma'am," he said. "I'll try elsewhere." He knew Joanna Joe had done her best to hide the soap wrapper inside a *woluta* and tie it in her hair, even if the brand's name was so common.

By noon he'd walked half of his circular plan, east and north, to the edge of town. Seven motels and one inn. At the next, a bellhop stationed at the entrance took the wrapper in his white-gloved hand and said no. At the third, the clerk told him to use the Yellow Pages.

Afterwards, he waded through snow in ditches, kicked at drifts with his boots, and searched for cans. Slow going. Better luck in the downtown alleys or along the road south to the Res. He counted his change, bought a burger and coffee, and walked to the library. Inside he watched people search in wooden cabinets full of drawers. He asked a librarian what they were doing.

"You mean the Card Catalog." She explained the index of all the books in the library. He found cards for the Federal Bureau of Investigation. Two books, numbered 363.25. He found the shelves, found the books: *My Life as an Agent* and *J. Edgar Hoover. Man of the Hour.* He read to learn their habits, styles, codes—all from their point of view. He'd only seen them as intruders on Turning Hawk land at his Sweat Lodge, carrying guns.

He went up to the librarian. She checked out a dozen picture books for a mother and toddler. After she finished, he asked, "I'd like to take these out."

She looked at him. "You want to read books?" Then she blushed. "I can read, ma'am."

"Do you have a city address?"

He smiled. Badger'd make up an Under-the-Bridge address for fun, but he'd use Auntie's in Lakota Homes. "Yes, 454 Gnugnushka Drive."

She handed him a form to fill out.

He hesitated. Harold Goggle Eyes, why not? He started writing.

"Do you have a driver's license? A letter addressed to you? Some identification?"

His face reddened. He felt like telling her he had no wallet, only coins in his pocket, but said nothing. He crumpled up the form and dropped it in the wastebasket. "Thanks. I'll read them here."

The library made him feel worthless. According to the books, the FBIs were heroes. They arrested serial killers and Mafia drug dealers. They made America safer for Americans His Captain Kangaroo and Mr. Rogers TV education hadn't taken him far enough into the upside-down-inside-out White World. He was raised in oral hands-on tradition, learning the Old Ways, useful for surviving Under-the-Bridge.

George chose the wrong person for the AIM mission. As a wanted criminal for evading a warrant, Alex couldn't interview Agent Trask or Slade. He couldn't interview anyone, couldn't show his face in Lakota Homes—someone might turn him in, even an AIM member, even the bums. Once they knew he was a wanted man, they'd turn him in for a bottle. Especially they didn't want cops searching Under-the-Bridge. He couldn't even be sure about Badger, so eager to take him on. No Moccasin telegraph out here. Just the bums' street rumor mill. He found it hard to ask questions, unlike Tate. How could he investigate anything? His training was to listen, using silent but keen observation. He had to try. He left the warm library and walked to the alley behind the FBI office. FBI agents dressed in suits, ties, and dark overcoats came in and out. Some wore dark fedoras or black lambs-wool hats. Indians said that all FBIs looked alike: light skin, light, short hair, and no mustaches, beards, ponytails or braids. He recognized Agent Slade by the long blond strand he kept tossing back, and Agent Trask by his swivel-head-radar searching for trouble all around him. Would Trask notice a *Passed-Out Wino* hiding behind a cart in the alley? Alex wished he'd worn the hideous black wig to hide his face, but even Trask seemed not to notice.

Soon he discovered that agents headed for the faded but elegant six-story old historic hotel nearby. His cousin Leila, who cleaned the sixth floor, had told him wild stories about the gilded ballroom large enough for society weddings and debutante balls, wood-paneled meeting rooms for important bankers and senators, as well as a large lobby and restaurant with exotic food like French snails and chocolate grasshoppers. Since 1975 after two of their agents had been shot, the FBIs had taken over the hotel as a base to search the Res for the killers. Their real headquarters lay inside, not at the dingy FBI storefront office with steel desks and file cabinets. Leila'd told AIM that the agents ate and slept at the hotel, and he'd checked out Trask and Slade's white Bronco parked in the rear.

After an hour, Alex left to find his own cardboard box. Behind the Sears store he found a collapsed, snow-covered refrigerator carton. He squeezed it into his cart, the top sticking up like an unwieldy sail, turning his cart into a boat with wheels. Leaning against it for balance, he pushed his cart into the wind and snow. All he had was a soap wrapper, but he kept thinking about *S-p-r-i-n-g*—

He tried one last outlying motel and discovered a curly-haired redhead painting her nails lavender behind the front desk. Redheads were rare on the Res. She had freckles on her upturned nose and wide rosy-pink lips. Her bell-shaped earrings jingled as she leaned far over her desk. "Looking for work? He's not here now."

He kept his glance sideways, away from rosy breasts bulging out of her low-cut lavender uniform. Nail polish and tangy-sweet perfume surrounded him. He took a deep breath and laid the crinkled soap wrapper on the desk top. "I'm looking for help."

She laid her brush down and blew on her nails. Then she smiled as she looked directly at him. "What kind of help?"

Caught off guard, expecting another rejection, he hesitated. She must have noticed his worn parka, old boots and ragged haircut. Indians must be as scarce in this part of town as redheads on the Res. Maybe she noticed his energy. He pushed the wrapper in front of her. "Trying to find the name of that motel."

As she picked up the crinkled paper, her hands brushed his. She pressed the slippery paper flat and squinted. "Well, there's not much here. But tell me the story. You're looking for a woman?"

He frowned. Young, strong, dark, hawk-nosed men must be scarce, too.

"She left you and you want to find her?" Her voice had a lilting accent.

"No—" He tried to stop her.

She raised an arched eyebrow. "An older woman? Your mother? Your auntie?"

Playing clairvoyant. Or else toying with him, curious? He reached for the wrapper in her hands. "I'm looking for that *motel*. Have you any idea where it might be?"

"Of course." With two fingers she picked up the wrapper and placed it in his palm. "I'm off work soon. I have a car and can drive you there—"

It was tempting: a warm car driven by an enthusiastic redhead with lavender fingernails. But Old Sam his mentor had trained him to notice when others were lying. Cold, wet and tired, he had no time for play. He might be a bum, but he wasn't a toy.

Discouraged, he headed back into downtown. He scoured the alleys Badger had showed him, but found no sign of his mentor or his squeaky cart. He did find enough cans and bottles to make the long walk to the dump worthwhile. Badger wasn't around, so he kept the cash.

On the way back at dusk he wondered if Iná had persuaded Tate to move into town. He shouldn't have left his wife alone. If only she'd been here, she'd have insisted that the self-important desk clerks find that motel. But how'd she have taken the redhead's offer? Then he remembered his Under-the-Bridge cardboard box, and was glad Tate was home, safe and warm.

He stopped at Woolworth's for soap, hairbrush, mirror, scissors, jackknife, and padlock. Tomorrow he'd finish the circuit, search west and south. Surely the Great Mystery would help him find the secret motel where Joanna Joe had once been held.

~~~

The next day Alex rose early, but this time he pushed his cart into the nearby Rapid City Park, faced east with the Rapid River at his feet and prayed with his small Pipe, asking the Great Mystery to help him find Joanna Joe's trail. He headed west in the pre-dawn along the deserted thruway toward *Paha Sapa*, the sacred Black Hills. Along the snow-plowed edge he searched for cans and bottles. As he passed the cluster of dark houses built for urban Indians, he caught a glimpse of light on at Auntie's house. If only for breakfast—but she'd told him not to come back.

Instead he pushed on, heading for the western edge of the city. Ahead lay rounded hills covered with evergreen trees dusted with snow, beckoning with hope.

Yet all day, at every motel or inn along the way, no one knew anything about the soap wrapper. One clerk squinted and asked, "*Spring View*, maybe? Try Spearfish or Sturgis."

Half an hour later Alex glanced at the thruway rising in the distance. Spearfish, thirty miles, Sturgis, fifty. He'd have to leave his cart and hitchhike. Reluctantly he turned back alongside the now-busy road, his parka splattered with slush from the semis. He skirted the city to the south to complete his plan. Motels were more run-down as he came to the road to the Res. No luck. More cans and bottles. Black clouds in the west. It grew darker and colder, too cold to snow. Alex's feet ached. He'd walked farther than Badger ever had. With his cart full and his stomach grumbling, he headed directly for the city dump.

The recycling man recognized him and laughed. "You got twice as many as Radio. Maybe you don't yak as much." He handed him a ten-dollar bill and change. Enough to eat, and more.

What else did he need? George's words filled Alex's mind: "I don't expect White-man justice. Spook 'em, drive 'em crazy, get 'em transferred." If he couldn't find where Joanna Joe'd been hidden, at least he could spook the FBIs by spray-painting red severed hands on their windows and doors. Spiritual harassment. If the FBI could terrorize AIM, he could terrorize Trask and Slade.

Much better than undercover in the alley as a *Passed-out Wino*, hoping for some clue as the FBIs walked into their parking lot and climbed into company cars with coded license plates.

He pushed the cart toward downtown, where he bought cans of red spray paint, a knife, and duct tape. He spent the evening as a graffiti artist. First he cut a cardboard silhouette of his own hands. Urban AIMs from the Lakota Homes used the red fist as their sign, but he kept his graffiti simple: two raised hands begging the FBIs to remember Joanna Joe. That way, the FBIs wouldn't raid Lakota Homes for teenage AIM hoodlums. He laughed at his own bad Indian joke: painting red hands without being caught *red-handed*.

The official FBI office in a one-story row of offices was two doors down from the Rapid City AIM lawyer's office. Very convenient. No wonder the FBIs had placed their office in a rundown set of buildings. AIM must know the FBIs had bugged their office. Perhaps AIM was playing a Harold-Goggle-Eyes game, talking legal strategy elsewhere. Each group was watching the other. He must make sure neither group recognized him. With AIM, he could lose his reputation as a medicine-man-in-training. With the FBI, he could lose his life.

Invisible as one of Badger's *Passed-out Winos*, he spray-painted red hands on the windows of their street office. He spray-painted red hands on the FBI car doors and windshields in the parking lot behind the hotel. He spray-painted red hands on all the doors of the hotel's third floor where the FBIs stayed. Outside, wiping away frost, inside, wiping away dust. He was exhilarated, invincible.

Sooner or later the Great Mystery would unleash Hawk Power to haunt them with red-hand nightmares and drive them crazy—unless. Unless he wasn't a graffiti artist but a hyped-up vandal.

When he returned to the bridge with his empty cans, his winos, who'd laughed at him when they found out he didn't drink, now teased him in that Indian joshing way to let him know that they accepted him as one of their own—a paint-huffer instead. If only he could accept them as well.

~~~

Wrapped in a blanket, curled in his box, Alex dreamed again of the Sundance. He stood in the center of the arbor, painted and ready to be pierced, but the piercing song faded away, drowned out by the roar of a river near his head. It surged forth again, off-key, slurred, unfinished. Badger was back, singing the sacred songs to keep him safe.

He climbed out to piss and pester Badger into silence, or at least ordinary talk. The squeaky-wheeled cart was empty. Either Badger had been rolled, or sold his stash to continue his binge. He shook the old man's box, bent in the opening and called, "Hey, Radio."

"Them bums," Badger muttered and poked his head out. "Don't start. I ain't *Radio* any more 'n you're *Harold*." He squinted at Alex. "*Hokshila*, ain't I yer elder?"

"Go to sleep, so I can sleep."

Badger sat up. "Roll me a smoke. I know you got some."

Alex pulled out thin papers and Bull Durham from his parka, sprinkled tobacco on them, and rolled up two with a lick of tongue. A peace offering. He lit one and handed it to Badger.

Together they smoked, breathing in, breathing out.

Badger closed his eyes and inhaled. "You did okay without me?"

He nodded.

"Where you from?"

Alex shrugged, motioned with his head southeast, toward the Res.

"I come from there, too. Porcupine."

Alex finished his smoke, rubbed it out in the snow. "A Badger from a Porcupine."

"*Hokala* is my real name, an old family name. Maybe you heard of Star Comes Out?"

Alex had heard of an Old Man Badger, descendent of Star Comes Out, one of the warrior hold-outs of Crazy Horse Band who refused to be penned in on Reservations and turned into farmers. Badger came from another honorable family. "What are you doing here?"

Badger shrugged. "No land. All the old ones died. No one's left." He pounded his heart with his fist and looked up. "You got family, I can tell. You cry for them in your sleep."

Was Badger putting him on? Had he called out Tate's name? Or maybe Iná's?

"Why're you here?" Badger asked. "Shiner's almost gone. Go back to your girl."

What could he tell Badger, the talking radio? That he hated being dirty? That he hated the smell of booze? That he was on a mission? Finally he said, "I can't find her. She's holed up in some motel around here, and all I've got is a soap wrapper with half the name ripped off."

"You can't remember where you got in a fight over her? You must 'a been really drunk, got knocked out cold and dumped."

Alex lit a match and held it so Badger could see the small paper once again.

Badger squinted. "Can't see. Read it to me."

"Where's your glasses?"

"Oh, them. Library props."

Maybe Badger couldn't read—or couldn't read much. "Get them."

"Tomorrow," a weary Badger said. "What color's the letters?"

"Green. Light green. *Springv—*"

"Lemme sleep on it. I seen something like that somewhere. If I see it, I remember it. So if we walk all around the city, it'll come back to me."

Alex hadn't the heart to tell him he'd already done that. Tomorrow he'd be a *neat-repentant-wino*. He didn't want Badger shadowing him as he nosed around City Hall and the FBI. Badger might be insignificant, but he wasn't quiet.

Alex would never become part of Badger's world. He'd live in it, yet not be of it. He listened to the men singing and joking around the campfire. In Lakota, his language. They were his people, an Indian nation Under-the-Bridge. Unseen, unnoticed by him until now. He could no longer look down on them, no longer fear them. He got up, stripped down to his jeans, found his small fasting Pipe and walked over to his new buddies.

They stared at him, at his bare chest and back, moving away to leave a space around the bonfire. Flames lit their faces. He saw that some recognized the Sundance scars on his chest from pulling free from the Tree of Life, the scars on his back from pulling the buffalo skull around the Sundance arbor. A murmur rippled through the circle of men. A few realized he'd sundanced and sacrificed for the People. One 'Nam vet pulled off his t-shirt to reveal he'd sundanced as well.

Some remained wary, wondering why a young holy man had come among them. He spread his arms wide and sang, a powwow greeting that honored the vets who carry in the flags to open the way. A few joined in. But others pulled back. One buzz-cut Marine vet in ragged camos cried in alarm, "Pipe? You carry a Pipe? Can't have a Pipe down here, bad luck. Pipe and alcohol don't mix."

A WWII vet with medals on his vest spat into the river. "He's a sundancer."

The dirtiest, most bedraggled Indian cowboy, limping on one leg said, "Yeah, we see him. He'll bring the Thunder Beings down on us, storms and lightning. Even Under-the-Bridge we'd get struck down. Or drowned in floods. Put your Pipe away, leave us alone."

Alex held up his fasting Pipe. "This small Pipe is closed with sage. I will pray for us all, and share it with anyone who chooses. The Great Mystery led me here, and will watch over us in the days to come." He sat by the fire until his new buddies left to bed down, one by one, until only coals gleamed in the night. He'd invite the scarred man to his Sundance. Or maybe his mission was here beside those with no land, family, or reason to live. The men feared him, not because he was a young, strong stranger, but because he'd awakened memories of their souls.

CHAPTER 16
TATE

THE CASE AGAINST Night Cloud wasn't closed for her. She had the poster, and George needed to see it. But Alex's pickup still wouldn't run. She went to find Lester. Outside the cabin door sat a stack of eighteen-inch logs, half cottonwood, half ash, covered with a blue plastic tarp. Lester was so annoyingly helpful. Forget his wild driving and insulting manner. She should be grateful.

As she filled her arms, she saw the top of a canvas tipi behind the Ceremony House that hadn't been there before. Smoke rose from the open flaps at the top. She stopped, startled. Alex couldn't have come back and put it up, he'd have come right to her in the cabin.

As she came closer, she saw the tipi wasn't Alex's. Large and new, it was painted with the same red and black AIM border design, and placed just west of Alex's firepit and pile of Sweat Lodge rocks. She peered inside it. The canvas lay taut and solid against the north wind, with a liner and fire pit. On the ground lay a backpack and sleeping bag on a mat of dried sage—who had dried sage in winter? This neat and orderly campsite had to be Lester's. He must have been up before dawn. She noticed he'd repaired Alex's smashed Sweat Lodge as well.

"You like it?" Lester spoke from behind her. "Tipis are warmer and easier to heat. I try to live by the old ways, round not square. Log cabins are so dark and dank."

She hated him sneaking up on her. "It's set too close."

He leaned closer. "Course, when it gets 40 below, and the water freezes in the cream cans, you might hear me knock on the cabin door."

She faced him. "You're crowding Alex's Sweat Lodge." She'd just fixed the altar the way it had been before the FBIs wrecked it.

"Not after I move the altar and fire pit out of the way."

She stared at Alex's rebuilt Sweat Lodge. Something was wrong. The tarps and blankets totally covered it. Then she realized Lester had changed Alex's entrance from west to east, the ordinary direction. But Alex was a sundancer, so his had faced west. She stepped in front of him and stared up into his face. "How dare you tamper with Alex's Sweat Lodge!"

He took a step back. "Faced the wrong way. I fixed it."

She pushed him backwards, first with one fist, then the other. "That's Alex's personal Sweat Lodge. You'll have to put it back the right way!"

He brushed her hands aside. "Sweat Lodge door always faces east. Like the entrance to the Sundance arbor is east, where the prayers begin."

She stomped around him and pointed west. "But the Sundance Sweat Lodges face west."

"That's because we go into the Spirit World for four days and nights. Even though we dance to the sun, we're in darkness, we've gone into the West."

"But—"

"You're new here. You don't understand the old ways."

She was so tired of hearing that. She knew the Old Treaty Traditionals who took sweat with Alex wouldn't go in if the lodge had been turned around. They'd hear the young bloods in AIM had taken over, and they'd stay home. Lester was too pushy, trying to take Alex's place.

Lester chopped the air in front of her with his hands. "I go by the teachings of Black Elk. If Alex built his Sweat Lodge to face west, he looks out at darkness all the time, maybe into black medicine, black tobacco ties—"

She put her right hand up to stop him. Alex was a Sundance leader, with different teachings. "I don't want to hear it."

"That's why I had to move it. For your protection, for Camp Crazy Horse's protection. We can't have black medicine come our way. We AIMs have enough trouble already."

"Wait till his mother finds out!" Tate wailed. "Iná will blame me for letting you!" She stood at Alex's buffalo skull altar. "Leave this alone! I don't care if it faces east or west, it belongs to Alex."

He said nothing, just walked away.

"Wait! The poster. Can I borrow—" She didn't know whether to chase him to the Sundance grounds and beg, or try to repair what he'd already ruined. Was Lester's frantic remodeling a way to avoid avenging Shuta's rape? No wonder he hated the poster.

She stared at Lester's changes. He was neat and thorough, not like the FBIs who had JJ buried before her body could be claimed. She spent the rest of the morning moving Alex's buffalo skull altar and Sweat Lodge back where they belonged, but left Lester's tipi for him to move back to the Sundance grounds where it belonged.

She was determined to stop Lester. If she hitchhiked into town, her mother-in-law, Iná, could intervene on her own land. But with Alex gone, Iná the Terrible would force her to live in town to avoid scandal. She'd be trapped with her mother-in-law, who'd supervise her every move until Alex returned. It would be a fate worse than death. She prayed for more thawed snow and mud to keep Iná away. For the first time she felt trapped out in the country. Although she was Alex's wife, everyone saw her as an outsider with little authority.

George needed to know that Night Cloud, aka *Patrick Stewart*, was back in Nebraska on a lecture tour to defame AIM. They'd put a stop to that traitor's lies. She'd catch a ride into town later after the AIM guys took sweat.

Around noon she heard a disturbance at the Sundance grounds: banging, pounding, grinding, revving, grating, rasping, male voices swearing. Alex didn't allow swearing in the sacred arbor; there were no swear words in Lakota. She wondered who had forgotten. She walked the path to look down at pickup engines grinding, mud splatting, and wheels sinking deeper as South Dakota gumbo triumphed over four-wheelers. The AIM guys from town had mired their pickup. Lester and Smokey were using chains to pull them out.

By the east entrance she saw a crew taking down the Sundance arbor. Half the arbor had been stripped of pine boughs, and four boys hauled crutches and crosspieces to where others dug postholes for a fence. She ran down. "Stop! Don't destroy the arbor!"

Chaské lifted a crosspiece down. "Lester told us to."

She stared up at him, arms akimbo. Lester was remodeling Camp Crazy Horse according to his own plan. She yelled, "Alex didn't say to, and this is his Sundance."

Chaské threw down another crosspiece. "He's not here."

But he will be. She asked Old Louie, who leaned on a posthole digger. "What's going on?"

He shrugged. "Improvements. Fence in the arbor, keep the four-leggeds out." He kicked at a pile of manure. "No more horses or dogs."

She felt helpless. She knew Lester must keep the AIM guys busy, but at what cost? Alex let the horses graze the Sundance grass down. Now who'd keep the grass down? "Chaské, we can't get new crutches and crosspieces every year."

"Lester wants everything old-fashioned, Traditional," Chaské said.

"Easier to fence horses out than fence them into a quarter-section," added Louie.

So this big change was Lester's Boot Camp. She picked up a crutch and put it back in its hole. "I don't like this. We'll end up with a puny fence, no arbor, and the sacred tree standing alone in the wind. Where's George?"

Old Louie crushed his cigarette butt on his sole and put it in his pocket. "Still on trial for burning down Custer Courthouse. Which he didn't do."

Tate remembered George had to be in court every day. "George won't stand for it, either." As she stomped across the arbor, she heard Old Louie's warning, "Lester's in drill sergeant mentality," but she didn't stop. She ran past the pile of pine boughs near the fire pit to Lester's muddy pickup, her boots slipping in the gouged-out tracks. She grabbed his door for balance and shouted above the noise of the engine. "I told you not to change anything!"

"Just in time to help push!" Lester revved the engine again. Mud splattered in her face.

"Or get outta the way. This is men's work."

She looked at the mud-coated crew behind the sunken pickup. The earth had thawed to piss-yellow gumbo. "Better push harder, guys, because I need to catch a ride into town after the sweat." She walked away, washed her hands in the cold stream below, and went inside the cabin. Let them remodel the Sundance grounds for now. The real work would start in June.

By dusk she noticed two plumes of smoke rising in the east. Not a Sweat Lodge fire! When she ran over to the Sundance grounds to check—no danger since snow blanketed most of the prairie—she was shocked that the round Sundance arbor had vanished, and its round meadow had been squared in by fence posts strung with strands of barbwire. Outside the fence, one bonfire burned black from old outhouse plyboards. Inside the fence, the other fire snapped and crackled from dry pine boughs blazing in the fire pit. All four Sweat Lodges, left stripped to the bare willow bones after the Sundance, had been turned around so their entrances faced east, and the nearest one was re-covered with canvas tarps.

Fortunately, Lester hadn't changed everything. The Tree of Life stood in the center, its tall branches crested with snow. She put her arms around the trunk, girdled now with faded prayer flags from the Sundance last August. Only this small spot left for the Great Mystery. She must guard Camp Crazy Horse as best she could.

She walked over to the men's Sweat Lodge fire pit and pulled out the poster to show the AIM guys. Smokey took it and bent to read it by firelight.

"That's Night Cloud, calling himself Patrick Stewart," she said, "but it's him. We have to stop him and his lies."

Smokey turned the poster in the firelight. "What the f—?"

Lester grabbed the poster and handed it back to her. "Don't bring bad news around the sacred sweat."

"OK," she said. "After the sweat, take me into town to show George."

"You know what he'll say?" Lester added, imitating George's deep voice, "We already took care of him. Let him spread his lies. Don't chase after evil. Work with the good, right here at Camp Crazy Horse."

Lester was taking it all apart. "If you don't, I'll call an AIM strategy meeting right here at the Sundance grounds."

"Without George?" asked Old Louie.

"If I have to."

~~~

She walked back. Winter meant short days and long nights. She went in, lit the kerosene lamp, put two logs in the woodstove and waited to heat the leftovers. Only Lester came over to eat, as if he'd taken over Camp Crazy Horse. Fortunately, she'd called a halt to his changes. He stood at the cabin door, dressed and radiating sage fragrance and heat. His face flushed, his hair damp, his drill-sergeant tightness mellowed.

She blocked the doorway, arms crossed. "Finished vandalizing for the day?"

He smiled as if they hadn't fought earlier.

She asked, "Aren't the AIM guys coming over?"

"Not tonight."

She remembered that yesterday, he'd made it so hot he'd given them blisters. Perhaps that's why he'd moved his tipi away from the rest of the AIMs.

"Hot one. Used all forty rocks."

Women never used more than twenty big limestone rocks. "What about Old Louie?" she asked. "Doesn't he have a heart condition?"

"He lasted a round. Longer than Chaské, who had it easy by the door." Lester took out his tobacco pouch, rolled a smoke and lit it.

She'd heard some medicine men's sweats raised blisters. "Another mourn sweat? You poured the water on all at once?"

"A tough-it-out sweat. These warriors are soft, not used to hard work."

Lester must have burned them badly. "So they left you and went back to town. Then you crawled out and came over here to eat."

He stared at her. "Even with nobody, I stayed and finished."

Lester acted so tough. Yet how lonely it must be for him to act so macho, driven to misuse the sweat and treat everyone harshly. "Will they come back?" she asked.

"Every day. George wants them away from alcohol and trouble, so I keep 'em busy."

"Sweats aren't for torture. Alex says *inipi* means *reborn-lodge*— hot and dark enough to cry, purify yourself, and emerge reborn."

"I'm sick of *Alex this, Alex that*—but he's not here now, is he?" He stood up and pushed away from the table. "You don't understand. You think I want to tear down the Sundance grounds? Burn up the outhouses? With snow on the ground, I got to find things the warriors can do, keep 'em occupied, get 'em in shape, prepare—"

"George should have sent you to find the killer!"

"Yeah, and why didn't he?" he shot back. "I know all the hideouts." She watched a series of expressions flicker across his face, shock, anger, doubt, ending in a smile. "I don't mind, though." He rolled another smoke.

Regretfully, she understood George's strategy: Lester the drill sergeant, tough enough to keep the AIM guys occupied; Alex the shape-shifter, resourceful enough to shadow the FBIs. But could she and Alex ever get Camp Crazy Horse back to the way it had been?

Lester sat in the far corner shadows at Alex's workbench. He'd made holes in the cedar, and now was sanding it smooth. Lester made cedar recorders for tourists. In contrast, Alex made breast-plates and chokers for grass dancers, eagle bone whistles for sun-dancers, and led sweats that healed people, and led Sundances so the People would be strong for the next three hundred years.

She brought Lester a cup of coffee.

"*Pilamaya.* Thanks." He put the cedar down and spread his hands across the workbench, swirling the designs among the red cedar shavings. "I don't mean to fight you," he said, "but George ordered me to guard Camp Crazy Horse."

So George had made him shadow her, as if she were a trouble-maker like JJ. She smiled inside. Poor Lester had a tough job. She sat on the piano bench and played without him asking. She filled the cabin with a Chopin polonaise. Her fingers flew over the keys.

Lester had moved to stand beside her. He held the flute sideways, not like a recorder.

She looked at them, surprised. "It's not a recorder?!"

"Please continue." He sat beside her on the piano bench. "I want to watch your hands."

She shifted away. "You're crowding me. I can't reach the notes."

He got up and stood behind her, then pulled away. "Keep play-ing." In his hands he held the cedar flute that he'd made to sell, dry now with a carved cedar bird below the mouthpiece.

"Can you play it?"

Instead of answering, he lifted it to his lips and blew softly. A breathy melody filled the air, rose and fell into a minor mode, fluttered like a bird, then soared to an upper octave, whistled and dropped to a throaty trill.

She closed her eyes to float with the sound so close to her. Not like the *ai-yi-yi* cadences of the Sweat Lodge or powwow drum songs. More like the wind in the pines, or a stream bubbling over pebbles. It ebbed and flowed with each breath he took.

Finally he paused and said, "What did you play?"

"A Chopin polonaise. It's a dance."

"Play it again for me."

When she reached the end of a cadence, he touched her arm again. "Stop."

She let her hands drop.

He played the melody back to her, almost breathing in her ear.

She played a longer arpeggio. Would he be able to repeat it?

He played it back exactly, the same intonation and tempo.

Faster now, she played a longer sequence.

He echoed her, an octave higher.

Lester had an ear, a natural musical ability. She had simple duets they could play together.

She closed the piano lid. She was tired. "It's late. Tomorrow please take me into town."

He sat at the table and poured two more cups of coffee. "Please sit down over here."

She wondered what he wanted now. But he'd said *please* for the first time, so she slid onto the bench across from him and waited.

He looked at her. "You don't need to have any more nightmares."

She stared at him. Had he spied on her, overheard her cries when she woke to nightmares, JJ without hands, hands floating in the Badlands, back to childhood fears, and tonight she'd see Leon's steel hooks as well.

Lester shook his head. "You found her. Who didn't have nightmares?"

"It's worse with Alex gone. It's her hands. I see her in the Badlands but then I'm back as a little kid and it's my hands gone. Once my mother read me a horrible bedtime story called *The Handless Maiden*. They cut her hands off with a silver axe and forced her to leave home and wander in the woods, helpless against the Devil. I told my mother to stop, but too late. I had nightmares for years. In them my mother makes me practice-practice the piano, but my hands are gone. I can only crash the piano keys with stumps. Now the nightmares have come back, only different. Worse."

Lester reached across the table and touched her hands. "I have nightmares from 'Nam. I'd have gone insane if I didn't learn how to control them. Some vets drink to forget, others can't sleep, so they pace back and forth all night, and some kill themselves. Not me."

She brushed her hair back and looked directly at him again. He was like an older brother that she'd never had. She'd heard they could be both cruel and kind.

He got up, opened the woodstove door, thrust another log on the fire, and sat back down. "What I do, is, I re-dream them. I dream my own endings. I make it come out right. I wake myself up just enough. Then I turn it around into a dream of power."

She shuddered. "I don't see how."

"I'll show you. In your nightmares there is a Handless Maiden. But she's not lost in the woods, or in the Badlands. Or if she is, she comes to a house and inside there is a table, and on this table are many pairs of hands—long-fingered, short and stubby, tanned, short-nailed, manicured—all kinds. Now, you're the Handless Maiden and you're amazed. Maybe one pair will fit you, and you'll become whole again. You nudge first one pair, then another, see if any might fit. Maybe one pair might be the very ones you lost."

He reached across the table to grasp her hands in his. "Suddenly large, warm hands reach out and take hold of your poor stumps. These hands begin to massage your stumps very slowly and carefully. You shiver at their touch. At first you feel some pain and cry out, but then you feel energy pass up through your arms and into your body. Afterwards you reach out your quivering stumps and realize that all the hands on the table are yours. You have only to claim them and put them on to become whole."

She couldn't see it, only the horror. "What about all the blood?"

"What blood? This is a dream without blood. No reds allowed. You erase the nightmare. Or you take a giant mop and wipe the blood away. It's your dream."

"I see. The Sorcerer's Apprentice tries to mop up the water, but the flood gets worse. The difference between a nightmare and your re-dreaming is willpower."

"If you lose it, you wake up again. And again. You get better at it, so you can sleep through the whole night."

"That's how you survived 'Nam."

"My buddy Leon, too. I brought him back and taught him."

How the evening had flown away. It was much too late now to go into town. But she'd learned something, how to take charge of her nightmares. She was grateful for Lester's gift of re-dreaming. She'd turn her nightmares into finding JJ's killer, re-dream the knife, turn it against Night Cloud and get JJ's RED POWER hands back. Or she could re-dream her hands as RED POWER and use his knife against him instead. A new sense of urgency filled her. She couldn't wait to try re-dreaming. If he'd take her into town, so they could call an AIM meeting and plan strategy for the raid, then she'd be fine. After she found JJ's killer she wouldn't have any more nightmares.

CHAPTER 17
ALEX

NOW THAT ALEX had learned to be invisible in Rapid City, he dressed as an alley bum to search downtown for *two White men* mentioned in the *yuwipi* ceremony. George had been sure they were FBI agents, but which two? Rapid City seemed full of agents. Which one had found Joanna Joe and kept her in some motel to interrogate? Who had her hands? All he had to go on was the ripped soap wrapper. He wondered if he shouldn't be back on the Res where he knew everyone and spoke the language. Here he didn't know the habits and ways of the White world. He could break into the FBI office to read files on AIM, but he was sure they'd installed security alarms as well as wire taps. He had no idea where they'd keep Joanna Joe's hands, probably in an evidence locker, but not with the local police, who resented the FBIs intruding on their turf. Maybe in a cold room at a morgue. Even if he knew where it was, he couldn't go there. Medicine men weren't allowed near dead bodies.

All day he observed the FBIs' reactions to the red hands. Some cursed AIM and yelled for turpentine, some took fingerprints, a few laughed it off as the *Red Phantom Strikes Again.* No one noticed the difference from AIM's fist-and-feathers logo. Hotel maids ended up having to wipe clean the FBIs' room doors. In daylight his spree seemed foolish. He'd given in to malicious mischief, but learned nothing. Going into the FBI office, Agent Trask looked haggard. Perhaps he'd dreamed of black birds that screeched and dove in the night sky. Perhaps he was unable to protect his eyes from the beating wings, slicing beaks, gouging talons taking out eyes that refused to see Joanna Joe wandering lost in the Badlands. Agent Slade, a 'Nam vet without nightmares, was not in the office. Probably off in the white Bronco interrogating someone, or meeting an informant.

Instead of painting hands, he must find the hands. The killer could have cut off Joanna Joe's hands to keep as souvenirs. The collectors didn't stop in 'Nam. Sick minds brought back souvenirs of tongues, teeth, sex organs, skin. Now, collectors of the perverse drooled over paid-for body parts, skulls and bones stolen from Indian graves. Possession gone berserk.

Both Trask and Slade had served in the military. Trask was by-the-book Mormon. Only Slade, who'd served in 'Nam, would have had a chance to collect enemy souvenirs preserved in formaldehyde or else stuffed like deer or elk heads. At the library he looked in the Yellow Pages for taxidermists, and found three. Would any of them preserve human hands? Surely it was illegal, open to charges of grave-robbing as well. How could he proceed? He could hardly walk in and say, "I'm looking for a pair of hands, dark-skinned small female hands."

By the third visit he had his inquiry down. He walked into the Deadwood store, looked around, rang the bell. A 'Nam vet dressed in uniform emerged from the rear, limping with a cane. His hands reeked of preservatives.

Alex, dressed in his borrowed vet uniform provided by Badger, leaned on the counter and said, "I was asking around and I—uh—heard that sometimes you take on special jobs that require delicacy and skill to preserve and mount, and I was wondering if you could do something special for me. Mine are getting all dried up and leathery, you know, souvenirs from Pleiku? Uh—do you ever work on things like that?"

"What'd you have in mind?" The vet's voice rasped. "Mounted?"

"Yeah, you know, there was this old lady gook—"

The guy stared at him.

"—all bayoneted to ribbons, she didn't run fast enough—" Alex could not go on.

"—and you brought 'em back, didn't treat 'em proper, and now you want me—"

"—to mount them. Yes." Alex took a deep breath.

"Sorry. I don't do that kind of work."

"They're small." Alex showed with his hands.

"Small ears vets just string 'em and let 'em dry. He swept his hand over his brushcut. "You Injuns come back from 'Nam want sumpn' bigger, and that don't come cheap. It'll cost you."

Alex whistled. "I need 'em fixed. They're all I got left from that hellhole."

"Two, three hundred bucks. Each. Cash up front. You got the cash, you bring 'em in."

~~~

Later that evening, wearing his new black topcoat and white shirt, in his best *Sober-Sinner Wino* disguise, Alex sat in the shadows of the ornate hotel lobby where the FBIs stayed. He hid behind a copy of the *Rapid City Journal*. Agents Trask and Slade emerged from the restaurant, but only Trask, the Mormon family man, walked to the elevator. Slade waved him goodbye, then slid into the Western bar off the lobby. Soon afterwards Slade sauntered out, turned down the hall to the rear and exited. As Alex opened the back door, he saw the taillights of a white Bronco zoom past. Slade, the California dude, spent his time elsewhere. To shadow him, Alex needed wheels.

CHAPTER 18
TATE

AROUND NOON the next day in the AIM House living room, Tate beat on the big powwow drum to get the attention of the guys sprawled on the living room chairs, couch and floor, immersed in a TV car chase. She waved the yellow poster.

"Yeah, yeah." Old Louie waved it aside.

"See this traitor?" She handed it to Smokey.

He squinted. "Some white guy with glasses and three-piece suit."

Shuta came out of her bedroom. "Gimme that!" She peered at the poster, now wrinkled. "Patrick Stewart, huh? That's Night Cloud. I'd recognize him anywhere, even with dyed hair, wire-rim glasses, three-piece suit—can't disguise shit!" She threw the paper down.

Tate rapped on the table until the room was quiet. "The FBI have him speaking at John Birch rallies to tell lies about AIM. We have to stop him."

Shuta turned off the TV and stood in front of it. She folded her arms. "You warriors better get him—the nerve, to come back here and black-mouth AIM! Right in our back yard!"

Lester stood up. "George left me in charge—"

"Of the Camp," said Shuta. "He left me in charge of this AIM house." She waved her hands around the room. "Go ahead, Tate."

Tate rushed over to stand beside Shuta. "I call an AIM strategy meeting."

Lester said, "George wants us to lay low."

Shuta said, "He'll be pissed if you don't go after Night Cloud. He fooled George worst of all, taking him on as AIM's own airplane pilot!"

Tate held the poster up so all could see. "We have two days to get ready. It's the same town where they killed old man Yellow Thunder. I wasn't here then, but you guys must remember how those cowboys made him dance naked at the Gordon Grange Hall."

"Bad idea." Lester rose and stood in front of Tate and Shuta. "Nebraska State cops? Federal offense? Think about it! Too dangerous."

"You want us women to crash that hall without you?" Shuta pushed Lester away.

Things were getting out of hand. Tate stepped between them. "Guys, we won't let them catch us. We'll use Night Cloud's own methods against him: We'll take away his mike, expose him as a liar, and zoom back across the Res line and get home safe."

Chaské jumped up. "Saturday evening bars'll keep the local cops busy."

Smokey pulled him back down on the couch. "The Birchers have their own security."

Tate glanced at Lester. "Keep it simple. No guns. No alcohol. Agreed?"

Some nodded, others grumbled. Lester looked down at his feet.

"Agreed, then," Tate said. "Smokey, four of you can stop the John Bircher gate-keepers. I'll grab the mike, and tell them what he is: thief, wife-beater, murderer."

Shuta added, "Six of you rush up, get him backstage, punch him out, and split."

"Drivers keep the cars gassed up by the back door, running," said Tate.

"What if you're cut off by a cruiser and caught, Tate?" asked Lester. "Ever been cuffed and beaten by a Nebraska State cop?"

"Brave-heart warriors never get caught!" said Shuta.

"We'll be like lightning! Those Birchers won't know what hit them," said Chaské.

"Red Power! Red Power!" The room resounded with their chants.

She'd unleashed the AIM guys' energy. She felt the group power flood through her. At last they'd do something about Night Cloud. All except Lester, who had backed off into the kitchen. She knew he wasn't afraid. He'd led men into battle. Perhaps he felt loyal to George, or was being cautious. She didn't know the territory. At least they were willing to take action to stop Night Cloud, even if he never confessed to killing JJ.

When the chants petered out, Lester stepped back into the room and held up his hand. "All right, you crazy AIM warriors. We need strategy. Anybody been in that Grange Hall?" He looked around. "Didn't think so. Here's why they gave me my 'Nam medals."

She watched him take over. He strode to the west wall, pulled down an AIM poster, turned it over and laid it on the linoleum. The warriors drew closer and crouched down to see, leaving Tate and Shuta in front of the TV. "Here's the layout." He drew the floor plan, marking entrances and exits, steps and barriers.

Lester lifted his head. "Anybody else led a lightning raid? Didn't think so. Don't want the usual barroom brawl—crash in, start a riot, get into fist fights. Personal satisfaction that ends up in cuffs and no bail. Agreed, no fistfights in the hall?"

Some nodded, others grumbled. Tate moved closer to see the diagram.

"Whoever wants to riot can drive to Scenic Bar. It's closer." Lester stared at the warriors. "Our plan is *in-and-out*. One action. One goal. Tate wants to stop the lies. We can throw leaflets around the hall with truth about AIM. Or we can deal with Night Cloud directly. What'll it be?"

Shuta cried, "Both!" Lester thought like a veteran strategist.

Lester looked up at her. "Tate, suppose you run in, grab the mike. Night Cloud grabs it back. You hit him and try to grab it back. He punches you out."

She frowned. "Of course, I'll need some help."

"So we rush up with you and haul Night Cloud backstage while you take over the mike. You talk until some Bircher cuts the power," said Smokey.

"I can yell without a mike," replied Tate.

"Meanwhile we're gone—and you're arrested," added Lester.

Tate hated to give up the onstage drama, but Lester had a point. "We need to kidnap him, question him and find out if he killed—"

Shuta interrupted, "We know he killed her."

"Then what?" asked Lester. "Turn him over to his FBI bosses? No justice there."

"We already run him off the Res, said Shuta. "Now we shut him up for good."

Tate grew alarmed. Shuta was escalating, but the idea was to take over the mike and stop lies about AIM. Maybe they should just flood the hall with AIM flyers about Red Power. No fights, no killing, just *in-and-out,* like Lester said.

Smokey said, "Beat him up—for personal satisfaction? That what you want, Shuta?"

"Kidnap him. Bring him back to the Res—" Shuta left the rest unsaid: *Now we take him out.*

"We could brand him. A.I.M. on his forehead," Chaské added.

"Think about it before we risk our lives." Lester strode out of the living room.

Tate realized he was leaving, so on the way out she said to Shuta, "We can ride together."

Shuta looked at her, wide-eyed. "I'm not going. I got a kid to watch."

Tate stared back. She'd though Shuta was her friend, but she didn't act like it now. Shuta had been the strongest supporter for the raid on Night Cloud. Without Shuta along, the warriors wouldn't listen to her, only Lester. What would George say? Alex, the peacemaker, was gone. She'd set something in motion and now it had a life of its own. How could she stop it now?

~~~

Tate, along with Chaské and Lester in his now-black pickup, led the AIM caravan down to the John Bircher rally in Nebraska. Behind them came a red van and two cars, each loaded with AIM warriors. Lester had checked: no guns, no alcohol. They drove off the Res into Nebraska and cut their lights when they neared the Gordon Grange Hall, drifting unseen into the parking lot filled with ranchers' pickups. Light filled the tall side windows of the white plank Grange Hall.

They eased their car doors open—dome lights masked by tape—and listened. Feet shuffled, chairs scraped, tinny piano strains of the *Star Spangled Banner* filtered out into the parking lot.

"Wait for them to settle in and get bored," whispered Lester.

The AIM guys inched their way into the parking lot. Dressed in black, the drivers stayed outside. They moved across the parking lot to disable the parked pickups and cars, peered with flashlights into open hoods, removed the distributor caps, and closed the hoods quietly.

Tate's team, the rally-crashers, wore cowboy hats and boots, jeans and pearl-button shirts. They snuck up to the rear of the hall and around the corner to press against the long west side. Lester and Smokey peeked in the high windows to check out each bodyguard onstage.

Behind them she asked, "What are they doing now?"

More feet shuffled and chairs scraped. "Shh. Introducing the speaker," replied Lester.

"Is it Night Cloud?"

Smokey said, "Can't tell yet."

"Let me see." She reached with her fingers to the sill and leaped up to glance inside.

"Stay down. They'll see your hat," said Lester.

She heard a deep bass voice start to talk. He didn't need a mike, but he used one anyway, and the sounds reverberated throughout the hall. She heard only phrases—*thieves and thugs—drunken orgies—welfare bums*—Ranting, denouncing AIM.

Lester nodded. "It's him. Can't change the voice."

More AIM guys crept alongside the building and joined them, pulling red bandanas over their faces. They inched toward the front corner. She knelt down and peeked around at two tall cowboys who strode back and forth in front of the big entry doors.

Smokey said, "Bodyguards. No holsters. Must'a left their rifles in their pickup gunracks."

Lester turned to the AIM guys behind him. "You Indian cowboys wait for Smokey and me to take those honchos out." He pulled Tate up, backed her against the wall. "You, too, Hothead."

At least he wasn't calling her *Sarge* any longer. Lester and Smokey tied their long hair up inside cowboy hats and sauntered around the corner, Lester hiding a wood bat behind him.

She peered around the corner again.

"Hi, y'all," said Smokey in his best Texan drawl. He reached out to shake the nearest guard's hand and flipped him around so Lester could knock him out. As the first guard collapsed, Lester swung the bat at the other, while Smokey ducked behind and chopped him in the neck.

She heard one *ungh* as she and Smokey dragged the two unconscious guards around the far corner away from the overhead lights. Hooray for AIM teamwork and karate chops. Later she'd get them to teach her those close defensive moves.

Lester leaped up the front steps and grabbed the door handle. "Now!" He pulled the door open and waved the rest of the rally-crashers forward. "Remember, in-and-out!"

They rushed in, pushed the ticket taker aside, and rushed up both aisles. Tate followed them, her long hair flying behind her. She loped to the stage and leaped in front of the speaker dressed in a gray three-piece suit and tie. He waited for her, mike held high, but she tackled his legs. He landed on his back with a crash. She grabbed the mike from him and faced the crowd, her borrowed cowboy hat knocked off. "This FBI informer is a thief, rapist, and murderer!"

From the corner of her eye she saw Night Cloud start to rise. She pushed him away, and before he could grab her, Lester jumped on his stomach. Night Cloud reached inside his suit coat toward a leather holster, but Lester twisted his arm and knocked the handgun loose to skitter across the stage. Smokey, struggling with a suited Bircher bodyguard, grabbed for it.

"He's got a gun!" Tate yelled. She saw another suited Bircher bodyguard in the front row head toward her. Behind him, cowboys and ranchers rose from their seats and pushed forward. As they tried to climb onstage, the AIM guys' feet and fists pushed them back.

Someone cut the power. The lights and mike went off. It was pandemonium.

She dropped the mike, oblivious to the scramble in the darkness behind her, and continued to yell at the distraught audience. "The American Indian Movement fights for our civil rights and treaty rights. We teach Indian history at the Red Schoolhouse, we feed the kids when there is nothing to eat at home. They gain pride in their Indian heritage and learn to speak their native language. We make regalia for the young powwow dancers."

Someone elbowed her in the back. Thrust forward, she stumbled over legs on the floor and fell to her knees. In the melee of thuds and whacks, curses and cries, she heard Smokey's voice call, "*Lechetu-ki-ya!*" Come this way. She crawled her way toward his voice, bumping and pushing, twisting and turning, to haul herself toward the cold air. Miraculously, the back door opened. She pulled herself across the lintel and rolled down the steps to the parking lot.

She ran across the parking lot to Lester's pickup, lights off but running, Chaské at the wheel. She yanked open the door and climbed in. "Get us out of here!"

"Where's Lester?" asked Chaské.

"I don't know. They cut the lights and everybody was fighting. Did you see Smokey? I followed his voice and crawled out on my hands and knees." She heard the other AIM vehicles idling, and boots scuffling as some AIM guys slid into their places.

"That's gotta be Smokey in the van," Chaské said.

She ducked down and peered through the window. Shadows flitted across the darkened parking lot. "Hey, that's Night Cloud over there climbing into that black car. I thought you AIM guys disabled them all. Follow him."

"Gotta wait for Lester."

Chaské had better take orders from her. She shouted, "Lester told me to catch Night Cloud. Go after him." She reached her foot over to press down on Chaské's boot on the accelerator. "Go!" The pickup engine thrummed. "Or get out."

Chaské pushed her foot away. "Hey, bitch—" Realizing he'd gone over the line, he closed his mouth and shifted into gear. At her signal to split, the other AIM vehicles, dark and silent, moved out. Some went left, others right, until they disappeared.

She pointed to the black car, squealing as it left the lot. "He's turned his lights on. Follow."

Chaské shifted again and followed the black car's tail as it turned west and headed past the streetlights, out of town. He hung back in the darkness until the car turned right onto another asphalt road leading toward the flashing neon of a motel.

"Stay behind until we see which room he goes in," Tate said.

Chaské drove by, turned around, and with lights off, idled beside a garage behind the motel.

"Keep the pickup running." She got out, strode toward the lighted motel and rounded a corner. Night Cloud's black car sat in front of a unit, its driver door open, the car empty. Running past it to the motel door, she grabbed the knob, the key still in it, door slightly ajar. Inside was dark. She slipped in against the wall and smelled blood. If only she had a flashlight. She reached behind her and found the light switch, but was afraid to turn it on. Night Cloud might be right in front of her, ready to grab an intruder, so she waited, listening.

The curtains swished and cold air rushed into the room. There was an open window at the back. Maybe he'd already jumped out and escaped. She switched on the light and blinked. The walls were sprayed with blood, fresh and dripping. Before her, halfway on the bed lay Night Cloud, his white shirt stained red. His face was pale, his mouth open, his throat slit, as if a second mouth had been carved there above his blue silk tie.

She watched the blood burble out of the wound and flow onto the white sheet, like hot gleaming red lava pouring, pouring down a mountainside in Hawaii, unstoppable. She stepped back, nauseated, immobile, speechless. She'd seen JJ dead and cold and without blood. This man was bloody and warm. He was dying, he was already dead.

She picked up a towel to staunch the flow of blood, or to protect her from it. There was so much. She was no EMT to check for breath or listen for a pulse. What could she do? How could this happen so fast? Minutes ago he drove a car. Call the cops? Run to the window to escape.

A car pulled up outside. Lester burst through the door. His face was swollen, one eyelid shut, knuckles bruised, jeans muddy. "You took my pickup, left me back there."

"*Shh,*" she whispered as she confronted him. "It's Night Cloud!"

He stood beside her and leaned over the body. "Cut from behind. Seen it before." He fumbled with the bedspread, searching. "Where's the knife?"

She pulled his arm back. "It was gone. Don't touch anything."

"Are you sure?" he asked. "Sure *you* didn't touch anything?"

She nodded. "Just the light switch and the windowsill."

He took out his bandana and wiped off the light switch. "Get in the pickup. I'll get the windowsill."

She stumbled toward the pickup and climbed in. Lester, too, had crossed the line. She glanced sideways at Night Cloud's black car, its engine running, the driver's side door still open, as if he'd expected to leave right away.

Lester emerged from the motel room, locked the door, wiped off the handle, and pocketed the key. Then he ran to the driver's side, shoved Chaské over against her, climbed in and backed out.

"Did you get him?" Chaské asked.

Lester paused. "No. Night Cloud jumped out the window and got away."

She stared at Lester, but said nothing. He must have lied for a reason. She'd find out why.

Lester drove east without lights, a madman along back roads. They escaped through the Sand Hill Crane refuge to the Res.

Why keep Night Cloud's death a secret? His John Birch Society speech had been posted all over Nebraska. Anyone could have known. But someone had been waiting, someone tall and strong and quick enough to slit Night Cloud's throat. Someone used to butchering hogs or cows. Someone in Special Forces or Navy Seals. Could one of the other AIMs have murdered Night Cloud? At the strategy meeting they'd mentioned about stopped him from speaking. A slit throat would do it.

If only she could go back to the crime scene. She'd search the room for the knife, look for a snagged thread on the window screen, and interview the motel clerk for check-ins. The bed hadn't been made. Was the window forced open from the outside? Were there toiletries in the bathroom? Clothes in the closet? She'd only seen the knife wound and gushing blood.

If only she could go back to *their* strategy meeting and call off the raid as foolish, pointless, and dangerous to AIM. Lester knew it, yet he went ahead with the plans. From now on she'd be like a missionary and just distribute leaflets.

Around 3am Lester pulled into the AIM house driveway behind Smokey's red van. Lights were on and people inside. Tate woke Chaské, who climbed out, stumbled up the steps to the kitchen and went downstairs to bed. Lester turned off the pickup and touched Tate on the shoulder. "Don't say anything about Night Cloud."

She brushed his arm off. "We have to tell George privately, before the FBIs come."

"I'll do it. It's on my shoulders. My fault I let you talk me into it."

"I'll tell him. It was my idea to defend AIM."

"No, it has to be Lakota way, man to man. He left me in charge."

She shrugged. She'd talk to George anyway to find out about Alex. She pushed ahead of Lester and entered the AIM house. The AIM guys played checkers in the living room, as if nothing had happened, except for Old Louie intent on his perennial game of cribbage with Smokey, played on an old hand-carved board.

Smokey asked, "Geez, we lost you. Where'd you go? We made it back hours ago, just about to send out a rescue squad."

Tate asked, "How did you guys get away?"

"Easy. The Birchers' cars didn't start, and the cops who came split right away to take another emergency call. Someone drew them off." Lester said.

Old Louie said, "You guys look bad. Night Cloud did that to you?"

"You catch him?" asked Smokey.

Lester looked around the room. "Who got his gun?"

They shook their heads. "After the lights went out, we split, in-and-out." Chaské said.

Smokey said, "We thought you got it. You took him down."

"I took him down, all right, but the gun flew over by you guys." Lester said.

Old Louie said, "You said no guns."

Lester sat down at the table and poured himself a cup of coffee. "Tate took my pickup and chased Night Cloud to his motel. Good thing, Smokey, you picked me up and followed, but by the time I got there, he'd escaped out the back window and we lost him."

She started to disagree, but swallowed her words. Lester was lying again, but why?

A bedroom door opened and slammed shut. George appeared in shorts and t-shirt, scowling. "Lester Bear Heart. Tate Turning Hawk. What did you accomplish? Nothing."

Lester stared at his coffee. Tate looked away.

"Nothing but more trouble." George said. "I come home to get some sleep, get woken up by AIM *warriors* who limped home, all cuts and bruises, stone cold sober and scared." He turned and glared at them. "Then you all had the nerve to tell me you escaped from a big fight at the Scenic Bar. You forgot I drove through Scenic on my way home from my trial."

George paced around the living room and turned off the TV. "From now on until the Sundance, you hothead warriors pack up and move out to Crazy Horse Camp—for sanctuary. When the FBIs come to ask about Indian vigilantes, no one but Shuta and the kids will be here. FBIs can't get you at the Sundance grounds unless they take off their guns. Which they never will."

The AIM guys groaned. "Live in tipis?" asked Chaské.

"No TV? No girls? No—" The refrain continued.

George sat down and faced Lester. "Bro, you get one more chance to get these boys in line, shape 'em up, Indian way. Hard work, sweats, Vision Hill fasts and prayers to the Great Mystery.

Then he turned to Tate. "And you will not mess with AIM plans. Move into town with your mother-in-law until Alex comes back."

That she would not do. Night Cloud had killed JJ. Now it was over. She didn't have to find out who killed Night Cloud.

George brought down the Pipe from its shelf in the living room. He cradled it in his arms. "I need you to pray for my acquittal. Every time I leave the courthouse to come home, I run the gauntlet of rednecks all the way to Buffalo Gap, then the Goons on that lonely stretch from Buffalo Gap to Oglala on the Res. Even with a body-guard and driver, I could get picked off at any time."

Tate asked, "And where's Alex? We should pray for him, too."

"Hiding out," George said, "like you *warriors* from now on." He stood up, picked up the empty coffee pot and gestured for her to follow him into the kitchen.

While she filled the pot with water and poured in fresh grounds, George stood behind her and whispered in her ear. "Be patient. Alex is okay, but you won't recognize him. Which is good." He patted her on the shoulder. "But Night Cloud couldn't have killed her. He's been speaking against AIM on the East Coast, got to Nebraska just two days ago."

George must have his own Moccasin Telegraph to keep ahead of the feds, but his news was devastating. All her work had been for nothing. She looked directly at him. It was her fault. "Night Cloud ran from the hall, got in his car and took off. We chased him back to his motel room. I was the first one inside and saw he was stabbed to death. I saw the body, but not who did it." She hesitated. "It couldn't have been any of us, because we were all at the rally when he was killed."

But it could be someone they knew.

George clenched his fists. "Be careful, Tate. Now the FBIs will be after AIM again."

She wished Alex were here. He'd have gotten Night Cloud into a Sweat Lodge like he'd tried with the FBI, and steam out a confession. But she had no idea how to investigate on the Res. Old-timers only spoke Lakota, others lied to strangers, anyone not born on the Res, and officials stonewalled or deliberately knew nothing. She didn't know who was related to whom, or what was going on. All her plans had gone awry, and she'd really angered George and endangered AIM.

She had been so sure about Night Cloud, she'd never looked for anyone else. Now, as an outsider, she'd suspect everyone. She didn't know the history of Eagle Nest. What had happened before she'd married Alex and moved to the camp lay like a mist over the land, vague outlines and feelings gleaned from Alex. Whose side? Indian or White, she couldn't tell. Some Indians were Apples, red-on-the-outside-white-on-the-inside, or paid Goons or BIA sellouts, and some Whites were AIMs. The FBI paid good money, and most people on the Res were poor. She felt a wave of paranoia sweep over her. Night Cloud must have had many enemies. Whoever killed him, she couldn't worry about that now. It was JJ's killer she was after. She'd have to start over.

~~~

Back at the Camp Lester surprised her at the door, alone with his cedar flute. It was very late, almost morning. After George had chewed out Lester, she'd expected him to be so angry that he'd refuse to talk to her. He seemed tight, tense, ready to spring. She backed away. But he came in, said he needed to unwind, needed to play. He picked up the flute, blew into it, played a sad, mournful tune. Minor key.

She played a similar tune from Brahms; he played it back to her.

Amazed, she played another motif from Beethoven.

He played it back an octave higher.

She played the opening notes of the Bach B Minor fugue.

He played it back to her two octaves higher.

Now she'd try counterpoint. She said, "If I play it, can you repeat it four beats behind?"

Instead, he played faster and caught up to her. He didn't get rounds.

She played and sang *Row, row, row your boat.*

"Everyone knows that," he said.

He must think it's a race, and played faster to catch up. "You start, and I'll come in second."

He played the phrase and stopped. "It's a stupid tune."

"You don't understand. Keep going. It's a round. We play in harmony. Together."

He played the tune again, phrase by phrase, then stopped and looked at her.

"Did you hear me playing? Did you hear the harmony?" Earlier he'd loved the Bach counterpoint.

He laid his flute on the piano. "I don't like it, *row, row, row.* People rowing against each other, White man way. We use the drumbeat for one voice, one mind, Indian way. Your music is beautiful—but strange. Many voices float away to other worlds, not centered on this earthly one."

She hid her disappointment. "You don't like to play together?"

"When we imitate, call and response, we're birds, finding each other, mating."

Making music together wasn't mating. She'd mated for life with Alex. But where was he?

Was he all right? She'd told him she'd find the second FBI informer—JJ's killer.

CHAPTER 19

ALEX

ALEX HADN'T FOUND the *Springv*— motel, but he had found a taxidermist who for $300 would preserve hands. Now he realized the killer might be a souvenir collector. Or have sold them to a collector. In any case, taxidermy, rather than the soap wrapper, might lead him to both the killer and the hands. Who'd want them? And who'd pay that much? The Kadoka Sheriff collected Indian artifacts, sacred eagle feathers and bone whistles, but nothing as monstrous as body parts. He'd heard that some 'Nam vets, numbed by war atrocities, returned wearing necklaces of teeth.

The bums said that the VFW Club didn't kick out vets that came for bottles and cans, and sometimes leftovers. He'd be careful because the bums swore one vet was a Fee-Bee, ate super-early breakfast, and drove away the bums waiting out back for handouts. Smart place to meet, in an empty private Club before the regulars drifted in. Could be Agent Slade, a 'Nam vet running a vet buddy as informer, somebody he'd known during the Vietnam War. The second FBI informer had to be a vet, since only vets with cash were allowed inside.

He'd chance it. Alex slid into the alley behind the FBI's downtown hotel to find a place to spend the night closer to the FBI's cars rather than Under-the-Bridge in his cardboard box. Slade's white Bronco sat inside sections of 10 x 10 steel fencing hauled in to protect the vehicles from more vandalism. He'd hoped to wipe off his childish prank with turpentine, but it seemed too risky. Instead, hidden behind his cart, he bedded down further away in the alley. This time he could follow Slade no matter how early he left.

Just before dawn he heard the hotel's back door slam. Slade appeared, dressed in uniform rather than black suit and tie, and unlocked a fence section. He swore at the red graffiti, got in his white Bronco, put on his VFW cap, and drove away, leaving the fence open.

Wearing his *Passed-out Wino* disguise, Alex pushed his shopping cart toward the VFW Club near downtown. Open early and closed late for shell-shocked vets with cash. The air was crisp and cold. He could see his breath with every step as he walked. The Club had an awning over the front door and a sign, *Vets Watering Hole.* All the windows were mirrored glass, allowing for privacy inside while letting in light.

He pushed his cart to the rear parking lot half-full of pickups. Past a fancy blue-and-chrome Dodge pickup mounted with deer lights, two rifles in its gun rack. Past a mud-splattered high-center Chevy pickup with stock rack, hay bales in the bed. Past a low-slung four-seat Camaro, half-pickup in the rear. Past a flat-black Ford pickup with a Res license plate in the rear window. Past a battered VW bus plastered with bumper sign, *Proud American Vet.* Some vets were hunters. Others were ranchers. Some slept in brick houses with neat yards. He could tell others slept in their cars.

Slade's Bronco wasn't among them.

From cover Alex surveyed the vehicles in the parking lot. In his mind he saw those of the AIM vets in Eagle Nest Housing: Smokey's Ford pickup was blue. Lester's Ford pickup was Red Power. Chappa had a banged-up yellow Dodge pickup. Who drove a dull black Ford pickup with a Tribal plate in the rear window? Must be a Goon from Pine Ridge Agency. Who else could find a scarce Oglala Sioux Tribal plate?

As he neared the back door, he saw crates of empties: squat brown beer bottles, tall slender wine bottles, square whiskey bottles. Bonanza. Enough to fill his cart, fill his pockets, fill his stomach. Canny old Badger, a WWII vet himself, had kept this spot secret.

As he lifted a crate into his cart, careful not to clink any bottles, he heard a growl from behind the tan dumpster, then a series of deep barks. He wasn't scared. On the Res, each house out in the country had a pack of loose dogs for protection. This ferocious city dog was chained. Maybe they turned him loose inside after closing time.

The back door opened. "No bums allowed. We got a pit bull for the likes 'a you."

Wrong disguise. He bent over his cart. "I'm just collecting bottles."

A grizzled man with tattoos on both arms stood in jeans and dirty white apron. His grizzled hair was held down by a net. He pointed to the crate in the cart. "Put it back. Our brewery truck comes on Fridays to pick up and restock."

He lowered the crate back to its pile. "What about pop cans?"

The cook squinted. "You ain't a vet. Kid, go home to mama."

Hokshila again. No one here knew he was grown up and married. Dirt didn't age him. Talcum powder could, but next time, ashes would do. "Could I look at the bulletin board for *Help Wanted* signs?"

"Can't let minors in. Try the Y."

He tried once more. "Any leftovers from breakfast?"

This time the cook laughed. "I get it. You been sent to bring your old man home. Can't do it, we protect our own. Sorry." He closed the door, then opened it again and tossed out an unopened pop can. The cook crossed his arms and stood in front of the racks of empty bottles. "I'm gonna stand here, lettin' in cold air, until you skedaddle."

Alex caught the pop can and put it in his coat pocket for later. "Thanks," he said, and pushed his cart past the teeth-bared pit bull and the dumpster surrounded by a chain link fence. No chance for bums to grab food. Beyond was a loading dock, and on the far side, as if in a reserved out-of-the-way spot, sat a white Bronco, smudged red hands on the windshield, on the spare tire. Slade was inside after all, with the *reluctant Indian* of Old Sam's prophecy, waiting to be paid.

Alex hadn't found him before Joanna Joe got killed, and hadn't had a chance since. The traitor was so close, but inside, protected by one-way mirrored windows. Had Slade and his informer looked out and recognized him, instead? His disguise as a wino bum with a cart must have worked. He turned into the alley and waited for the pit bull to stop barking.

He waited for Slade to emerge with the informer.

~~~

After half an hour, Slade emerged alone, not noticing the barking pit bull nor the bum asleep beside a cart in the alley. Slade drove off as if he'd had an emergency call, speeding toward the center of town. No one else came out. Alex realized that the FBI informer was either still inside, or had left by the front door. In the meantime he could study the black pickup with Tribal plates for clues.

As he crossed the parking lot, he heard claxons and sirens in the distance. In a great clatter, fire trucks and police cars zoomed toward downtown. A lone ambulance wailed past. Above the city rose a thin pillar of black smoke. Vets ran out to their jeeps and 4-wheelers in the parking lot, talking excitedly about a fire on the downtown thruway.

He was puzzled. The thruway couldn't burn, unless a semi crashed and went over the bridge. Or Under-the-Bridge, where he and the bums lived. If he waited, he'd miss the second FBI informer, who might not return for hours. But he worried that his friends Under-the-Bridge were caught in a fire.

Alarmed, he pushed his cart as fast as possible, past the crowds milling about, fire trucks and cop cars blocking the road. When he arrived at his home, Under-the-Bridge, he saw smoke rising from a pile of rubble on the Indian side of the river. Below, men in black jackets with FBI printed in white on their backs, stood on the cleared riverbank. Two firemen in waterproof coats hosed down the remains of the bums' homes and belongings. Another fireman raked out blackened metal cans and dishes.

All their refrigerator cartons, wooden pallets, footlockers and suitcases, winter clothes and blankets and shoes, boxes of commodity milk and powdered eggs, cans of beef and pork, packets of rice and beans—now flickering flames and wet ashes. The Great Mystery had stripped them of everything. He'd worn his *Passed-Out Wino* clothes that morning, but his *Sober-Sinner Wino* disguise, black topcoat and boots, even the wig he'd refused to wear, had vanished into the pillars of smoke.

Perhaps he could save the Pipestone bowl of his fasting Pipe from the ashes. He started to climb down, leaving his cart behind, but a fireman called out, "Stay back! We have it under control."

The men must have fled when the FBIs arrived, taking with them anything precious: photos, cigarette stash, gold wedding ring. He worked his way free of the crowd and down the embankment to the city's Riverside Park south of the bridge. Hidden in the thickets and bushes, behind the aspens and pines, the men had watched the destruction of their lives. He joined them.

One old man leered at him, his breath reeking of Red Turkey. "You set 'em on us. That's why you weren't here."

Another grabbed him from behind. "Look what yer Great Mystery prayers brought us."

Alex twisted away from him toward the river. He had no answers. Another failure. His tobacco ties hadn't saved Joanna Joe. He'd been beaten up, lost everything, even his reputation He realized that when he'd cut his hair, he'd lost power, and his hawk had stayed on the res. Yet the Great Mystery had led him to Slade's meeting with the second FBI informer. He was getting closer.

A WWII vet intervened, acting as the *eyapaha*, a town crier. "The FBIs come all pussy-foot and polite, with a warrant for Alex Turning Hawk."

How had the FBIs known to look for him here? Who had ratted him out? No one knew where he was, exactly, not even Tate. George only knew he'd gone to Rapid City. Had the FBIs already searched the Lakota Housing? Had they threatened Auntie Agatha, who'd told him to stay Under-the-Bridge? She wouldn't tell, regardless. Or had one of the FBIs followed him after he spray-painted their cars? Was the second informer close to George, who'd let his location slip?

It had been a controlled burn. The FBIs had trashed just the Indian side to smoke him out. Instead, they'd found men with no other home. Had one of them, raised Christian in a Mission School, decided he was a heathen, and squealed? For a carton of cigs? Red Turkey?

The WWII vet continued. "We told 'em, *You say he's twenty? We're all old geezers.*

"*Any newbies?* they ask. We tell 'em, *Just one oldie kicked the bucket, hauled off to the morgue.*"

Alex had slept in that dead man's carton.

A Marine with tattoos added, "They find red spray-paint cans in the trash, toss 'em in the fire, watch 'em explode. Except they kept one for prints."

Alex started to apologize, but the WWII vet stopped him. "*Vagrants*, they call us. We leave before they arrest us. Carts, pallets and refrigerator cartons, commodities and clothes, we can get them again—if we're not in lockup."

Alex looked for Badger. "Where's Radio?"

"Them FBIs got 'im," a toothless man called out.

The WWII vet said, "Radio was cool until them FBIs discover his padlocked bin. Then he runs and tackles the FBI boss, yelling, *You ain't got a warrant for my locker.* He swings his new baseball bat. So them FBIs handcuff 'im and carry 'im off for assaulting an officer, disorderly conduct, until Badger starts to swear and goes rigid, eyes bulge out, face turns red—heart attack. Them FBIs call an ambulance quick, take off the handcuffs, load him on a stretcher and order him to Hot Springs VA Hospital. Radio wakes up enough to cry, *Not there, anyplace but there.* One FBI says, all prissy, *I'm sure you've been there before. They'll recognize you.*"

He'd been so close to finding the second FBI informer, the *reluctant Indian* of the prophecy. He wanted to go back to the VFW parking lot to check out the pickup with tribal plates. But he owed Badger, who called the VA Hospital a *Death Trap*. Badger believed he'd die in there. The Placebo Effect. Medicine men knew long before White doctors named it, that belief was the most powerful medicine of all. Grandpa Henry, who'd had one lung removed, was fine until they told him to be careful since he had only one lung left. Then Grandpa Henry, who believed he needed two lungs to survive, panicked and died four hours later. Alex had to bring Badger back to the Res for doctoring with heart medicine tea.

Alex returned by moonlight to Under-the-Bridge and joined the other shadows, homeless men searching for remnants of their lives. He sifted through the ashes only to find his red Pipestone bowl smashed into a dozen pieces. He was glad the Turning Hawk Treaty Pipe was safe at home. Luckily, the FBIs hadn't found Badger's wood locker buried in the earth. Two days ago Badger had handed him the padlock key and told him, "If I die, open my locker and take my treasure home to my family in Porcupine."

The men gathered around, curious, as he dug up the lid and un-loaded Badger's stash. "This is Radio's *wopila*. Share this giveaway, to make up for what the FBIs burned up." Alex handed out shopping bags of treasures to the group. The men tore open the bundles of wool blankets, boots, jackets, caps, gloves, cigarettes, commodity rations, even a small camp stove, as if it were Christmas and they were trying on brand-new clothes.

"I will return," Alex said, "to bring wood and tin roofing to help you rebuild homes." He stuffed a set of Badger's clothes in his back-pack, dug to the bottom of the bin and tucked a heavy velvet bag—Badger's cash-worthy treasure—into his parka pocket. Leaving his cart behind, he waved farewell to life Under-the-Bridge and walked to an all-night pawn shop. From Badger's stash, he hocked the Black Hills gold—three rings, a watch, and a brooch—for a used Harley motorcycle.

On the road to Hot Springs Alex's ears rang from the roar of the cycle, his body wracked from the shaking of the engine. All to rescue Badger from the VA Hospital he feared so much, or at least bring him his belongings. What if that old fart, Badger, had been faking, just to get removed from the scene and not be arrested? Probably not. For Badger, jail in Rapid City wasn't as bad as death at the VA.

Crisp moonlit air kept him awake. So did the cry, "*kree–kree–,*" of a night hawk who circled above the winter wheat field beside him. He called back, "*kree–kree–.*" Yet this hawk didn't swoop down.

The town of Hot Springs lay silent. Only one neon sign lit the closed Texaco gas station. He rode past the usual cottages, Motel 6, and a Country Inn, closed until summer. Even the Evans Plunge spa was dark. As he slowed to find the road to the VA Center, he noticed an out-of-the-way strip of five green motel rooms at the end of a cul-de-sac street. No overhead sign, no lights. Not even tire tracks or boot prints in the fresh snow. He stopped. It looked deserted, but it didn't feel deserted. Some dark energy lay within.

He turned off the cycle and wheeled alongside the building. As he brushed past snowberry bushes, his boots nudged a large wooden sign propped against the wall. It had fallen off the roof, probably broken off and blown down. He brushed snow off the top, revealing chipped paint lettering, green on white. *Springview Motel.*

He laughed. The Great Mystery, must have a sense of humor. All his trips to find the soap wrapper motel had led him nowhere. Now that his conscience made him take a side trip to bring Badger his clothes and stash, here was his goal. He got off the Harley, hid it behind the sign and thanked the Great Mystery for guiding him. He edged around the corner onto a walkway beside a parking strip. Pulled up by the last room in the row, dusted with snow, sat a White Bronco with an FBI license plate.

Careful to brush out his tracks along the way, Alex sidled under the eaves to the last room to listen beside the door. No sounds of life inside. Almost dawn. He rounded the far side of the unit, no windows here, furthest from the street. He crouched down between a rusted air conditioner and a door-less gas refrigerator, and napped until dawn. Agent Slade had kept Joanna Joe here.

Awakened by slamming doors, Alex heard Agent Slade drive away in his white Bronco. He hoped that meant Slade was headed to the FBI office in Rapid City. Moccasin Telegraph said that the FBIs kept some Indians as witnesses in hotels outside Rapid City, holding them until they signed affidavits for upcoming AIM trials.

He stretched, rounded the corner and tried the double-locked door. Slade, the sun-tanned dude, must have come to the Hot Springs' famous spa and luxury lodge, and while there, found this dilapidated paint-peeled motel unit with rear entrances ideal for his witness holding site.

He knocked, in case Slade had left someone inside. No answer. He didn't have all day to get in, not with Badger in the hospital. He knocked again and listened carefully. He heard a faint groan. Female. Hung-over. Slade's shack-up? Local bar floozie or Joanna Joe replacement? Indian?

He leaned on the door and spoke in Lakota: "I've come to take you home." He waited.

"Sonny-boy, get away from me."

He'd guessed right. A full-blood. She spoke in the old cadences. He only knew one Sonny-boy from the Res. He felt for the unused flask Badger had given him to douse himself as a drunk, lodged in his inside parka pocket. "Got some White Lightning here." He used the Lakota word for fire-water. "Want some?"

He heard a low laugh that ended in a hacking cough. "Locked."

"Open the bathroom window."

"Nailed."

"I'm coming in anyway."

"No you ain't. Billy's comin' back an' he'll beat the shit outta you."

From a pile of junk next to a gas refrigerator Alex dragged a rusty barrel around back, under the high bathroom window, climbed up and hung onto the ledge. With Badger's pocket knife, he dug into the rotten wood of the transom, pulled out two nails and lifted the frosted glass outwards. He shed his thick parka and wriggled through the narrow opening, sliding down to the toilet seat and floor. Before he could stand up, the window banged shut above him, leaving the room semi-dark. He stood up, felt for a switch, found none, and opened the door a crack.

He blinked and stared up into the blotched face of a *Hang-Around-the-Fort* woman with a single streak of white hair running through her black disheveled hair. A red flannel bathrobe encased her bulk. She'd never fit through the bathroom window. Close to his ear, her right hand held a broken-edged green bottle.

"Sonny-boy don't speak old-time Lakota."

Behind her he saw cigarette butts stuffed in ashtrays, beer bottles, wine bottles, whiskey bottles, half-eaten pizza in take-out cartons, panties, bras, Kleenex, makeup, spilled nail polish.

Alex thrust his flask out.

She grabbed it. "Who the hell are you?"

He took a deep breath to fill himself with Hawk Power. "*Chetan Yuhomini.*" Alex announced himself in the old formal way. "Medicine-man-in-training to Old Sam."

She laughed. "Come here, *hokshila*, and bring me your medicine bottle." She grabbed the flask, twisted it open, tilted it up and swallowed three times. "Get outta here."

Ignoring her, he counted the take-out cartons to see out how long she'd been kept here.

She finished the flask, tossed it on the bed, and pointed her lips toward the bathroom. "I never go in there. Only in the dark. You bring me any more?"

He shook his head. She must pee sometime.

"Then go away. Can't talk to nobody. Billy's good to me. Lotsa times."

The TV was turned on so low he hadn't heard it. He walked to it and turned it higher to cover their voices. "Who are you?" he asked very slowly in Lakota.

She looked up at him, her eyes wide.

"It's okay to tell me. We're probably related."

"You know my cousin Sonny-boy? Sonny-boy Broken Rope?"

Broken Rope family in Porcupine. He'd heard that a Mabel Broken Rope had run off with a BIA lease check on a spree, deserted a passel of kids. Went missing. Nothing new. Alex remembered a chunky woman with a round pock-marked face and greasy black hair, with stair-step kids which Social Services threatened to take away. Gossip had her as an easy lay, a good-time bad-drunk. Beaten up, thrown from a horse, hospitalized, detoxed, tough.

"I like it here!" She swept her arms around the room. "Billy feeds me good, cigarettes, booze, all I want."

He remembered that four years ago during Wounded Knee Occupation, Mabel had been a BIA radio dispatcher in Pine Ridge. That must be where Slade had met her and found out she lived in a fantasy world of made-up stories. She'd have been easy to woo. He'd heard Mabel was *kinda sick in the head*, so far gone on alcohol that people got scared of her. Mabel'd sign anything.

She ducked her head, secretive and seductive, and said, "He's my boyfriend."

Family was important for Traditional Lakotas, so Alex used the old word for close-relations, female cousin, to remind her. "Your kids want you to come home, *hankashi*."

"I lost 'em already." She burst into huge drunken sobs.

Alex went to the door, turned the lock and yanked the handle. It didn't budge. He realized a second deadbolt kept the door locked. He rummaged around the bedside table for keys.

"Where does he keep the key to this lock?"

"I dunno."

He stared at the large new brass dead bolt. Unlike the bathroom window, the motel door was sturdy. He'd have to exit the same way he came in, and Mabel'd never fit. He'd have to come back later with more persuasive tools.

"You belong with your family, back on the Res."

She shook her head. "No-oo-oo."

Then her whole body shook. Not from the booze, but frightened to death.

"Won't go. If I run away, he take my kids an' hurt 'em."

"When's Billy coming back?"

"I-dunno."

"How long you been here?"

"I-dunno. He calls me that, *I-dunno*. Billy brings me booze, I sign papers. Once I didn't sign. He told me a man I never saw was my boyfriend. I said no, Billy, you're my boyfriend." She grabbed Alex's arm. "He showed me the picture on the mirror. I could get dead, too."

He looked around. No pictures on the big mirror on the wall. He went into the bathroom, leaving the door open to see. A black and white photo blocked the middle of the mirror. Fuzzy Polaroid. An Indian woman lay naked on a double bed, eyes closed. Joanna Joe, dead, complete with hands. He flipped open the pocket knife, sliced the tape, and slid the photo into his pocket.

He stepped back out to comfort Mabel, but heard the screech of tires, then a vehicle lurch to a stop before the door. Slade bringing Mabel more booze. In a flash Alex grabbed Badger's empty flask, dashed back into the bathroom, and slid its flimsy bolt in place. He heard the keys rattle in the locks, the deadbolt thrown back, and the door slam open against the wall.

"Who was here?" Slade's voice snarled out.

"I-dunno. The TV?"

Alex heard the TV click off, then a cry and thud as a body hit the wall.

"You talk to nobody," the voice said. "You let in nobody, or you're nobody. You forget, you go in and look at your face in the mirror."

"Nobody been here. You got the keys." Mabel whined.

"Got the gun, too. Quit blubbering and drink your breakfast." Slade banged the door open.

"Billy, don't leave—"

Her words said it all. Alone, he'd never get Mabel away from Slade. Alex heard the motel door slam, then Slade drive off in a rush. First he'd get Badger out of the VA hospital. Armed with cheap wine, Badger-alias-Radio could sweet-talk almost anyone into coming along.

Alex slowly unbolted the bathroom door, picked up his parka, and timed his leap out the window to coincide with thuds from inside the room. He hid the oil barrel, brushed away his tracks, and walked towards the Veterans' Hospital.

The VA Center on the hill stood lit like a military base or prison. He parked the cycle by the hospital's Emergency entrance, unstrapped his pack full of Badger's clothes, and went in. An Indian orderly in green scrubs sat in a chair dozing upright next to a hospital bed and stretcher.

Alex averted his eyes, shuffled his feet to wake him, and said in Lakota, "My mother sent me to bring my father home to Porcupine, name's Badger."

The orderly opened his eyes slightly, scrutinizing him, and replied in Lakota, "Second floor."

He took the stairs, checked the doors on each side for names of the occupants, but was drawn by a familiar Lakota voice and shouts of laughter from the big room at the end, an open area with large windows, lounge chairs, ashtrays, and TV. This was where vets well enough to walk spent their days. He thanked the Great Mystery that Badger was okay.

A nurse rushed in. "You don't belong here." She was all business, and all white: cap, hair, face, uniform, hands and arms, stockings and shoes.

Alex wasn't dressed as a clinic orderly, but he straightened up, looked her in the eyes, and showed her Badger's VA card. "Mr.

Ho-ká-la of Porcupine was brought in yesterday from Rapid City. The Indian Public Health Clinic doctor wants to check him out."

Badger wheeled toward him in a rickety high-backed wooden chair, pumping furiously.

He wore a tan bathrobe over pale blue pajamas, and brown leather slippers. "Having races," he said. "Lotsa bets." He panted. "I won." He coughed and pointed to his pocket. "Won cigarettes."

He grabbed the back of Badger's chair and wheeled him down the corridor. "Which room?"

"Here," Badger said. "Moccasin Telegraph said you'd get me outta here before I die."

"You're lucky I need your help." Alex pushed him in and shut the door. "Can you walk?"

Badger pushed the footrests aside and stood up. "You need help? I need help. DT's help."

Alex grabbed Badger and lifted him onto the bed. He opened his pack. "Put these on."

Badger shook out the wrinkled mismatched shirt and pants and put them on. "You brought me *sneakers*?" he asked. "What the hell happened to my cowboy boots?"

"Your headache'll pass when you see that White Bronco." Alex put Badger's socks and too-big sneakers on, lacing them tightly.

Badger stood shakily, grabbed Alex's parka, and shook him. "You found them bastard FBIs? I fought 'em." He looked sad. "They tore down our shacks, burned us out, looking fer you."

Tough old Badger, stubborn with sharp claws. Claws that once dug into dirt underground for root medicine and secrets. He asked, "You know any Broken Ropes from Porcupine?" Badger's face broke into a slow smile. "A streak of white hair down the middle of her back? Never forgot her, never forgot her mean brothers, neither."

Alex hid a smile. After all his struggles off the Res to find what happened to Joanna Joe, the Great Mystery was helping again. "Badger, you gotta stay sober, like a warrior on a raid to steal horses. But this time it's a horse only you can rescue." Then he explained his plan.

~~~

At the back of the motel, Alex pried the bathroom window frame loose and pushed Badger inside, sent the bottles of booze through, and then crawled into the small bathroom himself.

Mabel looked up from the bed, blurry-eyed. By now she seemed unfazed by men emerging from the bathroom. "Do I know you?"

Badger crooned in Lakota, "Remember me? Red Turkey?"

"You bring me some, I might." She peered at Badger.

Alex pushed Badger into the room and handed Mabel a bottle.

She grabbed the bottle and laughed. "Red Turkey? Him I remember from Scenic Bar, long time ago. I did call him that."

"Sweetie," said Badger, sitting on the foot of the bed, "I called you White Lightning." He handed her the second bottle. "Brought you some, too."

Red Turkey and White Lightning brought by an old Lakota drinking buddy convinced Mabel. It must have once been true love, since Badger kept his word and stayed sober.

When Mabel was well-lubricated and had to pee, they maneuvered her into the bathroom, Alex climbing out the window first, Badger waiting patiently, just outside the bathroom door.

From hauling drunks out of ditches, Alex knew how limp and flexible Mabel could be. He reached through the window, grabbed her arms, and pulled her out until her hips stuck tight. "Push!" he called to Badger. Slade could return at any time.

"Do the hoochie-hoochie," Badger begged Mabel, pulling her body from side to side.

She wiggled and slithered into Alex's arms, then clutched him in a huge embrace. When Badger climbed out, Alex handed her to him.

"Where's the convertible?" she asked.

"Right here, sweetie," Badger said, wheeling the cycle into view, "with the top down."

Before Mabel could change her mind, Alex draped his own parka around her, one pocket filled with a nearly-empty bottle of Red Turkey, the other a full bottle of White Lightning. He zipped up the parka, pulled the hood over her white-streaked black hair, gave her cheek a kiss and heaved her onto the Harley behind Badger. She linked her arms around Badger's waist, and propped her slippers against Badger's sneakers.

Alex told Badger, "Slade will be furious to get her back, so go direct to Camp Crazy Horse and hide her from the FBIs." He waved the honeymooners off, hoping they'd make it. His last night with Tate in the Vision Cave came back to him so strongly. He hadn't sent her a hawk feather, powerless in the city with spray paint and anger, but at least now he'd send her two people with news. He wished he could've zoomed home on the Harley with them. Instead, his mission led onward to find Joanna Joe's hands.

~~~

Alex understood now why his father had left Iná and him for the Under-the-Bridge bums. *Their disease was trying to live with two worlds inside.* Generations of Traditional full-blood Indians had been sent to Boarding Schools and the Army. Two worlds, Indian and White, always a river apart. Opposite values, spiritual or material: Be generous or greedy? Quiet and respectful or loud and demanding? Live amid *all my relations* or outside of *Nature*? Compete or share? No wonder split souls drowned themselves in firewater to forget the internal heart-break. Alcohol was called *spirits*. Alcoholism was a spiritual disease. Burning Breast was one of the first to die from it. When Alex finished training to become a medicine man, could he bring the split-hearts to live at Camp Crazy Horse and follow the Red Road? Crazy Horse had lived with only one world inside. Could they?

CHAPTER 20

TATE

TATE TOSSED AND TURNED in her sleep until the cold wind whistling in the eaves woke her. If Alex were here, together they'd figure out how to find JJ's killer. Like George, Alex wouldn't have approved of the failed AIM raid. If only she'd had known that Night Cloud had been in the East.

George had grounded her. "Stay hidden at Camp Crazy Horse," he'd said. She'd stumbled on two dead bodies already, and it didn't look like coincidence. Yet she couldn't quit. No one else would go to the Pine Ridge Agency to track down the missing autopsy report—if the mortician actually did one, rather than just billing the tribe—and her death certificate.

All the others believed in the *Yuwipi* prophecy, the words of Old Sam, as if a prophecy could solve the crime. George had sent Alex on a wild goose chase off the Res to track down the "two white men" in the prophecy, and he'd disappeared, for sure. No word, no hawk feathers, no hands.

Someone had it in for JJ because she knew too much. Tate had been so sure it was FBI informer Night Cloud—his style, his modus operandi. Yet he'd had a strong alibi—speaking on the East Coast. Unless George was wrong, or lying. She hated the thought. After Alex, George was the most honest AIM person she knew. He might keep quiet about private reasons for his actions, and he might be deceived, but he'd not lie. She'd check the John Birch speaking schedule and find out for herself. It was stupid of her to have forgotten about the second FBI informer. She'd let Shuta send her off track for her own personal reasons.

Growing up, she'd thought the FBIs solved crimes and caught se-rial killers, not infiltrated civil rights groups to destroy them from within. Now she knew better. Since Night Cloud couldn't have killed JJ on his East Coast speaking tour, it must be someone on the Res, the second FBI informer that JJ had been seeking. Alex had warned her that he the informer was in Eagle Nest.

Outside it had snowed. Damn, another blizzard. She needed one of the AIM guys, a better mechanic than Lester, to fix Alex's pickup. Above the wind she heard the buzz of a chain saw and the whack of axes in the distance where Lester had moved his tipi back to the Sundance grounds. Even with snow, he had them hauling wood for the Sweat Lodge. He was still a drill sergeant.

She filled a bucket with oats, put on her parka and boots, and slogged through drifts to the corral behind the Sundance grounds. The ponies waited for her, snorting and nudging each other at the wooden gate. They could smell oats from afar. She whistled like Alex did for Bloketu, but the buckskin didn't push his way to the front. She sighed. He only came for Alex. Her horse, Midnight, pawed at the gate, crowding out the smaller Appaloosa ponies, roans and blacks. She pushed her way to the trough and spread out the oats. "Back now, back now," she talked to them as she checked the horses out.

No Bloketu. She panicked. Had Bloketu jumped the corral fence? Had one of the AIM guys tried to ride Bloketu and been thrown off? She looked around. Lester's big roan Shayela, was also missing. Was it poachers? Lester would go on a rampage and blame her for not noticing. But he patrolled the camp every night, and he would have noticed. The blizzard had wiped out tracks.

Maybe Alex had come last night, whistled for Bloketu, and was hiding in the Badlands, or invisible on a far hill, watching the camp.

"Lester! Lester!" she called. When she'd reached his tipi door, he'd opened the flap, already dressed in parka and boots.

"You want to wake everybody up?"

"The horses are gone."

"Since when? I heard them whinnying last night."

"No, the ponies aren't gone, just Bloketu and Shayela."

"My roan?" He ducked under the tipi door flap and came out frowning. "Show me."

At least he didn't yell. She started back to the corral.

He caught up with her. "When did you feed them last?"

"Yesterday."

"All here? You didn't check them out?"

"Of course."

At the corral, ponies circled. "Well, dammit, they're gone now. Horse thieves take the best." He brushed loose snow off the mounds beside the corral gate. "Boot tracks—small—yours." He squatted down to feel the snow. "Fucking blizzard. Gotta be tracks. I don't believe in ghost horse thieves, *wanaghi* spiriting them away. And no horse trailer got past us, not in that blizzard."

She moved away, circled the corral and looked for disturbances in the snow. On the north side she found a loose fence rail, then another propped in place, baling wire removed. She called out, "Look here!" She bent and brushed new snow away from the posts.

Lester ran to examine the loose fence rails. "Sneaky bastards left no tracks at the gate."

They brushed away snow until they found a trail of hoof prints and large pointy-toed boot prints. Touching the prints, Lester said, "One horse thief came in on foot from the pines, or up the Badlands Wall." He looked up. "Hell, how'd they get near my horse?"

And how could anyone get near Alex's stallion, she wondered.

Lester grabbed her arms and shook her. "Has to be Alex. He's back, ain't he? He came back and you helped him!"

"Let go of me!" She broke loose and backed away. "He's not around or I'd feel it."

"Sorry." Lester brushed his hands in front of him, as if he could brush away his words. "Must be a hyped-up cowboy, able to rope 'em in the dark and lead 'em away single file."

How could anyone rope a horse in the dark? She stumbled on a loop of baling wire in the snow, pulled it free and held it aloft. Quickly they rewired the loose posts into place.

"Hell," Lester said. "Pickups will plow into the first ditch. We got no big horses left, and them ponies will sink in too deep. Gotta borrow some snowmobiles."

"We have to go now, before more snow covers the tracks."

Lester stared at her. "Bring us Alex's saddle and saddlebags, food and hot coffee." He loped back to the Sundance grounds and yelled, "Warriors! Get up!" He kicked the tipis and threw snow in sleepy faces. Five or six AIM guys emerged and followed him to the corral.

Back to the cabin she made ham and cheese sandwiches, filled canteens, and stuffed them into her saddlebags. No way was she being left behind. Her horse, Midnight, was still in the corral.

Chaské at the door grabbed the saddles, while she followed with bridles and saddlebags. Lester, impatient, had caught the largest of the ponies, a skittish pinto. She handed him Alex's saddlebags and took her saddle from Chaské. While Lester calmed the skittish pony to bridle and saddle him, she caught her own horse, bridled and saddled him, tied on her saddlebags and mounted, ready for the search.

Lester, busy adjusting Alex's saddle, looked up at her. "Get off. I'm riding that horse."

She nudged Midnight forward. "My horse and I know the trail out to the Badlands Wall."

Lester grabbed her bridle. "Off," he ordered.

She tightened the reins and pulled away. "I have to find Alex's horse."

"We can't wear out the only horse left." He grabbed her boot. "Look, I weigh two hundred pounds, you weigh a hundred. I ride your horse, you ride the pony. "

She hated to admit he was right.

He brought the pinto around and handed the reins up to her. "Unless this pony is too spirited for you. He might buck you off."

Now she'd have to prove herself. Gentle, easy Midnight had spoiled her. She wasn't used to skittish half-broken ponies, but a saddled pony was better than riding bareback, like Chaské. She'd hang on. She talked to the pony the way Alex did to calm horses, and stroke his neck. Let Lester and Midnight lead the way, and she'd count on the pony to follow.

While they switched horses, Lester motioned to the bareback riders, "Pick a pony and let's head out. Follow me."

Tate followed Lester out onto the drift-covered land. He led them along the ridges where the wind had blown much of the snow clear, but at times they dismounted and led their mounts through the drifted gullies.

They tracked the prints to the pines, where they disappeared. Lester split the group in half. He sent Smokey's crew west to search the pines until they hit the highway. She stayed with Lester at the drop-off into Redstone Basin, where the wind had blown the rocky trail free of snow—and of tracks. They filed down the Badlands Wall past the old fasting grounds. No one had been to the Vision Cave since she and Alex had hidden there a week ago.

She'd never been this far down the trail. At the bottom, all the arroyos looked alike, flat without shadows, branching off into crumbly striated layers that led to more crumbly striated layers carved out by the wind and melting snow. Some outcrops looked like riders on horseback, some like three hags on a broom, some like buffalo stampeding. She shook her head free from tired imaginings. The sky had turned gray. It would be so easy to get lost.

Finally Smokey's group rejoined them. They looked cold and tired from riding ponies bareback in the snow and wind. "Getting late," Smokey said. "We'll look again tomorrow."

Tate ignored them and rode further into the Badlands. Behind her, another horse snorted.

Lester, mounted on Midnight, raced ahead of her. "Nobody rides into *Mako Shicha* alone," he shouted, "or we lose two people as well as two horses."

She reluctantly agreed, and let him lead the way, since he knew the land from childhood.

They followed the old rutted wagon trail at the bottom of Redstone Basin into the canyons that led to the old site of Lip's Camp and the graveyard from the 1918 flu epidemic. No one went in there, not from fear of the old germs, but because of the mass grave, like at Wounded Knee, and the sadness—every Eagle Nest family had lost half their relatives. It was the perfect place for horse thieves—water from nearby Pass Creek and a track, no matter how rutted, out to the paved road.

Overhead she heard the cry of red-tail hawks, daytime hawks, not Alex's "kree–kree–" of night hawks. That meant water nearby, and she listened for the burble of stream against pebbles. Wind-carved canyons leveled out to a snowy meadow ringed by bare cottonwood trees.

Lester pointed ahead. "Hoofprints. Careful, they're here."

She rode closer and looked down. The snow was scuffled and bloody. Ice must have cut into the unshod Indian horses. "No tire tracks, but do you see any footprints?"

"There's another way out of old Lip's Camp, east. Maybe they're off-Res and free."

She rode ahead into the open meadow and down to the bank of the iced-over stream. Her horse snorted and whinnied. She heard a weak whinny in reply.

"Over there." Lester, behind her, pointed to two horses standing amid the cottonwoods, a buckskin and a roan. Bloketu and Shayela.

This made no sense to her. "Why steal horses and leave them here in the Badlands?"

"Not horse thieves, or they'd be in Nebraska. Wait here, don't spook 'em." He spurred Midnight, and breaking ice, rode across and around the copse of cottonwoods to check the snowdrifts for tracks.

Tate eased the pinto into the broken-up icy path, crossed the stream and halted. She called to Bloketu in the distance, "kree–kree–," but he didn't lift his head or whinny in return. Neither horse moved. Something was wrong.

Lester met her as he circled back around, his face pinched in fury. "Only one fucking cowboy did this, and that son-of-a-bitch walked out east." He dismounted, and grabbed Midnight's bridle. "Easy now. Hold my reins. Stay here and let me walk in closer."

Tate took the reins, but dismounted. He'd seen something as he'd circled around, and was hiding it from her. She tied both horse and pony to a nearby sapling and walked silently in his footsteps. He stepped carefully, as if approaching a rattler coiled to strike. She was better at catching the horses; she fed them oats all winter, and she talked to them.

"Goddam!" Lester's voice broke and his shoulders shook.

She caught up to him and stared. "Poor Bloketu!" He'd been beaten, he'd been hobbled so tight his hooves had bled, he'd—she gasped—his mouth had been barb-wired shut, his eyes wide with terror. Inching slowly forward, she crooned to him in a low, sing-songy voice to soothe him, until she broke into tears.

Lester sidled up to Shayela, swearing under his breath nonstop, "Fucking maniac." Then he blew softly on the roan's nose and snorted a greeting. He waited until Shayela stopped quivering and stroked his neck.

Tate reached out to touch Bloketu, but he didn't respond, as if his spirit had left only a buckskin carcass standing, eyes closed, withers whipped, so she stroked his neck and mane.

Lester came up with wire cutters from his belt. "Ease into him, get his halter. He can't kick or run, he's hobbled too tight."

Bloketu opened his eyes and shied away. She hooked her fingers around the wire halter.

"Easy does it, hold him steady." Lester slipped the wire cutters underneath Bloketu's nose and with a ping cut the barbed wire loose. Bloketu whinnied and reared upwards, lifting Tate off the ground, but she pulled his head back down. He snorted and chomped, shaking his head. Bloody snot spattered them both. "Next his feet."

Tate held Bloketu steady while Lester snipped the forefeet loose, then the back feet. Bloketu stood still, then aware that he was free, stumbled toward the creek and fell down.

"Get him up, get him up," Lester urged. You pull on his halter, I'll push from behind."

"Can't we let him rest for a minute?" Tate fed him snow. "He's so weak and thin."

Lester shook her shoulder. "No! Once a horse is down, they'll die. Gotta get him up."

She stood. "Don't hit him." She grabbed the halter and pulled Bloketu's head out of the snow. Lester lifted underneath the horse's shoulders until Bloketu struggled onto his knees and up.

"Pull!" Lester thwacked Bloketu's rump. "Lead him to the stream to drink."

Tate pulled Bloketu forward two steps, then four. His hooves bled, but she led him into the water, spread his forelegs and bent his neck down to drink. At first he left his head in the stream, but then he gulped down water, raised his head, shook it, and whinnied. Tate could feel water-life revive him. He stepped farther into the stream where the ice broke, soaking all four feet, and drank some more. Even though she wasn't sure he'd be okay, she turned back to help with Lester's roan.

Shayela shied away from Tate, raising his head above hers. Lester lunged in, grabbed the halter, and tossed Tate the wire cutters. She picked them up out of the bloody snow. Shayela was skittier, more frightened, maddened with pain. Lester pulled down the head. "Quick, now!"

Tate reached up and under Shayela's neck, but the wire was embedded in the skin. "I have to get him on top," she cried. "Lead him over to that log."

Lester shook his head. "He can't move, his muscles are frozen."

Shayela's muscles quivered. Tate ducked to the other side and raised the cutters as high as possible, pushing the blade up and under the embedded wire. Shayela jerked his head, blood spurted, but the wire pinged loose and flew into the air.

When Lester regained control over Shayela, soothing him, rubbing cold snow into the wound, she bent down and snipped the hobbled feet free. Lester stroked the stiffened hocks and hindquarters, then led Shayela to the stream to drink beside Bloketu.

Tate pocketed a strand of old barbed wire with a two-pronged twist like the straight horns of an African eland. Some of the fencing on Turning Hawk land was new and standardized, but some was old, strung in the 30s or 40s with unique twists to the barbs and woven patterns. Alex might be able to identify it.

Lester pounded the wire cutters against a tree trunk. "Who did this? Torture a horse when you're afraid to face a man. Only a coward stoops to this kind of payback."

"There's a madman loose, someone who tortures animals and enjoys cruelty."

"It's a warning." Lester pulled Shayela out of the stream and rubbed snow onto his hocks. "This is pure rodeo meanness. I heard about it once over to Red Skaffold, an old-timer way to say, *shut your mouth, back off.*

Tate led Bloketu out as well, so he'd not drink too much, and rubbed snow on his hocks and withers. "Alex must have made someone very mad."

"Not just Alex. Me," Lester said.

"Maybe the warning is for AIM."

"Maybe for you. You ask too many questions."

"He didn't wire my horse Midnight's mouth shut."

"Probably didn't recognize yours."

"It could be a crazy Pine Ridge Goon picking on AIM, harassing Camp Crazy Horse."

"Uh-uh. Goons use shiny new rifles in shiny new pickups. Gotta be a rodeo cowboy who knows our horses. Sure to be payback for the riot at the Grange Hall in Gordon."

Tate stayed with Bloketu and Shayela while Lester rode out to get the camp's horse trailer and return with the other AIM warriors. The poor horses shied away from her touch. She spoke to them in a soothing lilt, washed away the dried blood with snow, and rinsed out the deep cuts from the barbed wire.

The winter afternoon grew colder and dark clouds rolled in. More snow coming. She hoped the AIM guys would return soon. She wondered if Alex had hidden in the Badlands as everyone said. But he'd have sensed Bloketu's spirit and rescued him. No, Alex was far away. As dusk filled the arroyos, she shivered. Perhaps the mad cowboy would return—before Lester. Suppose Lester didn't return—no, he'd return for his own horse. She'd been scaring herself, left alone at dusk in the Badlands. She stamped patterns in the snow bank to keep herself warm and alert, and sang the only sacred Sweat Lodge song she knew, to keep herself and the horses safe.

After Lester returned with horse trailer and feedbags of oats, Smokey and Chaské lured both horses inside, bolted the trailer doors, and the caravan of pickups and horses left the Badlands at nightfall. Tate climbed in Lester's pickup and huddled by the heater while he drove slowly back to Camp Crazy Horse, careful not to jolt the horse trailer going over the cattle gate. When they reached the log cabin, he stopped and said, "We have to keep the horses inside overnight to make sure they don't lie down and die. It's either here—by the piano, like Mr. Ed—or the Ceremony House."

"Not in my house," she said. "No horses are going to muck up my polished dirt floor."

He shook his head. "Ceremony House could never be used again." He turned off the engine.

Either place, horses weren't allowed. All the tipis were too small. The woodshed was full of wood, and the outhouse fit only one person. The horses had to be kept warm. Only the cabin's Kalamazoo woodstove would do. Horses were more important than floors. She didn't like the only solution, but it was inevitable. Their cabin was solid and big, but crowded. They'd make do.

Lester yelled out the window. "Okay, warriors, time to unload."

She climbed out of the pickup, opened the cabin door, and re-kindled the coals in the woodstove, still warm from a stoked ash log. The floor wasn't slippery wood but polished dirt that could be re-polished. She pushed the table up against the sink and rolled the log stump seats underneath the drain board. Then she called out the door, "Chaské, help me move the piano!"

As soon as Chaské came in, they pushed the piano into the southeast corner, the double bed next to the northwest wall, and Alex's workbench against the northeast corner. Only the woodstove and stovepipe remained in the center.

"Ready," she called, opening the bag of grain.

Lester led Shayela in first, forcing his head down through the low wide door. Shayela backed up over the threshold, but Tate coaxed him farther into the cabin with a handful of oats. Chaské took the rope, led him to the east window and tied him to the workbench.

Tate ran to the door to get Bloketu, but Smokey already had him at the threshold. She took the rope and led him to the west window and tied him to the bedpost. Immediately he leaned against the log wall, sagged to his knees, and collapsed, head down.

Lester yelled, "Get him up and keep him up!"

"How?" she yelled back. No way could she lift him up by the rope. His nose was too sore. "Do I prod him all night?"

Outside, a pickup revved and took off. Smokey and Chaské had left just when she needed them. Had Lester sent them to get more supplies? Or were they on a wild chase after the thief? Lester looked up at the rafters, sturdy cedar beams. "Got any old denim quilts? The kind you sit on at outdoor feasts and giveaways?"

What did he have in mind? Denim quilts as trusses? Thank God her wool blankets and sleeping bags were too short. She pulled two denim spreads from the foot locker under the bed and handed them to Lester.

She found a hammer and nails in the workbench drawer, and handed them to him. He pocketed them, climbed the ladder and as she handed him a quilt, nailed sturdy denim onto a rafter above Shayela. Without being told, she backed the horse closer to the window, passed the denim under his belly and handed it back up to Lester overhead. Long enough. He nailed the other end to the rafter. "*Washté!* He's trussed up for the night."

Shayela whinnied and beat his hoofs, but Tate brought him a nose-bag of grain and left a pail of water in front of him. While Shayela chomped down his oats, Lester talked to him in Lakota and brushed him off with his eagle feather until the horse stood still.

Together they lifted Bloketu and trussed him to another rafter. In spite of the denim sling and nosebag of grain, the horse shivered and refused to eat. She wished she had Alex's eagle feather. "Lester," she said, "Please brush Bloketu off, too." Then she remembered Lakota had no word for *please*. She hated to beg.

He climbed down the ladder and smiled at her. "I care about all horses, even Bloketu," he said, and brushed the horse off with his eagle feather as well.

"*Pilamaya*," she said. She'd learned there was a Lakota word for *thank you* after all. But you didn't gush say, *thank you thank you thank you* and embarrass people.

After the horses settled down, Lester filled two large syringes with penicillin and handed her one. "Watch," he said, and demonstrated where to stand and how to plunge the big needle into the withers without getting kicked. Then they smoothed antiseptic salve into the deep cuts, and forced each horse to drink water. Oats were for later. Horse farts, nose slobber, and wet hair smell filled the crowded cabin.

To keep the all-night vigil, they sat around the woodstove and drank black coffee. The horses snored just like humans, a soft-breathed *whunny*. Breathing with the horses, Lester sang an ancient horse chant of encouragement.

During a break, she handed the piece of barbwire to Lester. It was old and rusty, yet had held the horses tight. Two-prong was an old style, two loose ends twisted as barbs along the straight wire of a fence.

"You kept a piece?" He examined the wire in his hands. "Looks like it came from the old Slow Bear land claim, out by Black Pipe. Has to be Jerry. Even as a bronc rider at rodeos, he was rough on horses. He's the only man in town who'd be cruel to get even. Who'd remember the old Lakota meaning of the trick: *lay off.*"

"I don't get it," she said.

"Alex must have accused Jerry of starting rumors about him and *Our Lost One*. And Jerry got mad. Felt threatened. Medicine men can be spooky, you know. So the payback."

"That explains why Jerry may have barb-wired Bloketu, but why did he barb-wire Shayela?"

"We're AIM, and he's got a Boss-Indians-Around house and wife."

"I'm AIM, too. Why didn't he bother my horse, Midnight?"

"Question Box." Lester stood up and checked on the horses, as if to end their discussion. "I made up my mind. Jerry's the second FBI informer who killed *Our Lost One*. Barbwire proves it."

Not necessarily. As a rodeo man, Jerry would have known how to steal horses away silently. He could have barb-wired the horses, but not necessarily have killed JJ. "Wait a minute," she said. "You're jumping to conclusions." Nothing was for sure yet. "Did you send Smokey and Chaské after Jerry?"

"What?" Lester looked confused. "No, I gave them gas money."

So that's why they left so quickly. In the middle of the night, the only station open all night was in Kadoka, thirty miles away. They'd probably gone elsewhere, and not for gas. "In the morning, I'm going in town to show the barbwire to Jerry."

Lester grabbed her shoulders. "Bad idea. Wait until Alex comes home. Let him deal with Jerry. They're old rodeo buddies. Jerry's a tough customer, liable to hit you if you accuse him, especially small women. Rumor has it he beats on his wife when she bosses him around too much, which is all the time. His brother-in-law deals drugs, no telling what might happen."

She stood up and faced him. "And when will Alex be back?"

Lester shrugged. "You're supposed to tell me."

"Go with me, then," she persisted. "He barb-wired your horse, too."

Lester turned away from her. "No way. I steer clear of that family. Don't go face-to-face with Jerry. Catch him later on from behind, pay-back for pay-back."

Not Lester, the 'Nam vet, the platoon leader. He'd go with a bunch of AIM warriors, but he didn't want her going there first. She didn't believe him. He was too insistent, too sure Jerry killed JJ.

Lester spread his hands out, as if there was nothing else he could do. "Besides, tomorrow—no, today when it gets light—I promised Shuta I'd make a run to Rapid City."

"At least take me into town on your way."

He didn't answer, which meant *no*. She'd find another way.

<p style="text-align:center">~~~</p>

At daybreak, she and Lester released the horses and led them with oat bags to the corral to recover. They whinnied to the rest of the herd.

"Good sign," Lester said. "They'll be okay. Watch them two, so they don't lie down."

She'd get Chaské to do that. Or one of the other AIM guys asleep by the Sundance grounds.

As Lester ran back to his pickup, she ran beside him. "I still need a ride into town."

"Wrong direction. Gotta return this horse trailer over to Kyle."

Lester was acting strangely. Usually he wanted to be with her, but now he wanted to get rid of her, strand her at the Camp. She ran ahead and climbed into the passenger side of his pickup.

"No way," he snarled. "Get out or do I have to haul you out?"

She got out. He couldn't stop her. She'd find one of the AIM guys to watch the horses, and hitchhike into Jerry Slow Bear's place. In time both horses would recover, but Bloketu's spirit had been broken, and only Alex could bring it back. Alex was far, far away. If he were dead— she stopped herself. Never dwell on what might happen, only on what *must* happen.

Tired, she returned to the cabin, swept out the manure, and smudged the room with cedar. She sat down to make a row of red prayer ties from Alex's stash of tobacco and prayed at his sweat lodge altar. But her fingers couldn't seem to tie the knots tight enough and the tobacco spilled out. It seemed as if everything she touched turned bad.

"Oh, Alex," she said aloud, as if her words might reach him somewhere, "you're not here to heal Bloketu. You've sent no hawk feathers. And I've heard nothing on the Moccasin Telegraph. Like JJ, have you disappeared, too? If only the Great Mystery could help us now."

She fell asleep amid the tobacco ties and tossed and turned, caught in barb-wire dreams.

When she woke, she drank the thick boiled-down coffee on the woodstove and strategized before accosting Jerry. This investigation was so complicated she had to sort it into separate questions. First, who choked out JJ and dumped her body in the Badlands? Next, who cut off her hands? Third, who was the second FBI informer? What part did he play in these crimes, if any? Last, who barb-wired the two horses? Were these all acts of one person, or were there accomplices? If she could figure out the reasons, she could fit the pieces together. She'd start with the last and easiest.

Jerry or his wife started the lie that JJ was last seen in Alex's red pickup. Had Alex threatened Jerry before he went off-Res, and Jerry got scared, and retaliated? Probably. Jerry was capable of torturing horses. Camp Crazy Horse was deserted when she and the AIM warriors drove to Nebraska to catch Night Cloud. Jerry could have taken the horses then. Maybe he'd been jealous of Alex. Maybe an AIM-hater paid him to do it.

But was Jerry the second FBI informer? How convenient it was that he drove an ambulance, both on and off-Res, so it would be easy enough for him to contact an FBI agent. He was always eager for money, trying to gouge people with his secondhand car parts. But Alex would laugh at the idea of Jerry the Spy. He'd say, *Jerry's too dumb, but watch his wife.* Lester was wrong about this.

And what about JJ? Jerry could barbwire horses but could he kill a woman? If Tate could get inside his ambulance, she could look for evidence to prove he'd killed JJ. But that wouldn't work. Jerry was so proud of his antiseptic ambulance that there'd be no traces of blood or hair left. Even if she found any, Jerry would say that it came from the time he transported the body to Pine Ridge. Yet ambulances were equipped with medical supplies, including surgical knives sharp enough to sever hands. Jerry could have killed JJ, dumped her body, and then officially carried her body away. If so, did he have a personal vendetta, or was he a hired thug? She didn't know him well enough.

But why would Jerry kill JJ? Perhaps the FBIs ordered him, and he followed orders to keep his job. Or for money. Or to keep his big-boy toy, the ambulance with siren and flashing lights.

And where was he when JJ was killed? And when *was* she killed? He could have killed her anywhere, taken her body in the ambulance and dumped it in the Badlands gully, cut off her hands with a scalpel or bone saw. Who would stop him? He wouldn't be considered suspicious, on a run here or there for accident victims. Could the FBIs and Jerry have been in cahoots? Again, why?

Maybe Jerry came along afterwards, saw the body, cut off the hands and traded JJ's jewelry at a hock shop for more Black Hills gold. Still, it would be pretty stupid to cut off JJ's hands just to please his wife. However, he could have cut them off for their flashy tattoos and sold the hands to a souvenir collector somewhere. Still, she wasn't convinced by Lester, who insisted that Jerry did it all.

Jerry wasn't subtle, but he was big and scary. How could she check him out, first, about the horses? She could buy a car part, saying that Alex's pickup wouldn't start, and maybe needed a new alternator? Or carburetor? Instead, she might fake an injury so that on the drive to

Pine Ridge she could question him. Flirting wouldn't work, though. His possessive wife would go on the warpath.

After finding a horse-watcher for the day, Tate hitchhiked to Jerry's place, the piece of barbwire in her hand. His ambulance idled just inside the gate, Jerry inside, ready to go off on a run.

She opened the passenger side and climbed in. "Can I hitch a ride?"

Before Jerry could reply, his wife stormed out from their house and banged on Jerry's window, yelling in Lakota.

Jerry rolled down his window and replied in a rough guttural voice. Then he turned on his flashers and siren, and zoomed down the road toward Kyle and the Pine Ridge Agency.

Startled, Tate braced herself against the dashboard. It was too dangerous to jump out, but she grabbed the door handle anyway. Locked. She put on her seatbelt. "Is this a real call?"

Jerry, hunched forward and intent on the road, drove faster and didn't answer.

Was he pretending to take her to Pine Ridge Hospital, as if she were a woman in labor? Merely to escape from his wife? Or was this an abduction? Lester's warning rang in her ears: *Don't go face-to-face with Jerry.* She caught her breath. Had this happened to JJ? Had he picked up JJ hitchhiking, and once in the ambulance, she'd never left it until dead?

As the ambulance bumped and swayed, she improvised. She rarely threw up, but she cried, "I'm really sick. Stop, I'm going to throw up."

He spoke in spurts, as if words cost him effort. "Not—in—my—ambulance."

She tried to throw up, but couldn't. She must not be pregnant, then. She could only spit on the floor, which made him madder.

He drove faster as the road curved past barren wheat fields. Eighty. Ninety?

Was there a weapon within reach? She opened the glove compartment, hoping for a gun, or at least a screwdriver, but found only logbooks.

"My pistol's under my seat," he said.

She fumbled to unclip her seatbelt, hoping to climb in the rear and find another weapon. Then she realized it was in her hand. She held up the barbwire, the blood now dried.

Jerry looked over at her. "Where'd you get that? You been cutting fence out to my place?"

"Someone has. Two of our horses were barb-wired to starve."

"Horse thieves," Jerry said, turning back to the road. "People know Alex ain't around. I say somebody been messing with the old Slow Bear homestead, probably antique wire collectors, 'cause nobody lives out there no more. Everybody moved into BIA Housing in Eagle Nest."

She waved the barbwire closer to his nose. "I say *you* tortured our horses."

"Hey, I'm a rodeo guy, know horses, treat my own herd well." Swerving, he grabbed the barbwire from her fingers. His hand was large and coarse, and the barbwire disappeared into it.

"Give it back. It's evidence." She reached across the stick shift to grab his wrist with one hand, using the other to pry open his fist.

He didn't wince. Instead he shook her hands off and yanked his arm back into her face. "*Your* barbwire? You saying your horses got tangled in your own barb-wire fencing?"

The ambulance swerved as she fought to get the barbwire back, cutting her own fingers.

He grabbed the wheel and steered left-handed. "Lady, you don't know nothing about fencing. Tight wire-stretching, that's men's work."

"I'll take it to the cops myself." If she ever got out of this ambulance alive.

They fought, he one-handed, she with both hands. The short ends pierced her fingertips. "Ouch," she cried, writhing in pain, curling her fingers to stop the blood from dripping on her lap. She'd kept her piano hands safe from injury for so long. Would she be able to play again? Would the scars twist her skin so she'd become clumsy? Would she survive to play at all?

Her fingers bled onto her jeans. His palm bled onto the steering wheel and streamed down onto his driver's pants. Blood flowed onto the seat between them.

"Hey, this is an ambulance," he said. "I gotta keep it antiseptic."

If the pain weren't so excruciating, and the gushing blood so scary, she'd have laughed. The two long barbs had gouged deep into Jerry's palm. He hadn't cried out or even flinched at the pain, but his wounds were worse. Ashamed of her pettiness, she let go of her end of the wire. "Stop the ambulance. You need bandages." So did she.

He slowed to the side of the road by a dirt turnoff and pulled the brake with his left hand.

Holding his right hand aloft, he directed her to the emergency kit bolted behind the driver's seat.

She found gauze, mercurochrome, tape and Band-Aids within.

Sitting beside him in the rear of the ambulance, she pried loose the barbwire embedded in his big palm and staunched the flow of blood with gauze. "Now hold your hand up."

"Lady, I do this every day. You do it like this. "

They swabbed each other's cuts with mercurochrome and bandaged each other's hands. They put back the supplies, then wiped up the blood on the front seat and floor.

This was the absurdity of it all, getting wounded by fighting over a rusty piece of barbwire. What had made her so desperate?

At last Jerry said, I wasn't gonna hurt you. Just wanted to show you sump'n.'"

He drove out to the town dump, just a gully in the prairie filed with old metal, tires and ripped-out sofas. Crows hovered overhead, and even one displaced seagull. It was a swirling mass of maggots, putrid smell, and papers ruffling in the breeze, carrying decay. There was no gate, just a dirt track leading off into the prairie. He stopped beyond the dump at a burned-out building, remnants of logs and tarred roofing. Once it had been a log cabin, like the one she lived in. Once there had been a dirt floor.

He got out and walked around. "I was born here. Rode ponies before I could talk."

No one went out to the old Slow Bear deserted spread, past the stench of the town dump. The corral was empty, the fence broken down. No horses. In the distance she saw the bare bones of a fallen-in Sweat Lodge, a staved-in wooden bucket nearby. Jerry stood forlorn, the wind blowing his driver's coat open. She sensed his loss of the old ways of respect and Honor. His wife had moved him into town and found him a job. No more rodeos. Who wouldn't be jealous of Alex and Camp Crazy Horse?

On the ride back past the town, she was silent. It was clear that Jerry wasn't the killer. Jerry was a simple man. Whoever the clever second FBI informer was, he was JJ's killer. But how could she smoke him out?

The ambulance had stopped. Jerry had driven her back to Camp Crazy Horse's gate. "You can get out now," he said.

She left the barbwire in the ambulance. "*Pilamaya.*" Thanks.

Before she closed the ambulance door, he said, "The FBIs took her body and disappeared it. Buried before anyone knew."

CHAPTER 21
ALEX

ALEX KNEW AGENT SLADE chose not to stay with the other FBI agents in Rapid City's historic hotel, much too public and cramped, without electric tanning, sauna or bikini girls. No, Slade took the white Bronco after work and disappeared, reappearing at work with his California tan intact. He wasn't getting tan anywhere in Rapid City in winter. His personal hideout was somewhere else.

The only spa and exercise center in western South Dakota, according to the Moccasin Telegraph, was on the way to Mount Rushmore, at the new Black Hills Estates that didn't hire Indians. But Lakota construction workers had told of a luxurious three-story central patio turned into a tropical paradise, with imported palm trees thirty feet high and potted orchids around an Olympic-size pool plus a spa with Jacuzzi, sauna, tanning and exercise machines. Slade, the dude in FBI clothing, could stay there in privacy.

Alex wore warm dark clothing with tools and binoculars in his pack. He hitched a ride after dark out to the Black Hills. As part of his training, he'd helped Old Sam with vision quests on Harney Peak. He'd come to know the land that had once been part of the Great Sioux Nation. From the highway he took a hidden trail around the bend from the resort and climbed up the steep ridge through the pines for a hawk's eye view. Nestled on top of a granite outcropping, he took out his binoculars and scanned the gated complex in the meadow below. The air was cold and crisp.

A ten-foot concrete wall enclosed the resort from the road to the cliffs, spikes rising along the top all the way around. Convenient for Alex to rope and rappel over easily, avoiding the gatehouse at the road. Night watchmen in electric carts circled the perimeter on a schedule, easily avoided. But there might be dogs. Or trip alarms.

Lights twinkled. Below lay the inn and restaurant, like a giant W on the land, separated by a glassed-in recreation area with two pools. Behind the W, snow covered the tennis courts, outlying buildings, and a housing circle dotted with clusters of apartments. One with a white Bronco in front. Slade's. The night air was so clear he could see red smudges on the windshield where he'd spray-painted red hands only yesterday. He waited until most of the apartment lights went out. By then the whole rear of the inn was dark. Only the windows of the three-story pool room remained lit.

He hiked down onto the close-cropped lawn, climbed over the outer wall and found the Bronco in slot 310. He looked at the balcony above, with sliding-door windows. No curtains drawn. A square of light shone out. Slade was there, thirty feet above him. Alex calculated the distance. He wished he had his good lasso, but he'd make do with a salvaged clothesline, long enough. He hunkered down to wait behind a row of cars, sending his heat energy out until he became nothing but a dark shadow, as dark as his fear of intruding on private White property. He'd wait all night if he must, until Slade took off in his Bronco to visit Mabel or check in at the FBI office.

~~~

Two a.m. Alex stirred when he heard the door to 310 slam shut. Twenty feet away, Slade unlocked the Bronco and took off. Above, Slade's third floor balcony door was dark. Yet Slade might have left someone inside. He'd be extra careful, his first time at breaking and entering. He prayed that his makeshift lasso worked.

Alex used his champion calf-roping trick — if he missed, the calf charged, so he never missed. This time he looped the iron grillwork of the second floor balcony with a soft whoosh. Gripping the rope with his arms, he hauled himself up and landed lightly without a sound. Curtains blocked any light inside.

In a minute he'd roped the third floor grillwork and hoisted himself up to Slade's dark balcony. Slade hadn't drawn the curtains, careless, overconfident. Perhaps he'd installed his own alarm system, only relying on his gun when there.

Alex peered in, but heat inside had steamed the windows. In the hush he sensed no movement, no guard dog. Probably no pets allowed, not even for FBI agents. He checked the glass doors. No wires he could see, no sliding bar on the floor. Only a latch to jimmy. He took out Badger's glass-cutting tool and incised a semi-circle around the handle, then tapped lightly—*chink-chink*—until it caved in. He reached his gloved hand in, opened the door and slid inside. He hesitated. No alarm. Perhaps Slade only set traps on his front door.

He felt the heat immediately. Slade must keep his rooms so hot that he'd feel he was back in California. Alex breathed in the heated air, caught the drifting smell of marijuana, and with it a chemical odor, not brake fluid, not anti-freeze, but perhaps recently printed photographs.

He shone his flashlight around the middle of a white-and-gold living room. He'd be careful not to leave footprints on the white shag rug, and tape the glass disc back in place. How had Slade's FBI salary paid for his expensive tastes? Before him sat two white leather couches and a white recliner that surrounded a white marble coffee table. On it—he moved closer and sniffed the source of fragrance—a bowl of shredded leaves and dried buttons. So Slade had a source for peyote as well as grass. The Native American Church kept tight control over their ceremonial buttons, so he wondered if Slade's source, the second FBI informer, was a church member gone bad.

Otherwise, the sitting room was stark and empty. No pictures on the walls, no books, no magazines, not even an ashtray. Certainly no souvenirs on display. Anonymous, faceless, unused except for a stoner's white-out party.

Slade must spend little time here. Alex passed by an equally un-used kitchen and shined his flashlight down the hall. He turned the knob of the first door carefully. It might be booby-trapped overhead. He pushed the door open, but nothing fell down, so he stepped in, closed the door and switched on the overhead light.

He was stunned by the room's darkness. The walls and ceiling had been painted shiny black, and in the middle of the ceiling, a large oval mirror reflected that darkness. He'd entered another kind of un-derground. Before him lay a big four-poster bed covered with black leather. Metal dangled from each bed post. Alex walked closer to check out the handcuffs. Above the bed hung the only picture in the place, a medieval knight in full armor, sword at his side. Alex won-dered why a knight instead of a naked painted lady. Then he realized: the knight was Slade the Lady-killer.

A heavy carved chest of drawers with a lava lamp on top filled the bedroom. He slid open the top drawer full of metal and plastic ob-jects he'd never seen before, plus chains—some light, some heavy—a piercing awl, jars of oils or creams, a pearl cigarette lighter, a scal-pel—he shuddered and shut the drawer. Weird, creepy. He opened other drawers looking for souvenir teeth, ears or hands, but found gauzy scarves, nylon panties, garter belts, a riding crop.

He turned around. Dark mirrors had been mounted every-where—on the back of doors, on folding panels at the window. Even the floor had been tiled with dark reflective surfaces. The room reeked of stale sweat, alcohol and cigarettes. Piles of wrinkled shirts and socks, half-filled glasses and ashtrays lay strewn on the floor. Slade kept this dungeon for the ladies of the night he met at classy bars or this resort. Where Slade played. Not for erotic sex, but con-trol. Alex turned off the light.

At the end of the hall he found another door. This time when he turned the knob, he felt a slight resistance. The door was locked. He slid his knife blade alongside the door frame until the latch released. He turned the knob and felt another slight hitch, as if something overhead released if he pushed the door open. He stepped back to kick the door open. The bottom scraped across the thick plush rug, and white flakes, soap flakes, it seemed, floated down into his flashlight beam and onto the floor. Not a very impressive booby-trap, easy to avoid.

He stepped over the flakes and shined his flashlight around the room. Slade's den, his workroom. Glassed-in cases lined the walls. Alex recognized a beaded lizard bag, a horsehair braided belt, and other artifacts. Slade's private museum. As he'd suspected, Slade was a collector, but not of pottery and woven baskets. Curious, Alex bent closer to the glass. Inside lay scalps, fetishes, skin pouches, strings of shells and teeth, and what seemed to be dried tongues and ears. On top at eye-level a badger, its teeth bared, glared mid-stride at him. Next to him, a black-tailed ferret and an erect watchful prairie dog. Higher on the walls heads of animals stared at him, a deer with an eight-point rack, a massive white bear with glassy red eyes. Hanging overhead a stuffed red-tailed hawk, wings outstretched. He reached up to touch its tail feathers, felt its interrupted flight to escape. The walls closed in on him, as if he too had been trapped and become part of the collection. He shook himself loose and forced himself to search farther.

Against the far wall, bookcases. Books held in place by bookends. Animal bones. Shoulder blades. Femurs. Skulls. On the shelf below, taxidermy. Bound human feet, toes bent, hidden beneath. And below that, human hands held leather-bound books upright. Small dark-skinned hands. Delicate woman's hands, palms outward. Were they Joanna Joe's? He caught a whiff of formaldehyde, which sickened him. He hadn't really expected to find them, and not like this, stuffed and felted at the wrist. Even with gloves on, he dreaded touching them, knowing they'd feel alive, clutch and beg, grab his neck and choke him. He needed a purification sweat first. Medicine men couldn't touch death; they might disappear because they lived so close to the Spirit World. But it didn't matter. He picked up the nearest hand and turned it around to see if it had been Joanna Joe's.

His hands shook, his body swayed. The skin on the backside was totally black, including the nails. Not Joanna Joe's, but a Negro's hands. Or were they? The palms and fingertips were light brown. He fixed his gaze on the pores of the knuckles. Underneath the black dye lay the blackened edges of letters. RED POWER obliterated—almost.

He took off his black sweatshirt and cocooned Joanna Joe's hands, talking to them as if they were a like a stillborn colt about to be revived, ready to take their first breaths, *easy now, easy.* He tucked the bundle into his pack, stepped over the white flakes by the door into the hallway and halted, stunned.

At the other end of the hallway a tall blonde in a sheer white gown held out handcuffs. She had large full breasts, and between them dangled a key on a heavy metal chain. Had a female FBI agent caught him? For a moment he panicked and backed down the narrow hall until he felt a closet door against his shoulders. Then he realized that FBI agents always had a gun nearby. This woman wasn't about to handcuff him. She was just another of Slade's women, left alone too long. She must have hidden in the bathroom, afraid of an intruder, but then decided he was safe enough.

She smiled. "Want some, Black Face? Under that paint I bet you're hung and handsome." Moving closer, she invited him with her hands, enticed him with her stance. Perhaps she wanted him to handcuff her. Lakota or English, he was speechless.

He took a deep breath. He could smell her heavy sweet scent, stronger than wild roses. He'd wondered about making love to a White woman with fuzzy blonde hair all over her body, not smooth like Indian women. A flush of lust rose through him, desire, curiosity, perversion. To handcuff a woman to a bed, helpless yet eager? Would it feel like rape? Or like bareback riding, bucking but never losing the ride? He'd never forced himself on anyone, but he loved the thrill of willing resistance. Some of the AIM warriors bragged about counting coup on wannabe women. How would it feel to bed a woman his size, with long fleshy legs to wrap around him?

In the bedroom were handcuffs and leather whips. He'd never whipped a horse, let alone a person. Traditionals never hit their children. They used silent disapproval. What if he became the handcuffed one, and couldn't escape? Medicine men were tempted all the time. Some gave in to elk medicine and were lost to the People.

Her large pale arms opened to embrace him. "Come on, Indian men are the best."

He snapped out of his reverie. What was he thinking? He'd just touched the sacred hands. He'd forgotten his mission and he'd forgotten his wife. He'd almost become like the first warrior who met the White Buffalo Calf Woman, the one who lusted and shriveled to dust.

He saw the traps clearly. The Great Mystery was testing him on a spiritual level. And Slade, on another level, had set him up. He'd hope to catch Alex spread out naked with his whore. Beside the blonde he saw his pack waiting next to the sliding balcony door. As she came toward him, he grabbed her arms, pivoted, and pushed her behind him.

He heard the click before he felt the snap on his right wrist. He looked down at his wrist handcuffed to hers. Just what he'd feared. Cuffed to an oversexed cow. Why hadn't he fled right away? Instead he'd let a horny woman hypnotize him.

He whipped his free arm around to fight her off, but she dragged him back toward the bedroom like a bull she'd roped, his boot heels scraping along the tiled floor. He'd have to knock her out to get loose, though he'd never hit a woman before. If he could reach the hacksaw in his pack, he could rip the handcuff key that lay between her breasts right off its heavy chain.

She backed him against the bedroom door. Her pouty red-lipstick mouth loomed and she thrust her tongue between his teeth.

He almost gagged at the sensation. So this was French-kissing. He felt invaded, not aroused. Their noses bumped. Disgusting. Her tongue tickled the roof of his mouth, unbearably. He twisted loose, breathing heavily, struggled to say, "Stop!"

"Stop it some more, buck? Hey, I felt your hard-on."

He pushed her away, and with his free hand, clutched her throat

"Hey, burglar, should I call the cops?" She winked a come-on blue eye. "More exciting."

Much too exciting. She had blue eyelids. The nearest phone sat on the white table in the living room. She didn't use it. Or maybe she was supposed to call Slade. He yanked her handcuffed arm toward the balcony door so he could bend down and grab his pack.

Before he could reach it, she pulled him onto the thick living room rug and said, "I love you 'fraidy men." She bent toward him, smiling. From her free hand dangled another set of handcuffs. Who wouldn't be afraid, chained to her in a slow dance, all tangled up. He tensed. She couldn't catch him a second time. He swung their linked hands, his right and her left, over her head so that he ended up behind her, with his free arm bent under her chin in a choke hold.

She struggled to break the hold with her free arm. She had long arms, but he held her down. She moaned. He released the pressure on her throat, puzzled. He hadn't hurt her. Then, as she gasped, he realized that his violent move had turned her on. She waited for more, and more only aroused her. He felt ashamed, defiled. He imagined Tate's face, frowning in disbelief. He could never tell her about this. Sex for them was gentle and sacred.

He tightened his choke hold again until she threw her legs around his and knocked them both down face forward onto the plush white rug. She went limp. He crawled off her and turned her over. In the scramble she'd hit her head against the marble coffee table. He checked the dent in her forehead—no blood, only a swollen bruise. He touched her neck to feel for a pulse. Knocked out, not dead. "*Pilamaya, Wakan Tanka*," he prayed. Thank you, Great Mystery.

The key around her neck released the cuffs around his wrist. Soon she'd come to. But he didn't try to move her. Instead, he took a white shawl draped on a couch and covered her defenseless body. He felt sorry for her. She'd only seen his blackened face. To her all Indian males looked alike. Yet she'd tell Slade. Or maybe not.

He grabbed his pack, opened the sliding balcony door, leaped over the railing and down his rope, slick as a circus aerialist. Before any white Bronco could reach the resort's gatehouse, he faded into the starless night. Though he'd been careful to leave no fingerprints or footprints, Slade would notice the broken glass door, then discover his bookends gone. He'd rampage through Lakota Homes in Rapid City and harass the AIM houses, and then turn to the Reservation. But Slade would find no evidence. By that time he'd unite Joanna Joe's hands with her body.

Alex zipped the sacred bundle securely in his coveralls, ignoring the faint smell of tanned leather. Joanna Joe's hands lay close to his chest and his Sundance scars. Sacrifice next to sacrifice, ready for his holy mission. Cutting across the fields and pastures below the Black Hills, he let the stars guide him along the dirt and gravel side roads to avoid Slade's white Bronco. He ran across White rancher country, Custer, to Buffalo Gap, tracing the remnants of the old buffalo trail south. The herd route was safer, straight as a hawk flies, with no moon to reveal his shadow, and light snow to cover his tracks. He followed his ancestor's path, from the Stronghold, place of the Ghost Dance long ago, past Red Shirt Table south toward Wounded Knee. Dogs barked in the distance, coyotes yipped nearer. He longed for a safe ride, but couldn't trust anyone. When cars and pickups drove past on the distant highway, he lay down close to the ground to be invisible.

Near dawn, almost to Oglala, a rusted-out dull blue pickup with two old men inside slowed down beside him. Still, it was dangerous to be out so late on deserted Res roads, back from the bar at Buffalo Gap. Baling wire held the driver's door shut. The driver wore a sheepskin jacket and an American Legion cap over short white hair. An old-timer, a veteran from WWII. Alex could trust a Traditional Indian decorated with medals of honor. The other man also wore medals on his jacket.

"*Tokiya hwo?*" the driver asked. Where you going?

"*Chankpe Opi?*" Wounded Knee?

"*Ohan!*" Get in.

Alex was grateful. The Great Mystery was helping him on his journey. He'd be at the Pine Ridge Agency cemetery before dawn. Alex put his pack in the pickup bed, between the woodpile and groceries, tucked next to a chain saw and tire iron. Then he squeezed in next to the other vet, hoping they didn't notice the bulge at his chest in the coveralls. Indian way, they asked no questions. Instead, they offered him a smoke. They'd been to a WWII memorial at the Veteran's Cemetery in Sturgis, and afterwards had headed home to be safe on the Res, no matter how late.

As he listened to their WWII stories, he dozed off until Wounded Knee. He shook their hands and got out. "*Pilamaya,*" he thanked them. He lifted out his pack, now cold and snow-covered, and took the tire iron as well. By now he knew where they lived, and he'd return it later.

He jogged along the road to Wounded Knee, swinging the tire iron like a warrior's coup stick, climbed the path to the old cemetery, and entered under the curved iron gate. All at once the snow stopped and the moon came out. In the quiet he felt he'd walked into a different world. Only *wanaghi* lived here, ghosts whistling on the wind, and he could almost hear their cries in the silence. He walked among the gravestones and wooden crosses surrounding the mass grave. He brushed snow off the historic plaque that told of the 1890 massacre and wandered over to the AIM and full-blood section, righting plastic flowers on graves that the wind had bent to the ground.

No new graves. None in the unmarked section. Joanna Joe must be buried in Pine Ridge, ten more miles to go. He sensed the hands' impatience, wrapped in his sweatshirt, wanting out, as if they knew they belonged in Wounded Knee along with the other victims left frozen in the snow. As he patted his chest, he spoke to the hands softly, "Quiet. Not yet. We have to find her." He lit a cigarette, said a prayer, and left a tobacco offering beneath the plaque.

He ran on, mile after mile, following the path of his breath form-
ing O's in the air. As he neared Pine Ridge Agency, falling snow
shielded him from passing cars full of young bloods cruising.

He cut across the creek and over the rise into the far end of town,
and stopped at a bank of pines that sheltered the public cemetery.
He waited under them until he was sure no one else was in the "unknown" graveyard below, far from the main plots. New snow cov-
1ered the graveled road and fell heavily on the gravestones, but not
enough to hide any dark earth of a newly-dug grave. He found one
heaped-up pile of earth, a white cross, no name, no date. A pauper's
grave. He circled it, felt the earth with his boots, knelt and prayed until sure this was where Joanna Joe lay. He took off his leather gloves
and warmed the icy lumps of earth in his hands. With the tire iron he
scraped away frozen dirt near the white cross at the top of the grave.
He worked carefully, ashamed to violate the grave more than he was
afraid to be caught.

His journey had taken so long, it might be morning by the time
he'd uncovered the casket buried deep in the earth. The mound he'd
piled up could be seen by cars entering the cemetery. He gave up
the idea of reaching the casket with her body encased in metal and
wood. Better to bury her hands, even if violated and preserved, in the
earth as near her heart as possible.

He dug a hole and placed the hands in it, still wrapped in his
black sweatshirt, and sprinkled frozen ice crystals over it gently, then
clods of earth. Crying softly, he pounded the earth flat, scraped snow
over the grave and brushed it smooth with his hands. Yet he felt uneasy. Things were not right. Had he made a mistake? He prayed to
The Great Mystery, and told Joanna Joe that when he got home, in
the Sweat Lodge he'd smoke the Pipe for her. At least she was whole
again, and her soul released so it no longer wandered lost in the Badlands.

He closed his eyes and sang the Traditional Lakota prayer releasing her soul to send her safe on her journey to the Spirit World.
Caught in a trance, he sang the cadences high then low, over and

over, keening the Lakota death song, "*Maka Shina, the earth it is our blanket.*"

Behind him Alex felt a breath on his neck. He opened his eyes and turned as someone's hands grabbed his shoulder and flung him to the ground. He hung onto his small Pipe. A knee jabbed into his back, knocking the wind out of him. He reached for the tire iron, but it was too far away. He twisted and kicked at boots beside him. Someone yelped. Someone else sat on him and pinned down his legs.

A gloved hand pushed his face deep into the snowy dirt. He breathed in slush and coughed. Two of them. One sat on him, the other pulled his arms behind him. As he hunched his shoulders and raised his face to breathe, he felt the metal cuffs snap shut.

They flipped him over and dragged him away from the grave. Standing above him, Agent Slade brandished a gun while Agent Trask waved a paper at him and said, "We have a warrant for your arrest. Murder."

All this time he thought he'd been invisible. Instead, Slade had gotten his partner and they'd waited for him here. He hung his head. He'd been so naïve.

While Trask read him his rights, Slade dug with the tire iron, its thuds shaking the grave until he unearthed the black bundle and shook it loose of dirt. "Here's the evidence."

CHAPTER 22
TATE

STILL GROUNDED at Camp Crazy Horse, Tate had to find JJ's killer. This time she'd focus on JJ's hands and the missing jewelry. JJ had worn a Navaho turquoise and silver bracelet and a ring on a necklace made by Whitebird, each one of a kind, inscribed inside with a small script V, a winged bird in flight. Tate pictured the scene of death in her mind: blue-black bruises on JJ's neck, but no ring on a necklace, and no bracelet. Whoever had cut off her hands hand wanted them either for the tattoos or the jewelry.

Perhaps it was a hired killer, ordered to bring back hands rather than head as proof, as they did with Che Guevara's hands resting on a Colonel's desk in Bolivia. Someone who wanted to send a message to AIM: *RED POWER, you're dead.* Or it could have been two separate people: one person to kill her and leave her body on the Res in the Badlands, and another to come upon her body who wanted to take the jewelry, which was probably frozen to her body, so in a rush the thief chopped off her hands to get the pieces to keep or sell. No Traditional touched dead bodies. Maybe a wino did it for booze. The nearest hockshop was Scenic Bar, a few miles away, just off the Res.

She negotiated with Smokey to borrow his pickup for the day, and drove to the off-Res Scenic Bar, a hole-in-the-wall service station that pumped gas unwillingly for customers. Vern, the owner, made his money off booze and pawn. Everyone went there to hock, trade, or sell anything, especially Sioux beadwork and Navajo silver jewelry.

She'd never been inside. Traditional medicine men's families didn't mix with drinkers. They lived in separate worlds. But Smokey probably had been here before. She hadn't thought about Reputation. If anyone saw her in Smokey's pickup, gossip would grow. *The hell with it,* she thought. She was on a mission. Whoever had taken JJ's probably hocked it here, not in Rapid City a hundred miles away. Vern, the owner, was more greedy than careful. She'd heard he'd take anything valuable, no questions asked.

She pulled into the empty parking space in front. Three battered ranch pickups clustered around the side door to the bar itself, but no sedans or tourist campers. She recognized Yellow Elk's pickup. On the Res you knew everybody by the vehicle they drove. Out on the open prairie you could tell for miles who was headed your way. She hesitated, hoping not to be seen, but she realized any Yellow Elk would be in the bar next door.

She hated to go in underneath the sign, faded now but legible. Once, Scenic Bar had been a tourist spot. It was famous for its double sign above the door which said: *No Indians Allowed* in English, and underneath, in Lakota, *Indians Welcome.* Alex laughed, thought it funny as well as ironic, but she hated the racism and self-serving dishonesty.

As she entered, cow bells on the door jangled, and she cringed. Now she'd be noticed as she looked around. Yet the hock shop was empty. It was a collector's dream come true. Fantastic treasures had been hocked here over the years, and because Vern charged outrageous prices that only tourist collectors paid, they gathered dust in glass cabinets or on the walls. Fascinated, despite the price tags, she felt as if she'd entered a museum rather than a store. The history of her People, all their most precious possessions, lay before her:

Fossil turtle eggs, whole fossil turtles, oreodont teeth, mastodon bones, all dug illegally out of the Badlands. Buckskin dresses decorated with elk teeth or dentalia, beaded tunics and leggings, fringed leather vests, ribbon shirts, jingle dance dresses made from bent tobacco tins. Once-worn prom gowns and wedding dresses hung on racks. Painted shields, bone breastplates, fancy dance feathered bustles and large family sacred Pipes hung on walls behind the counters. The practical items sat in the back corner: chain saws, engine hoists, car jacks, fence stretchers; along with the necessary items: radios, TVs, CBs, tape players, reading glasses.

She walked between rows of glass cases filled with Lakota beadwork. On one side hung Pipe bags, vests and belts covered with geometric designs, mainly in white and red, but some in dark green, blue, and yellow. On the other side, rows of moccasins were laid out in pairs, some turned over so the beading on the bottom showed. These were burial moccasins, either never used, or stolen from graves on a hill where red scaffolds had once stood.

"Want sum'pn?"

She looked up, startled. A big, burly man stood before her, a Santa-Claus figure in red suspenders. A cigar poked through his streaked grey beard. He was not friendly but surly, not fatherly but miserly. He must be Vern, the tough old-timer who ran both bar and store. She'd heard he was his own bouncer.

"I'm looking for some Navajo silver."

He walked back toward the rear and gestured to a case of jewelry beside the cash register. "What ya see is what I got."

He stood there as if guarding the case. He must think she wasn't buying. Indians never bought, they sold. Only a few rich BIA Indians ever bought anything, and not at Vern's tourist prices. She stared through the glass to the black velvet shelves crowded with Lakota beaded earrings, hairclips, porcupine quill medallions, and black and white braided horsehair hatbands.

She laid her purse on the countertop and repeated, "Do you have any Navajo jewelry?"

After giving her the eye, he unlocked the glass door and laid a rough hairy hand on some shiny pieces. "Got lotsa nice Black Hills gold. Collector quality. Rings, earrings, pins."

Down at the bottom lay a few pieces of Navajo turquoise-and-silver. Silver squash blossom necklaces, a row of turquoise rings, a few inlaid turquoise bracelets. All were burnished with exact patterns turned out by the dozens. She stared at them. None of them were like Whitebird's, handmade designer quality. She was both disappointed and glad not to find JJ's jewelry on display. Vern could have it stashed away, hidden because it was hot. It was no accident that Vern's store had survived for thirty years. "I'm looking for a turquoise-and-silver watch bracelet to replace this one." She showed him her frayed leather watch band, then tapped her purse. "I can pay."

His eyes showed a flicker of interest, but remained wary. He closed the case and locked it. "S' all I got. It ain't tourist season, lady."

She didn't believe him. Vern always wanted a sale, and he always took in stolen goods. From his unease, she wondered if he'd kept JJ's jewelry back in his office. She couldn't leave until she was sure, but she'd have to wait. As she strode out of the Scenic Bar, the door clanged behind her from the cow bells hung on its frame.

Smokey had wanted her back before dark, before the bar got rowdy when Rednecks and Indians drank and fought. She knew she was reckless, but one person wearing gloves acting in silence could take JJ's jewelry without getting caught—provided it was there. Vern trusted in bodyguards and reputation rather than newfangled strobe lights and electronic alarms. His fears centered on bar fights. He'd installed bars on his office window, but the boards above and below looked flimsy.

~~~

In the Badlands Monument Tate parked behind a huge knife-edged wall of stone on a remote gravel road, and slept until midnight. The moon emerged from behind clouds, transforming Badlands outcroppings into shapes of horses and warriors. She felt like a warrior, too. Her luck was changing. She waited until 4am, then drove back through the Badlands without headlights. The town of Scenic was so small it had no street lights, and the hock shop and bar lay shuttered and dark. Only coyotes yipped out on the prairie.

She parked Smokey's pickup behind the main building, away from the oil tank and grain silo, and used his tire iron to pry loose the bottom boards of Vern's back office. She worked slowly, so the nails didn't screech. Pulling back musty insulation, she pried the inside boards away, propped the sill up with the tire iron and crawled underneath the steel bars.

It was easy—so far. She stood up, turned on her dim flashlight, and surrounded by the heavy odor of cigars, surveyed the room. At the rear he'd stacked metal shelves with items in clear plastic bags, like evidence bags at the morgue. A cold wind swept through her. She shone the light on them. Bones. She looked closer. Oreodont bones from the Badlands. Fossils. No boxes, no jewelry.

Vern was smart. His steel bars were all for show. He kept his valuables somewhere else. Here there was nothing but a wooden cigar-butt-strewn desk. She searched the cubbyholes on top, touching each item. A single worn beaded moccasin lay there, useless. A geode, cracked in half, had been left unpolished alongside broken dentalia no longer useful for sewing onto a dance dress.

She tried the drawer, which pulled out crooked. It was empty, except for a black ledger. She turned the pages, looking for recent entries. She found nothing since 1966. Yet the desk top wasn't dusty. It was odd, as if he'd only used the room as a retreat to smoke cigars.

As she turned to leave, she caught a flicker of light from inside the lone moccasin.

She shook it and dumped the contents out on the scarred desk top. There it lay, partially wrapped in tissue, a silver ring inset with turquoise, and beneath it, a silver and turquoise bracelet. A winged V was engraved on the back.

The bracelet burned like dry ice in her hands. She felt the silver weight dent into her skin and braced herself. Her arm felt numb. She slipped the bracelet and ring into her pocket. Each turquoise stone carried part of JJ's fighting spirit. It would be hard to wear the jewelry to get people to notice, but she'd watch their reactions, let them reveal themselves. She'd shock the killer.

She pulled out her neckerchief and wiped everywhere she'd touched clean, including her conscience: stealing from a liar wasn't stealing, merely recovering stolen goods. Alex might not agree with her, but he was far, far away, no help at all.

~~~

Back at Camp Crazy Horse by dawn, she put on JJ's jewelry—the turquoise and silver bracelet, the turquoise ring now strung on a chain around her neck—before she fell asleep. She'd never worn jewelry since she'd come to Camp Crazy Horse, since it got in the way of hauling cream cans and chopping wood and fixing fence.

She woke to a banging on the cabin door. Smokey wanted his pickup back. She'd parked it in front of the log cabin, gas on empty. Before he could chew her out, she gave him the keys, and handed him a twenty from her purse. "No gas stations were open."

Smokey stared at her, looking her over. She thrust her right hand in front of his eyes. They widened. Then she bared her whole arm. She watched his face as he figured it out.

"Wear those, and you'll get reactions," he said. "Not the kind you want. Somebody'll offer you a drink and roll you. Or think Alex gave it to you to hide, and stupid-like, you have to flaunt it in front of everybody. Nobody else wears a dead person's jewelry."

Sure they did. All the heirlooms in the world were jewelry from the dead. "I found her jewelry, didn't I?" Alex would be proud of her. "Now I'll find her killer."

"Or he'll find you."

That's what she hoped. She'd be ready.

Smokey looked alarmed. "License plate? Vern will have his thugs looking for my pickup."

"It was dark. No one was there."

"You don't know Vern. He's got his own network of informers."

"Smokey, I'll bring you gas and a new license plate."

She'd continue to wear JJ's jewelry and visit Jerry Slow Bear. George didn't like her leaving Camp Crazy Horse to investigate, but then, his sleuth Alex hadn't found the killer, or sent her hawk feathers, or come home.

~~~

Tate roused the AIM guys at the Sundance grounds to find the best mechanic. She waved her hands, dangling them in front of her. They couldn't help but notice the turquoise ring and bracelet. Yet none of them said anything. It was typical of the Res—no comment. Instead, they avoided her.

Finally Smokey said, "Chappa's the mechanic, not me."

Tate looked at Chappa. He averted his eyes. Something was wrong.

When no one else responded, Chaské said, "Hey, I can do it. I studied the auto books in mechanic class, and my dad says I'm good."

Again, no one among the work crew replied, but looked down and laced up their boots.

She'd heard the guys say that Chaské did almost anything to avoid digging post holes. She'd give him a try. "Come with me." She saw him give the guys a grin as he walked away with her.

"What's with the jewelry?" he asked as they neared the cabin. "Never seen you wear any."

"Aren't they beautiful?" she asked, turning to catch the sun as she brushed snow off the pickup. "Alex keeps his tools behind the seat. I'll bring you coffee and scrambled eggs."

By the time she came back out with breakfast, Chaské had propped open the hood with Alex's toolbox, crawled on top of the engine, and opened up the carburetor. "Got the keys?"

"Agent fucking Trask took them," she replied. "I know how to hot-wire. But something else is wrong. Whatever it is, Lester couldn't find it." She climbed in the cab, grabbed the screwdriver from the glove box, reached under the dash and touched the two wires together.

Nothing happened. If you had electricity, you connected your pickup to a bolt heater. If not, you covered the hood with a tarp and left a lit kerosene lamp underneath to keep the engine warm. Instead, Alex's pickup had sat neglected in a snowdrift for days.

"It'll start," said Chaské. "I just fixed it. But the oil's sluggish. I need hot water to pour on the engine block."

She didn't believe him, but brought out the teakettle anyway. When it was empty, she went back inside to boil more water. She heard the *unhun-unhun* of the starter, then the *clunk-clunk* of the engine almost turning over. She rushed back outside.

Chaské sat behind the wheel, grinning. "You give her another try, and I'll jiggle the carburetor, give 'er a little gas until she catches."

She sat in the driver's seat, clutch down and tried again. It almost caught. At the third try, the engine caught and backfired. She gunned it to clear water from the gas line. Another miracle: no one had used a siphon hose to drain out the gas. She'd make it into town. "How'd you do it, Chaské? Lester said it needed parts."

Chaské hesitated. He looked embarrassed rather than proud.

"What's the matter?" she asked.

"Some cables, distributer cap got banged loose. You must'a drove the pickup too hard."

Alex always babied his pickup. What Chaské meant was that somebody had loosened them to disable the pickup. Tate felt herself heat up with fury. Only Lester had been around when Alex's pickup wouldn't start. Lester had been both friendly and hostile. She'd thought of him as the older brother she'd never had. She'd been so focused on hiding her pregnancy that she'd dismissed his efforts. She felt foolish that she'd been so lonely that she'd let him push his way into her life.

"Where's Lester?" she asked.

"Not back. Said to start the sweat without him."

She'd tell George to move Lester back into town. No more duets. She'd bar the cabin door.

She jumped into Alex's pickup and zoomed up to the camp gate to head into town for George. Before she crossed the cattle gate bars, she stopped. A second thought turned her rigid. Lester hadn't only tried to count coup on her, he'd pried at her for Alex's whereabouts. What if Lester wasn't jealous of Alex? Instead, what if he'd been planted at Camp Crazy Horse as the second FBI informer?

Lester was older, a 'Nam vet. He knew how to kill. He was a mean drill sergeant with the AIM guys. Among the vets, only he had money for a fancy pickup. He was always taking off in it to Rapid City. And he was such a good liar.

Yet George trusted him, enough to make him his right-hand man. Lester was gentle with horses. He'd been helpful and kind to her when she'd had nightmares. And only he had helped her try to get Joanna Joe's body. She wondered if JJ had been his woman.

Who really knew Lester? There was only one way to find out. She drove back to the cabin. She'd confront him when he returned. She'd wear JJ's jewelry and watch him.

When she opened the door of the cabin, she caught a glimpse of iridescent highlights above her head. At the top of the door, slipped into a crack between the boards, fluttered a small dark feather. She caught her breath. It was a hawk feather, Alex's sign. He must be nearby. She climbed on a chair to catch it in her hand and hide it next to her heart.

She cleaned the cabin, smudged it with sage to clear out remnants of horse manure from the all-night doctoring ordeal. She folded up the denim quilts and aired out their double-zipped sleeping bag. She hauled water to heat for washing her hair. After she bathed, she smudged herself with cedar, and put on her best blouse and skirt. She laid out dried meat and prairie turnips to make *papa* soup, a special meal for Alex, but stopped. She hid her excitement. None of the AIM guys must know he was near. Instead, she made the usual pot of beans and *kabuk* bread, ready if they came over after the sweat to eat. And she changed into her usual work clothes, worn sweatshirt and jeans.

She needn't have worried. Only Smokey stopped by after the AIM guys' sweat to let Tate know that George had called them into town. He stared at the cedar flute on the piano. "That Alex's?" he asked.

"No, Lester made it," she replied.

He hesitated by the door. "Uh, Tate, that's a Lakota love flute. Used for courting."

Shocked, she realized what Lester had done. Lakota way, he'd gotten her alone. Unaware of the custom, she'd played along and had let Lester get too close to her. It was shameful. She picked up the cedar flute, beautiful but deadly, and thrust it at Smokey. "Put it in Lester's tipi!"

Smokey slid it into his parka pocket. "Didn't Alex warn you that some Lakota warriors try to count coup on medicine men's wives?"

That's why that lecher had disabled Alex's pickup. He wasn't being helpful. He hadn't fallen for her, a JJ clone. He was jealous of Alex, out to destroy him—them. How stupid she'd been to think that she could keep him distant because he was a talented musician who liked classical music.

"Alex told me to stay and guard the Camp." She listened to her words echo in the cabin rafters. "That's why you guys never came over after the sweat to eat the meals I cooked for you. You thought I—" She couldn't say the words. Had she ruined her reputation by staying on alone to guard the Camp? "He bragged, didn't he?"

Smokey hunched his shoulders and looked away.

"Lester lied." She stared at Smokey, willing him to believe her. "Alex and I—" she closed her eyes at the memory in her head "—we were married by the Pipe." When she opened her eyes she saw that Smokey understood what that meant: *faithful unto death.*

He put his hand out. "Tate, I'll take you into town, let you off at your mother-in-law's."

"Thank you, Smokey," she said, backing him out the door, "but I'll be okay." She could hardly wait until he left so she could touch the hawk feather beside her heart.

He looked doubtful. "You'll be alone. I can't stay, you know."

Yes, now she knew. No male could stay, not even young Chaské. No wonder Iná had been so insistent that Tate move into town. Maybe Tate had ruined her reputation. Iná was the worst, always reminding her about Turning Hawk Honor.

Smokey looked at her, worried. "I'll send Shuta back out to be with you."

She frowned. She didn't want Shuta for company, not with Alex hiding nearby. Then she had it: her protection. "Smokey, I'm not alone." She pointed to the far cabin wall. "See the Turning Hawk Pipe watching over me? That's the most powerful protection there is." She added, "Just in case, I'll bar the door." Still, she wished Alex were already waiting outside.

CHAPTER 23
ALEX

ALEX ACHED ALL OVER, his head, neck, back, knees, wrists and ankles burned raw. He lay sprawled face down on a cold cement floor. It smelled of piss. He raised his head and opened his eyes. After the red flashes of pain receded, he stared at the grayness around him. He felt trapped, enclosed. A coffin, a grave—no, a Rapid City jail cell—in solitary.

Gradually he remembered. He'd been lying in the back of the FBI Bronco, handcuffed and chained, his ear to the floor filled with the throb of tires, the Badlands darkness whizzing by outside. Slade speeding through the night while Trask sat shotgun. They'd forgotten about him in the back. He'd lifted his head with great effort to see Trask open the bundle on his lap and ask, "How'd Turning Hawk get these hands?"

Slade answering, "He killed her."

Then Trask, disbelief in his voice, "Stuffed, with velvet bottoms?"

Slade replying, "My informant says Turning Hawk wanted trophies."

Trask flinching. "Don't think so. More likely bookends for your collection."

Trask had been appalled at what he held. Slade must not have told his partner that he'd found Joanna Joe and kept her in a secret motel. Nor told Trask that when she wouldn't cooperate, he'd hired someone to get rid of her and bring him the bundle of hands as proof.

Trask wasn't stupid, but what would he do? Could there be one honorable FBI Agent? Alex despaired.

Slade had yanked him out into the blinding yard lights of the jail parking lot, where he stumbled as the chains bit into his legs. Trask, holding the bundle of hands, had watched from the other side of the Bronco. Alex had demanded an AIM lawyer, until Slade had kicked and punched him into blackness.

He moved his arm. No handcuffs, only wrists scraped raw. His elbow burned. He flexed his knee. No chains, only knees and ankles and toes bruised. No boots. Yet he wasn't naked, just wrapped in rough cloth. A jail jumpsuit. He touched his chest. He'd been stripped, everything taken. Except for the incriminating photo of Joanna Joe. After he'd been handcuffed, he knew he'd be searched, so out of desperation he'd slipped it under the floor mat in the back seat of the Bronco.

He opened one eye. Solid walls, floor, ceiling. Nothing else. Not a cell, no metal bars, only walls. No mattress, no shelf for a bed. No food. No water. A hole in the corner that reeked. He listened for sounds of others nearby, but heard only distant clangs and whirrs, an incessant muffled roar. No human voice. He was in solitary.

Though Agent Slade had killed Joanna Joe, the FBI would convict him instead. They had the hands back, with his fingerprints on them as evidence. "Caught red-handed," Slade had bragged.

He pushed himself up off the cold floor and stood up. He could almost touch the walls with arms outstretched. But he couldn't touch the ceiling with its light fixture overhead, covered with metal mesh. He banged on the solid metal door set with rivets and bolted lock. Faint light filtered through a slot. No bars. No window.

Beside him, near the lock, marks had been gouged into the wall, i's and x's, someone who'd waited by the door for release, keeping count. How many Indians had been buried in here, and for how long? No one knew he was here. He could send his mind out to Tate and Iná and George and Old Sam, but if they came looking, his name wouldn't be on the jail roster. No lawyer for Indians.

He paced barefoot in his cement cage, three steps by two, three steps by two, like a hawk caught in a net, round and round, his heart beating faster and faster, the walls crowding in, crushing him. No sign of the sun or moon or stars or sky overhead or grass underfoot, not even darkness, only a filtered grayness, hard and square and dead. He couldn't breathe. He slumped to the floor and put his head on his knees. Would he ever see Tate or his home again? Had the FBI come back and harassed her? Suppose the AIM warriors gave her a hard time and took over the camp? What if the Goons came back while George was gone and started a firefight? He felt so helpless. Why'd he cut his hair for a disguise? He prayed, "*Tunkashila, unshimalaye.*" Take pity on me.

As he prayed, he took deeper and deeper breaths. He felt the breath of *Wakan Tanka* surround him, fill him. They had taken everything from him—except his body. His mind. His faith in spiritual power. With the help of the Great Mystery, he'd rescue himself.

Day or night? He never wore a watch, told time by the sun or moon. He could sense which way was up and down, but which way was east? How could he pray without facing east? He focused his mind, let his bare feet reach through the cement floor, row on row of cement floors, down past the jail basement into the earth. Slowly he turned toward his left shoulder—East. He reached out to embrace East, yellow as the sun, with both hands, sent his prayers through the walls, and greeted the Great Mystery. He was not alone.

He looked around. No tools. He had only the zipper of his jumpsuit. And his fingernails. He sat down to work, unzipped his jumpsuit and leaned forward. He used the zipper pull to sketch a design on the East wall.

Much later, he heard muffled footsteps in the corridor outside. Cart wheels creaked, then stopped. He smelled bean soup. The slot below the window slid open. On a plastic tray sat a bowl of brown soup, a slice of white bread and a cup of brown water—coffee.

Alex reached up and took the tray. He was hungry, though the food looked unappetizing. He grabbed the spoon, disappointed that it was plastic, useless for gouging out his altar design faster. He swallowed the soup without thinking, then stopped himself. He'd forgotten to pray over the food. Other prisoners might think jail food awful, but for him, it was sustenance. Commodity fare. Nothing new—beans and bread—not good *kabuk* or frybread, but still bread. Not good thick Res coffee boiled on the woodstove, but weak tea-water. He'd survive jail food. His whole *tiyospaye*, his clan, had survived hard times on flour gravy and dried berries.

That wasn't the problem. He'd forgotten to pray, forgotten who he was, how he lived, walking the sacred path, the bright Red Road. They had walled him into a cement tomb, but he'd transformed it into a Vision Cave, high in the solitary wing of prison.

He'd give his body back to the Great Mystery, cry for a vision. Go on *Hanblechia*. Vision Quest. Even if he wasn't at the Vision Cave overlooking the Badlands. Even if it was winter, not the usual time in June. No Sweat Lodge, no *kinnick-kinnick* or Pipe or red felt or sage. No Old Sam to take him out, to watch over him for four days, to bring him back safe. No matter. His guardian spirit, Turning Hawk, took him to the Spirit World.

He had no sense of time, it too had been taken away—a tray of food was shoved through the slot. He refused it. He was fasting.

"Take it or leave it," said the guard.

To the East he carved out a white buffalo skull. Above it floated a sacred Pipe, and below, the scraped-loose white particles formed a small mound for his gopher hill altar. Not too deep, unnoticeable to anyone who passed by.

He began his Vision Quest. No Sweat Lodge, no hot rocks, *tunka oyate*, the Born-and-Ancient-Ones, no fresh spring water to drink, no sage to rub himself with. He created it all in his mind—the musty smell of ash on hot rock, the crush of damp sage in his hands. He took off his jumpsuit and ran in place, leaped into the air, and raced from wall to wall. The roof became bent willows overhead, enclosing the steam. He leaped to touch the branches, then dropped to the soft dirt floor, inside Mother Earth's womb now—naked we come into this world, and naked we leave it—until he'd raised a film of sweat over his body and his face flushed. He sang the Sweat Lodge songs, one after the other, no opening for fresh air—a mourn sweat, pour on the whole bucket and cry.

He improvised. His orange jumpsuit became soft green sage for him to sit on. His zipper pull, sharp from all-night scraping, became his knife. Four hundred drops of blood became his red tobacco ties that would surround and protect him when he entered the Spirit World. He prayed with each bead of blood, pressed his left thumb to the floor, and created a row of red marks—forty, eighty, a hundred, switching to fingers when his thumb quit bleeding, until hundreds of blood-red offerings marked off a sacred center. He stepped carefully into the *Hochoka* and knelt before East, his buffalo skull altar at the wall.

Then he raised his arms high until he felt the weight of the fasting Pipe in his hands, its soft red Pipestone bowl and smooth cedar stem wrapped in sage, and sang: "*Kolá, le-che-e-le-chu—*" calling to the Spirit World, crying for a vision, asking his Turning Hawk to come and help. He sang over and over, turned to the four directions, let its mournful cry fill his body and reach the heavens.

His *Hanblechia* began. He left the worries of this world, rose and soared above it, turning and turning. Everything became small, and then, with a flick of wings, he entered the Spirit World.

The day jailor left him alone, the food slot untouched.

The night jailor told him to eat—in Lakota. "*Wana wota.* Eat or they'll tie you down and force-feed you. They won't let you starve, but they'll try to kill your soul."

He heard the familiar words from far away, but did not answer. He sang and prayed. He chewed imagined sage and soothed his sore mouth. Two guards thumped on the glass window.

One said, "Stop that noise and eat. We can't let Injuns starve."

The other answered him. "Can't you see he's meditating? Gone into a trance?"

"He's gone over the edge," replied the first. "Your choice, Injun, the loony bin or sick bay."

Alex heard them from far away. He sang and prayed.

The guards unlocked the door, entered, and yanked him upright. He didn't resist, his body in solitary, his mind in the Spirit World. His knees descended two flights of metal stairs, his legs walked across a closed-in yard and down a lighted corridor to a solid metal door. It opened. His body stumbled inside. His nose smelled Clorox and stale sweat. His eyes saw the mirror window and Agent Trask standing beside it. Agent Slade grabbed his body, shoved him onto a bolted-down chair, handcuffed him, and sat opposite him at a narrow metal table. His eyes closed.

"Who helped you? Where's her rifle?" asked Slade.

His body remained in the deep trance.

Slade reached across and slapped his head.

His body did not respond.

Slade stood up and stood behind him, shouting questions rapid-fire in his ear. "Why'd you cut off her hands? Where'd you hide her rifle?"

His mind sang and prayed.

Then Trask spoke from his corner. "Grave-robbing is a felony. But murder is life. Meanwhile, your wife is in good hands."

Alex caught his breath at the words, but his hawk came and flew him away.

Slapped awake, hauled back into his cement cell, Alex sang and prayed, stronger than ever. His body had been dragged back to solitary, but his mind and soul had stayed at his *Hochoka*, his sacred circle. He hadn't left the Spirit World, hadn't broken his fast.

From far away he heard a rat-a-tat-tat on his door. Again. He stirred from his trance. The AIM signal? George? His heart quickened. No way. George must stay away from prison. An FBI trick? He'd heard the FBI had rats in prison. Then he heard the same Indian guard say in Lakota, "Brother, give them an empty tray, dump the slop down the shit hole."

Maybe the guard was AIM. But he couldn't reply. If he left the Spirit World, his *Hanblechia* ended. He wondered if the guard recognized the ancient fasting songs. He resisted the temptation to use Hawk Power to soar above the earth and swoop down to see his wife in her small world. Instead, he turned his mind away and prayed some more.

Still in the Spirit World, Alex's hawk brought him juniper berries to slake his thirst. He crushed them in his hands and soaked them in spring water to drink for his achy joints. Still facing East, he ignored the clank of guards striding down the hall, the click of his cell door opening. Let them drag him to the infirmary, no one could force-feed him. He filled his mind with sacred songs.

From behind him Agent Trask spoke. "Turning Hawk, you need to answer some questions."

Although he sensed that Agent Trask had come alone, he remained in his deep trance.

Trask squatted down beside him and asked quietly, "Where did you find her hands?"

Alex opened his eyes. Trask's polished shoes had stepped on the red gate made for protection. The agent hadn't noticed the blood. Or maybe he had, and deliberately intruded, not worried about getting too near a *dangerous* prisoner. Alex wrapped himself in a cocoon of energy so Trask couldn't reach in, touch his shoulder and break the fast. He sang and prayed in his head.

Trask rocked back and forth on his haunches. "I'm looking for evidence. You have a photo of the victim."

Alex remained in his deep trance, hardly aware that Trask was searching the cell for it.

Trask shifted his feet and braced himself with his hands on the floor inside the *Hochoka*. He leaned in closer and said in his ear, "Kidnapping a government witness is a felony."

Alex concentrated on the hands resting on the cement floor. Trask had no idea his hands had reached into the Spirit World, and that he'd never be the same. Alex smiled inwardly. The Great Mystery worked in unseen ways.

As if his hands burned from contact with the concrete floor, Trask stood up. "I need that information to help you."

The words *help you* resonated inside the *Hochoka*. When had the FBIs ever helped Indians? Yet *help you* filled his mind: he could help Trask, partnered with a rogue FBI agent.

Trask shrugged his shoulders and walked over to the cell door. "We're no longer interested in your wife as a witness." He banged twice on the metal door. "Remember: Grave-robbing is a felony. But murder is life."

Alex caught his breath at the mention of Tate, but pushed his fear down, and called his hawk to fly him away. He couldn't leave his *Hochoka*, the Spirit World, even for her.

Later, he heard the AIM rat-a-tat-tat signal again. Then, very faintly, he heard an echo of the *Hanblechia* song. The Lakota guard knew the words, knew the song, knew why he fasted. Alex turned around to face the door, and from the Spirit World asked, "*Tokiya hwo?*"

"Edgar. Four Horns, out of Red Skaffold."

That meant he knew the Turning Hawks, maybe his grandpa.

"I saw you, Turning Hawk, when you rode at Rapid City Rodeo and won the bareback."

Alex remembered that day, a good day to die, trampled underneath a wild pony's hooves, but miraculously he'd hung onto its long mane and hoisted himself back up when it reared and plunged around the arena until the buzzer sounded.

"I bring you food every day, but you don't eat. I see you dig at the walls with your fingernails, rock back and forth crying. I worry you might turn into a basket case. You got to get outta here before they come and move you to the crazy ward, electro-shock your mind. They'll say you cut yourself, spilled blood all over the floor, gone crazy and sing *ai-yi-yi* over and over."

He was still cautious around Edgar, who might be a snitch, another informer for the FBIs. Why else did they plant a full-blood rather than an Apple Indian on night duty? But he decided to trust him, and said aloud, "The Great Mystery keeps me sane."

Edgar shook his head. "If you think you can escape, they got too many lockdowns, electric eye, gates, razor wire, dogs—"

"When you sing with me it helps. *Pilamaya*." Thanks. Alex heard Edgar's footsteps go down the corridor. The pungent smell of sage floated into the room from the tray slot in the door. Alex knew from his last vision that he must stop the trouble coming to Camp Crazy Horse. Tate was closer than ever to danger. He'd left her alone for too long. He needed to fly home.

~~~

Ready to leave the Spirit World, Alex filled his imagined Pipe with *kinnick-kinnick* and smoked it to the four directions. His final prayer was for the People to continue strong for the next three hundred years, seven generations. He sent his hawk cry, "*kree–kree–*," out into the sky and rolled up his fence of tobacco ties to be burned in the Sweat Lodge. He stepped back into his concrete world, ran in place to work up a sweat all over his body, singing the *inipi* songs.

He hated to trick Edgar, his new friend. He'd made his preparations to time it right. He shredded his jumpsuit into strips for a makeshift rope, lassoed one end around the metal base of the overhead light bulb, and rigged the other end in a loose slipknot around his neck, ready to pull himself up, one hand underneath the noose to keep him from choking. He cut one arm with his sharpened jumpsuit zipper and let drops of blood cover the cement floor. Then he waited for the AIM rat-a-tat-tat on his door.

"*Mielo.* " It's me. Edgar slid the dinner tray through the slot. "*Wana wota.*" Time to eat.

Alex didn't answer. He pulled himself up to the ceiling and hung there, tilting his head at an odd angle, his mouth open, tongue hanging out.

"You okay?" Edgar looked through the slot, let out a wail, unlocked the door and rushed in to cut Alex down.

Alex kicked Edgar in the gut, then dropped down on top of him, swung a fist into Edgar's jaw and knocked him out. He tied Edgar's hands behind his back with the bloody cloth strips, and when Edgar moaned, stuffed some in his mouth.

Alex looked at his own hands, now bloody—hands dedicated to carry the sacred Pipe, to brush sickness off people with his eagle feather, strong hands to soothe wild horses and chop firewood, to heal not hurt. Forgive me, Great Mystery, he prayed silently, help me beat him up so he won't lose his job. Alex closed his eyes and pummeled Edgar. When he opened his eyes again, Edgar lay on the floor, curled on his side, his face puffy and bruised. Alex shook his shoulder. No response. This time the Lakota warrior had passed out.

He stripped Edgar of his uniform, socks, and boots, and dressed quickly. Then he picked up the key ring. "So long, friend. You must not be blamed, but end up in the hospital to get sick leave."

Alex stood, found the bit of sage Edgar had left him the night before, and placed it in his friend's tied-up hands. "I'll pray for you, and I will return your pickup and keys."

Alex opened the heavy metal door so it didn't rasp or clang, and stepped into the dark silent corridor. He pushed the food cart down the hall, thanking the Great Mystery, that all Indians looked alike, especially late at night.

CHAPTER 24
TATE

ALONE IN HER CABIN Tate couldn't sleep. She held the single hawk feather and waited for Alex's *kree–kree–* call. In her parka she walked from the cabin door to the outhouse, holding the rope guideline used for blizzards. Outside, cold and silent, millions of stars overhead kept her company.

When she returned, she pushed the door open and hesitated. Inside, something had shifted. She fumbled her way to the sink, struck a match and lit the kerosene lamp. Behind the open door stood Lester. He was supposed to be in Rapid City. She backed against the sink. "How dare you sneak in?"

"Been waiting to see you." He held his arms up as if in surrender.

She saw through his fake move. He wasn't harmless. "Bastard! You sabotaged Alex's pickup." She grabbed the heavy iron skillet and moved toward him.

He smiled. "How else could I get to know you better?"

Fat chance he could get her in bed. "You told everybody you'd counted coup on me and ruined my reputation."

He looked outraged, as if innocent. "Who said?"

"Watch out! This skillet can count coup on you." She swung it in front of her.

He backed around the piano. "I just came to get my flute. Where is it?"

He thought he was safe behind her piano. She advanced toward him. "Smokey put it in your tipi. Get out!"

"Put down the frying pan. I got news about Alex. An APB."

She was onto his ruse. Why didn't Alex rush in? Where was he, whatever was an APB? She held her breath and tightened her grip.

"Nobody told you?" Lester laughed. "Alex is stuck in Rapid City jail."

Lies. Alex would never get caught. He was invisible. He was nearby. She raised the skillet over her shoulder like a baseball bat.

"I came to warn you the FBIs are headed here, and Goons, too. You gotta get away."

More lies. She backed him away from the piano toward the workbench.

He reached his hands out. "I came to get you, so you don't get caught in the crossfire."

Crossfire? She was still frightened by their flight from the Goons at Pine Ridge Agency, bullets whizzing by, shattered window glass. But there'd be no crossfire here. Furious that he'd scared her, she shouted, "You want to save me?"

He moved closer, staring at the turquoise and silver bracelet on her arm, the arm holding the skillet. It was as if he'd seen a ghost. "The FBIs think Alex killed her. They caught him burying her hands. Now you're wearing her jewelry, more evidence. They'll say he gave it to you."

His voice had hardened. He'd come to get her, all right, so he could turn her in. She kept Alex's workbench between them. He made it all sound plausible. But it didn't matter. If Alex had found JJ's hands, then he must know who killed her. Stuck in jail, no wonder he hadn't sent hawk feathers—till now.

Lester edged closer and shouted, "You're the one who found Joanna Joe. You took her jewelry! Did you chop off her hands to get it?"

Lester had twisted things around again, but he looked genuinely puzzled.

With her free hand, she pulled out the large turquoise ring dangling from a chain around her neck. "I found where the killer hocked them."

He reached across the workbench for her arm. "Last time I saw her, she had them on. I want them back. It's all I have left of her."

So he had been JJ's lover. With her hip Tate pushed the workbench over onto him. "You gave her the bracelet, and the ring."

His voice was bitter. "You keep the ring. It belongs to George."

George? Tate felt an icy wind enter the cabin. The lamp flickered, casting Lester's shadow on the log wall, as if he were shaking with grief. Or regret. She said sharply, "You must have been the last one to see her."

He kicked the workbench and tools away. He loomed over her, fixated on the turquoise and silver bracelet that glowed in the lamplight. "Who gave it to you?"

She glared at him. Let him be confused. "JJ," she said, raising the skillet between them. "You must have killed her."

He shook his head. "Whoever took this bracelet killed her."

He was lying. She flexed her arm, felt her power grow, as if JJ's spirit had taken possession of her and unleashed her to seek revenge. She raised the skillet higher. "Tell the truth!"

Raging like a wild bear, he ducked down and knocked her in the stomach. Caught by surprise, she doubled over and retched. He wrestled the skillet from her hand and threw it with such force that it bounced off the cedar log wall and clattered under the bed. She crawled underneath to retrieve it, emerged on the other side, and whacked his knee with such force that the skillet flew out of her hands. He moaned as he fell on top of her and forced her down on the earth floor and wrenched the bracelet from her arm. She twisted beneath him, slipped out of her parka and eluded his grasp. Desperate for her skillet, she crawled toward it near the woodstove.

"Uh, uh." Limping from behind, he dragged her up and turned her around. With his bowie knife he slit her long johns neck to waist, exposing her faintly nicked skin. He stared in her eyes and let out an unearthly triumphant yell.

Deafened by his cry, too terrified to feel any pain, she clutched her ripped long johns and backed against the cabin wall. If only she could melt into the cedar logs and disappear. She pressed against the cedar logs and felt them warm against her back, as if they were alive. Above her hung the Turning Hawk Pipe in its beaded Pipe bag, left behind by Alex to protect her. She believed in Alex and he believed in the Pipe. Now was the time to pray with it, even though she felt unworthy. She was afraid to touch it, but she reached up and prayed, "Help me, Alex. Help me, Turning Hawk. Help me, Great Mystery."

Lester pulled at her raised arm. "Uh-uh."

She pulled the beaded Pipe bag down between them.

Lester clutched it in his hands. "This won't stop me!"

She heard a muffled shriek. Lester stood, paralyzed. He couldn't let go. His mouth opened in a terrified cry. As he bent to shuck off the leather bag, his hands and arms shook, but his fingers seemed glued on. His whole body trembled, as if a magnetic force had taken hold. She watched his hands melt into the old leather of the Turning Hawk Pipe bag, which pulsed and throbbed with life.

Once Alex had said, *the Pipe, it has me.* Now she understood what he'd meant. She believed in its spiritual power.

Lester stared at Tate as if he'd seen a ghost. "Joanna Joe, you've come back to me," he cried, his eyes fixated on Tate's face. His trembling hands thrust the Pipe bag at her, but it remained stuck to his arms.

Goosebumps rose on Tate's skin. He'd gone crazy, his eyes fiery, hallucinating. She knew then that he'd killed JJ, felt it in her body where the bracelet had burned like a brand.

"They wanted you dead—" His voice broke.

She didn't ask who, afraid to break the spell.

He backed away with his Pipe-hands and fell to his knees. "I loved you even after you left."

She didn't need a weapon — the Pipe had him. Had taken him over and broken him. He lay before her, helpless in the Pipebag's grasp. He'd killed what he loved, the saddest thing of all. He'd need forgiveness. The JJ she'd known hadn't forgiven him.

Could she, strong from the love she and Alex shared, give it? She let all her rage and self-righteousness flow out into the cabin's polished earth floor. Only then could she touch the Pipe. She hesitated. Fear rose in her again, fear of the Pipe's power to take over a person. After she stood tall and centered herself, she reached down toward Lester, placed one hand underneath to receive the Pipe bag. With the other she stroked his fingers sunken into the old leather. Only The Great Mystery could forgive him.

His fingers loosened, unclasped, freed. She let the Pipe bag drop into her hands, now just an old leather Pipe bag. Before it had glowed like a burning brand, filling the cabin air with crackle. Now in the dim lamplight, she could breathe again. Relieved, but without the power to pray with the Pipe itself, she re-hung the Turning Hawk Pipe bag on the cabin wall.

She looked at Lester, aware that despite whatever had happened, he was a liar, a lecher, and a murderer who'd sold his soul for a shiny red chrome pickup. "You have to turn yourself in!"

He looked up at her. "Never."

CHAPTER 25
ALEX

ALEX PULLED EDGAR'S PICKUP into the AIM house driveway in Eagle Nest. He'd escaped solitary, but still wore Edgar's prison guard uniform. George needed to know that Agent Slade was the killer. He'd had Joanna Joe's hands. Weak from four days of fast, yet strong in mind, the Great Mystery had kept him invisible from cops on the road. He gave the AIM knock on the kitchen door.

George opened it, stared at the uniform, and half-closed the door. Then he yanked Alex inside and gripped his shoulders. "Thought you was the law. Crazy man! FBIs have an APB out on you!" He took Alex into his bedroom and gave him jeans and a shirt. "Spill it, Bro."

As Alex changed clothes, he told George how he escaped from solitary, taking Edgar's uniform, keys and pickup.

"You been off our AIM radar, no word from the Moccasin Telegraph."

"I made myself invisible. Old Badger from Porcupine taught me to be a bum. No one sees drunk Indians in alleys. Until the FBIs raided their camp and burned them out, looking for me."

George called down to the basement, "Wake up, warriors, we got news."

When the AIMs came upstairs, Alex told them that he'd found where Slade had kept *Our Lost One,* helped by the *woluta* Joanna Joe had tied in her hair, a soap wrapper from Spring Valley Motel in Hot Springs. There he'd found Mabel Broken Rope, held captive by Slade to sign affidavits for the FBI cases against AIM. Slade had terrorized her with a photo of the dead woman—hands still on. How Badger'd rescued Mabel on his motorcycle. How he'd found the hands in Agent Slade's apartment in the Black Hills Estates, turned into bookends, part of a collection. How he'd stolen them and reburied them in Pine Ridge with her body. Only to be caught by the FBIs and arrested for grave-robbing and then, for her murder. So he'd broken out of jail to report the truth.

"Did you catch the second FBI informer here on the Res?"

When no one answered, Alex added, "I almost caught him meeting with Slade at the VFW Club. Agent Trask doesn't know his partner's gone rogue, and Agent Slade still has the hands. He'll use them as evidence against me, even though he's the killer."

George leaned across the table. "Camp Crazy Horse is the first place they'll look for you. You lay low on the Rosebud Res. Meanwhile we get our AIM lawyer on the case."

Alex shook his head. He'd lost his evidence. The photo hidden in a locked white Bronco. The hands hidden in a FBI evidence locker. A traumatized Mabel hidden with Badger. He said, "The FBIs are untouchable."

The kitchen door shook from a sudden pounding. Not the AIM knock. Had the FBIs tracked him down? He should have hidden Edgar's pickup behind the house.

"Hide under the stairs," said George.

More banging. In between, a horse whinny. Federal marshals on horseback? He ducked halfway down the basement stairs.

Chaské unlocked the door.

His wife burst in, hair mussed, parka muddy, smelling of horse. She looked straight at George, missing himself on the stairs. "George, it's Lester," she cried, "He was going to kill me. He's the killer." She caught her breath. Then she noticed the room full of AIM warriors. "Why are all of you up? What's going on?"

Alex ran up the stairs and embraced his wife. Her clothing was ripped. He pulled off his shirt and wrapped it around her. He brushed back her hair. "Who did this?"

"Lester," she cried, "He told me he killed JJ. He tried to rape me, but I got away." She flashed her eyes at him, as if seeing him for the first time. "What are you doing here? I saw the hawk feather and waited at the Cabin for *you—you*, not Lester!"

He'd been in solitary, starved for days, and had driven all night back to the Res. Of course he'd reported first to George. Urgent news about Slade. He'd found JJ's hands and her killer. Instead, Lester had been waiting—for his wife. Tears came to his eyes. He felt both impotent and furious that he hadn't protected her. He stuttered, "I'm s-sorry."

Noticing Joanna Joe's jewelry, he took Tate's hands and led her to the table. They sat down across from George. "You're wearing her jewelry."

She pulled away from him. "Not for me! To trap the killer!" She buttoned up the shirt. "You think I had time to dress? Start a dead pickup? Find a saddle? I barely got on my horse and rode bareback ten miles into town. And I'm supposed to look like Miss Indian America?"

George said, "Calm down, Tate, and explain." The AIM warriors gathered around them.

"Quick, he's getting away!" Then, realizing no one understood, she took a deep breath. "I found the jewelry at the Scenic Hock Shop. I wore it to find the killer—and I did. Lester's crazy, he thought I was JJ, and he tried to kill her again."

Her words made no sense. Alex said, "Agent Slade's the killer. I found his photo of *Our Lost One*, and then I found her hands used as bookends—"

"It's not the FBIs, it's Lester!" She pounded on the table. "He's the informer inside AIM. Just now he confessed to me that he killed her."

"Inside AIM?" Smokey seemed puzzled. "We got rid of Night Cloud."

She pounded her foot. "Lester is the *second* informant. You all still don't believe me?"

Now Alex was confused. Lester's Red Power pickup hadn't been in the VFW parking lot. He said, "Slade's informer drove a black Res pickup."

Even Tate remained silent. Finally Smokey said, "Lester had to repaint Red Power black after he ran into some Pine Ridge Agency Goons."

Tate stared at George. "Lester is the *reluctant Indian* in Old Sam's prophecy." She took the turquoise ring from the chain around her neck and handed it to George. "Lester said it was yours. He's gone crazy with remorse. He can't run far because he's wounded."

Alex yelled, "*Hoka hey,* warriors, after Lester!" He grabbed Tate and ran for Edgar's pickup.

Old Louie called, "Warriors, load up the guns from the basement."

～～～

Alex was so angry he ground the gears of Edgar's pickup as he headed for Camp Crazy Horse at full speed. Tate sat silent and brooding on the far side of the front seat. The fingers of both hands were bandaged. Her piano hands. Even more enraged, he asked, "How did he hurt you?"

She looked away and muttered, "Don't worry. I did it to myself."

Had Lester made her cut herself? Did they fight over the axe? He tried to imagine what would make Tate cut her own hands.

"Dammit," she said. "You sat there and drank coffee all night while you left me with her killer! Why didn't you come home first? Some hawk feather told me to wait all night. Then I wouldn't have had to fight off Lester myself."

He couldn't get used to the idea that Lester was the second FBI informer. It was Lester in his now-black pickup who'd met Agent Slade at the VFW Club. He would never have guessed. George hadn't, either. Why would Lester, George's right-hand-man, betray AIM? He lived by the military Code of Honor. He *was* AIM. He'd lose it all after they caught him in the Badlands.

Had Slade ordered Lester to kill Joanna Joe and cut off her hands for Slade's collection? He tried to explain. "I just escaped from solitary—I was sure Slade was the killer. He still has them."

She didn't reply. As they neared the gate to Camp Crazy Horse, she said, "Lester didn't cut my hands. I went to see Jerry Slow Bear. I took him a piece of that old barbwire and we fought over it. In the ambulance. His wound was worse. We bandaged either other's hands."

What else had happened to Tate while he was gone? He'd heard about the failed raid in Nebraska, and Lester attacking Tate, but cutting Jerry with barbwire while he was in solitary? What good was gaining Hawk Power compared to being home to protect his wife?

"I wounded Jerry," she said. "I meant to hurt him. Payback is a terrible thing." She reached across the pickup and touched his arm. "I don't want AIM to go after Lester. Can you stop it?"

Like water over a dam. He'd always tried to stop the flood of violence, but now? He shook his head.

"You've changed, she said. "Letting guns on Turning Hawk land."

He'd had no choice. Guns had already been on Turning Hawk land. First, Joanna Joe's, then Lester's. George had ordered the chase, and he'd agreed, angry that another man had touched his wife. Angrier now that Lester had betrayed them all as well by turning against AIM. "Don't you want Lester the killer, the informer, the seducer, caught?"

Again she didn't reply.

"Had to, to get back here. I knew you were in trouble." He couldn't have been in two places at once. Whatever he did, it would have been wrong. He had no answers. He'd been so blind. Now, on the warpath, would AIM take out one of its own? Payback for betrayal?

~~~

He focused on the road and raced in the gate to Camp Crazy Horse. George and Old Louie in one pickup, and Smokey with Chaské carrying Midnight back to the corral, followed. Behind them came the

'Nam vets' car with Ben, Dave and Willie, and the local hotrod with Chappa and Yamini. Enough for an AIM posse decked out with rifles and red bandana headbands, accompanied by war whoops.

He and George drove directly to the cabin and Ceremony House. Behind them, Smokey, with Chaské, led the other AIM cars to search the Sundance grounds, Sweat Lodges and tipis.

Their cabin door hung wide open. Leaving the pickup running, Alex ran in. No Lester. "Gone," he yelled out to George and Old Louie. But his home had been violated, a kerosene lamp smashed, his worktable overturned, his carving tools scattered on the floor, an cracked iron skillet beside the woodstove. Fortunately, Tate's piano in its corner and the Turning Hawk Pipe bag on the wall were unharmed.

Tate stood at the threshold. She'd fought Lester off. No wonder she looked so disheveled, so angry that he hadn't come home first.

"Go after him," she said.

"Bar the door and stay here until we catch him." He sensed her resistance. "Please. Or else I'll have to stay here with you."

Angry, Tate flashed her eyes at him. "Go."

Let her stay behind in the cabin. That didn't mean she'd stay. He hugged her and left, but waited outside until he heard the door bar clunk into place.

~~~

George and Old Louie searched Alex's small Sweat Lodge, the outhouse, and the Ceremony House. George yelled, "His pickup's behind the Ceremony House, but it won't start. He's on foot."

"He'd head for the horses," Alex said, revving Edgar's pickup. He drove over the rutted path to the corral behind the Sundance grounds. George and Old Louie followed. Ahead of them were two carloads of AIM warriors fanned out to search the Sundance Sweat Lodges and outhouse.

Smokey had gotten there first. "Over here," Smokey yelled from the corral. "Bastard got Shayela and turned the rest loose."

"Pile into the pickup, warriors!" The 'Nam vets and the locals climbed into the bed and George drove the ruts to the open gate of the corral.

The pony herd had spread out over the pasture, pawing under the snow for grass, but spooked at their approach, and headed over the rise. Alex found his own horse, Bloketu, standing listlessly by the water trough. He looked nearly dead. No time to check him out. "What happened?"

"Long story," said Smokey. He handed Alex a bag of oats. "Bring the ponies in."

Alex stood at the top of the nearest hill and nickered. The herd raised their heads, smelled oats and quickly surrounded him. He caught Chaské's red pony easily and led the herd back into the corral. Chaské leaped on, grabbed the tawny mane and raced out toward the pines.

Meanwhile Smokey had unloaded Tate's horse. He said, "Midnight's yours."

No time for saddles or bridles. Alex cried, "Bareback riders, leap on a pony and ride out with us!" In a flurry of snow he and Smokey raced to catch up with Chaské following Shayela's tracks.

When Alex reached the second hill, he turned to look back. Below, three pickups full of urban AIMs and local hot-rodders had driven up the first hill and down into the first gully, where they'd plowed into waist-high deep snow. Shouldering their rifles, they were following George on foot. He urged Midnight forward to catch up with Chaské and Smokey half a mile ahead.

Near the pines Alex saw a rail-thin roan grazing among the stubble. Had to be Shayela, as worn out as Bloketu. Cautious, he searched the thick pines for a sign of Lester.

Smokey rode up beside him. "He's gone. Once he got his Winchester 30-30 that he'd tied in this pine, he turned his horse loose. No damn good in Badlands shale. He'll leave no footprints once he's beyond the snow, down in Redstone Basin."

Chaské rode up. "Watch out. He's a sniper."

The three dismounted, let their horses graze with Shayela and studied the tracks. Lester had limped, leaning on a stick or rifle. He'd be easy to catch up with, but hard to get near. Cautiously they followed his tracks to the Badlands Wall. From below they heard shale break loose, slither and drop far below into Redstone Basin. Treacherous terrain, ice under light snow.

Behind them, George and Old Louie had slogged on foot to the crest of the ridges free of snow, and made it to the pines. Alex waved the armed warriors on foot to stay back. Why didn't George keep them in line?

Plodding through the last drifts, George caught up and asked, "Which way'd he go?"

Alex nodded at the old trail to where Vision Caves had been dug into the Badlands Wall.

George called out into the clear air, "Brother, we come to help you." The call echoed off the rocky escarpments down into Redstone Basin.

Behind them one of the ponies neighed.

Alex said, "He's far enough down, he can't hear you."

George waved the warriors nearer. "Then we move in until he can hear me."

Alex started single-file down the slippery trail he knew so well and paused at the first outcrop of striped lavender and ochre shale.

A rifle shot rang out.

Warriors dropped flat into the snowy prairie stubble. Alex scrambled up the slippery trail and back beside George.

Another rifle shot.

"Warning us off." George grabbed Chaské to hold him back and called out, "Lester, hold your fire." He turned to the warriors beside him and stood. "I'll go in alone, unarmed."

Alex pulled George back down. "We can't let him shoot you. What would AIM do without its leader? I'll go—he knows medicine men never touch guns."

George replied, "Even unarmed, he'll kill you."

Alex realized he didn't know the 'Nam-drill-sergeant, ruth-less-sniper, greedy-Red-Power Lester. Who knew what a guilty FBI informer, a desperate traitor, would do? Or what Alex would do to Lester.

Alex led the AIM warriors away from the trail and onto the east ridge to strategize. George took over, pairing the men into teams. Silence for a few heartbeats. Lester was hoarding his ammo. Sound carried in the cold crisp air. Below, Alex heard gears grind as a semi climbed Quiver Hill in the Badlands three miles away. Then he heard a distant throbbing, a helicopter coming nearer, loud and insistent until almost directly overhead. He looked up at the grey-green army camouflage that circled above them. FBI—coming for him. An agent in combat gear leaned out with a megaphone and told the AIMs to stay back from the copter.

Instead the warriors all stood up and raised fists and guns at the FBIs.

The copter landed fifty feet away on the flat bare crest of the oppo-site ridge, spooking the horses into the pines. A SWAT team poured out and formed a line on the west side of the pasture, M16's at the ready.

In response, the warriors lined up on the east hill and faced the FBIs, deer rifles poised.

Despite the SWAT team's camouflage, Alex recognized Agent Trask with an M16. Agent Slade wasn't with them. He heard Trask tell his men, "Subject headed down toward a cave."

Another rifle shot from below.

Agent Trask ordered George, "Stay back! We'll take him."

George leaned toward Alex's ear. "All Indians look alike to them. Let them take Lester, while you disappear."

Alex realized the FBIs thought he, Alex, was holed up for a shootout. They'd come for him, a jail escapee wanted for murder. He dreaded being returned to solitary. Yet he'd chosen to escape.

He must stop the confrontation before it turned into a shootout. He cried, "They only want me."

Before George could stop him, Alex stepped ahead of the AIM warriors toward Agent Trask and the FBI SWAT team. He walked west across the gully, hands outstretched, and cried, "Welcome to Turning Hawk sacred land and Camp Crazy Horse! You came on my land two years ago, smashed my altar and Sweat Lodge, looking for the man who killed your partner. This time you invade us looking for me. Here I am."

CHAPTER 26
TATE

TATE STAYED in the Turning Hawk cabin. No one had listened to her, not even Alex. She'd wanted Lester caught, but not by a manhunt. Besides, the AIM guys couldn't catch Lester, a veteran sniper, with guns. He wouldn't come in. He'd pick them off, one by one. It would be a massacre.

Guns had no power to heal. She'd seen the Turning Hawk Pipe catch Lester. She'd bring it to him again. Nothing could stop another shootout but a sacred act. Lester would shoot Alex or George, or even JJ's ghost, but not the White Buffalo Calf Maiden, the one who long ago had brought the sacred Pipe ceremony to Her People. All the AIM guys, Lakota or not, would recognize Her. Even Lester must recognize Her, accept the sacred Pipe and drop his gun.

She knew the story: Two warriors had greeted the White Buffalo Calf Maiden. One warrior, who lusted after Her, shriveled to bones and dust. The other warrior saw Her sacred light and accepted Her Pipe as a gift to bring back to the People.

Tate prayed for courage. She wasn't a warrior or spiritual leader, and hardly knew her language, but she was *Lakota*. As she prayed she unpacked her white buckskin wedding regalia, laced up the leggings and pulled on the soft white leather tunic, then her beaded moccasins. She braided her hair, and put her wedding wreath of dried sage on her head.

Lester might recognize her as Tate, and shoot her, or act like the first warrior. But she'd witnessed the power of the Pipe. The old

Turning Hawk Pipe, passed down for generations, had protected her.
She'd held it only once before, at her wedding, when the spread-wing
hawk on the bowl had overwhelmed her—as if only Turning Hawks
should hold it, and she wasn't a hawk.

She hesitated to pick up the beaded Pipe bag. Only hours ago it
had glowed with such life that it swallowed Lester's hands, and it
might swallow hers, too. She asked the Great Mystery, for permis-
sion, and lifted the Pipe bag off the wall. It lay in her hands as before,
just a beaded bag. She withdrew the Pipe, and held it in both arms
across her chest. Unafraid now, she let its power fill her hands, arms,
shoulders and flood her body. She stood tall. She became the Pipe;
the Pipe became her. She understood that when Alex said, *I carry the
Pipe* in English, he always meant the Lakota words, "*Chanupa leha…
the Pipe, it has me.*"

CHAPTER 27

ALEX

ALEX RAISED HIS HANDS to the Great Mystery to pull power from the sacred Black Hills, the power to erase the bitterness and pain of loss, the healing power from the land. Would Agent Trask feel it, too? He clenched his fists, wrists ready for handcuffs.

Agent Trask recognized Alex striding toward him but looked confused. "I thought you were in the cave below."

"Here I am," Alex repeated, holding his hands out to be cuffed.

George yelled across the dividing gully, "You FBIs are on Res lands. No jurisdiction."

Trask shouted back, "Don't jerk me around, George. He's a federal escapee from custody—our problem. Put down your weapons and leave."

George jerked his hand down. The warriors behind George lowered their rifles.

Trask whipped Alex's hands behind his back and cuffed him.

Alex faced the FBI SWAT team police. Though he couldn't free his hands to gesture while speaking, the Great Mystery surrounded him and filled him with words. "All we want is our Treaties honored, our Black Hills returned, our buffalo renewed, our Indian rights honored."

Gunfire ricocheted in the Badlands below. Trask said, "Who *is* down there shooting at us?"

"Lester, your informer. He killed Joanna Joe, and now he's running from us. We won't kill him, just drive him off the Res, like we did with Night Cloud."

Silence for a moment. Then gunfire broke out again. Two guns.

Trask grabbed his binoculars. "Who else is out there?"

With his long-distance hawk eyes, Alex stared down toward a flat promontory to the west of the Vision Cave trail. He caught the glint of sun on glass, binoculars beside an FBI agent three hundred yards to the north lying sniper-style on a flat outcrop, rifle aimed at the Vision Cave. Even in camouflage, his blond forelock shone in the sun. Alex shouted at Trask, "Agent Slade! Your partner! He's trying to silence his informer."

Another fusillade. Lester and Slade shooting at each other.

Trask shuddered. He'd just figured it out. He'd seen the bookended-hands. Now he saw his own partner going rogue. He took command. He pointed the megaphone at Slade and shouted, "Halt your fire." Then he called to George. "AIM, you stay back. We'll take care of this. We're going down after them."

CHAPTER 28
TATE

TATE LEFT THE CABIN and walked out to the AIM warriors after Lester. She wore her buckskin regalia and carried the Turning Hawk Pipe, her family's Pipe, the Peace Pipe of forgiveness. She'd prayed for it to protect them all. A great silence surrounded her.

As she neared the pines she heard a whirring in the air, as if many eagles were descending to accompany and protect her. Wind blew through her dried sage wreath. She walked down the trail to the Vision Cave, oblivious to the cold seeping into her moccasins, oblivious to the men with guns. Past the pickups, past the ponies turned loose, into the draw between the hills where the two armed groups faced off over turf and Treaty rights. She strode straight ahead, carrying the Turning Hawk family Pipe high in her outstretched hands. She felt the wings of the hawk on the bowl of the Pipe lift her off the frozen ground. She walked over prairie grass stubble, snow patches, slick ice, but felt nothing, as if she glided into a lighted tunnel into another world. She kept her head high.

She passed between the lines of warriors on each side, FBI to the west and AIM to the east. She saw their guns raised but could not hear their voices. A faraway voice cried, "Hold your fire."

Her walk between the AIM guys and FBIs had stopped them from shooting each other. Now to stop Lester. She did not hesitate, but entered the white tunnel and floated past them down the trail, past the Badlands Wall to the Vision Cave. She was inside an older time where no bullets could touch her. She sang the sacred song Alex had taught her: "*Chanunpa leha—The Pipe, it has me. I bring you the sacred Pipe.*"

CHAPTER 29
ALEX

HANDCUFFED TO AGENT TRASK, Alex heard a woman's voice in Lakota singing. He recognized the song before he recognized the voice. Before him came a vision of the White Buffalo Calf Maiden carrying a sacred Pipe and walking out singing.

Across the gully, the AIM warriors, those who knew the ancient story, stood at attention, silent and amazed. She floated on the air as if from an older time. Even Trask didn't stop her. She kept walking down toward the Vision Cave, into gunshot range.

She was carrying the Turning Hawk Pipe. Unmistakable. His wife was walking in a sacred manner between the FBIs and the AIMs down the Badlands trail, singing the old Lakota Pipe song he'd taught her. Helpless to grab Tate as she disappeared, he yanked at his handcuffs. "That's my wife! Stop the shooting! They're going to kill her." The Great Mystery was carrying her, singing, into great danger.

CHAPTER 30
TATE

TATE WALKED DOWN the trail onto the ledge that led to the Vision Cave. An overhang protected the entrance. She ignored Lester's rifle poking through a slit in the leather door flap, and kept singing. From behind her, a shot whined and split the rock wall above her into fragments. Shards fell down in front of her. Someone was shooting at her, someone with no respect for the Pipe. Not the AIM guys. Not the SWAT team. Someone else was shooting at Lester.

Cradling the Pipe in her hands, she ducked, pushed the leather door flap aside, and entered into shadow. Across from her in the small round cave sat Lester behind the door flap, his eye against the rifle. He knelt, braced against the rock wall, focused on movement across the arroyo. His answering shot shook the Vision Cave and echoed off the arroyo walls of the Badlands. Sweat dripped down his bruised face. He snarled, "What the hell are you doing here?"

She didn't expect him to swear, but he recognized her as Tate, not the White Buffalo Calf Maiden. No longer afraid, she said, "I carry the sacred Pipe. I carry it to you to stop the gunfire."

He reloaded his rifle. "Stupid! You think you can stop this? Once the shooting begins, it never stops until all are dead—or out of ammo."

She leaned forward and held her arms out to him.

He stared at her. "You dressed and came all this way to fuck me at last? In the Vision Cave? You are out of your mind." Another sniper shot drew his attention back to his rifle.

Above the ricocheting echoes, she shouted, "I came to help." Lester didn't understand her at all. He was *unshika*, pitiful. He'd betrayed all his friends, the AIM cause, and he'd killed his love. Thrown away everything, and for what? A fancy Red Power pickup. Holding the Pipe filled her with calmness. She had cared for him as if he were an older brother, both kind and cruel.

"You want to help? Distract Slade so I can get a bead on him, take him out before he takes me out." Then he stared at her hands. He saw the Pipe at last.

She held the Pipe out to him again and said, "The Pipe for the gun."

He laughed harshly. "You want to trade my gun for the Pipe? You're kidding. The Pipe will protect me from Slade? *The bullets will fall away*— you believe that crap? Didn't work for the Ghost Dancers in 1890. Won't work now." He fired another round, but his shoulders shook, his aim off. "Slade has a dark soul. He has penetrating shells, more ammo. He'll get me, no matter what."

She'd never seen him afraid. He'd always hid behind his 'Nam drill-sergeant mask. She held the Pipe out a third time. She waited, the Pipe heavy on her outstretched arms.

He reloaded. "I'm not touching that Pipe. You saw what it did to me before!"

She inched closer and knelt before him. He might be afraid of the Pipe bag, but not the Pipe itself. "That was then, this is now. I'm giving it to you four times. You cannot refuse the Pipe."

The rock floor of the cave shook from more volleys outside. The air became dense with an electric charge.

Lester let go of the rifle and took the Pipe from her hands. She noticed the change in him immediately. He stared at her, but saw through her to something bigger, as if the White Buffalo Calf Maiden had come inside the Vision Cave and knelt before him. He whispered, "You came to forgive me. To help me on my way. I did it for my sister, Shuta. Our family honor."

Tate hardly heard him. She pulled the rifle to her. It felt hot and hard in her hands. It wanted to be used. She could shoot him, knock him out. Like the Pipe, it wanted to be used.

He reached out and touched the turquoise and silver bracelet on her arm. "Forgive me, Joanna Joe. I always loved you."

She moved back from his touch, into a different stance, not with open arms, but crouching. She rested the heavy rifle on her knees, then braced it on her shoulder. So this was how it felt, solid. She could aim to make things right.

Then he said, "Forgive me, Tate. I told the guys I slept with you, gave you a child. I bragged about counting coup on a medicine man."

How dare he? An inner fury rose inside her. She put her finger on the trigger. If she pulled it, it would penetrate and kill. She felt a dark rage wrap her like a cloak until she saw nothing but death. Bam-bam-bam, anger released with every shot. What had come over her? He was asking her forgiveness, and she was ready to kill him.

He held the Pipe in front of her. "I don't deserve to hold this, yet you walked through bullets to bring it to me." He opened the door flap, stepped out onto the ledge, and stood underneath the overhang.

She closed her eyes and took a deep breath. Like the sacred Pipe, the gun had power. God-like power. The Gun, it *had* her. She stared at her hands gripping the stock. Appalled by its power, she crawled outside beside him and threw the rifle over the ledge, down into a deep arroyo, where it clattered and bounced out of sight. Lester stood in front of her, out in the open. She grabbed his body to pull him back into the Vision Cave.

He stood facing East. He shook her off and said, "*Chanunpah leha.*" He raised his arms to the Great Mystery. He held the Turning Hawk Pipe aloft, unafraid. His chest swelled and he opened his mouth. Out came a tortured, twisted high cry of pain, anguish, and strength, a song she'd never heard, a song that made her cry, so piercing to the heart. Its cry floated high on the wind, wailing down, down, deep and strong. "*Chanunpah leha—*"

A rifle shot whizzed by her and hit Lester. It echoed off the arroyo walls. "*BOOM-boom-boom*." Holding the Pipe aloft, he kept singing.

She cried out. How could the Pipe not protect him, as it had protected her?

Another shot hit his back. He slumped against the rock wall, but kept singing.

She realized he was on his final vision quest. He was singing his death song, having chosen Honor in death rather than capture and prison. She tried to staunch the flow of blood. When he choked, no longer able to sing or stand, but still clutching the Pipe, she dragged him back into the Vision Cave. He was bleeding profusely, his eyes fluttering, his breath heavy, his pulse uneven. She lay down beside him and rested his head in her lap. Blood covered her white buckskin tunic. She didn't know the song, couldn't keep it going to the end.

Then she heard men's voices, Alex's voice, too, from afar, singing in Lakota. They must have heard Lester crying to the Great Mystery, and were finishing his prayer song for him.

CHAPTER 31
ALEX

TATE HAD DISAPPEARED. Alex couldn't bear the silence, then the gunshots from Slade. Amid the echoes bouncing off the Badlands Wall, he heard a shout. "Lady, move away." He knew the voice. Agent Slade had been shooting at his wife. He jerked the cuffs at Trask. "Stop your partner!"

Agent Trask called, "Anybody have a visual?"

Down among the arroyo walls, rifle shots echoed. "*BOOM-boom-boom!*"

Agent Trask shouted down to Agent Slade, "Hold your fire! We're heading down!"

All Alex could do was to call his hawk to protect her. He gave a great cry, "*kree–kree–.*"

A single rifle shot echoed off the arroyo walls. "*BOOM-boom-boom!*"

Below them a Lakota warrior cry rose from the Vision Cave, the start of a Traditional victory song. But Lester must have been hit badly, because it was a victory-in-death song. When the high-pitched cry choked off, Alex, raising his shackled hands in the air, sang the rest of the Lakota victory cry. Loud and clear, the AIM warriors joined in, but he wondered how many of them knew what it meant. Lester was dying. But was Tate safe? Had she been hit, too?

And where was the Turning Hawk Pipe? Even without it he was not helpless. He had Hawk Power. He swelled his chest and called for his hawk, "*kree–kree–,*" and prayed. Above them, as if startled by the shots, a dark shape loomed like a thunderhead and rose in the air. It circled higher and higher overhead, the outline of a hawk's dark wings etched into the sky.

"*Kree-kree-,*" Alex called to his hawk in warning, afraid that the FBIs might shoot his bird.

Instead of fleeing, the hawk circled directly over Agent Slade, who lifted his sniper rifle upward to catch the bird in his sights.

With his mind Alex sent out a Hawk Power command. His hawk gave a sharp cry in response, "*kree-kree-,*" folded its wings, and dived, a hundred miles an hour, straight at the sniper below. As the hawk plummeted toward the rocky promontory, Alex saw Agent Slade dodge and roll backwards to aim, then slip and fire shots wildly. Off balance, Slade fell into a deep gash in the rocks, and tumbled with a hoarse cry down the steep crevice into Redstone Basin a thousand feet below. Then silence.

Handcuffed and chained to Agent Trask, Alex walked with him to look out over the Badlands Wall. Far below them Slade's body lay twisted at an unnatural angle, unmoving. Hawk Power circled above, then spread its wings and landed on the promontory. As its cry, "*kree-kree-,*" echoed off the Badlands Wall, the gigantic hawk rose again and vanished.

CHAPTER 32
TATE

AFTER THE FBIS had taken away the bodies of Agent Slade and Lester Bear Heart, the AIM warriors had gathered at the Sundance grounds for a purification sweat, where an evening peace settled over Crazy Horse Camp. They'd pray for the lost souls, Indian and White, and banish the evil from the land. Balance would be restored. Camp Crazy Horse would continue. She'd make sure everything was back in place when Alex returned.

She heard gears grind on the road leading down to the camp. It had to be a rattletrap Reservation car. All the AIM guys were already at the Sweat Lodge. She left the stew cooking on the woodstove and walked over to the Sundance arbor.

An old motorcycle crested the dip in the trail and slithered down toward her. With a bang and a wheeze, it pulled up to the Sundance fence and died. Two figures climbed off.

"*Hau!*" A wrinkled codger walked towards her. "You Alex's *tai-chu?* Name's Badger, Ma'am." Was this someone Alex had picked up on his mission? He bowed to her, more like Chinese-style, certainly not Lakota. "He said you'd hide Mabel. FBIs are still after her. Told us how lovely and loyal and musical you are."

She was suspicious. He was sweet-talking her already. The driver didn't look like AIM, not even close to Old Louie, who knew all the articles of the Treaty rights and Lakota history.

Here comes more trouble, she thought, double trouble. A shape-less woman with a white streak in the middle of her long black hair

299

climbed off the cycle. She wore a black fur coat that had probably come from a thrift store. Her bare feet were blue from the cold.

"Now, Mabel here, can teach you Lakota—women's Lakota, not men's. Knows all about picking and drying wild plums and choke-cherries, wild turnips and herbs and sweetgrass— " He paused for breath. "— butchering and drying meat and *tanigha* and *wahanpi* and *wojapi*." He stopped and swept his arm toward the AIM guys around the firepit. "Feed the warriors good."

She turned to Badger, shook his hand and checked his breath. "You're just in time for a sweat. Sweat out all that alcohol in your veins."

"That, too. We come to get away from booze."

Alex had talked about some day Camp Crazy Horse becoming an AA rehab center. She'd let Smokey handle this one.

Mabel asked, "You got a bathroom here?"

Tate pointed to the Sundance outhouse. "I'll find you some shoes."

"A shit-house?" Mabel cried. She beat Badger with her large purse. "You promised I'd have hot and cold running water and a bathroom so I can put on my makeup."

Tate stifled a laugh. Though Badger cringed and ducked, Mabel, at less than five feet, landed whack-whack blows with every curse word, then disappeared into the outhouse. She'd not intervene.

Without a word Badger stumbled over to the safety of the AIM guys around the sweat, where he recovered with a cigarette in his mouth, talking nonstop in Lakota.

"Tate," Smokey called from the fire pit. "Feed Mabel at the cabin."

If Smokey knew who she was, the woman must be okay. She walked over to him and whispered, "Who are they? Where will we put them, with me in the cabin, or in the Ceremony House?"

"Figure it out later. Try to make Mabel at home. Get her talking, ask her anything, but keep her away from the sweat."

She led Mabel, barefoot, to their log cabin where coffee and beef stew waited. Mabel sat in a chair by the woodstove and faced the door, braced as if expecting someone to burst in. Perhaps Mabel was afraid of Smokey. She certainly wasn't afraid of Badger.

"Alex says you'll hide me from Billy," Mabel said at last.

While Mabel drank hot coffee, Tate searched Alex's clothes for wool socks and a pair of moccasins to fit Mabel's large feet. "There's no *Billy* here," Tate said, "not even in Eagle Nest."

"You don't know Billy. He said he'd kill me." Mabel looked around for a place to hide.

"Eat your stew and put on these socks and moccasins," said Tate in a calm voice. "I'll hide you in the Ceremony House. No one dares search there." Except the FBIs, which Mabel didn't know about. Tate gathered bedding in her arms and led Mabel to sleep there, hidden beneath old blankets. On her way back to the cabin, Tate saw a black pickup pull up to the Sundance grounds. Someone had come too late for the men's sweat. Not Alex, still not out on bail. Better not be a *Billy*.

After their sweat, the AIM guys came over to the cabin for stew, frybread and coffee. Usually the men ate first, talked and smoked later, but with a new audience for his stories, Badger ate and talked all at once.

As she stood by the sink, Badger said, "Yer old man was in solitary. The winos overnight in the drunk tank said somebody sang *Hanblechia* songs all night. Had to be him." Badger handed her a newspaper, the *Rapid City Journal*. The front page read: *Prisoner Escapes*, and below it, his name, *Alex Turning Hawk*. She wished he hadn't become famous. Now Alex would have to go to trial, maybe even out-of-state, gone as much as George was from Shuta.

Badger laughed. "Figured he'd come home to you first. Got himself in lots more trouble. I come to warn him."

"You're too late. He's come and gone." Badger had brought more trouble. She couldn't see Mabel moving into one of the AIM tipis at the Sundance grounds. She wasn't ready to turn Crazy Horse Camp into an Indian Alcoholics Anonymous Center, no matter whoever Alex had said could come and stay. The Ceremony House had almost been used as a horse stable. Since Alex was gone, it looked like the old couple must stay in the cabin. She couldn't take Mabel into Iná's house in town. Or—she could move into town. Which was worse? She had a feeling she'd find out.

~~~

Before the AIM guys left for town, Tate took Smokey aside. "Who came late to the sweat? Mabel's afraid of a guy called Billy."

"George don't know it yet, but Shuta's over to the Sundance grounds, putting on rocks, waiting for you to take sweat with her. Asked me to tell you, but it's late. You don't have to go."

But she did. Everyone but Shuta had seen her wear JJ's jewelry. She'd kept it in a leather parfleche under the bed, waiting until Alex returned to bury JJ with her jewelry out on the land. She slid the turquoise bracelet on her arm and the ring strung as a necklace around her neck. Armed with JJ's *bank account*, she walked into the night to confront Shuta at the Sundance grounds.

Lester's black pickup had been transformed by four new tires and stock rack that held Lester's horse, Shayela, tossing his head and pawing at the slat floor. Lester's canvas tipi cover had been folded to fill the passenger side. His red cedar flute lay on the dash. Shuta must be leaving his tipi poles and clothes behind. All Lester's possessions had been shoved into one black pickup.

Tate ran over to the driver's open window. Shuta must have finished bleeding from her miscarriage. She'd cut her long hair short. "Can you go in the sweat yet?"

"I've been waiting for you. Just the two of us."

Tate didn't have a long dress to wear, but even naked, wrapped in a towel, she felt strong enough in such a sacred space to ask Shuta questions that needed answers.

"I rebuilt the fire." Shuta climbed out, and wearing a long loose dress for the Sweat Lodge, walked over to the fire pit. She kicked one of the logs aside to peer in at the now-glowing rocks. "*Wana*. Ready. You haul in the rocks. I'll lead, since you don't know Lakota."

Tate was as Lakota as Shuta, but she ignored the insult. It didn't matter who led, she'd have Shuta just where she wanted her. "We'll get Badger to watch our door."

"No! No men!" Shuta waved her arms back and forth, as if to protect her empty belly.

"Okay, I'll watch the door, since you want to be alone." Tate picked up the pitchfork and watched Shuta's reaction. Perhaps they both wanted a confrontation.

"No, you come in after you bring in all the rocks," Shuta said, "unless you're too weak to haul them."

Tate ignored the jibe. Shuta was the weak one, her face blotched with fever.

Shuta crawled into the sweat, circling around the center pit to the leader's spot.

Tate carried hot rocks, one at a time at first, and raked each into the pit, then several at a time. There were so many, she lost count. The tines of the pitchfork turned as red as her face and her arms burned from the rocks' heat. Finally she scraped the last hot rock onto the steaming mound in the center.

Flushed, she crawled into the Sweat Lodge opposite Shuta, undressed, and wrapped a big towel around herself. Beads of sweat poured into her eyes as inside the lodge grew dim.

Shuta pulled the door flap down and tied it tight with rawhide strips. "Plug that hole on your side," she said, "so no light, no air gets in."

Tate pressed the leather flap into the earth so only the glowing rocks lit the walls. Before she tuck her feet in, water hit the rocks, spitting and hissing. Billows of steam rose to the roof and rolled down the curved walls. She ducked her head and waited for the first Lakota song and prayer to start.

Shuta's voice scraped like metal on rock. "Where'd you steal that jewelry?"

Tate didn't answer. Every sweat began with a song and prayer, not a loaded question.

Shuta must know she'd found it at the Scenic Hock Shop.

"Answer. Once you're in the sweat, you're in," Shuta said, pouring more water on the rocks.

Tate knew that wasn't true. You could always mumble *mitak-weahsne* and be allowed to crawl out. Tate ignored her burning toes, the scalding steam. This was no bonding, a gathering of women in the darkness of the earth, but a contest. A contest she herself had chosen. Would Shuta turn this sweat into a torture chamber, like Lester'd done with the AIM guys? She hunkered down, curled into herself and readied to tough it out.

Shuta poured water on the rocks and prayed in Lakota. "Sing!" she commanded.

Sing? She could hardly breathe. Her lungs were full of hot air. Still, she started the only Lakota song she knew, until overcome, she fell into a fit of coughing. So much steam rose from the rocks between them that she couldn't see Shuta's face, only a flash of metal from the bucket.

Shuta poured the rest of the water on the rocks and prayed in Lakota. Not the usual words, *Tunkashila, unshimalye*, but something else, harsh and jerky, not like the flowing ancient phrases. The rocks hissed and crackled as if they'd become angry as well. It felt like descending into Hades, the darkness hot and oppressive, not warm and comforting. Tate sent her fear down into the earth beneath her, sank into the moist damp caress, let her body and pores expand and embrace the heat. The heat scalded, intense and sharp. She felt blisters form on her shoulders and back. JJ's ring burned between Tate's breasts, and JJ's bracelet singed hairs on Tate's arm. Shuta must feel it, too.

Shuta said, "My name! Don't you remember what that means in Lakota? *Tough*."

Steam rose, super-hot. It means *unforgiving*, Tate thought. "Why pour on all the water?"

"Mourn sweat," Shuta replied.

AIM had already taken a mourn sweat for JJ. She didn't understand what Shuta meant. "Mourn for whom?"

"My brother. No one else will mourn him," she cried. "He did it all for me."

Now Tate understood that when she handed Lester the Pipe in the Vision Cave, that's what he'd meant by Family Honor. He'd acted to protect Shuta. She said, "So Lester choked out *Our Lost One*, all for Family Honor."

"Don't say his name out loud," Shuta wailed. "Don't call him in here!"

"Shuta, I'm leaving." Tate pulled one of the rawhide strips loose from the door flap.

Shuta yanked the knots tighter. "This is a mourn sweat, closed till the end."

Closed till the end. That was what Tate wanted: the two of them in a small enclosed sacred place where she could ask questions. She braced herself against the heat. "Lester was her driver, the last person to see her alive." By now she knew to phrase her questions as statements, so that silence meant *yes*. "You pretended to be *Our Lost One's* friend."

Shuta laughed bitterly. "You don't know what it was like. We stayed inside Wounded Knee and loaded rifles, while you lounged inside a warm house and read books." Steam hissed. "We got arrested together, put in jail together."

"So what changed?"

Shuta burst into a fit of laughing. "That ring you're wearing? She gave George that ring, but I made him give it back."

No wonder George had gone berserk when he'd found out JJ was dead. No wonder when Shuta'd heard about it, she'd faked a crazy fit, while inside she'd been glad. No wonder she hadn't come to JJ's burial. "You got her kicked out of AIM." It was an accusation not a question.

"She asked too many questions. Like you." Shuta leaned over the rocks as if to grab her arm. "You asked your questions. Now it's my turn. I got an old Lakota story for you. You're so tough—you took a skillet to my brother, maybe you'll get its meaning. How we are. Not like you European weaklings in those fairy tales you talk about so much, who blindly obey their fathers. We do not wander around the Res crying for an Indian mother. We defend ourselves."

A story was supposed to be a gift, not a punishment. Burning from the heat, Tate listened, even though she had one more question.

"Long ago, but not so long ago," Shuta began, "a *washichu*, a White trapper, rode into a friendly Lakota camp to get himself a woman. He stood before the chief to ask for one. As he looked around, he saw a beautiful woman kneeling nearby to butcher a buffalo. It was the chief's daughter. He said, *I'll take that one!* and put his hands on her rump, as if she were already his."

Shuta upended the empty pail onto the rocks. Acrid smoke filled the Sweat Lodge, burning Tate's eyes. She closed them for a moment.

"Before the trapper could take a breath, the chief's daughter whirled around and with her bloody butcher knife cut off both his greedy hands."

Like Shuta. It all made sense. Lester had been so puzzled when he found out that JJ's hands had been cut off, and he'd had no idea where her turquoise jewelry had been hocked. Shuta had made it all happen. She'd used *Family Honor* to goad Lester into killing JJ. She'd cut off JJ's hands and stolen her jewelry. And she'd killed Night Cloud for raping so many Indian girls. Then Tate remembered Lester's words in the Vision Cave about Family Honor. Had Shuta had done it all herself?

"Did you kill Joanna Joe?" Tate asked.

A knife blade flashed in Shuta's hands. Had this knife killed JJ? Had this knife cut off JJ's hands? Shuta had hocked the jewelry. Shuta had delivered the hands to Slade. Lester had been her minion. Shuta was the second FBI informer. Had this knife killed Night Cloud, too?

Shuta was slicing the rawhide strips to get out. Then, in one swift thrust, her knife flicked across Tate's wrist, scraped against the turquoise bracelet, and left droplets of blood up her arm.

Tate flinched, but it was a trifle, nothing compared to the barbwire cuts on her fingers. She gave thanks to the Great Mystery, who protected her always.

Shuta scrambled out of the Sweat Lodge, started the pickup and yelled as she drove away, "This Red Power pickup was always mine!"

Shuta might get away with it all if she fled far enough. But at what cost? Her husband? Her son? Her relatives? Bear Heart Honor? Whatever was consuming Shuta—envy, jealousy, guilt, old tribal hatreds—it was eating her up, no matter how many purifying sweats she took. All that remained of her were bare footprints melting in the snow.

CHAPTER 33
ALEX

ALEX, HIS SHORT HAIR parted to one side, dressed as a clean-cut Indian cowboy, entered the Rapid City FBI office in the old storefront across from the Howard Johnson building. Behind him, Frank Fast Wolf, his AIM lawyer in a three-piece grey suit, followed with his briefcase in hand.

The young male receptionist looked up, unfazed by their united Indian front.

"We have an appointment with Agent Trask," said Frank in a no-nonsense voice.

The receptionist led them down the dark wainscoted hallway to Trask's office. As they entered the room, Trask, wearing a black arm band, remained seated. The office was small, crowded with a big wooden desk and two straight chairs, a shelf of books, and cardboard boxes piled neatly in one corner. He read one title: *The Book of Mormon.* Alex noticed photos of Trask's wife and children on his desk, all short-haired blondes with wide smiles. Church-going family. On the wall, framed FBI citations for sharpshooting and other skills. On top of a pile of papers Alex fixated on a beaded eagle feather. By the pattern, Alex recognized it as his own, but resisted the impulse to pick it up. He wondered how Trask had gotten it from the Kadoka Sheriff's collection. Alex remained silent, according to plan.

"Sit down." Trask said to Alex. "You're here to give evidence, sign a statement of guilt."

Frank countered, "We're here to plea bargain. A dozen witness-es, including yourself, saw your partner Agent Slade kill his infor-mant, Lester Bear Heart, who had confessed to killing Joanna Joe and bringing her hands to Slade for proof. Charges against my client are null and void."

Alex remained silent, detached. He watched the ping-pong game between agent and lawyer. He knew who he'd wronged, and later he'd make it up to Edgar. Tate. Joanna Joe.

"This man broke the law. The charges have been reduced to im-personating a corrections officer and eluding capture."

"For an illegal arrest for a crime he didn't commit," Fast Wolf add-ed without missing a beat.

"Turning Hawk's arrest was right and proper. He was read his rights. If he had waited, we'd have released him legally."

Frank shifted forward and leaned on Trask's desk. "My client has seen the bookends. I believe you have seen them as well."

Alex watched Trask's face flinch and his body swivel. Joanna Joe's hands were the key.

"At trial we'd force the prosecution to produce them as evidence. We'd also produce evidence against Agent Slade—a naked photo-graph of the victim, dead—embarrassing for the FBI. My client's insignificant trial could drag on so long, keeping you in court hin-dering you in your primary task, finding who killed your old FBI partner at Jumping Bull's Camp."

That case was personal, Alex knew. Trask's first loyalty was to the rookie FBI agent he'd left without backup who'd unwittingly walked into danger.

Trask leaned forward. He didn't seem intimidated. "We're on the trail of my old partner's killer. We're collecting unassailable evidence at this time."

The lawyer replied, "That we'll see. We know of another collection of artifacts besides a County Sheriff's, much more comprehensive."

Trask, his face flushed, pushed back his chair and stood up. "This interview is over."

Alex stood up as well. "Wait. I have come in willingly, to bring you a gift."

"The FBI does not accept gifts, bribes, or money," Trask replied stiffly.

"Perhaps an exchange?" Frank suggested.

"Turning Hawk's release for the name of my old partner's killer?" Trask's eyes gleamed.

"My client was never at Jumping Bulls' Camp. He is not an eye witness. He cannot name someone he does not know."

Alex stood up. Time to end this stalemate. "Perhaps something for your collection of sacred books?" He pointed at the row of Mormon books on the shelf. Before Trask could decline, Alex unwrapped his parcel and placed a worn leather Bible on the desk in front of Trask. "My grandfather's Lakota Bible. He was a lay reader at Red Leaf Episcopal church. We are not all pagan savages. Some of us worship your God and live by your savior's teachings, and all of us practice your Golden Rule, the same as our Buffalo Hide sacrament. We, too, have Honor."

Trask picked up the musty volume and flipped through the pages of Lakota words until it opened at a bookmark. Not a bookmark, but the photo of Joanna Joe, once taped to a Springview Motel mirror. It had waited for him underneath the floor mat in the Bronco when Trask took him back to jail. Trask's eyes widened. He closed the book and turned to the lawyer. "Leave us."

Alex looked at Frank, who frowned, but Alex put his hand on Frank's shoulder. "*Washté.*"

"If you say so," Frank replied in Lakota. "You remember what we agreed on earlier?"

Alex nodded his head, unafraid to be left alone with his old enemy.

"Yell if he handcuffs you." Frank left, shutting the door firmly.

~~~

Alex and Trask stared at each other.

Trask broke the silence. "I've been told you are a leader of your people. That you are a carrier of the Turning Hawk treaty Pipe, that you are a truly peaceful man working to civilize AIM. That because you carry the sacred Pipe, you will never carry a gun."

"True. I only carry a rodeo rope, which often allows me entrance to strange and miraculous places with palm trees and black bedrooms."

Trask winced. So he knew about Slade's lair. From a pile Trask picked up the top cardboard box and placed it on his desk. "I never wanted these. Something I believe you've been looking for." He shoved the box toward Alex.

Alex could feel the energy from inside the box, smell the faint odor of formaldehyde. As he touched the box he could feel a cold wind blow through his veins. He let the chill wash over him. He remembered Trask saying *bookends* with such loathing in his voice.

"Sometimes a box from the FBI evidence room cannot be found," Trask said. "Sometimes a rope can hang a man, sometimes it can free him—if he forgets about palm trees and black bedrooms and collections."

"I see you have found something from another collection as well," Alex felt the beaded feather call to him, but he hesitated to pick it up.

Trask picked it up instead, held it a moment, and said, "I once stepped on this feather, ground it into the dirt as something evil. Now I know it is a symbol of honor as powerful as my FBI badge. Neither are artifacts." Trask tapped the badge on the desktop. "I removed the feather from another collection where it did not belong. No trouble, since possession of eagle feathers by persons other than of Indian heritage is a criminal offense. The current possessor did not wish to be prosecuted."

Alex reached across the desk to take his old eagle feather, weathered and bent but not broken, from Trask's hands. "Thank you. I use it to bless and heal others." He hesitated. Would a Mormon stand still for an eagle feather blessing?

From Trask's stiff shoulders, Alex knew this wouldn't happen. In-stead he said, We're from different traditions, but we each follow a Code of Honor: justice, not vengeance. In the future I hope we can learn to work together to re-establish law and order to both of our worlds."

~~~

Alex caught a ride back to Camp Crazy Horse in front of the Sundance grounds, where Edgar's pickup still sat waiting to be returned. Bloketu whinnied from the nearby corral. Alex called softly, "*kree–kree–*," and heard his horse nicker in reply. As he entered the corral, Bloketu shied away. His horse was wounded. Raw flesh over the nose and jaw, raw flesh above the hoofs, covered with ointment. In a few places, scars had begun to form. He sang softly as he drew nearer, a keening song, and caressed his withers and flanks, reached for the halter, soothing Bloketu so he'd remember his touch. Who had done this?

He examined the wounds closely—barbwire cuts gouged in deep. To wire a horse to starve to death—meant *shut up, lay off.* He knew only one cowboy who would beat a horse or ride it to death, so used to cruelty as to feel nothing, whether horse or human. Jerry Slow Bear. No one else knew the old meaning of the deed, and no one else treated his horses mean. Jerry'd been mad at him for threaten-ing to take away his ambulance, and Bloketu had taken the torture meant for himself. Alex stroked Bloketu from his nose, along the black stripe down his back to his black tail, reassuring him. He felt his own body heat with rage, rising through his gut.

Without a second thought, he leaped into Edgar's pickup, drove into Eagle Nest until he reached the ambulance parked in Jerry Slow Bear's driveway, and slammed into its rear bumper. He jumped out of the pickup and pounded on the front door of their BIA house. When it opened, he threw a rope loop over Jerry's head, and yanking it tight, pulled him down the steps into the snowy yard, where he looped Jerry's feet and trussed him like a bawling calf. Alex yelled, "I could've barb-wired you, but I don't torture snakes-in-the-grass."

Jerry gagged and clawed at his throat. "Cuz," he wheezed, trying to loosen the noose. "Yer wife—"

Alex didn't want to hear more. He knew he'd explode if he didn't control himself. He kept the noose just tight enough so Jerry could answer his questions. But beating Jerry because Jerry beat Bloketu would only create more cruelty. He wanted justice instead.

"You saw it was Joanna Joe, and didn't tell me."

"*Hiya*! Body was already wrapped up in a blanket."

Alex replied, furious at Jerry's lie. "Not a blanket, just an AIM coat."

"Dark, couldn't see. I backed up and got rid of it quick. Same night as the Eagle Nest firefight, so I stayed away."

So that's why there was no ambulance that night to take Shuta to Pine Ridge before she miscarried. Alex glared down at Jerry, "All this time you *knew*!"

"I do my job good, mind my own business. Took it to Pine Ridge when they called me."

Alex pushed him down flat and threw snow in his face. "You're wheezing a lot. As you get older but not wiser, you get short-winded. Can't chase horses, can't rope 'em, can't stay on 'em."

Jerry shook snow out of his eyes and gasped. "Yer wife already came. What else d'ya want?"

"AIM won't burn down your house. But we will take the Eagle Nest ambulance, move it to the CAP office and paint it red. Red Power!"

Jerry ground his teeth and muttered, "No—"

"As of now you got a new job, barb-wiring cars. Everybody with a Res car needs a mechanic. You got it all: big yard, central location, a wife to bring in customers. And dollars." He could see Jerry thinking, *wife likes dollars*. He added, "Before I untie you, there's one more thing."

"Whazzat?"

He glanced at Jerry's shed. "I want the ponies you keep hidden over to Wakpamini Lake. Cuz, every kid in Eagle Nest wants a horse, but they can't keep them in town. Kids will swarm out to Camp Crazy Horse. You teach them to make halters and bridles. Teach them to gentle-break and ride their own ponies. Then take sweat with us, learn the old ways and respect all living beings. You know the prayer: *Mitakuye oyasin.* All my relations.

CHAPTER 34
TATE

EARLY THE NEXT DAY Tate rebuilt Alex's personal Sweat Lodge behind the Turning Hawk cabin. She took care to place the door and altar exactly as it had been, facing west, even though she knew he'd notice the new willow branches and new tobacco ties inside. She laid logs and rocks in the fire pit to make his sweat ready. He'd want that first. She sensed someone behind her. Only Alex walked so silently. There he was, but so thin. Yet his sunken eyes gleamed, and his short hair was trimmed neatly, with an eagle feather tied in it.

He carried a pail of water. "We need to start anew." He sat opposite her around the fire pit, lit the kindling beneath the logs, and let the flames warm his hands.

Tate said, "You stopped the shootout. How brave to turn yourself in."

"No," he said, "*You* stopped the shootout. You walked out with the sacred Pipe."

"No, it was the Great Mystery walking me."

He carried the rocks into the Sweat Lodge, returned to the fire pit full of glowing coals, and untied his eagle feather. "I wanted to purify you ever since you touched that tobacco tie in her hair."

She stood to let him brush her off with his eagle feather. "How'd you get it back?"

"The Great Mystery brought it back to me. Now we can purify ourselves together."

"You know I don't like sweats." She'd survived their marriage sweat, even though she'd felt trapped in that hot dark space and couldn't breathe and felt like dying. She'd survived Shuta's sweat as well. But could she survive another sweat?

He squatted by the altar and laid down a string of tobacco ties from his pocket. Not looking at her, he said, "This time Mother Earth will heal you. Something happened when you were very small. Your hands were slapped, and you were thrown in a dark closet for a long time. Then you were taken away and adopted. So when you found *Our Lost One,* the nightmares came back. But Lester taught you to re-dream them."

She nodded. Had Lester taught the AIM guys, too?

He looked up at her. "Can you do that now, re-dream this memory-before-memory? They say about the Sweat Lodge, *Naked we enter Mother Earth's womb. Naked we leave, reborn.* He set the pail of water inside. "This sweat will be different. We're different." His voice cracked, but when he whispered, *"kree–kree–,"* she knew he'd recover, and so would she.

He handed her the deer antlers to grab the hot rocks and slide them into the round pit. His touch was just like his first touch at the courthouse in Minneapolis, electric, as if by touching, he'd *had* her ever since. Yet the power of his touch was so different from the power of the Pipe, or the power of the Gun, more than *possession.* With them it was a two-way power, flowing back and forth, a power-together, as if by touching they could strengthen each other. They *had* each other.

She took his hand, no longer afraid to go into the small dark space, crawled in opposite him and took her clothes off. His face was lit by the glow of rock-faces shimmering red. The rocks felt alive, with pulsing eyes that winked on and off.

He said, they're called *Born and Ancient Ones, in the Center of All That Is.*

He hung another string of tobacco ties over the willow branches, closed the door flap and poured on water. The hot steam curled around her back, a caressing breath from the rocks. Hot darkness covered her like a blanket. His deep voice comforted her, the old songs calling in the Spirits. She sank into the darkness until she felt enclosed in Mother Earth's womb. There was the mother she'd never known, who gave her away. The foster-mother she'd known, who treated her as a toy. Alex's mother, who treated her like a servant. Now she was enfolded in the Great Mother, her *real* mother all around her. Now she understood what *inipi* meant: the Sweat Lodge was a *born-again* lodge, and when she emerged, she'd be born anew. Whole enough to become a mother.

Afterwards they went into their tipi, laced shut the canvas door flap, and lay on sage.

"You've grown up," she said.

"I was given great gifts. At first I was *unshika*, pitiful. I thought I was better than the winos Under-the-Bridge, but I learned to be humble and appreciated their gifts. Then I was thrown in solitary, but I learned to create my own *Hanblechia*. I fasted, entered the Spirit World and claimed my Hawk Power." He stroked her hair. "You've changed, too."

She touched his face. "I don't have Hawk Power, but learned about two others: the Power of the Pipe and the Power of the Gun."

He wrapped his arms around her, nuzzling close.

She sat up, crossed her legs and frowned. "You've never touched a gun, but I have. I understand why the AIM guys are gung-ho to carry a rifle. You caress the wood stock. It's warm and smooth. You touch the cold metal shaft, hard and smooth. You sight along the bore, rest it on your shoulder and it becomes a third arm, one that reaches far out ahead of you. It gives you power. It brings you solid safety. You think you own the gun, but it owns you, and nothing else matters. For Camp Crazy Horse to offer sanctuary, we must break the spell of Gun Power."

He pulled her down to him. "I've been listening. You've grown wise." He stroked her belly. "And grown bigger, too."

She said, "Yes, I am pregnant. And I'm glad."

He didn't look surprised.

"How could you know when I hardly figured it out?"

"Old Sam told me the Spirit People said—"

"That night, at the *Yuwipi*? Old Sam knew I was pregnant then?"

"They said someone would come into our family. I thought they meant Até coming home at last. My father."

"Oh, Alex—" She put her hand over his heart, aware of his unspoken longing. "Perhaps your friend Badger could find him."

He laughed. "Not a good idea!"

"I don't know how long I'll be able to build fence or ride—"

He hugged her tight. "You will have to stop work on fence crew. Men work with men, women with women. We'll move you and your piano into town."

By now she knew what that meant: let her mother-in-law Iná teach her how to butcher and make dry meat and frybread, how to bead and quill and sew quilts. Join the Lakota women's world. She caressed her stomach and felt a small life inside her. It was time.

"We'll name her Joanna."

Alex grinned. "Maybe just Joe."

~~~

Tate was proud of her husband, now recognized by Old Sam as a full-fledged medicine man. Though his hair was still cut short, he stood taller and his voice had deepened. He'd retrieved the body from the Pine Ridge Agency cemetery and taken charge of the burial. Now he led the AIM warriors down the Badlands trail of crumbly purple shale to a hidden meadow ringed by clumps of yucca. He carried the red felt bundle, his eagle feather, and the Turning Hawk Pipe. George and Smokey brought the big tribal drum, and Chaské the bag of drumsticks. Coming last, she held the turquoise and silver jewelry in her hands. She'd worn JJ's "bank account" to catch the killer. Now she carried it to rest with the hands.

At the meadow the AIM warriors formed a circle around the plain wood coffin beside open grave. They stood with knuckles out to show that RED POWER had not disappeared. Alex brushed each one with his eagle feather and tied a red prayer cloth amid the yucca spines. Yucca was for protection, sharp and tough.

Large snowflakes drifted down covering them all with pure white. George and Smokey lifted the rough wooden lid. There lay *Our Lost One*, wrapped in a star quilt, honored at last. Everyone sighed. Tate slipped the jewelry to Alex, who laid it with the red felt bundle in the coffin. Hands reunited with the body. Now complete, her soul would no longer haunt the Badlands below.

George closed the lid. Carefully, the warriors lowered the rough box into the grave. Each person took a handful of earth and dropped it into the grave, saying private goodbyes. When it was her turn, lacy white designs landed and melted on the cold dirt in her hands. The earth was so solid, the snowflakes so fleeting. Yet she would never forget how Joanna Joe had found her on the streets and brought her into AIM, taught her to be proud to be Indian, and introduced her to Alex. She'd been like an older sister, and now she'd still be near, safe on Turning Hawk land.

The AIM warriors took up shovels, refilled and mounded up the grave. George set a white cross at the head with large black letters: JOANNA JOE, AIM WARRIOR. Alex marked each corner with a red prayer flag, and she scattered dried sage over the mounded grave.

Alex stood at the simple grave marker and lifted the AIM Pipe to the four directions to pray. Drumbeats filled the air. Chaské's high-pitched cry floated out into the clear air. So began the traditional Lakota farewell: *Maká Shiná, the earth is our blanket.* Tate didn't understand all the words, but she knew the feeling. She loved the sacred songs, sad and ancient, which started high with a wail and dropped down deep into the earth, carrying her soul with it. The song swept her breath away.

Alex raised his hands to the west. His booming voice echoed over the land. "This brave AIM woman gave her life for truth and freedom. Now her spirit can join her body, no longer haunt the Badlands. Yet her RED POWER hands will always be with us, help us, guide us, lead us, point the way on the Big Red Road, encourage us to be strong. Like the Chief who sacrificed his arm so that the Hand stars would always reappear in the spring to bring new life to earth. When we make things, when we comfort a child, when we tie a knot in tobacco offerings, when we open a door to our hearts, when we Sundance this year, *Napeshni* will be with us."

Hechetuelo. So It Is.

HISTORICAL BACKGROUND

In the Spirit of Crazy Horse, Peter Matthiessen, Viking, 1980, 1983.

For the purposes of this novel's time and place, one history book covers not only the Oglala Lakota from 1835 to the 1980s, but focuses on Pine Ridge Reservation and the village of Wanblee, SD, as well as including testimony from my husband, other relatives, and friends. Not only is it written by a master nonfiction storyteller, the book is so accurate that it survived a libel suit against the author and Viking Press, despite being temporarily banned in South Dakota.

Sample chapter from the next *Lakota Mystery*

THE BLACK CRADLEBOARD

Chapter 1

Camp Crazy Horse
Pine Ridge Reservation
Early June, 1977

ALEX TURNING HAWK woke before dawn in the old log cabin at Camp Crazy Horse and reached over to stroke his wife's hair. But the pillow was empty. When his mother, a midwife, learned that Tate was pregnant, she'd come with Big Al to move Tate and her piano to be safe in town. Tate had protested, but when Iná said in English, "Barely married and already so big!" Alex knew better than to oppose his mother when she was on the warpath.

He'd stayed at the camp to prepare for *hanblechia,* a four-day Vision Quest. Babies were dying on Pine Ridge Res and no one knew why. As a young medicine man, he had to fast for guidance from the Great Mystery for a cure. He had to be strong, calm, and wise for those who came to ask for help and healing. But he'd put off going to his great-grandpa's vision cave ever since Lester Bear Heart had been killed there. He must purify it first.

He pulled on overalls and cowboy boots, picked up his sacred pipe and went out to greet the sun. Its rays lit up the bare poles in the sundance arbor and the tree of life in the center. He prayed to the four directions, east to the sacred Sundance grounds, south to Rattling Water Creek, west to the pines, and north to the Badlands Wall, where Turning Hawk land dropped off into Redstone Basin.

He called for his hawk, "*kree, kree—*," the only one he could talk to about his worries, fears, and strategies for the future of Camp Crazy Horse and the Lakota People. Overhead a dark shape circled, as if an ancestor hovered above to keep him strong, perhaps his great-grandpa who'd lived on this allotted land and kept his clan, together in the terrible shoved-on-the-reservation days of sickness and despair.

His hawk swept down and buzzed him, "*kree kree- kree kree-*," as if on an urgent mission as zoomed in, then he rose and flew off north. Alex put away his sacred pipe, shouldered his pack of work tools and followed the cries. At the Badlands Wall he paused to let silence and space fill him. Below, Redstone Basin's maze of barren arroyos twisted and turned out of sight.

His hawk buzzed him again, "*kree–kree–*" and disappeared down the trail. Alex followed him onto the narrow ledge in the rock wall where his hawk sat on top of his grandpa's buffalo skull altar, staring at the faded red tobacco tie offerings as if he were a magpie collecting shiny pieces of ribbon. Strange behavior for a hawk.

An odd buzzing came from behind the altar. Alex stared at the elk hide doorflap covering the opening to the small cave dug into the rock wall. Could be rattlers coming out of hibernation. Have to find a stick. Then the slight breeze shifted, carrying the smell of blood, decay and fear. Had some animal crawled into the darkness to die?

Alex pulled his neckerchief over his nose and stepped past his hawk still on the altar. The smell surrounded him and he hesitated. He'd brought only a jug of water, not enough to wipe away whatever was inside. Should he go elsewhere to dig a new Vision Cave for his *hanblechia?*

His Turning Hawk ancestors surrounded him, outraged by the violence and death that had entered this sacred space. For them he must purify it all and rebuilt the sacred altar—or else it would be haunted forever.

He put on his leather work gloves and lifted the doorflap. Black flies stirred and buzzed in the heavy darkness. No sunlight entered—Vision Caves always faced west. He anchored the doorflap on top with a rock. He took off his jacket and whisked the flies out.

Before him lay an old cradleboard with a beaded lizard bag tied to it for protection. Someone had made the bag to hold a baby boy's umbilical cord to remind him he was always connected to the earth. The cradleboard itself was charred at the edges and the beadwork was odd—pink beads, not the usual sacred colors. Then he saw it—the Vision Hill design: red- yellow-black-white striped hills in two rows down the cradleboard. Only the red beads had faded. It was Turning Hawk's design, the same beadwork on his own cradleboard. Had this belonged to one of his ancestors, saved from a prairie fire?

He lifted the cradleboard's head cover. Inside was a baby, his face turned black. Alex listened—no breathing—a baby wearing a black necklace—he leaned closer—no, a string of *wolutas,* cloth tobacco ties, but black not red. For a moment he thought he was staring at a life-size doll painted black, put there to scare him, but the fetid smell told him no. The dead baby and the black ties, each tie full of prayers, black prayers, were real.

As real as the live baby inside his wife Tate. Were they safe in town with his mother? He backed away, repelled, afraid. Whose baby? Dead how long? Why hide it here? Who else knew of this place?

Someone had sent evil into the most sacred Turning Hawk place, out to destroy him and his family: his mother, wife, and unborn child. The Badlands wind chilled him to the bone. He looked around for his protection, his sacred pipe, but he'd left it hanging on the log cabin wall. He must keep this desecration of Turning Hawk land a secret.

Read more about this book and find out more about The Lakota Mysteries on Dorothy Black Crow's website:
http://dorothyblackcrow.com.

WHY I WRITE

I write to share a world no longer with us.

I write to honor the elders, record the passing of a culture, share the loss and encourage its retrieval. I write to show the young ones that a lost culture can be revived through storytelling to bind and heal. Even far from the Land, native values can be lived.

I've been blessed to live in times when only Lakota was spoken, when Honor meant doing things right—via feasts and memorial dinners, when anyone who came to the camp left with a handmade gift. We lived close to the Earth and appreciated the Creator's gifts: water life and air.

It is as if the elders have spoken in my sleep, asked not to be forgotten. Sometimes it is not my voice. I am merely a "translator" as the Spirit moves through my heart into my typing hands.

— *Dorothy Black Crow*
dorothyblackcrow.com